Mel Bay Presents

Handbook for American Musicians Overseas

— *with* —

The Dictionary of Contemporary Music Terms in English, French, German and Italian

Anthony Glise
Urtext Editions

1 2 3 4 5 6 7 8 9 0

© 2003 by A. Glise. International Copyright Secured.
Copyright reassigned, Mel Bay Publications, 2003. All Rights Reserved.
No part of this book may be reproduced or transmitted in any form or by any
means, electronic or mechanical, including photocopying, recording, or by any
information storage and retrieval system, without written permission from the
author or publisher. For author contact in the USA., address:

Ævia Publications, Ltd.
PO Box 7242
St. Joseph, MO 64507, USA
www.AnthonyGlise.com
Cover Photo: Classical guitar, "Sirius," constructed for Anthony Glise
by Gioachino Giussani, Anghiari (Arezzo, Italy).
Photo by A. Jeannine Borngesser-Glise, © 1997. Used by Permission.

Printed in the United States of America

—Table of Contents—

Important Numbers to Know Overseas:
(Fill this out and keep it by your telephone)

Emergency family contacts in the U.S.

International Telephone Information

U.S. Embassy in your Host Country

U.S. Consulate in your Host Country

Local Police

Local Fire Department

Local Ambulance Service

Local Tax Advisor

Local Travel Agent

CHAPTER ONE—
Studying or Working in Music Overseas as an American Citizen

If you are thinking about studying or working as a musician overseas, there are a number of subjects of which you should be aware. Keep in mind that this book addresses predominantly France, Germany and Italy.

For all practical purposes, the statements about Germany also apply to Austria and Switzerland. Belgium is similar to France, Liechtenstein is similar to Germany, Luxembourg is a cross between Germany and France (though slightly more French) and the Netherlands are similar to Germany.

However, these other countries vary depending on which border is closest to the specific city. For example, near the Holland/German border the Dutch music schools are more like Germany, but near the Holland/Belgian border they're more like France.

Needless to say, the languages are sometimes different in the same country. The most extreme example is of course Switzerland where, depending on the region you're in, you might need to speak either French, German, Italian or (however unlikely), Romanisch—all with a fairly heavy dialect. In short, the statements here are valid for

France, Germany and Italy. For other countries, check the situation at each specific school since it may be different.

Overview of Schools in Europe

Music schools in Europe have a very different system than in the U.S. First, the schools are divided into different categories. This in itself is a grotesque mass of confusion and I've never been convinced that even the Europeans understand their own systems. All this is complicated by the fact that some schools (especially in Italy) offer additional diplomas that are exclusive to that school and have absolutely no parallel or relation to any other diploma or degree from anywhere else.

Europeans are obsessed with receiving pieces of paper (*degrees, diplomas, diplômes, Zeugnisse, attestati, attestations, etc.*) and virtually every time you sneeze you can get some sort of diploma for it. Frankly, these lesser diplomas don't mean a great deal back in the States but they look good if you list them on a résumé and can be pretty impressive if you hang them all on your wall—and of course you do learn something in the process.

Keep in mind that throughout most of Europe, a university is exclusively for academic studies—*not* for music performance. In general, the only reason that a musician would be interested in the European university system is if he wants to concentrate on academic aspects of music such as music history, musicology, *etc.* Anything having to do with actual music *performance* is targeted in the *Conservatoire, Konservatorium, Hochschule, Conservatorio,* or *Accademia* systems.

Remember that a university, in all three countries, is the only institution that can grant a doctorate and again, this would be in some *academic* area of music. However, all three systems can grant various other degrees which basically parallel with degrees in the U.S. [1]

---

1. None of the three countries have the equivalent of our "college." However, note that in France they do have a word, *"collège,"* but a French collège is the same as our junior high school (or middle school).

In Italian, the word *"collegio"* also exists, but this is a boarding school for elementary students. The term *"collegio unversitario"* also exists in Italian, though this is essentially a dormitory, so don't let these words confuse you.

Fig. 1. Parallel of Schools.

U.S.	France	Germany	Italy
Music School (elementary)	École de Musique	Musikschule	Scuola di musica (Istituto musicale)
Conservatory	Conservatoire (Municipal or Régional)	Konservatorium	Scuola di musica or Conservatorio di musica
Conservatory	Conservatoire (National)	Konservatorium	Scuola di musica or Conservatorio di musica
Conservatory	Conservatoire (National Supérieur)	Hochschule or Konservatorium	Scuola di musica or Conservatorio di musica
University	Université	Universität	Università

Ten Steps for Moving to Europe

1) Decide which country you want to study in. If possible study at a summer masterclass with a teacher from that country in the country.
2) Get a letter of acceptance from the teacher.
3) Apply to the school and include the acceptance letter.
4) Find out the audition date and book and open-end round-trip ticket.
5) Apply for Visa.
6) Go to audition.
7) Find housing (ask around at the school).
8) Register with the foreign police.
9) Work hard (also on the language!) and make contacts.
10) Enjoy and learn from your new adopted country!

CHAPTER TWO—
France

Schools in France

In France an *école de musique* is more for children while a *conservatoire* is basically everything else but there are several types of conservatoires. A *conservatoire régional* (which is basically the same as a *conservatoire municipal*) is for children as well as serious students but these also have classes for amateur adults. [2]

A *conservatoire régional* or *conservatoire municipal* is usually not advanced enough for serious foreign studies but it depends on the school. These smaller conservatoires (as well as the écoles) are however, good possibilities if you decide to stay and teach in France after your studies.

The next highest level is the *conservatoire national* which usually offers the same programs and classes as a conservatoire régional, but these schools are supposedly more "serious" because they are supported and endorsed by the national government rather than simply by

---

2. The only major difference between these two types of French conservatoires is that a *conservatoire municipal* is supported by the city and a *conservatoire régional* is supported by the region.

the *département* (the state). Consequently, a conservatoire national can be a good option for foreign studies.

Keep in mind that some of the *conservatoires nationaux* frequently offer courses for students only through age 18, so (depending on your age) you should check with the individual school to find out if the one you're interested in will accept older students. Most of these conservatoires take students through age 26 though France tends to be lenient about age requirements. If you get the teacher on your side you shouldn't have any problems.

A *conservatoire national supérieur* is the highest level and is targeted for continued serious studies. There are currently only a few of these in France (in Paris, Lyon and Bordeaux) but I have honestly never been convinced that the teaching is any better at the conservatoires nationaux supérieurs than at the hundreds of conservatoires nationaux.

However, if you're planning on staying in France to teach it is *essential* that you do at least some study in a conservatoire national supérieur—especially since this can help you break into the labyrinth of French musical politics. You *have* to play that game if you intend to get a teaching job in France.

Degrees in France

In France performance-oriented studies (*i.e.* actually playing an instrument) are done in a conservatoire, while "*musicologie*" (which from their standpoint means basically anything that is not performance-oriented) is studied in a *université* under a degree program called the *C.A.P.E.S. (Certificat d'Aptitude Professionnel d'Enseignement Supérieur*—pronounced as one word: *c'apes*) which takes four years and accredits you to teach music in a *primaire, collège* or *lycée* (grade school, middle school or high school).

However, the C.A.P.E.S. is awarded in stages and you are "certified" at the end of each year with a different diploma (all of which—in theory—leads up the final C.A.P.E.S.). The specific stages are: *D.E.U.G. 1, D.E.U.G. 2, License,* and finally, the *C.A.P.E.S.* ("D.E.U.G." by the way, stands for *Diplôme d'Enseignement Universitaire Général*—but almost no one knows this and it is usually simply referred to as a "Deug," said as one word and followed by the appropriate number).

After the License (usually the third year) students chose to do the final year to receive either a *C.A.P.E.S.* or a *Maîtrise.* Both of these final diplomas (like the previous levels) usually take one year but students who opt for the Maîtrise normally plan on going one year further to do a *D.E.A. (Diplôme d'Enseignement Approfondis)* which is more advanced.

Actually this is a good system because it means that—even if you study a short time—your work is still recognized and awarded with a diploma. This is in contrast to the American system where you either do the entire prescribed 4-year degree program and get the final degree or you get nothing at all for your trouble.

To avoid any more confusion than I've already put you through, below is a figure that shows the steps leading to a C.A.P.E.S. and beyond.

Fig. 2. Basic Parallel Between the American University System and the French "C.A.P.E.S."

America	France
1st year university	D.E.U.G. 1
2nd year university	D.E.U.G. 2
3rd year university	License
4th year university	C.A.P.E.S. *or* "Maîtrise"*
	(if you do a maîtrise, you
	usually go on to do the
	D.E.A.)
first year graduate school	D.E.A.

* *N.B.* The term *Maîtrise* in French sounds like "Master's" in English, but the two degrees are not *remotely* similar! Be sure when discussing your previous studies in the U.S. (and also on your French résumé, *etc.*) that you specify that an American Master's is equal to a C.A.P.E.S. *plus 2-3 years!* This could obviously make a *tremendous* difference to a potential employer, as well as to any school to which you are applying.

If you think you understand all of the above I have bad news for you because it's not quite that simple. What I've told you is basically correct but in France—if you're talented enough—you can begin your musical studies *anytime* (through a conservatoire).

Thus, if you began musical studies very early, by the time you reached the age to begin working toward your final French music degree (*i.e.* university age) you would be much younger than the average conservatory student in the U.S. In that case, the proficiency and maturity would probably be lower. There's simply no other way to make a direct comparison. The chart above is the easiest way to understand the system in-general but don't take it 100% literally.

As I said before, for performance-oriented studies, you usually begin at a conservatoire (or école de musique) in a level called *Moyen*. This can take several years but is usually considered very basic, so if you're going to France with some musical background this level won't apply to you.

After the Moyen, the next level is a *Diplôme Fin d'Étude (or "D.F.É.")* which usually takes one year. In principal, this establishes you as capable of teaching and this is often the best option for foreign studies since (if you have some strong musical background) you can often complete a D.F.É. in one year.

However, most French musicians tend to work toward a diploma called the *Médaille d'Or* (also called *"Supérieur"*) which can take longer (sometimes 2 or more years). This has more prestige and can be much more valuable if you're trying to get a teaching job in France.

After the Médaille d'Or, you can go on to two other levels: *Perfectionnement 1* and *Perfectionnement 2*. Each of these levels (in principal) takes one year although this varies with the school and the level of the player.

Again, to try to clear the air, below is a rough parallel of how the different French levels can be equated to the American conservatory system.

Figure 3. Parallel Between the U.S. and French Conservatory Degrees.

America	France
preliminary studies	Moyen
1st year conservatory	D.F.E. (Diplôme Fin d'Étude)
2nd year conservatory	Médaille d'Or (or "Supérieur")
3rd year conservatory	Perfectionnement 1
4th year conservatory	Perfectionnement 2

Keep in mind that "Moyen" is the name of a level that says you're working *toward* a D.F.E.— it is not a degree in itself. To say that you have a "Moyen" would be the same thing as (in English) saying that you have completed you "pre-Bachelors studies." It doesn't make any sense in French. You are "Moyen" until you receive your D.F.E.

I should point out that France has several additional levels of certification for teaching called a *Diplôme d'État* ("*D.É.*") and a *Certificat d'Aptitude* ("*C.A.*") but these are not degree programs—they are simply a series of tests that you take and are then awarded the certificate. However, these can be *extremely* important—even more important than a regular degree depending on your future plans—since a D.É. or C.A. are often required by a school if you plan to teach in France. The D.É. is the lowest level teaching certificate and the C.A. is the highest level.

Both the D.É and C.A. certificates are awarded after passing a test that is administered sporadically throughout the country. These tests usually include a solfège exam, a playing exam (on your instrument) as well as written and oral sections similar to "comps" (comprehensive exams) at many U.S. schools for a Master's program. [3]

The Diplôme d'État and Certificat d'Aptitude are in addition to the normal course of studies and are, in principal, a way that the French attempt to maintain a consistent level of quality in their teaching system. Because of this, they are not necessarily tied to any of the above degree programs.

In short, if you can pass the test, you can get either a D.É. or C.A. immediately. However, like the various required music education classes in U.S. universities, a D.É. or C.A. only means that the teacher has passed the test—it does *not* guarantee that he can teach any better than someone else. The French haven't figured that out yet any more than we have in the States.

This certification (a D.É. or C.A.) is not obligatory to teach in France but more and more conservatoires are requiring that their faculty have a C.A. (though they will occasionally accept a D.É.). The only real advantage (as far as I'm concerned) is that if you have a D.É. or C.A., you can usually command higher pay for your teaching. The first pay hike is for the D.É. and the next highest is for the C.A., so from a practical standpoint they're worth having.

---

3. If you plan to take the French exams, which almost always includes a solfège exam, remember that all of Europe uses a "fixed-do system" in solfège, where the note C is always "*do*."

This is in contrast to the "moveable do system" used in the States where the tonic of the key center of the piece is always *do*. For example, in the U.S., for a piece in F major, you would call the note "f" *do*. In Europe, the same tonic in the same piece (the note f) would be called *fa*.

If you are interested in staying in France to teach, I *strongly* suggest that you find out about the testing for the D.É. or the C.A. immediately when you arrive at the school. This is important, not only so your professor can target your studies toward the test, but because these tests are usually given only once a year—sometimes once every two years depending on the instrument. You need to plan ahead!

CHAPTER THREE—
Germany

Schools in Germany

In Germany a *Musikschule* (like a French école de musique) is oriented toward children and adults who are taking lessons for fun after school or work. As an American it is useless to study at a Musikschule since they have no set curriculum or degree program and the level of teaching is often juvenile. However (like the French école de musique and some conservatoires), a Musikschule *can* be a good option for securing a teaching job overseas.

The different upper-level music studies in Germany are:

1) Universität
2) Musikhochschule
3) Konservatorium
4) Pädagogische Hochschule

The German Hochschule system (like the French conservatoire national supérieur) is generally considered more advanced than the Konservatorium system although both a Hochschule and Konservatorium are for college-age students. There are different Hochschulen in many different categories, *i.e.* for the fine arts, architecture, design, music, *etc.*, and there are hundreds of private and state Hochschulen throughout Germany.

A *Konservatorium* is geared for serious studies and offers various advanced classes and degree programs. These can be very difficult or very easy depending on the school and the quality of teaching can vary just as drastically. If you're trying to complete a foreign degree in a short period of time, a Konservatorium may be the best option since they tend to be more lenient about accepting credits from classes that you've had in the States.

The primary difference between these two is that a Hochschule is usually supported by the government, while a Konservatorium is usually supported by the *Stadt* (city) or *Bundesland* (state). Because the Hochschulen traditionally pay more they often attract higher-level faculty.

Thus, Hochschulen tend to have a stronger reputation and the curriculum is traditionally more rigid. However, because of this fewer credits will probably transfer from your previous U.S. studies. The quality of teaching is, however, not necessarily higher than a Konservatorium and both a Konservatorium and Hochschule have degree programs similar to American undergraduate and masters programs.

There is another option for musicians who are less performance-oriented but this is highly impractical for one year of study overseas. This is a school called a *Pädagogische Hochschule* which awards a diploma that is similar to our Bachelors of Music Education. This is a general course of study (usually 8 semesters) where you can choose emphasis in music. Graduates usually go directly to teach in a Musikschule or to teach general music in a grade school or high school.

While a Pädagogische Hochschule could be an option for overseas study they tend to not have a particularly strong music reputation and the odds of being able to complete the degree in one year are virtually nonexistent because of the required general education classes. Plus, if you get a diploma from a Pädagogische Hochschule, you are usually limited to teaching only lower-level students.

However, if you get a degree from a Hochschule or Konservatorium you can teach lower-level students (such as in a Musikschule) as well as possibly land a position at a Konservatorium or Hochschule. Your options are simply greater with *any* kind of degree from a Konservatorium or Hochschule. You will find them to have more flexible degree programs and more active, professional-level music circles.

Degrees in Germany

The German system of education is fairly well-organized and because much of the confusion occurs at the elementary level, it won't apply to your foreign university-level study.

Like all other European programs, the *Universität* (University) is for academic music studies (research, music history, *etc.*). Performance-oriented studies are targeted only at the Konservatorium or Musikhochschule.

However, for our purposes you must understand that to enter a Universität, Pädagogische Hochschule, Musikhochschule and virtually any Konservatorium, the German student must have passed his *Abitur*, referred to in conversation as an *"Abi"* (pronounced as one word).

The Abi is a large final exam (including written and oral testing) given at the end of the study in the Gymnasium which is the equivalent of our high school. For this test, the student usually has two "majors" or subjects that he has studied in-depth and usually intends to continue studying at the university-level.

The problem the Germans face is that the decision to go to Gymnasium must be made around age 10-11. If a student did not have the required grade point average, foresight or interest to go to a Gymnasium (which is traditionally more difficult than the other options), he simply can't go to a Hochschule (or even a university).

In order from the highest level of respect to the lowest, the options for elementary education are:

1) Gymnasium
2) Realschule
3) Hauptschule.

Only a Gymnasium can administer the Abitur. Sometimes a Konservatorium will admit students without an Abitur. However, coming from the States, this virtually never poses a problem since the Germans view an American high school diploma (of *any* sort) as the equivalent of the Abitur.

The different degrees awarded by both a Musikhochschule and Konservatorium are given below.

Fig. 4. Parallel Between U.S. and German Music Degrees.

U.S.	Germany
Applied Musical Studies	
(Conservatory or University)	(Hochschule or Konservatorium)
Bachelor of Music	Ordentliche Prüfung
Bachelor of Arts in Music in Performance	Diplom
Bachelor of music in Performance and Artist Diploma	Künstlerische Reifeprüfung (also called a Konzertreifeprüfung)
Musical Academic Studies	
(Conservatory *or* University)	(Pädagogische Hochschule *or* Universität)
Bachelor of Music Education	Staatsexamen mit "Schwerpunkt Musik" (*i.e.* Diploma with an emphasis on music)

These different degrees can take anywhere from 4 to 10 semesters depending on the school and the required courses. Again, you may be able to transfer credits from your studies in the States which could drastically reduce this amount of time. Make sure you find out the specific requirements at the specific school where you want to study.

CHAPTER FOUR—
Italy

Schools in Italy

Like France and Germany, the *Università* (university) in Italy is for academic musical studies rather than performance. In Italy there are essentially three types of applied (performance-oriented) musical studies. Those at a *Scuola di musica,* a *Conservatorio,* and an *Accademia.*

A scuola di musica (or *istituto musicale*) is similar to the French *école de musique* and the German *Musikschule.* A scuola di musica can be geared for very elementary studies (often for children or adults who are studying an instrument for fun) but unlike the German or French schools, they also have courses of study that are geared toward professionals and serious musical studies.

A scuola di musica may be either private or supported by the *Commune* (the city), the *Provincia* (the county) or the *Regione* (the state). These may be your best option for landing your first teaching job in Italy although they are less practical for serious study abroad as I'll explain below.

The reason a scuola di musica may be less practical for foreign study has nothing to do with the level of teaching. In fact, I know of many such schools who have *brilliant* faculty and the level of training is *extremely* high. The problem is, if you want to earn any type of diploma that is recognized by the Italian government, the testing for these diplomas can only be given in a *conservatorio*. This means if you end up studying at a scuola di musica you will still need to do your *testing* at a conservatorio. While many Italian students do this, you may simply find it easier to do your study at a conservatorio but this doesn't necessarily affect your chances (positively or negatively) of passing the exams. It merely simplifies the logistics of already being at the school where the exams are administered.

Another option for study is at a *conservatorio,* usually supported by the city or region. In Italy, a conservatorio is the same as a conservatoire in France. The various Italian conservatori contain both elementary studies and advanced studies that parallel the American conservatory system and they go through the equivalent of our undergraduate/graduate studies although the program begins at an earlier age since the full course of study can last up to ten years.

Usually a child will begin studying at a scuola di musica or conservatorio at the same time that he is doing his regular study at a grade school or high school. He then finishes his normal studies at high school and after that, concentrates more heavily on his musical studies for several years to earn his final music diploma.

Like France, each phase of musical study is awarded with a degree. Then after passing the various tests administered by a conservatorio, the student is awarded the title of *"Maestro."* Formally, that's as far as you can go in Italy. However, because most musicians want to continue study, either to perfect their skills or to specialize in a given field of performance (such as 19th-Century performance practice, contemporary music, *etc.*), they often enter an *Accademia.*

The Italian accademia system doesn't parallel with any other country. The concept of the accademia actually stems from the Italian Renaissance when artists would band together to trade ideas, work on specific projects, *etc.*

The music accademia today are somewhat the same. Each accademia has a specific "theme" which can be *very* specialized. For example, I teach in Italy at the *Accademia degli Studi Superiori "L'Ottocento"* (The Academy for the Study of 19th-Century Music) where my specialty is Viennese music from 1790-1830.

These accademie may be either private or supported and accredited by the city or region. Some are even formally or informally connected to a conservatorio. Because accademia are highly "free-form" (there is often no rigid organization or degree programs) an accademia may award all sorts of various diplomas *("attestati")* that have absolutely no parallel to any other degree in any other country *or* to any other accademia.

The Italian accademia system is a *very* confusing and changes drastically from one accademia to the next. However, for that very reason, an accademia can provide you with a chance to study in a highly specialized field of music. It can also be a chance to pick up some sort of diploma in Italy *very* quickly—sometimes even after a summer course of study at an accademia.

Degrees in Italy

The Italian degree system is more complicated than any other in Europe. Like a U.S. university, the degree program usually lasts 4 to 5 years although again, study at an Italian università is only for academic aspects of music. After your 4 - 5 years of study at a università you receive a degree, the *Laurea,* which is essentially a cross between a Bachelor's/Master's in the U.S. and gives you the title of *"Laureato Dottore,"* which qualifies you to teach academic music in any institution—including the university or conservatory levels.

While working on your Laurea you are under the guidance of a teacher called a *Professore* who is a specialist in your field of study. This is similar to the tutorial system used in England at Cambridge and Oxford universities.

After receiving the Laurea you may be able to continue working (usually doing research, *etc.*) for your Professore in the università. At this point you are given the title *"Dottorato"* which means you are working at essentially the same level as our concept of "post-graduate study." Unless you are extremely well-connected and can immediately land a teaching job at a università, you can remain in this "assistant" position for your entire career.

Frequently what happens is when the teacher (for whom you are acting as assistant) retires or dies, you then move into his position, though this can be heavily dictated by the "politics" of the school.

For musicians who are interested in "academic" studies in music (music history, research, *etc.*) there are several major universities in Italy:

The first is the *Istituto di Paleografia Musicale* in Cremona. Here you follow a course of study that concentrates on music theory, analysis, *etc.* This tends to be highly theoretical and usually takes 4 years.

Since this course of study is fairly directly applied to music, it is usually necessary to have a solid musical background.

Another form of academic musical study in Italy is the *D.A.M.S.* (*Dipartimento delle Arti, della Musica e dello Spettacolo*) in both Bologna and Torino. These tend to be less technical and concentrate more on historical and research aspects of the arts but you can specialize in music. Again, a solid musical background is expected and, again, this type of study is not performance oriented.

With these schools, as well as numerous others which are somewhat less recognized, you ultimately get a "Laurea" which is the highest level of formal university study in Italy but you don't get another title with this degree (such as "Maestro" or "Dottore").

In the conservatorio, you usually begin your studies very early (during high school or even before) and continue for several years after you are out of high school. Or at age 13 (the age when you can legally choose to quit your general education in Italy) you can simply quit school and concentrate totally on your musical studies.

The length of time required to finish a diploma in the conservatorio varies with each instrument but is generally between 7-10 years. However, coming from the States, particularly if you already have a Bachelor's or Master's, you may be able to complete a degree in a year or two. It simply depends on the school and whether you can pass the various exams.

To explain *performance*-oriented music studies in Italy in detail, first let me say that nothing is quite as bewildering as trying to figure out the Italian diploma system. Some of this is due to the fact that much of the Italian music education system was designed by the various governmental departments under Mussolini and they haven't gotten around to changing the system. So if you're into *serious* confusion, read on.

As I said before, you can begin your formal musical studies in Italy (as in France) while still a child. This is fine and much of the confusing explanations can be avoided because they happen at this early level and none of that will apply to you if you're going to Italy in your teens or later.

For older students it's a little easier to understand, but not much. If you go to Italy to study at "college level," you have basically one simple choice... which branches off into a dozen or so confusing options.

If you're studying performance, you *have* to go to a scuola di musica or a conservatorio. That's the simple part. From there it gets bizarre. Because they assume that you have started studying music at an early age (during grade school or high school) the length of time required to complete a degree is *much* longer than in the U.S. and changes irrationally with each instrument (*i.e.* the total time for wind instruments is generally 6-7 years; contrabass is 9 years; guitar, piano, strings are 10 years, *etc.*).

During this time there are various exams you must pass and (as in France) each time you pass a different exam you get another diploma. However, in Italy each of these diplomas have titles which sound fantastic but are very confusing, so I'll list the most general ones below.

Fig. 5.   Various Diplomas Given for
         Music Studies in Italy.

   • *Solfeggio* (3rd year)

   • *Compimento inferiore* (usually 5th year) This is also called
   "Diplomino" if you're doing a course of study for one of the
   instrument that takes less total time [*i.e. cf.* "winds" in the
   previous paragraph].

   • *Materie complementari* (6th or 7th year for music theory, music
   history, *etc.*).

   • *Compimento medio* (8th year of guitar, piano, *etc.*).

   • *Diploma* (10th year) This is essentially the same as a bachelor's
   in music in the U.S.

This final *Diploma* gives you the title of *"Maestro."* Obviously if you're going to Italy with some advanced musical background such as one or two years of U.S. conservatory or university, you could complete these exams in a much shorter time but you will *still* have to take the exam. This is different from Germany (and sometimes France) where they will often look at your university transcripts from the U.S. and simply award you credits toward the final foreign degree.

So... what do you do if you want to go to Italy and get some sort of degree to take back to the States? The answer is simple: *Go to Italy and study.* At some point, probably in a fairly short period of time, you will certainly be able to pass the exam for at least one of the above diplomas.

I know that sounds *extremely* vague but all this is complicated by the fact that the music courses in Italy vary from school to school. However the *exams* administered by the conservatories are regulated by the government and are all the same.

The very best thing to do is get in touch with a *specific* Italian school or a *specific* teacher, find out about their *specific* requirements and go from there—*always keeping an eye on your goal of passing the various exams administered by the conservatory.*

In my opinion, while Italy can appear *highly* disorganized, there is no country on earth more conducive to doing exactly what you want and if you're a little self-driven, you can accomplish academic *miracles* in Italy while still enjoying life with a passion that most countries have *never* learned. The second thing you should do is to simply do what the vast majority of Italian music students do: *don't worry about it...* it will work out!

Final Comments on Degrees

Often a foreign institution will accept some of the study that you have done at the university level in the U.S. and simply award you credit for that previous study which will apply toward your foreign degree. Thus, it may be possible to complete a degree in one year. Again, this depends on how many credits you already have and what credits the foreign school will recognize.

Obviously the same can be said for which credits will transfer from your foreign studies back to a U.S. music school. As I have said before, this varies greatly and the only safe move is to talk to *both* the foreign and U.S. institutions and see what they will accept.

If the foreign school will not accept some of your credits and insists that you take some classes you have already had, *don't panic.* First of all, it won't cost you any more money since in virtually all European schools your tuition covers any and all classes that you take that semester as opposed to the U.S. where you pay per credit hour.

Second, retaking a class can actually be an advantage since you will be studying a subject that you already know, which will be easy, but which will give you a chance to concentrate on that subject's vocabulary *in the foreign language.* Especially if you decide to stay and teach a while in that country, you will *desperately* need that vocabulary!

CHAPTER FIVE—
Getting Into a School

Through a Program or On Your Own?

You have basically two choices when you decide to study in Europe. First, your U.S. university or conservatory may already have a European extension or some affiliation or exchange program with a foreign school. Second, you may opt to simply go to a European school "cold" and rough it on your own like the European students. Each approach has advantages and disadvantages.

If your school has a European affiliation, the complication of getting into a school, trying to transfer credits, finding housing, getting a visa, *etc.*, are minimal. Your school in the States will usually help you out and may even do much of the paperwork for you.

Unfortunately, this *also* means that you could go to Europe, do all your classes in English, end up spending time at the extension with only Americans in a *very* sheltered situation and never get into the "European experience." However, this might be the best option if you're not too big on taking risks, have no way to make the necessary contacts in Europe, or if you're a little nervous about the whole thing and want the support that's built into a pre-designed program. I would also strongly suggest this type of program for younger students.

On the other hand, if you opt for going directly to a European school—*completely on your own*—you may have complications transferring credits back and forth, finding housing, getting a visa, *etc.* However, if you're a little adventuresome, this will definitely give you a more "real life" European experience and depending on how much musical study you've already done in the States, you can often finish a European degree in one year, which is almost never the case if you go through an extension or exchange program.

Naturally, it can be a bit more complicated to set out on your own but it can also be much more beneficial since you'll learn more (I'll admit, probably the hard way) but in spite of the slight complications, hundreds of Americans do this every year. If they can do it, you can do it. So for the rest of this section we'll assume that you've decided to go study in Europe "cold" without any outside help.

Contact with the Teacher

Many Americans tend to not understand that when you study at a foreign music school (with the general exception of the universities) you are studying with:

a) a *teacher*, who is teaching
b) at an *institution*
   —*in that order!*

If the teacher accepts you as a student, the institution automatically (in most cases) accepts you in their school, after an audition, which is little more than a formality. There is virtually never any sort of written entrance exam to the school.

This is a *drastic* contrast between the U.S. and European systems. In the States, you get into a school and are usually "assigned" to a teacher if you don't already have one. This is rarely the case in Europe. As a result, it is *essential* that you already have a strong contact with the teacher before you go to a foreign school. If not, you can find yourself in the terrifying situation of going to the foreign country, auditioning to get into the school, and finding that no teachers have room or are willing to take you as a student.

The best way to make contact with a teacher is through summer music festivals or masterclasses given by the teacher with whom you want to study. Attending a masterclass in the country of your choice is also important because this will give you a good idea of how you manage with the language (assuming they don't speak English in the class) and how you will get along with the teacher, which is probably the single-most important factor of studying music in Europe.

After the summer course or masterclass, try and get a letter from the specific teacher saying that he will take you as a student in the school where he normally teaches. Send a copy of this letter, along with your application for admission to the school, in one package and simply wait until the school tells you when the auditions will be. [4]

With rare exception, this will insure that you get accepted by the teacher and subsequently accepted into the school. The entrance auditions are almost always in person which means you must go to the country, but if you've taken the steps above (talking to the teacher, and applying to the school), there should be absolutely no risk and you can simply stay in the country and study at the school after the audition.

Tuition fees in most European music schools are a *fraction* of the American system. The tuition in most state-supported music institutions is roughly between $100 and $500 per year—a vast difference from the inflated tuitions in the States. The reason is that virtually all these schools are supported by the national or local government. This is obviously one of the greatest advantages of studying overseas, especially long-term.

Keep in mind, that if you plan to complete your entire degree in Europe and then return to the States to teach music in public schools (elementary or secondary education), some U.S. states may not accept the European degree. You will probably have to take an equivalency test and there will undoubtedly be some classes that you'll have to make up in the state where you will teach (usually music education and general education classes). The best thing to do is to talk with an official in the accrediting office in your home state and find out these details before you go to Europe.

If you plan on completing your degree in the States and are simply using your time overseas to take some extra classes, many classes (or credits) will usually transfer back to a U.S. conservatory or university though sometimes this also requires an equivalency test.

---

4. Don't feel uncomfortable about calling the foreign school office periodically to find out about the audition date. Since you're coming from the States, they are usually pretty understanding about the complicated logistics and your need to know the audition date as soon as possible to plan your flight, *etc.*

Conversely, many university credits from the U.S. will transfer to European schools which can speed the completion of a foreign degree. However, this varies from school to school so it's impossible to make a generalization. As I said before, the only solution is to talk to both schools in the U.S. *and* in Europe and find out what will transfer both directions.

If you're going to Europe as part of a pre-designed study program organized by your U.S. school, none of these complications should arise. In this case, they probably will have already decided which classes you can take and what will transfer (safe, but boring)— I personally *hate* "safe and boring!"

Classes in Europe

Assuming that you've gone to Europe on your own, bring a transcript from your U.S. school and *immediately* talk to your advisor in the European school to find out what classes will transfer toward a European degree (from your previous U.S. studies), get a list of what you are lacking to receive the foreign degree and ask what classes you should take.

If at all possible, the first semester you should take fairly easy classes that you have already studied (in English). As I mentioned earlier, you'll probably have to retake a few classes since they usually won't accept all the credits from your U.S. studies. Now is the time to retake those classes. Again, this is important since it will give you a chance to concentrate on the foreign vocabulary in a subject that you already know.

Also, get involved in the activities in the school. Play in ensembles, sing in the choir—anything you can do to start making contact with other students—*quickly*. This will not only integrate you into the system but will strengthen your vocabulary and help ward off any slight twitches of homesickness or culture shock.

A final word of warning about classes. Most of the European music schools have *very* lax attendance requirements. Because of that, many European students skip class often and simply "cram" before exams. If they don't pass an exam, they simply retake it the next semester. This is part of the reason that many European students stay in school several years longer than we do in the U.S. The problem is, as a foreign student, you probably don't have this luxury. You will need to get the exams out of the way *quickly* before you have to return to the U.S.!

Since attendance usually doesn't effect your grade (as long as you pass the exams) you can get away with skipping and cramming but it's not a good idea for a number of reasons.

Skipping classes and then cramming for exams is difficult in your *own* language. You don't learn the subject as well and the long-term retention of a subject is poor. However the main problem with this approach is that you miss out on much of the vocabulary in the language.

You'll need that vocabulary to pass the final exam (*especially* if you plan on taking the exam for the French teaching certificates [either the D.É. or C.A.]) and you will need the vocabulary even more if you decide to stay and teach in the country. Plus, the regular contact with the professor and fellow students is important to help you adjust to the country and these contacts can be *extremely* important in the future if you decide to start looking for teaching jobs or concerts.

My advice: *go to class!*

The Student/Teacher Relationship

It may come as a shock, but the student/teacher relationship throughout Europe is *much* different than in the U.S. The applied teacher is (by our standards) almost a dictator. He often tells you what to practice, what to play, when to play a recital, what classes to take and even suggests what books to read, films to see, *etc.* Conceptually, he is honestly trying to shape your musical and personal growth in the direction that he thinks will be most productive for you and your career.

From an American standpoint this can seem like an infringement of personal rights. Yet if you get used to the system and work within it, this can be *highly* beneficial. To the European mind, this dominance of the teacher is accepted because they assume that the teacher is in that position because he has earned it and is highly qualified to tell you what to do. Thus, he knows what's best for each student.

Obviously this may not be the case but often it is. Regardless of what you think of this system, you had better get used to living with it or you will have some *very* uncomfortable confrontations with your teacher. A teacher (or "professor" as they are virtually all called) wields *unbelievable* power and can make your life very easy or very difficult. *Stay on the good side of your teacher!*

Because of this rigid student/teacher relationship, be sure to talk to you teacher about any move you make—*professional or personal.*

Check with the teacher before you start working on a new piece, before you schedule a recital, before you break up with your boyfriend or girlfriend, *etc.* It may sound absurd, but venturing out on your own without first discussing it with your teacher—even with minor decisions—can be considered a *serious* insult and irreparably damage the relationship.

Also—just for the—record, *always* use the formal "you" when addressing your teacher (French = vous, German = Sie, Italian = lei). Using the familiar form of "you" can be so out of place that it borders on *extremely* offensive. In Italy the term "Maestro" is common for any music teacher and "Maestro" is *always* used throughout Europe for a conductor.

There is a formality in Europe between the student and teacher (and between a musician and his superiors) that we simply do not have in the States and you would be very wise to *never* overstep this boundary.

CHAPTER EIGHT—
Getting There and Other Details

Getting There [5]

When you check with the airline or your travel agent there are a couple basic things you want to ask:

1) "Open-end round-trip ticket" Remember, you may be staying for quite a while and in the course of the year your schedule may change. An open-end ticket (one that has a set departure but not a set return date) will be a little more expensive but still less than if you buy a set return date and have to change it.

2) "Excess baggage" Ask about any extra charges for excess baggage or weight. Some airlines are very strict and you can get hit with some hefty additional fees right there at the airport.

---

5. There are some travel agents that specialize in working with musicians. They are *definitely* worth being in touch with since they can give you info on baggage requirements, info on frequent flyer programs (make sure to use a frequent flyer program that lets you keep your miles over a long period of time), easily adapt to changing schedules, *etc.* Check with local musicians in your area to find who does such bookings.

The other option is the internet travel organizations. If you have a bit of flexibility in your schedule, these can often be the least expensive tickets.

Visas, etc.

Most European countries have two types of visas which apply to musicians. The first and most obvious, is a *student (study) visa.* This says that you are permitted to stay in the country for a specific period of time as a student. *It does not permit you to work in that country!* Permission to work in Europe (as for foreigners in the U.S.) requires a *work visa* which is infinitely more difficult to get.

Getting a student visa is relatively easy. Once you are accepted by the teacher, the next step is to apply to the school then immediately call the nearest embassy or consulate of that country and ask what you should do to get a student visa. Virtually all countries have an embassy in Washington, DC, but there may be one closer to your home and these smaller embassies can often be more helpful and friendlier. The requirements for a visa differ greatly from country to country and change constantly so you'll have to simply get the most current information from them. [5]

If you've landed a job in Europe, you have to have a work visa. In this case, you probably had to have a live audition and/or interview with the employer in that country and you may be able to apply for your work visa there rather than returning to the States to apply.

This is especially true if you already have a valid student visa since much of your documentation and paperwork will already be on file at their visa office.

A work visa usually requires the same type of documentation as a student visa so make sure you keep a copy of that application and a duplicate of all the materials you were required to submit. Most countries require that you reapply for all types of visas each year so don't forget to keep copies of everything—it will save you a lot of time!

The list of required documentation for a student or work visa changes from country-to-country so you'll *have* to talk to the embassy.

To get a work visa *then* try and find a job is almost impossible. If you want to work in Europe but have no contacts, I would suggest going to the country as a student (on a student visa) and make as many contacts as possible, work hard on the language and usually within one year you can land some sort of teaching or playing job. It's a rough way to go but it is still very feasible.

---

5. Telephone directory assistance for Washington, DC is 1-202-555-1212. Ask the operator for the number of the specific embassy, then call the embassy and ask them if there is another embassy closer to your home. If not, deal directly with their DC embassy.

This may be obvious, but remember that there is a great difference between a *passport* and a *visa* and one does not take the place of the other. Several of my American students have confused the two and had serious problems. *Note:*

1) A *passport* is a small booklet *issued by the U.S. government* that simply says who you are. You must have one of these before leaving the States (your local post office can tell you where to apply). It can take up to six months to get a passport so do this early.

A new passport is currently valid for up to ten years. If you lose your passport overseas or the date of your current passport begins to run out, you can get a new one from the local U.S. Embassy or Consulate overseas. If you do lose it, it will speed the application process if you know the passport number of the lost passport so keep this written somewhere safe—or better yet—have a photocopy of the title page (the one with your picture on it). It can also greatly speed the replacement process if you have a certified copy of your birth certificate. Otherwise you may only be issued a "temporary passport" that you will have to renew in three months.

2) A *visa* is *issued by the foreign country* (usually valid for one year) and says that you are permitted to stay in that country as either a student (in the case of a student visa) or as a worker (in the case of a work visa). The visa is a little piece of paper (usually with some really fun designs and colors—Germany and France even have a hologram) that they glue into your passport. Frankly, I've always found the system of visas a little stupid but every country requires foreigners to have a visa and besides, they make your passport look impressive!

Remember that a visa is *not* the same as the stamp you get at the border (or airport) when you enter the country. This "entry stamp" (sometimes called an "entry visa," which is what confuses some people) only says *when* you came into the country. Beyond that, it's useless.

Many European countries have started requiring foreign students and workers to apply and get the visa in their home country. *Do not assume that you can go to the country and then get a visa!* As ridiculous as this sounds, several people I know have had to return to the U.S. to simply pick up a visa. Be sure to check with the embassy of the foreign country. All these regulations are different for every country and change frequently and irrationally so don't take any risks because it could cost you a *lot* of time and money—*talk to the embassy!*

I should point out that most countries in Europe currently allow American citizens to enter and stay in the country (usually for three months) without a visa. This is referred to casually as a "tourist visa" (although no visa actually exists or is pasted into your passport). It is an "unwritten visa" that permits you to stay there short-term and in many cases (such as summer festivals, masterclasses, *etc.*) this will allow you to study briefly in a foreign country without the lunacy of getting a "real" visa. Generally, they base the 3-month period on the date stamped in your passport from the "entry stamp."

Because of this, some students stay in a country for the 3 months on a "tourist visa," then go across the nearest border for an afternoon and on the way back into the country, get another entry stamp in their passport with a new date. This establishes that they are, again, legal to stay in that country as a "tourist" for another 3 months.

Yes... this is "legal" but it's a very gray area and could cause you problems, especially since many schools have recently started asking to see your visa before they will let you enroll. I wouldn't suggest playing the "three-month-tourist-game," but in very extreme situations—for a very short time—this might be an option.

The only other visas you may encounter are a *tourist visa* or a *transit visa*. These used to be required by the former east-bloc countries but are rarely used now. However this changes periodically. If you're going to an out-of-the-way country, be sure to check (at the embassy of the specific country) if U.S. citizens must have a tourist visa to visit or a transit visa which simply permits you to travel *through* the country on the way to another one. A tourist or transit visa can take several days to get and is usually pasted in your passport.

Sometimes you can get a tourist or transit visa directly at the border before entry into the country (even on the train), but there's less chance of a problem if you go to an embassy in the town where you live in Europe and get it there in advance.

With the solidification of the European Union and the reorganization of the former east-bloc, tourist and transit visas are increasingly rare, but always check with that country's embassy to make sure because these requirements can change—*literally*—overnight.

Driver's License

The only other formal document you might want to invest in is an *International Driver's Permit*. You will need one of these if you plan to drive in Europe but you must get it in the U.S.

Contact your local AAA (American Automobile Association in the Yellow Pages) and they can issue you an International Driver's Permit in about five minutes. Simply show them your U.S. drivers license, give them two passport-sized photos of yourself, pay a few dollars and go home a sanctioned international driver. *Note that you must have your U.S. license with you as well as the International License while driving in Europe.* An International Permit requires no test, is valid for one year, is recognized by virtually every country on earth and is usually required if you're renting a car in Europe. *Important:* If you stay in your host country for over one year, the license may not be accepted *after* this initial year. Check with the embassy!

Depending on the country, with the driving classes, licensing fees, *etc.*, you can spend well over one thousand dollars just to get a local driver's license—a wee-bit higher than in the States!

In a few countries you can simply exchange your U.S. license for a local one in your host country but this often depends on the state in which your U.S. license was issued and most countries change their requirements frequently and irrationally.

For example, in Austria (since part of their test involves a basic overview of the mechanics of the motor), they will (this week...) accept licenses from Nebraska, Louisiana and a few others, since Austria has decided that these U.S. states have a test similar to their own. However, in reality the tests aren't even *remotely* similar and I'm convinced that what they really do is chose the accepted states by throwing darts at a map of the U.S.

If you *honestly* can't get by without a car and want a local license, call their embassy in the U.S. and ask about driver's license requirements and go from there.

Obviously, one solution (beyond the International Permit) is to find out which U.S. states are accepted for a direct license "exchange," go visit a friend in that state, and transfer your license, using their address as your "new U.S. address."

Simply get a license in that state and when you arrive in your host country, exchange it for a local driver's license. Note that this can foul your voting rights in your home state since in doing this, you are establishing residency in the new U.S. state—but you can always transfer your legal residence back when you return to the U.S. I doubt that I need to remind you that this is a grey area so of course I'm not advising this option...

Cars in Europe

If you plan to own a car overseas, remember that maintenance on a car in Europe is *easily* twice as expensive as in the U.S.—this is especially true for gas and insurance prices. Also, if you opt to own a car in Europe, I *strongly* suggested that you get an official driver's license in your host country which in many instances requires certification that you have taken a driving course in the host country and take their driver's test (both of which are insanely expensive and obviously in the native language) This may also mean brushing up on some new vocabulary.

If you want to go to the trouble, you can ship a car to Europe. There are several shipping firms who do this regularly. The cheapest shipping firms are in New York and the price is usually around $500. Check a New York City phone book under "overseas shipping." The shipping firms which are based in Europe are usually at least twice as expensive so deal with an American-based firm.

To ship a car to Europe, you fill out some forms at the shipping office, drop the car off at their dock and pick it up a few weeks later at any number of ports in Europe. Bremerhaven, Germany and Rotterdam, Holland are usually the cheapest if you're shipping from New York. I suggest shipping a car *only* under the following conditions:

a) Check with the embassy of your host country and make sure that you can legally drive with valid U.S. license plates. Otherwise you'll need to *immediately* re-license the car in the host country and as I'll explain later, this is a mess.

b) Make sure that you can legally drive with these U.S. license plates *for at least one year.*

c) Plan on selling the car *(at a loss)* as the end of your legal year approaches. You may need to resell the car in the former east-bloc (Hungary, Poland, Czechoslovakia, Romania, *etc.*) because their requirements for foreign auto resale are very lax. However, if you do this you should have some contacts there to help you because of the language, *etc.*, and the price you'll get will be lousy.

d) Don't plan on shipping the car back to the U.S. This is because the EPA (the U.S. Environmental Protection Agency) requires that any U.S. car that has been shipped out of the U.S. then shipped back, must be tested for pollution emission and various other tests to establish that the car has not been mechanically altered in any way that could make it incompatible with U.S. safety standards. These tests are expensive and they almost always find something that needs to be fixed.

Also, remember that if you have mechanical problems with a car you've shipped from the States, you may have *unbelievable* difficulty getting parts. I can tell you this from personal experience.

To ship a car over and re-license it in the host country is also possible but this is complicated and expensive because if the car is new enough you may get hit with some hefty import taxes and most importantly, to re-license a car, it must meet the local requirements. Depending on the country, "local requirements" can mean rewiring the car with fog lights, changing the color of blinker lights, changing the tachometer to read in kilometers-per-hour, *etc.*

Frankly, unless you have something like a vintage 1932 Jaguar, shipping a car to Europe isn't worth all the trouble. However, I did ship a car to Europe from the U.S. a few years ago and this *can* be an option if you're a little adventuresome, don't mind spending the money and you meet the requirements (a, b, c & d above).

The best solution is to simply do without a car or rent one on the rare occasions that you may truly need one. In Europe, you can *easily* spend as much on a car per month as you do on your apartment so unless you really need a car, you're probably wise to do what most European students do: use a train, bus, subway, taxi, bicycle—or walk. It will save you a fortune.

Driving Overseas

There are minor differences when driving overseas but it's pretty much the same as in the States (except of course in Britain where the drive on the *left* side of the road). However virtually every country in Europe has one MAJOR difference called "Priority from the Right."

Priority from the Right means that whoever is on the right (even if it's a small country road entering onto a larger state road) THEY have priority unless they have a stop or yield sign. If they pull in front of you and you hit them it's your fault.

This is *totally* irrational and Europeans even joke about it but be careful! A dangerous corner may be marked with the signs below but often it is not. Get a local drivers manual and be sure to ask the locals in your area about any corners with Priority from the Right!

This sign means you   *This sign means you*
DO have priority.   *DO NOT have priority.*

Additional Documentation
Photos

This is a minor point, but make sure you have about a dozen extra passport photos of yourself. Nearly every time you turn around in Europe you need your picture on something. This includes subway cards, registration forms with the foreign police, transit and tourist visas, student identification cards, *etc.* If you have some extra photos on hand it can save time and trouble.

School Transcripts

Bring a notarized copy of your transcript of your U.S. university-level studies. In the U.S. this is referred to as an "official transcript". This will show the various classes you've had, your grades and grade point average (which won't mean anything to them in Europe). However, you will need your transcript to establish what classes you've already had so you can (with luck) transfer these credits toward your European degree.

Letters of Introduction

If you're planning on doing any musicological research in Europe, remember that most of their libraries are government or university institutions (though some are private). There are two major differences between European and U.S. libraries: first, most are "closed stacks," especially in historical archives with very old music, manuscripts and first editions.

If you're not familiar with this system, in a closed stack library, you go to the card catalog (or occasionally the catalog computer), make a list of what you want to see and they bring it to you at your assigned seat. You cannot simply browse through the aisles and skim through anything that looks interesting.

The second major difference is that many old libraries are private. Especially in Italy, some libraries are still owned and housed by the original family dating back hundreds of years or owned by some other non-governmental institution (such as a monastery or school). These private libraries are sometimes open stacks but this poses additional problems:

Getting *in* these private libraries can be difficult. Make a visit, be *very* polite and bring a letter of introduction *in the language that they will be speaking.* A letter of introduction is simply a brief note on official stationary from your university or a professor that says you are doing serious musicological research and asks that you be permitted entry into the libraries.

Remember, these are *not* public institutions—they are doing you a *great* favor by allowing you to work with their materials, so act accordingly. The holdings in these libraries are their private property and often (in the case of Baroque, Renaissance or Medieval manuscripts, *etc.*) these items are irreplaceable so don't expect them to be thrilled about your request. However, *normally,* they are helpful and if this type of work interests you, be aware that it's still possible to find unknown, lost, or extremely rare music and books quite accidentally— *so keep your eyes open!*

Obviously, in the case of historical materials, if you do happen to find something they will not let you photocopy it since *a)* they probably won't have a photocopy machine and *b)* the heat from the light in a photocopy machine can damage old materials. As a result, be sure to bring a stack of blank manuscript paper and a notebook since you will probably have to hand-copy anything you find. Some music researchers I know use a good camera with very fast film and a macro lens to photograph manuscripts without a flash. This can save time and you end up with a facsimile of the original which can be used in publications, *etc.* Just make sure the director of the library gives you permission before you start snapping pictures.

Remember to document *everything.* Not only the materials themselves, but where they came from (including the row, shelf, size of the tome, color of the cover—*everything*). Since some of these libraries are highly disorganized, materials can easily get lost or mis-shelved from one day to the next.

INS Pass

This program was initiated in 1995 by the U.S. Department of Immigration and Naturalization (abbreviated, INS). If you make frequent trips between the U.S. and Europe, you can go *crazy* waiting in line to get cleared through U.S. customs when you return.

A rather high-tech solution to this problem has been established by the U.S. Department of Justice, is a little card called an INS Pass ("Immigration and Naturalization Service Pass"). Ask about this at the customs office in any U.S. international airport. The INS Pass is currently only used in a few airports but they plan to expand the program to all U.S. international airports.

You fill out a form, they check your passport, take your picture and make a "scan" of your right hand (sort of like the things used to identify alien monsters in science fiction movies). You are then issued a card and the next time you enter the States, rather than waiting in line with the hundreds of other blithering U.S. citizens, you go directly to the INS Pass machine, put in your card, put your hand in the scanner and it gives you a little ticket (like a grocery store receipt). You simply give that ticket, along with your customs declaration card that they give you on the airplane, to the customs official at the exit and you're finished. No lines, no hassle.

Remember that an INS Pass does not take the place of your passport but it saves you time since you don't have to wait in line to have your customs declaration checked.

There are several problems with the INS Pass system. First, the computer that they use to download the information to Virginia (where the main computer is located) is frequently "down." In fact, the last 4 times I've tried to get my pass updated, they haven't been able to get the computer to work. These technical problems seem to have infected the INS Pass machines themselves and *they* frequently don't work. However, when a machine is down, the customs officials often post an agent to stand next to the machine, look at your card, passport and customs declaration form, so you still get through the lines more quickly.

Unfortunately this program is not yet widely in use and it often doesn't work like it's supposed to but if you're frequently entering the States at an airport which offers this service, it can make your life infinitely more calm. Especially if you're on a concert tour and have some tight flight connections, the time saved can be critical.

Electronics

You're probably aware that the U.S. uses 110 volts while Europe uses 220 volts. Just to remind you, while 110 volts can hurt and can kill you, the European current is twice as strong. If you're not sure what you're doing, don't mess the electricity.

This is especially true in some apartments, since people usually buy their own light fixtures, *etc.* When you move into an apartment, there may be a number of loose wires hanging from the walls. Assume that these have live current and ***DON'T TOUCH THEM!!!***

Some electronic items from the U.S. (hair dryers, razors, *etc.*) have a 110/220- switch that you can simply flip, get a plug adaptor and plug right into the European 220 wall sockets.

If you're appliance doesn't have this switch, you need to have

1) a transformer AND
2) the plug adaptor (so it will fit into the European outlet).

On the other hand, it may be more practical to simply buy a new unit in Europe.

Larger items (computers, *etc.*) are *much* more expensive in Europe so if yours doesn't have a 110/220 switch you should invest in a large transformer (available at any electronic supply company). Get a good one, which will be about 4-6 inches square and weigh around 30 pounds but this size is stable enough to work safely with larger appliances.

On the other hand, some large equipment such as portable recording studios (particularly those made in Japan) are constructed identically for the U.S. and Europe. The only difference is the "power source." The power source is a little box (actually a transformer) with cords coming out of both ends. One side plugs into the wall and the other plugs directly into the machine.

However, since the machines for the U.S. and Europe are often identical, the *only* difference is the transformer. A transformer will:

1) in the U.S., convert 120 volts to 9 volts and
2) in Europe, the transformer will convert 220 volts to 9 volts.

What this means is you *may* be able to take your U.S. unit to Europe, contact the European branch of the manufacturer and get a converter that takes 220 to 9 volts (or whatever the converted voltage should be for your specific equipment).

This can save you a *tremendous* amount of money since professional electronic gear of this nature is usually *at least* twice as expensive in Europe and this also saves you from dragging around a 30 pound transformer.

I should point out that most manufacturers won't be too helpful if you explain what you're doing (they'd rather sell you two different units - one for the U.S. and one for Europe...). Talk to a professional electrician to make sure you'll be o.k. with this suggestion, but 99% of the time, this works.

CHAPTER NINE—
Finances Overseas [6]

As a foreign student, there are few ways to make money in Europe. You should have a set amount of money saved and transferred to a bank account where you will be living. To be safe, this should be enough to sustain you for your entire stay but that's a fairly idealistic suggestion. For example, when I first moved to Vienna, I had slightly over $300.—an amazing mixture of courage and stupidity! The best thing is to have the money in-hand that you'll need for your entire stay.

Most countries require that you have a bank account (with a required amount) to get a visa so you will probably have to do this anyway.

Naturally, as a musician there are many "unofficial" possibilities to make money overseas. You can always pick up "gigs" playing for parties, perhaps do some sub work with the local orchestra, or teach private music students.

Many Americans opt for teaching English (privately or through a school) which is a popular way to earn some extra money. However, keep in mind, if you do any of this without a work visa you are "working

---

6. At the end of this chapter are a few ideas for finding financial support. Note that there are *hundreds* of assistance programs for overseas study.

black" which is illegal. "Working black" is the common phrase used in virtually every European language for anyone working without a work permit and if you work black and get caught, you *could* be thrown out of the country (although this practically never happens). Many Americans work black while they are studying overseas and the decision is simply up to you. If you do chose this option, be careful! The well-known book, *Let's Go* (listed in "Suggested Reading") gives a few ideas for finding summer work in Europe with and without a work visa but this sort of thing is usually incompatible with studies and the pay is minimal, so don't count on this too much.

Again, the best thing is to make sure you have enough money to get by for the entire time that you'll be studying in Europe, then— if you happen to get some unexpected work—you'll simply have more money than you planned on. You can buy some extra wine in France, chocolate in Belgium, go to Oktoberfest, make a weekend trip to La Spezia or just treat yourself and a friend to a dinner at an expensive restaurant in your new town. There are a *lot* of things to spend extra money on in Europe!

There are many scholarship programs available to assist with foreign studies. For starters, I would suggest contacting:

Council for International Exchange
3007 Tilden St. NW
Ste. 5 M
Box GPOS
Washington, D.C. 20008-3009

This is the organization that administers the Fulbright Grants and numerous other foreign study programs. Remember, if you are currently studying in a U.S. institution, you must apply for a Fulbright through your school. If you are not currently studying in a school, you can apply for a Fulbright independently.

For short-term studies (such as summer festivals and masterclasses) you should contact the *Fund for U.S. Artists at International Festivals and Exhibitions (at the same address above)*.

Foundation Center
79 5th Ave.
New York, NY 10003

This is a library which houses a *massive* collection of grant information. If you are having trouble tracking down the address of a specific grant or need additional information, try contacting them.

In addition to these sources, talk with your dean, counselor and especially the financial aid office at your music school. They often know what programs are currently available, as well as any possibilities for funding at the local level that might not appear in national listings.

CHAPTER TEN—
Housing

Most larger towns will have some sort of student housing such as dormitories where you can live. These may or may not include meals and can be—in either case—an expensive but simple solution. [7]

Apartments can be a good situation depending on who you live with. Schools often have bulletin boards where other students list roommate (flatmate) openings. Finding an apartment on your own is a bit more complicated because the apartment rental contracts are usually for at least one full year and apartments are often unfurnished.

By "unfurnished" I mean that in *some* cases there won't even be an installed toilet. Because so many Europeans live their entire lives in an apartment (sometimes the *same* apartment), they often prefer to install exactly what they want—from toilets to door knobs.

---

7. This is especially true in France. There, once a student has a *carte de séjour* (foreigner residence card), the French government will often pay up to half of your rent as long as you are studying at a recognized institution—even if you are not a French citizen.

Unfortunately what *often* happens is the owner of a dormitory (recognizing that half the student's rent is often paid by the French government) has nearly doubled the rent. You end up paying the same as if you were renting a normal apartment, but the landlord makes more money. Be sure to check local housing prices so you know what you're getting into.

If you decide to rent an apartment, make sure you get one that is "finished" or you can spend a fortune just making it livable. Still, if you're staying for a year or more, an apartment can be a good option and fully-furnished apartments exist but you'll have to shop around.

You might also consider living with a family as a boarder. Boarding with a family (especially for short-term studies) is *much* more common in the Europe than in the U.S. and while it can seriously limit your privacy, it can be cheaper and also give you the opportunity of experiencing "real life" in another country, using the language on a daily basis and your host family can help out if you encounter any real problems overseas.

Many schools have a list of families who take boarders but beware of the prices. Some of these are highly inflated and boarding can be either a fantastic experience or a nightmare, depending on your host family. From their standpoint, you are truly becoming a member of their family and as we all know, not all families are "stable."

If possible, try to get to know them or talk to a previous boarder before you make a decision.

Once you have found housing, you need to register with the foreign police (or "immigration police"). *Every* country has a special division of the police called the foreign police. Their job is to keep track of foreigners living in their country. The foreign police in most countries have three distinct characteristics: they are often:

1) *unfriendly*,
2) *unhelpful*,
3) (and frequently) *not very smart.*

One of the few slightly unpleasant experience of your stay in Europe will be visiting the foreign police. It's nothing serious so don't let them ruin your opinion of a country. The foreign police are unfriendly, unhelpful and not very smart in *every* country (even the U.S.) and they seem to be proud of it. Don't give them any problems but also don't take their inhospitality too seriously. [8]

8. In all fairness, I should point out that the only two countries where I've had problems with the foreign police were Austria and Germany—but these problems were very extreme and *highly* irrational. Italy is usually very friendly and when I got my *carte de séjour* for France, the director of the foreign police even invited me (with members of his staff) for a glass of champagne to celebrate! Through the entire process, smile a lot! The bureaucracy can be a nightmare, but it's still a people-to-people situation. If you get the officials on your side, it should go smoothly.

To register with the foreign police, there are usually several forms to fill out. They always check your passport to make sure you have the proper visas and (depending on the country) they usually make you buy some tax stamps (for a few dollars) that are put on a piece of paper that says you really live where you told them you live. Then they usually give you a copy of this and they keep one copy in their files. *Both copies have to have the tax stamps.* I'm convinced that they do this just so you have to buy twice as many stamps. I agree, this is stupid, but they make the rules.

If you are staying for a short time and do not have a visa, you generally don't need to bother registering with the foreign police. Some countries (such as Belgium) require registration of any foreigner who is staying for more than a few days.

The school, your host family, landlord, or even hotel clerk can tell you who to talk to so you can find out the current local requirements. As a last resort, the U.S. embassy in your host country will know what you need to do.

Important note: anytime you talk to someone "official" (especially the foreign police) be friendly so they will remember you. Since most people are unfriendly to the foreign police, being friendly is usually enough to make sure that they will *never* forget you!

In fact, most people are so unfriendly to the foreign police (with good reason) that they will be completely aghast if you even smile at them. Friendliness makes them very uncomfortable—which is sort of a fun psychological game to play. Also, if at all possible, *shake their hand.* Again, this will help them remember you (more about hand shaking later...).

Also, try to find out their names. First, this helps them remember you. Second, if there is a problem later you can always say, *"...but Mr. X told me..."* which will nearly always help the situation.

Anytime you're dealing with anyone official, try to find out if they have a title *and use that title every time you talk to them.* For example, in French, the head of a conservatoire is *"Monsieur Directeur X"* (fill in the last name at the "X"). I realize this sounds absurd in English but they are used to it and *not* using a title can be considered a very grave insult.

The same is frequently true of academic titles. In Austria (and often in Germany), someone who has the equivalent of a master's degree is called *"Herr Magister X,"* while in Italy, virtually every music teacher has the title of *"Maestro."* I agree it's all a bit overly-formal but that's the way it is. And again, *always shake hands with everybody!*

Just as a passing note, *everyone* shakes hands in Europe—men, women and children—so get used to this. Other similar traditions are kissing and hugging (men, women and children). For the record, it's sort of interesting to note that in German-speaking countries you usually *only* shake hands.

In Italy you shake hands, and with good friends, often hug or trade one kiss on the cheek (sometimes both cheeks).

In France you shake hands, sometimes hug (good friends) and trade kisses on the cheek with friends and always with children. However this custom varies with each region in France. In southern France it's traditionally one or two cheeks—in central France it's usually both cheeks—and in northern France, traditionally, it's four kisses on the cheek (left, right, left, right, or *vice verse*).

Until you get used to this (especially in the North), you'll probably feel like a bird pecking frantically back and forth trying to catch a squirming worm. It's a nice custom and once you get used to it, kissing everybody becomes so automatic that when you go back to the States you will probably have to make a conscious effort to *not* kiss everybody you meet—this makes many Americans *very* uncomfortable. [9]

---

9. *Ps.* Do *not* try to kiss the foreign police. They will *not* consider themselves your friend, they have absolutely *no* sense of humor and they *won't* think it's funny...

CHAPTER ELEVEN—
Working Overseas

If you decide to live and work overseas, you are joining a rather elite handful of Americans, who for various reasons have decided to keep U.S. citizenship but live and work in another country.

These people are commonly referred to as *"expatriates"* (or *"ex-pats"*). The title means nothing since it is rarely a political decision or a question of patriotism but this has become a catch-all phrase and you hear the term "ex-pat" a lot overseas.

There are numerous advantages and disadvantages to being an ex-pat, some of which are important to understand in detail.

As I mentioned earlier, working overseas, *in any job whatsoever*, requires a different visa than simply a student visa. A work visa can be *insanely* difficult to get, depending on the country. The most obvious and important thing for working overseas is that you be fairly comfortable with the language, which I'll discuss later.

Generally, you must establish that you have an employer who wants to hire you. Your employer will give you the proper documentation for this. Then, the employer must prove that you are the only person qualified for the job and that no other applicants (from that country) could possibly fill that position.

Obviously, in the case of teaching English this is simple since you are a native English speaker and the locals are not. In music it is almost as simple because music is so subjective that your employer can simply say, "...*we liked the way he played...*" and that basically does it. This also naturally applies to securing an orchestral position.

One good option for students wanting to stay and teach is to try to find a post at a *Musikschule* (in Germany or Austria) an *école de musique* (in France or Belgium) or a *scuola di musica* (in Italy), or at any of the elementary-level music schools in other countries. Even though you will be teaching probably 50% children, if you enjoy this sort of work, it can be a good way to secure a steady income and stay longer than your initial studies.

The pay for this type of job is good—about the same as an average 40-hour work week in the U.S.—but a full-time music teaching post in Europe is usually around 25 hours a week. Often you can arrange the lessons in 3 to 4 days which leaves plenty of time for your own practice, composing, travel, *etc.*

Once you have found an employer, if they are familiar with hiring foreigners such as an orchestra, they can tell you how to secure the necessary visa. In some cases they may even do the paperwork for you. In the case of an école de musique, Musikschule, or scuola di musica, this can be more complicated because they are less used to hiring foreigners. They should still be able to at least tell you what office to go to in order to get the correct information.

Keep in mind that getting a work visa—especially with the recent European Union—is more and more difficult for citizens of non-E.U. countries such as the U.S. Obviously, they will first hire someone from their own country (exactly the same as we do in the U.S.), or (second choice) from another E.U. country. However, working and especially teaching overseas, is a *very* realistic option if you have a decent command of the language.

Working overseas as a musician has *tremendous* advantages over the same situation in the U.S. Although taxes are higher, in most cases (such as with a large orchestra or teaching—even at the lower-level schools) you are considered a government or state employee, complete with all the benefits including paid holidays and *unbelievable* health and social programs.

For example in Austria, if a working woman is having a baby, she can take up to two years leave and the husband can take up to one year leave. This is rarely taken advantage of and such extreme programs are the cause of the *highly* inflated taxes but virtually nothing compares to the welfare systems in most European countries.

Also, musicians are considered *very* special people in Europe. Because Europeans are more familiar with classical music, they tend to treat musicians with *much* greater respect than we do in the States.

This in itself can be a gratifying feeling. In the States if someone asks you what you do and you say, *"I'm a classical musician,"* they often respond with a look that seems to say, *"...but what are you going to do when you grow up?!"* In Europe when you tell someone that you're a musician, it's as if you have told them that you are a leading brain surgeon. The respect and appreciation of musicians is undeniably higher in Europe.

I should however point out again that simply getting a visa—because of the European Union—has become increasingly difficult. The worst situation (as of the writing of this book) is in Austria. To apply for a work visa, you must do the following:

1) Have your birth certificate translated into German by a "licensed translator." A licensed translator in the U.S. often works for the CIA, State Department (A.I.S. [American Information Service] or the Secret Service... try finding them in your phone book...). The best solution is to call your local congressperson in the U.S. and ask for help. They can usually get you in touch with someone.

2) Have a letter from the local police station in the town where you were born saying that you have never been arrested and have that translated into German by a licensed translator.

3) Have a full medical examination (also translated).

4) Know your correct address in Austria and the size of the apartment where you will be living. The apartment must be at least 50 square meters per person if you have flatmates and the foreign police actually send someone around to check the size of the apartment.

5) Get a document from your insurance company saying that you have health insurance which will cover you while you are in Austria. Of course health insurance is normally provided through your Austrian employer, but until you are employed, they can't give you the documentation saying that you're insured. This *can* mean that you must buy health insurance which covers you in Austria, before you're allowed to be there. No, this is not logical but it gets worse...

6) The application must be made to the embassy in your home country (*i.e.* in the U.S.) and then there is a six month waiting period before you find out *if* you've been approved to get the visa.

7) Then (if you are approved) you have to go to the embassy in your home country (*i.e.* in the U.S.—at their embassy) and let *them* paste the visa into your passport. No, they will not just mail it to you...

Needless to say, this is insane. Especially with regards to numbers 4 and 5, this makes it very difficult since to know your correct address you must already have an apartment there, which means—officially—that you must go over, rent an apartment, return to the U.S., apply for the visa, and wait six months (while paying for an apartment that you are not living in and health insurance that you can't possibly use) and then (with luck) get the visa. By the way, *you are not permitted to be in Austria during the six-month waiting period.*

I should add that this absurd law changed 4 times in the first 6 months since the Austrian Parliament passed the original version and it will probably change another dozen times before this book goes to print—I hope with much more lenient requirements. However, this does point out the extreme attitude taken by some countries.

In short—find out the most current information from the foreign embassy in the U.S. and act on that. It truly is not as severe as it sounds and they *frequently* bend the rules but things are changing so quickly in Europe (because of the E.U.) that it is *essential* that you know what to do, depending on the country where you want to study or work.

As with any of the subjects in this section, if you are already overseas and have questions and simply don't know who to ask, call the nearest U.S. embassy or consulate and ask them what to do.

Keep in mind that many U.S. foreign embassies have a "cultural attaché." This is someone who is involved in various artistic activities in the diplomatic circles of that country. As a musician, it can help tremendously to know a cultural attaché since he/she will be familiar with the many legal details from an artists' standpoint. A cultural attaché is also often responsible for arranging entertainment for diplomatic parties, cultural events, *etc.,* so they can help set you up with periodic performing opportunities.

On the other hand, if you are in the U.S. and have questions, call the embassy of the country and if you still can't get a straight answer, call your local congressperson and they will help you out.

CHAPTER TWELVE—
Taxation Overseas

U.S. Taxation

If you take a post to work in a foreign country and establish your residency there, your "tax base" (as defined by the U.S. IRS) will be in *that* country which means you will pay taxes to *their* government.

The current situation (as of 2001) is such that the U.S. government permits you to earn up to $74,000. per year in a foreign country and not pay taxes on that money in the States. Anything over that is *also* taxed in the U.S. but at a slightly lower rate. All this, however, is only true if you can prove residency in that country (a work visa is usually sufficient for this) *and* prove that you pay taxes in your host country.

This may not sound fair but it's a *major* improvement over the "double taxation" that existed until very recently. Under the older system, ex-pats were taxed by both the local *and* U.S. governments on *all* their income. Under the new U.S. laws, you still need to file your foreign earned income to the IRS but odds are you will only have to pay taxes on that money *once* (to your host country).

The important thing to remember is each time you are paid, *immediately* call your bank in the host country and ask for the exchange rate between U.S. Dollars and "X" (the currency that you're paid in).

This is absurd, but the U.S. IRS *can* require you to compute your foreign earned income based on the exchange rate *on the specific day that you were paid* and this obviously changes daily.

Note that the IRS has recently begun accepting an "average conversion rate" which is an average of currency fluctuations throughout the fiscal year. You can usually use this exchange rate to report your foreign earned income but they can change this ruling, so the only 100% safe method is to document the exchange rates on the day that you're paid.

In either case, the bookkeeping is only a minor complication and once you get the routine down it's actually very little trouble.

Remember that the U.S. also has a "financial information disclosure agreement" with virtually every country on earth, so if the IRS gets *really* nosy they can get information from your foreign bank as to your income and foreign assets. This is especially true in Western Europe, since your employer always pays your salary directly into your local bank account. [10]

For musicians, a complication arises when you return to the States for concerts, *etc.* and earn money there as well. The question then is, where do you pay taxes on *that* money? The only solution is to have a tax consultant in *both* the U.S. and your host country.

In the long-run a tax consultant can save you a lot of money and a lot of headaches. Unless you're earning a lot of outside income overseas (which complicates the filing procedure), you can usually have a tax consultant in the U.S. file your U.S. taxes one year and simply use those forms as an example of how to do the forms yourself thereafter.

In all honesty, the difficulties aren't that great but I would suggest that if you get a job in Europe, one of the first things you should do is write the IRS and have them send you the booklet 1040-7. This booklet will explain what you need to do insofar as declaring your foreign earned income.

This booklet also includes all the required forms which ex-pats must use to file if they are living overseas (notably the forms 2555 "Foreign Earned Income" and "Foreign Earned Income Exclusion" and the form 1116 "Foreign Tax Credit").

---

10. This is not always the case with banks in Switzerland and Liechtenstein, who are famous for their "secret" bank accounts. However, unless you plan on keeping a fairly steady cash flow going through a secret account, the service charges for this type of account make it impractical. Unfortunately, most classical musicians don't earn enough to make this sort of bank account necessary.

In spite of the imposing girth of the 1040-7 booklet (there are hundreds of pages), it is written to be understood by anyone with the I.Q. of a fruit fly so don't be intimidated when it first arrives.

Thereafter, the IRS will automatically send the necessary forms top your foreign address to file your foreign earned income each year. The instructions for these forms are updated annually to include any changes in tax laws as they effect U.S. citizens overseas.

Remember, you're living and working in a foreign country *but you still have to file with the U.S. IRS.* However, in most cases it means that you don't have to *pay* anything to the IRS. Don't let this slide because it can cause you some serious problems if you happen to get audited in the States.

Local Taxation and Benefits

As I said above, if you're living and working in a foreign country you still have to file with the U.S. IRS. Conversely, even though you're an American citizen, because you are earning in another country, you must *also* file with your host country.

There are two basic categories of employment in Europe. The first is "Full Employment" and the second is as an "Independent worker." [11]

Being employed for "full employment" means that your health insurance, taxes, social security, *etc.,* are automatically deducted from your paycheck. Also, half your health insurance is usually paid by the employer. You work, get your pay check and that's it. However if you want to save some money, you *may* be able to opt for the second type of employment as an "Independent Worker."

The subject of health insurance will probably be the pivotal factor when you decide if you want to work as "employed" or as "independent." Buying insurance privately can be expensive though you can sometimes negotiate a higher salary with your employer and you can often take more deductions on your income taxes. If you opt for the full employment package and your employer pays half of your health insurance, you may earn a bit less but the paperwork is all taken care of. This is an important decision so talk to your employer, a private health company, your tax advisor and a few other local musicians to get their opinions.

---

11. The terms for these two types of employment are different in each country. However, a good tax advisor in your host country will know immediately what you mean if you ask him about these two categories of employment.

The major difference between these two categories of employment is how you are taxed and what social benefits (in your host country) you want to take advantage of—*and pay for.*

Unless you are planning on staying in the host country for the rest of your life, you may save money if you contract with your employer as an "independent worker." Again, this means that you will need to independently buy into a health/medical plan and file your taxes yourself (with the help of your tax advisor) as opposed to the taxes automatically being taken out of your pay check.

Be *sure* to talk to a local tax advisor before making this decision because the pros and cons vary from country to country. As I said before, in either case, I *strongly* advise having a good tax consultant who can do the paperwork for you.

This may sound a bit overwhelming (especially since you're going to be dealing with all this in the foreign language) but in the long-run it can save you a considerable amount of money, as I'll describe below.

Avoidable Taxation Overseas

Depending on your host country, there are usually several taxes that you can avoid. As I mentioned earlier, you *must* pay income taxes in the country where you are working. However, some of the inflated taxes for social benefits can be dropped if you arrange with your employer to be hired as an "Independent Worker."

In order of the most useless to semi-useful, these taxes are:

1) *Retirement Welfare Tax.* This is only useful if you plan to stay in your host country for the rest of your life. This is similar to our Social Security retirement tax, but depending on the country, it is sometimes only paid back to you if (after retirement) you still maintain permanent residence in your host country.

However, in Europe (as in the States) there was a "baby-boom" in the 1950's-60's which dropped off shortly thereafter. This means that when the "baby-boom generation" reaches retirement age, the younger generation (who are still working and paying into the social welfare system) will not be able to pay enough into the system because there are so few of them in relation to the copious baby-boomers. As in the U.S., this means that the actual return on the money that you paid into the social welfare system may never come back to you in retirement.

Thus, unless you plan on retiring in your host country and have an overly-optimistic faith in that country's social welfare system, talk to a tax advisor and try to get out of paying into the retirement tax fund and set up your own retirement saving account.

2) *Health Coverage.* You must have health coverage! This is not only true for your own protection but documentation of health coverage is usually one of the first things that they will check when you apply for your visa. However, you can normally drop the medical coverage offered by your host government if you buy into a *private* health care program in Europe. These health programs are not cheap but you may be able to save money and have equivalent (or better) health coverage.

Keep in mind if you have a family, this may not be advisable since the amount of money you have to put into private health care may exceed what you would have to pay into the government program. However, for a single person or a young married couple, you can usually save money and if the time comes that you *want* the government coverage, you can always switch back.

3) *Unemployment Tax.* This tax assures that you will be paid unemployment benefits if you happen to lose your job or are sick for an extended time. Most private health care programs (which I mentioned in #2 above) include the sick leave coverage for a slight additional fee.

If you have a family and are permanently settled in Europe, you may want to keep the unemployment tax since it's obviously a good security. This insures that you can continue to pay rent, expenses, *etc.* if you are sick for an extended period.

However, often ex-pats are only working in Europe for a few years and when they leave their European jobs, they will be moving back to the States. Also, if they become seriously ill, many ex-pats prefer to return to the U.S. to be near family, *etc.* You'll simply have to decide what is most applicable to your own needs. Think this one through carefully since, depending on your situation, it could be a good thing to have or it could be a total waste of money.

Some countries will allow you to drop selected portions of their social welfare program while others countries require that you either take the whole "package" of social benefits (and taxes) or take none of them. As in the U.S., these rules can change annually so you'll simply have to talk to a tax advisor.

If you do decide to drop these social benefits, you must establish that you are employed as an "Independent Worker" (the contract with your employer will define this status), buy into a private medical coverage program and arrange your own retirement fund. Unfortunately, this *also* means that you must file the paperwork and pay taxes directly to your host country's government instead of having them taken automatically out of your pay check.

Taxation for Independent Workers is sometimes on a quarterly basis, which means you're going to become pretty good friends with your European tax advisor. No matter how you're required to file, a good tax consultant can take care of all the paperwork for you and in the long-run, a tax consultant will save you time, money and *serious* frustration.

The social welfare system in most European countries is *tremendous*. It covers virtually every aspect of health and welfare from the moment you're born to the moment you die. If you plan to work in Europe for a short time, it will probably be easier to simply go with the system that they have.

However, if you're going to be working for more than a couple years, you can save a great deal of money if you venture out on your own (as do many Europeans) and decline some of their marvelous—but marvelously expensive—social welfare programs.

CHAPTER THIRTEEN—
Legal Matters and Emergencies and Saftey Overseas

Legal Matters

Frankly, taxation (if you're working overseas) and your visa (either a student visa or a work visa) are the only formal obstacles facing you when you make a move to Europe. The only other thing I should mention is the use of drugs overseas.

In spite of the American fairy tale concept of Europe (especially Holland) being "drug friendly," *don't believe it.* While you are overseas, you are subject to *their* laws. Being an American gives you no special privileges, and their drug laws can be *much* harsher than ours in the U.S.

Even in Holland, where small amounts of heroin "for personal use" is considered legal, you can get into some terrifying situations if you get caught. Even being in the wrong place at the wrong time— innocently—can result in hefty fines, long jail terms and will virtually always get you thrown out of the country permanently. Often your personal belongings *such as musical instruments* will be confiscated.

Aside from the fact that this sort of activity can destroy your life and career—in Europe *or* the U.S.—in Europe it can land you in the middle of a personal, financial and legal nightmare.

In short—*don't even think about it.*

Emergencies Overseas

Unfortunately sometimes things happen back home in the U.S. that make it necessary to return immediately. This may be a death in the family, a sudden illness, *etc.*

There are a number of U.S.-based airlines who are fortunately sympathetic to these situations and have developed programs which make it easy to book flights in an emergency.

One well-known example is Continental Airlines who has a tremendously helpful program. In this case, if a family emergency arrises, you simply call Continental, explain the situation and they will waive the charge for booking your flight on short notice.

They will ask a few simple questions:

1) the exact nature of the emergency,
2) the name and telephone number of the hospital,
3) the name of the attending physician, *and*
4) your credit card number.

Have all this information on-hand when you call.

From there, they call the hospital to verify the situation, book your flight, debit your credit card and they wire your airline ticket directly to the airport, where you pick it up immediately prior to your departure—often within only a few hours.

I recently had the unfortunate situation of needing this service and they managed to get me from Stuttgart, Germany to Kansas City within 24 hours.

Again, this is *not* a free flight, but the charge for booking the ticket short-notice is waived, which, on a flight from Europe, can save you over a thousand dollars. They take care of all the flight arrangements so — with the stress of an emergency hanging over you — at least your travel arrangements are simplified.

I would suggest that you call the airline's main office in New York. Simply get the number from international directory assistance in the country you are staying. The U.S. offices tend to be friendlier and are immediately familiar with this program. In the midst of an emergency, it can also be comforting and more effecient to be able to speak English with someone about your travel arrangements.

Saftey Overseas

Since the terrifying and inexcusable terrorist attacks in the U.S. on September 11, 2001, things have gotten slightly more complicated for ex-pats while traveling. Some good general rules:

1) Assume you will be searched at the airport.

2) Don't carry anything that could be used as a weapon, even in your checked baggage. Bad news for bassonists and other wind players who make their own reeds. Plan on buying a new reed knife when you arrive in your host country.

3) Electronic equipment (metronomes, condensor shotgun microphones, *etc.*) must have the batteries taken out. Anything with wires (mic cables, wire to bind double reeds, extra sets of strings, *etc.*) will probably look strange on the xray machine and your baggage will be searched.

4) Finally, remember that these slight inconvieniences are for your own saftey. Any rational person would rather be slightly detained than have a disaster happen.

For ex-pats who have been in Europe a while, we've noticed very little difference in Europe since September 11. There's been slightly heightened security in Europe, but since 1945 Europe has already had a very high awareness of terrorist activity. Ex-pats (and all Europeans) are used to seeing state police with machine guns guarding buildings, airports, walking down the street, *etc.* We've been very lucky in America but also perhaps a bit naïve and that changed drastically after September 11.

A few more tips while overseas:

1) Stay in touch with the U.S. embassy or consulate—especially if any conflict or situation arrises (in Europe *or* the U.S.). When you arrive, drop by the embassy and ask that your name be put on the list of U.S. citizens living in that country. In the case of a severe emergency, they will contact you and give you instructions as to what to do.

2) Fit in. First you're in a foreign country as a guest. Second you are there to learn from being in that country so you should naturally try to fit in but blending into your surroundings can also help avoid becomming a "target" for anti-Americanism.

3) Don't argue politics. It makes you stand out and some people in Europe can be just as irrational about their political views as some people in the U.S. Read #2 again...

4) Keep a list of important telephone numbers next to your telephone (a checklist is given at the beginning of this book).

In all honesty, Europe is a very safe and friendly region. There's no reason to assume that you will have any problems or confrontations while you're there, but there's also a level of common sense that goes with being safe in Europe *or* the U.S.

Use good judgement and be aware of your surroundings.

CHAPTER FOURTEEN—
The Language

For many Americans—particularly those who have never spent much time overseas—the idea that people *truly* don't speak or understand English is a shock. There's a lingering belief that, even though Europeans don't use English regularly, surely they must speak at least *some* English.

Believe me, *they don't speak English* and the little that they may speak is usually nowhere near enough to make much difference.

Many countries (as of the mid 1980's) have made English a required second language in schools and students have usually had 4-6 years of English by the time they graduate from high school. I admit this sounds impressive but it means basically nothing. Occasionally they will speak fairly well but in all honesty this is rare, so don't fool yourself into thinking that you can just slide by with English.

If you work hard, in one year you can get a foreign language up to a functional level before you leave the States. "Functional" means you can carry on daily chores painlessly (shopping, your private music lessons, *etc.*) It also means that when you do get stuck on a word, you can logically figure it out based on what you already know.

Music classes and lectures are another thing. As we do in America, they talk rapidly and they use technical musical terms that are rarely learned in a normal language course, but again, with minimal background you'll be fine.

However, even with one year of foreign language study before you go, the first few months will be a bit perplexing. I'm not saying this to scare you—only to let you know that the slight confusion you'll have is normal. The better prepared you are, the less complicated it will be.

Another aspect of most foreign languages is that they sometimes use dialect. A true dialect will provoke you to lunacy faster than any other element of life on earth but it can also be one of the most fascinating adventures of your new language.

In the States we have regional accents. They have accents in Europe as well (which can be confusing in itself) but a dialect is a *totally* different thing. It's more than a different sound or vocal inflection— a true dialect involves different words—*many* different words and because a dialect is only spoken (never written), you can virtually *never* find these obscure words in a dictionary.

For example in Hochdeutsch (High German), "a shutter latch" (the little clip that keeps a window shutter open or closed) is called a "Fensterladenklappe" (which is logical since *fenster* = window, *laden* = shutter and *klappe* = latch). But in the western Austrian Montafon mountain dialect, the word for a shutter latch is a "Gödälödäleila." Try finding *that* in a dictionary!

The list of words in dialect is endless but let me stress that a dialect is not even *remotely* close to the pure language. In mountain regions, which usually have the most extreme dialects, many words will be totally different from one valley to the next!

While dialects can be a shock for the new arrival, they are fascinating! They often stem from ancient languages used by the various Celtic, Gaulic, Germanic or Frankish tribes from over 2,000 years ago. One of the best known languages/dialects is Romanisch which developed shortly after the fall of Rome in the mountain regions of Northern Italy and neighboring Switzerland.

In this case, the Roman soldiers who were stationed there decided there was no reason to go back home and share Rome with the invading barbarians. As they bred with the local Allemanisch tribes, the languages (Latin and Allemanisch) mixed—to the extent that (even today) if you speak classical Latin you can understand much of the Romanisch language!

If you end up in a region with a heavy dialect, carry around a small notebook and jot down any words that come up in conversation that you don't know. Then you can ask your landlord, friends or bilingual students what these words mean. This is tedious but there's no other way to deal with a heavy dialect.

Children (usually up to about age 7) who live in a region where there is a heavy dialect will usually not understand if you speak in the pure language. One of my first teaching jobs overseas was at a Musikschule in a mountain region of Austria and several of my younger students actually had to have their mothers come to the lessons to translate from my extremely good (but "pure") German into dialect because the children truly couldn't understand me.

To give another example, if someone from the Alpine regions of Austria, France, Switzerland or Italy is interviewed on national television (even though they will be speaking in the "correct language") because of their dialect, the television station will often subtitle the interview in the "pure" language because no one outside of that region can understand them.

With or without a dialect, a new language is an adventure and a *tremendous* learning experience. Once you become more comfortable, it becomes very automatic and fun—almost a game.

Another language will also change the way you think and many multi-lingual people I know have commented on different aspects of their personality that emerge when they use another language. It's as if you take on a bit of the "personality" of the country when you become more fluent in a language.

However, even after you are fairly comfortable in a language, you will make some "memorable" mistakes. A brilliant Australian 'cellist I know (who speaks German fluently) was at a restaurant and after the waiter explained all the specialties on the menu, my friend (wanting to tell the waiter to simply pick something for him), very politely said *"I place myself in your hands"* (or, in German, *"Ich begebe mich in Ihre Hände."*). Unfortunately he accidentally confused one word and instead of *begeben* (to place), said *übergeben* (which means to vomit). Thus, he told the waiter—quite politely— *"I, myself, vomit in your hands."*

Talking on the telephone offers one of the best opportunities to make mistakes in a new language because without any visual contact (as when you're talking to someone in person) it can be much more difficult to communicate.

Shortly after I moved to France someone called on the phone for my landlady. Being in the midst of practicing, with a rather impatient and exasperated tone of voice, I said *"...she's not here, she's teaching in Dunkerque today—she always teaches in Dunkerque on Wednesday!"* However, instead of using the French verb *enseigner* (to teach) I slipped and used another verb that in French sounds very similar, *saigner* (to bleed). The caller was rather shocked to hear that my landlady couldn't answer the phone because she habitually went to Dunkerque every Wednesday to bleed.

He never called back...

The important thing is to get as far along as possible with the language before you go to Europe because English simply *won't* carry you through. After that, the slight blunders and complications that you'll encounter will usually be more amusing than truly problematic. Maintain a good sense of humor about the whole situation and everything will be fine.

CHAPTER FIFTEEN—
"Living" Overseas

Because of the language barrier American overseas often find themselves spending most of their time with other Americans rather than "locals." This can be a comfort if you're a bit homesick or you simply need to "rattle" in English and I certainly don't mean to discourage this.

However, I would like to express a word of caution: remember you are going to a foreign country to learn from *living* in that foreign country. Particularly in parts of France and Italy (which can be so incredibly Americanized), it's very easy to change countries but never really get into the life-style of your new country. This is especially true with the language because if you are around other students, they will be anxious to practice their English and you may have less opportunity to use the local language.

If you honestly get homesick, find the nearest bowling alley. As absurd as this sounds, I occasionally have guests or students get homesick and this is truly the fastest remedy. To explain:

Bowling alleys all over the world look the same. They're virtually all manufactured by the Brunswick Corporation in New Jersey. They all sound the same, look the same and smell the same.

Terrifying, but true. They all have the same quasi-level pool tables and everyone dresses in the same short-sleeve bowling shirts (although depending on the country, the shirts will have names like "François," or "Wilhelm," or "Giuseppe" embroidered on the back instead of "Joe-Bob," or whatever). You can close your eyes and imagine that you are in virtually any city in America.

In all seriousness, homesickness is a very real and scary feeling that can strike even the most seasoned expatriate. If you have an attack of homesickness, grab an English-speaking friend, find the local bowling alley and spend a few hours. I *guarantee* it will work!

On the more positive side, to help you get into the local life, simply going to the neighborhood *café, Gasthaus, trattoria,* or sitting around talking with your neighbors about their garden, or complaining about the price of eggs, can give you more insight into a country and the language than hundreds of hours of formal study. Be careful that you don't neglect this aspect of your time overseas. *Get to know your neighbors!* Asking the old lady across the street if you can pick up a loaf of bread for her on the way home will make you one of the most popular people in the neighborhood!

If you are new to living overseas, I would also suggest that you *quickly* get into some professional or social organizations. For students, there are clubs (usually through the local university) for almost every sport and hobby as well as various student organizations.

If you are working overseas you may want to take an adult education class. These classes are *extremely* popular throughout Europe and exist in virtually every city and village. If your command of the language is a little weak, take a class in a subject that you already know. Like students who are re-taking classes that they've already had (in English), this will give you a chance to concentrate on the vocabulary in your new language without worrying so much about learning the subject—*and* make some new friends.

Cooking classes are one of my personal favorites for meeting people in a new city because there's a *lot* of interaction between the students and when you move back to the U.S., you can use what you learned to create some *great* cross-cultural meals. Most local specialties (such as French brazed horse steak, Italian deep-fried baby eel or an array of German Knödel) are very rare in the States and they are *fantastic.* A well-prepared foreign meal will amaze (or terrify) your friends and family, which can be fun in either case! Get to know the local cuisine. The food will truly help you to understand the culture!

Churches are also a good source for finding new friends and the sense of support in these circles can be extremely high. Particularly in smaller villages, the church is the center of almost every social activity. Moving quickly into these circles will help you become accepted—which can be quite a task in some of the more rural areas!

Most cities have American/English clubs that meet regularly. Sometimes these are Americans or British ex-pats but just as frequently they are locals who simply enjoy meeting once a week to practice their English with each other—in which case, a native English speaker (such as yourself) will automatically be *very* popular! These people will also know of many other local activities that you can take advantage of.

This leads me to another important subject which is the openness that you should have when studying and living overseas. We are *all* different. Everyone in every country has different preferences, likes and dislikes, all of which are normal. *None are more correct or incorrect than any other.*

Above all else, you *must* stay open and non-judgmental of these qualities if you are going to learn the most from your experience overseas.

In spite of these slight differences, I guarantee you will find—at the core—we are all very much alike. We all want to eat, have a roof over our heads, be loved, feel useful, productive and needed, *etc.*

If you go to Europe with an attitude of sheer equality, you will learn more and make more friends—sincere friendships that will last your entire life.

Frankly, if people went through life with this attitude, we could probably avoid many of the short-sighted international conflicts that have cost millions of lives. That—in my opinion—is truly the most valuable thing that you can learn overseas.

Understanding and tolerance of others makes us stronger and wiser and there are *very* few of us who couldn't use more of those two traits.

CHAPTER SIXTEEN—
A Final Word of Encouragement

There are dozens of good reasons to study music overseas. Naturally the experience itself can be tremendous. As an American, there is also a belief (whether it is justified or not) that a classical musician must "do time" in Europe since that is the proverbial Motherland of classical music.

However, because of that attitude there is a great fallacy that European classical musicians are more talented than Americans. In short: *not true.* I know many American-born classical musicians who are equally—or more talented—than Europeans. The difference is that classical music is more common there. The average European grows up with classical music and knows more about it. But that doesn't mean they are any better at it—only more familiar with it.

This is a true story: Once in Vienna I was at a corner bar—a dumpy and fairly dangerous-looking place; the kind where most of the customers have leather jackets, enough body piercing to set off a metal detector at 100 yards and a various array of tattoos and scars. A television in the corner above the bar was raging at full volume. [12]

---

12. Just to clarify, this is *not* my usual neighborhood in Vienna, but a friend picked it as a spot to meet because she said, "...it looks interesting..." (she was right...).

There was a game show on the TV with different Austrian personalities as guests and one contestant happened to be the lead soprano from the Vienna State Opera.

In the middle of the program, the game show host paused the game and asked the soprano if she would sing something for the audience. She broke off into the beautiful *"O zitter nicht, mein lieber Sohn,"* the famous aria from Mozart's *The Magic Flute*. The commotion in the bar stopped. *Dead silence.* Suddenly, everyone in the place— leather jackets and all—started to sing along, *word-for-word* with the soprano on TV. Again, this *is* a true story.

This is what I mean: that situation would be *extremely* rare in the States. Yes, everyone—even the bikers—knew that Mozart aria by heart and could sing along with it but I guarantee that none of them could *perform* it. Europeans might *know* classical music more instinc- tively but that doesn't mean that they can perform any better, at a professional level, than anyone else.

I suppose what I'm trying to say is don't be afraid that you're getting into a situation that you can't handle! If you have worked hard then you'll be fine. Naturally don't be over-confident but more than likely you will have very few problems during your stay in Europe.

Studying or working overseas will expand who you already are, personally and musically. It will, *without a doubt,* be one of the most valuable and enlightening experiences of your entire life. I wish that for you more than you could possibly know.

Sincerely
Anthony L GLISE
10, April, 2003
Sainghin-en-Mélantois, France

Suggested Reading...
(available through your local bookstore)

• *Let's Go!* (Cambridge: written by Harvard Student Agencies, Published by E.P. Dutton, [updated annually]).

This has become the "Bible" of budget travel and I highly recommend getting a copy of the most recent edition of *Let's Go!* Each section (for each city) is written by people, usually Americans, who live in that city or know it extremely well. There are additional volumes of *Let's Go!* for specific countries and in selected languages but I suggest the general English edition for all of Europe to start with.

I have found *fantastic* restaurants, bars and cafés—even in the cities where I have lived or know well—that I didn't know about until I ran across them in this book.

If you are traveling, this also lists good cheap places to stay, with the telephone numbers and often the owner's names. It also gives the addresses of laundromats and more seriously, first-aid clinics and hospitals. *Let's Go!* also suggests local sites, festivals, and the hours of various museums, *etc.*

• *Access* (Access Press, New York: Prentice Hall Press)

This is a more "up-scale" traveler's guide, available in separate volumes for selected cities. If you happen to be living in (or visiting) a city for which this guide is written—*get the book!*

These list many out-of-the-way places, including specialty shops and restaurants that you won't find otherwise. Though some of these can be a bit expensive, this series includes considerable detail and historical background to many sites that can be fascinating. It also has "walking guides" with detailed maps that can make your visit to a new city a *tremendous* experience.

• *Michelin Guide* (published in various languages).

This series of books is one of the standard tourist guides, written by the Michelin Tire Company in France to encourage tourism throughout Europe (I suppose with the assumption that you're going to drive everywhere, wear out your tires and buy new Michelin tires...). Michelin is also the same company that established and still administers the famous "Four-Star" rating system for hotels and restaurants, so their information is *very* current and reliable.

There are hundreds of *Michelin Guides* for various countries, regions, and specific cities. The guides are updated periodically, highly accurate and give *exceptional* historical and fine arts information, detailed maps of the various cities as well as survival vocabulary in the appropriate language. They're not great for a true budget traveler but the information is *exceptional*.

Author's Biography

—Anthony Glise

for further information see:
www.AnthonyGlise.com

The only American-born guitarist to win First Prize at the *International Toscanini Competition* (Italy), Anthony Glise is a product of the *Konservatorium der Stadt* (Vienna) and the *New England Conservatory* (Boston) with additional study at *Harvard, Université Catholique de Lille* (France) and the *Accademia di Studi "L'Ottocento"* (Italy).

A *Pulitzer Prize Nominee* for composition, Anthony has been awarded diplomas and performed at such festivals as *Festival des Artes* (Hautecombe), *Ville Sable* (France), *ARCUM* (Rome), and the *Nemzetközi Gitárfesztivál* (Hungary). In addition to traditional classical repertoire, concerts often include 19th-Century works performed on a priceless 1828 Staufer Viennese guitar.

Anthony's commitment to the art has led to many diversified activities. His writings have been published extensively in *The Soundboard* (U.S.), *Guitar International* (England) and *Gitarre und Laute* (Germany). He has acted as an Artist-in-Residence and Touring Artist for a number of U.S. state arts councils and similar European programs. He is also the editor of the internationally-acclaimed series of guitar music and books, *"The Anthony Glise Editions,"* published by Willis Music Company and *"The Anthony Glise Urtext Editions"* by Mel Bay Publications.

An active composer, Anthony's original compositions have been premiered in such cities as New York, Chicago, Rome, Vienna, Lille (France) and Esztergom (Hungary).

His recordings include traditional works (solo, chamber, orchestral and ballet) as well as original compositions for such labels as Éclipse (France), Young Recording Artists (USA) and Dorian Recordings (USA). His first album, *Overview,* was chosen as one of the year's "Top-5 Classical Releases" by *Vienna Life Magazine.*

Anthony lectures at the *Academy for the Study of 19th-Century Music* (Italy) and *Festival Sablonceaux* (France), and when not on tour, he lives and teaches part-time in the Flanders region of Northern France, part-time in the Black Forest region of Germany and part-time in the US.

Mr. Glise proudly endorses:
Classical Guitars by: Gioachino Giussani, Anghiari (Arezzo), Italy
Acoustic Guitars by: C.F. Martin (Nazareth, US)
Strings by: E&O Mari—LaBella (New York)
Microphones by: Audio Technica (US)
Amplifiers by: Marshall Amplification (London)

Selected critiques...

"Anthony Glise offers us a totally different 'rhétorique' than we normally hear; his is a language of delicate effects, pure sensitivity, and contemplative emotions.

"The playing and sonority of Glise is not only clear and varied: it's a highly individual and spirited voyage.

"His style is not only that of power and decisive virtuosity: Glise seduces us by the grace and emotional intelligence of the phrase."
Le Diapason
(Paris, France)

"...pure musical genius."
Classica
(Rome, Italy)

"...Glise has produced (re-discovered?) a radically different way of playing the guitar. His constantly evolving articulation makes every phrase a revelation. His fastidious attention to phrasing creates a *chiaroscuro* effect that I have only heard from the very best pianists or lute players."

"...a revelation, and should be heard by any guitarist who wishes to play 'expressively'."
The Soundboard
(Guitar Foundation of America)

"...so rich, so profound, so sensual, that every note tells a story."
Luister
(Amsterdam, Holland)

"Glise's playing is strikingly individual and blends and unbelievable dynamic range and ravishing tonal colors.

"Seldom have I been so impressed."
Vienna Life Magazine
(Vienna, Austria)

Dictionary of
Contemporary Music Terms
in
English, French,
German and Italian

by Anthony Glise

Introduction to the Dictionary—

Being born and raised in the U.S. but studying music throughout Europe and ultimately teaching music in the U.S., Austria, Germany, France and Italy, I realized *years* ago the language difficulty that American musicians face overseas.

Even if a musician has studied and has a brilliant command of a foreign language, he has rarely had the opportunity to learn *daily* musical vocabulary. The terms in this dictionary are used constantly by musicians but these terms are often so specialized that they *never* show up in a typical foreign language class or bilingual dictionary.

Obviously we all know the standard foreign musical terms (such as *forte, da capo, langsam, bouchée, etc.*) so these have been left out to avoid unnecessary clutter but sometimes the simplest *daily* musical terms have escaped a musician's attention.

This daily musical vocabulary is often so far from the English equivalent that you would never accidentally come up with the right word. For example, "stage fright" in German (Lampenfieber) translates literally "lamp fever;" a "tuxedo" in French is a "smoking," *etc.*

This is not to degrade traditional language studies. It's simply to point out that we musicians have an absurdly specialized vocabulary—as subjective as any other profession such as medicine. For example, who but a doctor would use the term "acute lower abdominal gastric distention" which means simply "a bad stomach ache with gas"?

Who but a musician would understand the terms "prepared piano" or "cork grease," or "hypomixolydian mode"? These highly specialized words are rarely found in even the largest foreign language dictionaries.

The traditional study of a language is *critical* before you go to Europe to either study or work, but this dictionary will help fill in some of the gaps that probably exist in your daily musical vocabulary—whether you'll be speaking French, German or Italian.

Because of that, this dictionary assumes a working knowledge of traditional musical terms in English, thus no musical terms are defined—*this dictionary was designed to help you to take the musical terminology that you already know and apply it to your new language.*

Since this dictionary assumes that you have a basic knowledge of the language that you will be using (like all standard foreign language dictionaries), only the root form of a verb is given with the assumption that you will know how to further conjugate the verb. It also only gives the singular form of most nouns assuming you will know how to construct the plural, *etc.*

Naturally the gender of all nouns is given in each language. In some cases, where there could be confusion, the plural and/or different gender constructions are given as well.

Keep in mind that a language is a living thing. Many words creep into a vocabulary from other languages (most often from English). This "popular" usage of a word is usually *far* from the original and is often frowned upon linguistic by purists. However, this is how a language continues to grow. As a result, if there is a popular word in common use I have given this first, followed by any alternate words that would be equally—more traditionally—recognized.

I consider this contemporary usage of a language to be critical. For example you could translate the English word "gig" to the French "engagement" (rather than the common "cacheton")—and people would understand you. However, it would be much the same as if someone asked you to go to a film and you responded with "Golly, that would be hunky-dory!"

Of course they would understand you, but languages constantly evolve and using words that are understandable, but highly dated, can make you sound like a neighborhood kid on some 1960's television sitcom.

Thus, the most common (though sometimes impure) language has been used in this dictionary. However, if a term is highly slang, that is also indicated.

I should also point out that this dictionary only goes from English to the other languages—*not* the other way around. This is logical since if you need the correct foreign word, you can find it here.

On the other hand, if you hear a word that you don't know in context (in a conversation) you would presumably ask what it means immediately—rather than (in the middle of a conversation) pulling out your dictionary and searching for the English translation. Life in a foreign country simply doesn't work like that. So for the sake of brevity and accessibility, I opted to work directly from English.

There are also a few sections that are not intrinsically musical but contain subjects that are important to musicians studying and working abroad (*i.e.* Anatomy, Financial, Instrument Repair, *etc.*). This specialized vocabulary is given in both the dictionary and in the List Section.

Finally I would like to encourage you as you begin your time in Europe. It's a region full of tremendous musical and personal opportunities. No matter how long you stay, Europe will shape your musical and personal growth—perhaps more than any other single experience. Stay open to new ideas, work hard *and take time to enjoy where you are!*

With Very Best Regards,
Anthony L. GLISE

Utilization of this Dictionary and
Details of French, German and Italian

Key:	*abv.*	abbreviated
	adj.	adjective
	adv.	adverb
	n.	noun
	pl	plural
	sl.	slang
	v.	verb
Gender:	*m*	masculine
	f	feminine
	n	neuter
Languages:	F	French
	G	German
	I	Italian

Some entries in the dictionary may seem redundant. For example "video" is "video" in all three languages but in French, "video" is *feminine*, in German it is *neuter*, and in Italian it is *masculine*. For the sake of clarifying the gender, these "redundancies" are listed as well.

Following the main portion of this dictionary is another section of "Lists." Here you may look up any number of primary subjects (given at the beginning of the Lists section on this book) and find all related terms *grouped together*. Entries in the main part of the dictionary cite when an entry is also found in the lists.

A Final Word About French

In July, 1998, the *Académie française* —the organization founded in 1635 by Armand Jean du Plessis Richelieu (1585-1642) under Louis XIII to monitor and regulate the French language—decided that a majority of French titles may now be both masculine *and* feminine if a feminine form doesn't already exist. For example, before 1998, the title *Professor* (which is masculine) was a problem in French when addressing a *woman* professor.

In the old system, the phrase was "Madame *le* Professeur." Since 1998, it is now legally acceptable to say "Madame *la* Professeur." This obviously changes (for the better) many titles listed in this dictionary so they may now be used as both masculine *and* feminine.

However, in a few instances this sounds simply wrong to the French ear in spite of the legally-correct feminine version. In these cases I have left out the feminine form but the reader should remember that — at least legally — *all titles and occupations in French may now be used in feminine*.

Note that when I say "legally acceptable" I mean that *literally*, since the French language is regulated by the French government for all official use. This won't mean anything to you in daily life. They're not going to throw you in jail if you use "Franglais" (Anglicized French) but it's a *fascinating* aspect of the French culture and their concern with keeping the language pure.

A Final Word About German

As of the year 2000, there was a standardization of written German called *"Neuerechtschreibung"* ("New Correct Writing"). This was the subject of considerable debate among German speaking countries but it was a noble (if not slightly over-done) attempt to simplify the German language to be more "user friendly" due mostly to the solidification of the European Union.

I have maintained the traditional spellings of words since they are more easily recognizable and anyone dealing with German at this level will have no difficulty in mentally adjusting the entries in this dictionary to the minor changes of the *Neuerechtschreibung*.

A Final Word About Italian

Ah, Italian!... While Italian has a *tremendous* number of dialects and accents, it is one of the most rational languages on earth. It changes when it needs to and everyone just accepts it — the whole point is to simply communicate, no? *Vedete, non c'e' problema?!* A pretty basic and friendly concept...

A special thanks to the following people who helped proof this book and offered countless suggestions for the following languages:

◇ **French**

Dr. Laurent Delevoye—research scientist in NMR (Nuclear Magnetic Resonance) *Université de Lille I* (Lille France), classical guitarist; trombonist (Bourghelles, France).

Dr. Yvonne Turrell—research scientist in Human Neuropsychology (Lille, France); French/English translator; violinist (Bourghelles, France).

Dr. Sylvia Turrell-Delevoye—professor of Raman Spectoscopy, *Université de Lille I* (Lille France); bassoonist, (Sainghin-en-Mélantois, France).

◇ **German**

Thomas Reuther—classical guitarist; pedagogue (Ulm, Germany).
Dr. Ingrid Benzino—Dr. Medicine; pianist (Ingolstadt, Germany).

◇ **Italian**

Maestro Stefano Abrile—classical guitarist; President, *Coro Polifonico "Turbo Concinens;"* faculty, *Civico Istituto Musicale,* (Pinerolo, Italy) and *A.G.I.F.* (Vigevano, Italy).

Maestro Antonio Battista—classical guitarist; film composer; recording artist; French/Italian/English translator (Lomello, Italy).

Maestro Mario Bricca—classical guitarist; professor, *Istituto Musicale "Arcangelo Corelli"* (Pinerolo, Italy).

◇ **English**

Tamara Glise-Filbert—writer; library science (Cedar Rapids, USA).
A. Jeannine Borngesser-Glise—Special Education teacher; pianist (St. Joseph, USA).

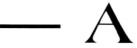

— A —

a *n.* (name of note) —*cf.* also Note
Names List
F la *m*
G a *n*
I la *f*

a 2 (English bastardization from the
Italian) —*cf.* also Orchestral Terms List;
divided in 2; — 3; — 4
F à 2
G zu 2
I a 2

a-double flat *n.* (name of note) —*cf.*
also Note Names List
F la double bémol *m*
G ases *n*
I la doppio bemolle *f*

a-double sharp *n.* (name of note) —
cf. also Note Names List
F la double dièse *m*
G aisis *n*
I la doppio diesis *f*

a-flat *n.* (name of note) —*cf.* also Note
Names List
F la bémol *m*
G as *n*
I la bemolle *f*

a-flat major *n.* (key center) —*cf.* also
Keys List
F la bémol majeur *f*
G As-dur *n*
I la bemolle maggiore *m*

a-flat minor *n.* (key center) —*cf.* also
Keys List
F la bémol mineur *f*
G as-moll *n*
I la bemolle minore *m*

a major *n.* (key center) —*cf.* also Keys
List
F la majeur *f*
G A-dur *n*
I la maggiore *m*

a minor *n.* (key center) —*cf.* also Keys
List
F la mineur *f*
G a-moll *n*
I la minore *m*

a-sharp *n.* (name of note) —*cf.* also
Note Names List
F la dièse *m*
G ais *n*
I la diesis *f*

a-sharp major *n.* (key center) —*cf.*
also Keys List
F la dièse majeur *f*
G Ais-dur *n*
I la diesis maggiore *m*

a-sharp minor *n.* (key center) —*cf.*
also Keys List
F la dièse mineur *f*
G ais-moll *n*
I la diesis minore *m*

absolute music *n.* (≠ program
music) —*cf.* also *program music*
F musique absolue *f*
G absolute Musik *f*
I musica assoluta *f*

accent *n.* —*cf.* also *agogic accent*
F accent *m*
G Akzent *m*
I accento *m*

accidental *n.* (sharp; flat or natural

not in the given key signature); *cf.* also
chromatic
F altération accidentelle *f*
G Versetzungszeichen *n*
I accidente *m*; alterazione *f*

accompaniment *n.*
F accompagnement *m*
G Begleitung *f*
I accompagnamento *m*

accompanist *n.* —*cf.* also Professions List
F accompagnateur *m*; accompagnatrice *f*
G Begleiter *m*; Begleiterin *f*
I accompagnatore *m*; accompagnatrice *f*

accompany *v.* (to accompany on the piano, *etc.*)
F accompagner
G begleiten
I accompagnare

accordion *n.* —*cf.* also Instruments List (Historic & Ethnic Instruments)
F accordéon *m*
G Ziehharmonika *f*
I fisarmonica *f*

accordionist *n.* —*cf.* also Professions List
F accordéoniste *m* / *f*
G Akkordionspieler *m*; Akkordionspielerin *f*
I fisarmonicista *m* / *f*

acoustic *adj.* (non-electric instrument, *etc.*)
F acoustique *f*
G akustik *f*
I acustico *m*; acustica *f*

acoustics *n.* (properties of sound in a hall, *etc.*)
F acoustique *f*
G Akustik *f*
I acustica *f*

¹action *n.* (the mechanical movement of a keyboard when playing) —*cf.* also *touch*
F mécanique *f*
G Mechanik *f*

I meccanica *f*

²action *n.* (in an opera; play, *etc.*) —*cf.* also Voice List
F action *f*
G Handlung *f*
I trama *f*

advanced *n.* / *adj.* (level of a student) —*cf.* also Teaching List
F avancé *m* ; avancée *f*; supérieur *m*; supérieure *f*
G vortschritend *m* / *f*
I livello avanzato (*N.B.* This term implies *ability* more than a specific *level* and is rarely used in Italian in this sense.)

aeolian *n.* (church mode) —*cf.* also Modes List
F éolien *m*
G Äolisch *n*
I eolio *m*

aesthetics *n.*
F esthétique *f*
G Ästhetik *f*
I estetica *f*

agent *n.* —*cf.* also Professions List
F agent *m* / *f*; impresario *m*
G Manager *m*; Manager in *f*; Agentur *f* (this implies more a company than an individual)
I agente *m* (usually more for theater); manager *m* (usually more for music)

agogic (accent, *etc.*) *n.*
F agogique *f*
G Agogik *f*
I agogica *f*; accento agogico *m*

Alberti bass *n.*
F basse Alberti *f*
G Alberti-Bässe *f*
I bass albertino *m*

aleatoric music *n.* —*cf.* also Historical Styles & Periods List
F musique aléatoire *f*
G aleatorische Musik *f*
I musica aleatoria *f*

allemande *n.* —*cf.* also Musical Forms List
F allemande *f*
G Allemande *f*
I allemanda *f*

alphorn *n.* —*cf.* also Instruments List (Historic & Ethnic Instruments)
F cor des Alpes *m*
G Alphorn *n*
I corno delle Alpi *m*

¹alto *n.* (singer) —*cf.* also Voice List (Traditional Types); Clef List
F alto *m*
G Alt *m*
I contralto *m*

²alto clarinet *n.* —*cf.* also Instruments List (Woodwinds)
F clarinette alto *f*
G Altklarinette *f*
I clarinetto contralto *m*

³alto clef *n.* —*cf.* also Clef List
F clef d'ut *f*; clef d'ut troisième ligne *f*
G Altschlüssel *m*
I chiave di contralto *f*

amature *n.* / *adj.* (level of a student) —*cf.* also Teaching List
F amateur *m*
G Amateur *m*; Amateurin *f*
I dillettante *m*

ambassador *n.* (in an embassy, *etc.*) —*cf.* also Legal List
F ambassadeur *m*; ambassadrice *f*
G Botschafter *m*; Botschaftlerin *f*
I ambasciatore *m*; ambasciatrice *f*

amplifier *n.* (for electric guitar; sound support, *etc.*) —*cf.* also Recording List
F amplificateur *m*; ampli *m* / *sl*
G Verstärker *m*
I amplificatore *m*

anacrusis *n.* (pickup in a phrase, *etc.*)
F anacrouse *f*
G Auftakt *m*
I anacrusi *f*

analog *adj.* (non-digital recording) —

cf. also Recording List
F analogique
G analog
I analogico

analysis *n.* (musical; harmonic, *etc.*)
F analyse *f*
G Analyse *f*
I analisi *f*

anatomy *n.* —*cf.* also Anatomy List
F anatomie *f*
G Anatomie *f*
I anatomia *f*

ancient music *n.* —*cf.* early music

antecedent *n.* (phrase) —*cf.* also Musical Forms List, (antecedent / consequent)
F antécédent *m*
G Dux *m*
I antecedente *m*

antiphon *n.* —*cf.* also Musical Forms List
F antienne *f*
G Antiphon *f*
I antifona *f*

antique cymbal *n.* —*cf.* also Instruments List (Percussion Instruments)
F cymbale antique *f*
G Antike Zimbel *f*
I cimbalo *m*

anvil *n.* —*cf.* also Instruments List (Percussion Instruments)
F enclume *f*
G Amboß *m*
I incudine *f*

applaud *v.*
F applaudir
G klatschen
I applaudire

applause *n.*
F applaudissement *m*
G Beifall *m*; Applause *m*
I applauso *m*

appoggiatura *n.* —*cf.* also *double appoggiatura*
F appoggiature *f*
G Vorschlag *m*
I appoggiatura *f*

appoyando *n.* (guitar fingering) —*cf. rest stroke*

arabesque *n.* —*cf.* also Musical Forms List
F arabesque *f*
G Arabeske *f*
I arabesca *f*

arch *n.* (of a finger, *etc.*)
F cambrure *f*
G Bogen *m*
I curvatura *f*

archive *n.* (in a library) —*cf. open-stack; closed-stack;* also Research List

archlute *n.* —*cf.* also Instruments List (Historic & Ethnic Instruments)
F archiluth *m*
G Erzlaute *f*
I arciliuto *m*

aria *n.* —*cf.* also Musical Forms List
F aria *f*
G Arie *f*
I aria *f*

arm *n.* —*cf.* also Anatomy List
F bras *m*
G Arm *m*
I braccio *m*

arpeggiate *v.*
F arpéger
G arpeggieren
I arpeggiare

arpeggiated *adj.* —*cf.* also *broken*
F arpégé
G arpeggiert
I arpeggiato

arpeggiation *n.* (This is used almost exclusively in English as a noun. *N.B.* French, German and Italian all tend to use this word in the adjective form—

"the chord is arpeggiated" or in the verb form—"arpeggiate the chord.")
F arpège (en arpégeant) (*N.B.* The accent is different between "arpéger" as a verb and "arpège" as a noun.)
G Arpeggio n
I arpeggiare (arpeggiare l'accordo — l'accordo é arpeggiato)

arpeggio *n.*
F arpège *m*
G Arpeggio *n*
I arpeggio *m*

arrange *v.* (to orchestrate a piece, *etc.*)
F arranger; orchestrer
G arrangieren; bearbeiten (This is often used to indicate editing of a piece.)
I arrangiare

arrangement *n.* (of a piece, *etc.*)
F arrangement *m*
G Bearbeitung *f*
I arrangiamento *m*

arranger *n.*—*cf.* also Professions List
F arrangeur *m*; arrangeuse *f*
G Bearbeiter *m*; Bearbeiterin *f*
I arrangiatore *m*; arrangiatrice *f*

artery *n.* —*cf.* also Anatomy List
F artère *f*
G Ader *f*
I arteria *f*

¹articulation *n.* (of a finger, *etc.*) —*cf. joint;* alsoAnatomy List

²articulation *n.* (in phrasing, *etc.*)
F articulation *f*
G Artikulation *f*
I articolazione *f*

artificial harmonic *n.* —*cf.* also *harmonic; natural harmonic*
F harmonique artificiel *m*
G Flageolettgriff *m*
I armonico artificiale *m*

artist *n.* —*cf.* also Professions List
F artiste *m/f*
G Künstler *m*; Künstlerin *f*
I artista *m/f*

ash *n.* —*cf.* also Instrument Repair List
(Various Woods)
F frêne *m*
G Esche *n* ; Eschenholz *n*
I frassino *m*

aspirated attack *n.* —*cf.* also Voice
List (Vocal Attacks)
F attaque murmurée *f*
G gehauchter Einsatz *m*
I attacco sul fiato *m*

assignment *n.* (weekly assignment,
etc.) —*cf.* also Teaching List
F devoir *m*
G Aufgabe *f*
I compito *m*

[1]**at the bridge** —*cf.* also Orchestral
Terms List
F sur le chevalet
G am Steg
I sul ponticello

[2]**at the fingerboard** —*cf.* also
Orchestral Terms List
F sur la touche
G am Griffbret
I sul tasto; sulla tastiera

[3] **at the frog** —*cf.* also Orchestral
Terms List
F du talon
G am Frosch
I al tallone

[4]**at the point (of the bow)** —*cf.*
also Orchestral Terms List
F de la pointe
G an die Spitze
I punta d'arco

atonal *adj.*
F atonale
G atonal
I atonale

atonality *n.*
F atonalité *f*
G Atonalität *f*
I atonalità *f*

audience *n.* —*cf.* also Concert List

F public *m*
G Publikum *n*
I pubblico *m*

audition *n.*
F audition *f*
G Vorspiel *n*
I audizione *m*

augmentation *n.* (of interval, *etc.*) —
cf. also Intervals List
F augmentation *f*
G Vergrößerung *f*
I eccedente *adj.* (For intervals, one
usually says "eccedente," but modifying
the noun "intervallo," *i.e.* "intervallo
eccedente."); aumentazione *f* (This is
used mostly for rhythmic augmentation.)

augmented *adj.* (interval) —*cf.* also
Intervals List
F augmenté
G übermäßig
I eccedente

authentic cadence *n.* —*cf. perfect
cadence;* also Cadence List

autograph manuscript *n.* —*cf.* also
Research List
F manuscrit autographe *m*
G handschriftlich Manuskript *n*
I manoscritto autografo *m*

[1]**avant garde** *adj.* (style)
F avant-garde
G Avantgarde
I avantgarde; AvanGuardia (*N.B.* In
Italian, this is often spelled with the
capital letters, but still as one word.)

[2]**avant garde music** *n.* —*cf.* also
Historical Periods & Styles List
F musique d'avant-garde *f*
G avantgardistische Musik *f*
I musica d'avanguardia *f*; musica
d'AvanGuardia *f* (*N.B.* In Italian, this is
often spelled with the capital letters, but
still as one word.)

award ceremony *n.* —*cf.* also
Competition List

F remise des prix *f*
G Preisverleihung *f*
I premiazione *f*

— B —

b *n.* (name of note) —*cf.* also Note
Names List
F si *m*
G h *n*
I si *m*

b-double flat *n.* (name of note) —*cf.*
also Note Names List
F si double bémol *m*
G hesis *n*
I si doppio bemolle *m*

b-double sharp *n.* (name of note) —
cf. also Note Names List
F si double dièse *m*
G hisis *n*
I si doppio diesis *m*

b-flat *n.* (name of note) —*cf.* also Note
Names List
F si bémol *m*
G b *n*
I si bemolle *m*

b-flat major *n.* (key center) —*cf.* also
Keys List
F si bémol majeur *f*
G B-dur *n*
I si bemolle maggiore *m*

b-flat minor *n.* (key center) —*cf.* also
Keys List
F si bémol mineur *f*
G b-moll *n*
I si bemolle minore *m*

b major *n.* (key center) —*cf.* also Keys
List
F si majeur *f*
G H-dur *n*
I si maggiore *m*

b minor *n.* (key center) —*cf.* also Keys
List
F si mineur *f*
G h-moll *n*
I si minore *m*

b-sharp *n.* (name of note) —*cf.* also
Note Names List
F si dièse *m*
G his *n*
I si diesis *m*

b-sharp major *n.* (key center) —*cf.*
also Keys List
F si dièse majeur *f*
G His-dur *n*
I si diesis maggiore *m*

b-sharp minor *n.* (key center) —*cf.*
also Keys List
F si dièse mineur *f*
G his-moll *n*
I si diesis minore *m*

baby grand (piano) *n.* —*cf.* also
Instruments List (Keyboards)
F crapaud *m*
G Stutzflügel *m*
I pianoforte a un quarto di coda *m*

[1]**back** *n.* (of the body) —*cf.* also
Anatomy List
F dos *m*
G Rücken *m*
I schiena *f*

[2]**back of the hand** *n.* —*cf.* also
Anatomy List
F dos de la main *m*
G Handrücken *m*
I dorso della mano *m*

backbeat *n.* (a beat which falls between the metric pulse) —*cf. off-beat*

backdrop *n.* (for a stage) —*cf.* also Stage List
F toile (de fond) *f*
G Hintergrund *m*
I fondale *f*

background music *n.*
F fond musical *m*
G Unterhaltungsmusik *f*
I musica di fondo *f;* musica di sottofondo *f*

backstage *n.* —*cf.* also *wings;* Stage List
F coulisses *f / pl* (*N.B.* French normally uses the same word for "backstage" as "wings.")
G Hinterbühne *f*
I dietro le quinte *f / pl* (*N.B.* Italian normally uses the same word for "backstage" as "wings.")

bagatelle *n.* —*cf.* also Musical Forms List
F bagatelle *f*
G Bagatelle *f*
I bagatella *f*

bagpipe *n.* —*cf.* also Instruments List (Historic & Ethnic Instruments)
F cornemuse *f*
G Dudelsack *m*
I cornamusa *f*

balerina *n.* (female dancer) —*cf.* also *dancer* (*i.e.* male dancer); *prima balerina;* Professions List
F danseuse *f;* danseuse de ballet *f*
G Tänzerin *f*
I ballerina *f*

ballad *n.* —*cf.* also Musical Forms List
F ballade *f*
G Ballade *f*
I ballata *f*

[1] **ballet** *n.* —*cf.* also Musical Forms List
F ballet *m*
G Ballett *n*
I balletto *m*

[2] **ballet company** *n.* —*cf. corps de ballet*

[3] **ballet master** *n.* (male ballet instructor) —*cf.* also *ballet mistress;* Professions List
F maître de ballet *m*
G Ballettmeister *m*
I maestro di ballo *m*

[4] **ballet mistress** *n.* (female ballet instructor) —*cf.* also *ballet master;* Professions List
F maîtresse de ballet *f*
G Ballettmeisterin *f*
I maestra di ballo *f*

[5] **ballet music** *n.* —*cf.* also Historical Periods & Styles List
F musique de ballet *f*
G Ballettmusik *f*
I musica per balletto *f*

bandwidth *n.* —*cf.* also Recording List
F largeur de bande *f*
G Bandbreite *f*
I larghezza di banda *f*

[1] **bank account** *n.* —*cf.* also Finances List
F compte *m;* compte en banque *m*
G Konto *n*
I conto bancario *m*

[2] **bank card** *n.* —*cf.* also Finances List. (This exists less in the U.S., but is very common in Europe. In the U.S. it is usually referred to as a "debit card." It is used exactly like a credit card, but the billing is automatically debited to your bank account.)
F carte bancaire *f;* Carte Bleue *f* (trade name)
G EC-Karte *f* (trade name)
I carta bancomat *f*

[1] **bar** *n.* —*cf. measure*

[2] **bar line** *n.* (measure line)
F barre *f;* barre de mesure *f*
G Taktstrich *m*
I barra *f;* stanghetta *f*

³bar number *n.* (measure number)
F nombre de measures *m*
G Taktzahl *f*
I numero di battute *m*

barcarole *n.* —*cf.* also Musical Forms List
F barcarolle *f*
G Barkarole *f*
I barcarola *f*

baritone *n.* (singer) —*cf.* also Voice List (Traditional Types)
F baryton *m*
G Bariton *m*
I baritono *m*

¹Baroque *n.* (Period) —*cf.* also Historical Periods & Styles
F baroque *m*
G Barock *m*
I Barocco *m*

²baroque guitar *n.* —*cf.* also Instruments List (Historic & Ethnic Instruments)
F guitare Baroque *f*
G Barok Gitarre *f*
I chitarra Barocca *f*

barrel organ *n.* (organ grinder's organ) —*cf.* also Instruments List (Historic & Ethnic Instruments)
F orgue de Barbarie *m*
G Drehorgel *f*
I organetto *m*; organetto di Barberia *m*

¹bass *n.* (singer) —*cf.* also Voice List (Traditional Types)
F basse *f*
G Baß *m*
I basso *m*

²bass bar *n.* (in a violin, *etc.*) —*cf.* also Instrument Repair
F barre *f*
G Baßbalken *m*
I catena *f*

³bass clarinet *n.* —*cf.* also Instruments List (Woodwinds)
F clarinette basse *f*
G Baßklarinette *f*
I clarinetto basso *m*

⁴bass clarinetist *n.* —*cf.* also Professions List
F joueur de clarinette basse *m*; joueuse de clarinette basse *f*
G Baßklarinetist *m*; Baßklarinetistin *f*
I clarinettista *m*/*f*; suonatore di clarinetto basso *m*; suonatrice di clarinetto basso *f*

⁵bass clef *n.* —*cf.* also Clef List
F clef de fa *f*; clef de fa quatrième ligne *f*
G F-Schlüssel *m*; Baß-Schlüssel *m*
I chiave di basso *f*

⁶bass drum *n.* —*cf.* also Instruments List (Percussion Instruments)
F grosse caisse *f*
G Große Trommel *f*
I gran cassa *f*

⁷bass player *n.* (double bassist) —*cf.* also Professions List
F contrebassiste *m*/*f*
G Kontrabaßist *m*; Kontrabaßistin *f*
I contrabassista *m*/*f*

basset-horn *n.* —*cf.* also Instruments List (Woodwinds)
F cor de basset *m*
G Bassetthorn *m*
I corno di bassetto *m*

bassist *n.* —*cf.* bass player; Professions List

basso buffo *n.* (singer) —*cf.* also Voice List (Specialty Types)
F basse bouffe *f*
G Baß-Buffo *m*
I basso buffo *m*

bassoon *n.* —*cf.* also Instruments List (Woodwinds)
F basson *m*
G Fagott *n*
I fagotto *m*

bassoonist *n.* —*cf.* also Professions List
F bassoniste *m*/*f*
G Faggottist *m*; Faggottistin *f*

I fagottisto *m*; fagottista *f*; suonatore di fagotto *m*; suonatrice di fagotto *f*

baton *n.* (of a conductor)
F baguette *f*
G Taktstock *m*
I bacchetta *f*

¹ beam *n.* (between two eighth notes, *etc.*) —*cf.* also Notes List (Parts of a Written Note)
F barre *f*
G Balken *m*; Notenbalken *m*
I linea di raggruppamento *f*

² beam *n.* (wooden reinforcement in an instrument) —*cf. brace*

beat *n.* (in a measure)
F measure *f*
G Taktschlag *m*
I battito *m* (For a beat in general. However in describing a *specific* beat in a measure, one uses "movimento." *Ex.* The second beat would be "secondo movimento.")

beech *n.* —*cf.* also Instrument Repair List (Various Woods)
F hêtre *m*
G Buche *n*; Buchenholz *n*
I faggio *m*

beginner *n. / adj.* (level of a student) —*cf.* also Teaching List
F débutant *m*; débutantante *f*
G Anfänger *m*; Anfängerin *f*
I principiante *m*

bell *n.* (of a trumpet, *etc.*)
F pavillon *m*
G Stürtze *f*
I campana *f*

bellows *n. / pl* (of an organ)
F soufflerie *f / pl*
G Bälge *m / pl*
I mantice *m / pl*

¹ bells (chimes) *n. / pl* —*cf.* also Instruments List (Percussion Instruments)
F cloches *f / pl*

G Glocken *f / pl*
I campane *f / pl*

² bells in the air —*cf.* also Orchestral Terms List
F pavillon en l'air
G Schalltrichter auf
I campane in aria

belly *n.* (N.B. French, German and Italian all distinguish between "stomach" (the organ) and "belly" (the outer portion of the body), while in English we often use "stomach" for both.) —*cf.* also *stomach;* Anatomy List
F ventre *m*
G Bauch *m*
I pancia *f*

bench *n.* (for piano, *etc.*) —*cf.* also *stool*
F banc *m*; banquette *f*
G Bank *f*
I sedile *m*; sgabello *m*

bend *v.* —*cf.* also Instrument Repair List (Common Verbs)
F dévirer
G biegen
I piegare

Beta-blocker *n.* —*cf.* also Concert List
F bloqueur-beta *m*
G Beta-Blocker *m*
I Beta bloccante *m* (Usually used in plural—"Beta-bloccanti.")

bi-tonality *n.*
F bi-tonalité *f*
G Bitonalität *f*
I bitonalità *f*

binary form *n.* —*cf.* also *two-part song form;* Musical Forms List
F forme binaire *f*
G zweiteilige Form *f*
I forma binaria *f*

birch *n.* —*cf.* also Instrument Repair List (Various Woods)
F bouleau *m*
G Birke *n*; Birkenholz *n*
I betulla *f*

"black" (to work) *v./sl.* To work "black" is to work illegally in a country without a work visa.) —*cf.* also Legal Subjects List
F travail au noir
G schwarzarbeiten
I lavoro in nero

blocking *n.* (in an opera, *etc.*) —*cf.* also Stage List
F mise en scène *f*
G Regieprobe *f*; Blocking *n*
I movimenti (di scena) *m / pl*

blood *n.* —*cf.* also Anatomy List
F sang *m*
G Blut *n*
I sangue *m*

bolero *n.* —*cf.* also Musical Forms List
F boléro *m*
G Bolero *m*
I bolero *m*

bone *n.* —*cf.* also Anatomy List
F os *m*
G Knochen *m*
I osso *m*

bones *n.* —*cf.* also Instruments List (Percussion Instruments)
F tablette *f*
G Brettchenklapper *f*
I taboletta *f*

bongo *n.* —*cf.* also Instruments List (Percussion Instruments)
F bongo *m*; tambourbongo *m*
G Bongo *n*
I bongo *m*

boom *n.* (extension for a microphone stand; lighting, *etc.*) —*cf.* also Recording List
F perche *f*
G Galgen *m* (modfied with the specific type, *i.e.* Mikrophongalgen, *etc.*)
I asta *f*

bore *n.* (shape of a conical wind instrument, *etc.*)
F perce *f*
G Bohrloch *n*; Bohrung *f*

I fori *m*

bounce *v. / sl.* (a check) —*cf.* also Finances List
F faire un chèque en bois *sl.* (to make a wooden check)
G platzen *sl.* (to explode a check)
I assegno scoperto *m*

bourée *n.* —*cf.* also Musical Forms List
F bourrée *f*
G Bourrée *f*
I bourrée *f*

bout *n.* (upper; lower; of guitar; violin, *etc.*) — *cf.* also *side*
F courbe *f* (corube supérieure *f*; courbe inférieure *f*)
G Bügel *m* (Oberbügel *m*; Unterbügel, *m*)
I volta *f* (volta superiore *f*; volta inferiore *f*)

[1] bow *n.* (at the end of a performance) —*cf.* also Concert List
F révérence *f*; salutation *f*
G Verbeugung *f*
I inchino *m*

[2] bow *v.* (at the end of a performance) —*cf.* also Concert List
F révérence *f* (In French one usually "gives" or "makes" a bow : "donner / faire une révérence.")
G (sich) verbeugen
I inchinarsi *m*

[3] bow *n.* (of a violin; viola, *etc.*)
F archet *m*
G Bogen *m*
I arco *m*

[4] bow arm *n.* (of a violinist *etc.*) (*N.B.* This concept exists almost exclusively in English.)
F archet *m*; le bras droit *m*
G rechte Arm *m*
I braccio dell'arco *m*

bowing *n. / down bow* *n. / up bow* *n.* (violin, *etc.*)
F coup d'archet *m* / tirer *v.* / pousser *v.* (*N.B.* In French, one usually uses the

verbs for up and down bowing.)
G Bogenführung *f* / Abstrich *m* /
Aufstrich *m*
I arcata *f* / arcata in giù *f* / arcato in sù *f*

box office *n.* —*cf.* also Concert List;
Stage List
F guichet *m*
G Kasse *f*
I biglietteria *f*

boy's choir *n.* —*cf.* also Voice List
(Choral Types)
F chœur de garçons *m*
G Knabenchor *m*
I coro di fanciulli *m*

[1] **brace** *n.* (in an instrument, *etc.*) —*cf.*
also Instrument Repair List
F contre-éclisse *f*
G Balken *m;* Sturtz *f*
I catena *f*

[2] **brace** *v.* (to reinforce a section of an
instrument) —*cf.* also Instrument Repair
List (Common Verbs)
F consolider
G stützen
I irrobustire

branle *n.* —*cf.* also Musical Forms List
F branle *m*
G Branle *m*
I brando *m;* branle *m*

[1] **brass** *n.* (material for horns, *etc.*) —*cf.*
also Instrument Repair List (Various
Materials)
F cuivre *m*
G Messing *n*
I ottone *m*

[2] **brass** *n.* (section) —*cf.* also Instru-
ments (Brass Instruments)
F cuivres *m* / *pl*
G Blechinstrumente *m* / *pl*
I ottoni *m* / *pl*

brassy *adj.* —*cf.* also Orchestral Terms
List
F cuivré
G schmetternd
I metallico

[1] **break** *n.* (in a voice) —*cf.* also Voice
List
F mue *f*
G Stimmbruch *m*
I muta *f*

[2] **break** *v.* —*cf.* also Instrument Repair
List (Common Verbs)
F casser
G zerbrechen; zerreißen
I rompere

[1] **breath** *n.* (in a phrase, *etc.*)
F souffle *m*
G Atem *m*
I fiato *m* (for vocal); respiro *m* (for
instrumental)

[2] **breath** *n.* (in singing) —*cf.* also Voice
List
F souffle *m*
G Luftstoß *m*
I fiato *m;* respiro *m*

[3] **breath support** *n.* —*cf.* also Voice
List
F appui du souffle *m*
G Atemstütze *f*
I appoggio sulla maschera *m*

breve *n.* (British name for double
whole note) —*cf. double whole note;* Notes
List

bridal song *n.* —*cf.* also Musical
Forms List
F chant nuptial *m*
G Brautlied *n*
I canto nuziale *m*

bridge *n.* (of an instrument) —*cf.* also
Instrument Repair
F chevalet *m*
G Steg *m*
I ponticello *m*

broadcast *n.*
F émission *f*
G Sendung *f*
I trasmissione *f*

broken *adj.* (arpeggio; chord; octave
etc.) ≠ straight *adj.* (not arpeggiated) —*cf.*

also *arpegiated; straight*
F brisé
G zerlegbar
I spezzato (In Italian, one usually
simply says *arpeggiato, i.e. arpeggiated.*)

budget *n. —cf.* also Finances List
F budget *m*
G Haushaltsplan *n;* Budget *n*
I buget *f*

builder *n. —cf.* also *luthier;* Instrument Repair List (General Terms);
Professions List
(*N.B.* All three languages distinguish
between a"luthier" [someone who
makes smaller instruments; *i.e.* violin;
guitar] and a "builder" [someone who
makes larger instruments; *i.e.* piano;
organ.])
F facteur *m /f* (facteur d'orgue, *etc.*)
G Bauer *m;* Bauerin *f* (Usually
preceded with the specific instrument
name. *Ex.* "Klavierbauer," *etc.*)
I construttore *m* (Usually followed by
the instrument name. *Ex.* "costruttore di
pianoforti," *etc.*)

bull roarer *n. —cf.* also Instruments
List (Percussion Instruments)
F planchette ronflante *f*
G Schwirrholz *n*
I legno frullante *m*

burlesque *n. —cf.* also Musical Forms
List
F burlesque *f*
G Burleske *f*
I burlesca *f*

buzz *v. —cf.* also Instrument Repair
List (Common Verbs)
F sourdonner
G summen
I vibrare

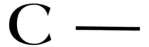

— C —

c *n.* (name of note) —*cf.* also Note
Names List
F do *m*
G c *n*
I do *m*

c-double flat *n.* (name of note) —*cf.*
also Note Names List
F do double bémol *m*
G ceses *n*
I do doppio bemolle *m*

c-double sharp *n.* (name of note) —
cf. also Note Names List
F do double dièse *m*
G cisis *n*
I do doppio diesis *m*

c-flat *n.* (name of note) —*cf.* also Note
Names List
F do bémol *m*
G ces *n*
I do bemolle *m*

c-flat major *n.* (key center) —*cf.* also
Keys List
F do bémol majeur *f*
G Ces-dur *n*
I do bemolle maggiore *m*

c-flat minor *n.* (key center) —*cf.* also
Keys List
F do bémol mineur *f*
G ces-moll *n*
I do bemolle minore *m*

c major *n.* (key center) —*cf.* also Keys
List
F do majeur *f*
G C-dur *n*
I do maggiore *m*

c minor *n.* (key center) —*cf.* also Keys
List
F do mineur *f*
G c-moll *n*
I do minore *m*

c-sharp *n.* (name of note) —*cf.* also
Note Names List
F do dièse *m*
G cis *n*
I do diesis *m*

c-sharp major *n.* (key center) —*cf.*
also Keys List
F do dièse majeur *f*
G Cis-dur *n*
I do diesis maggiore *m*

c-sharp minor *n.* (key center) —*cf.*
also Keys List
F do dièse mineur *f*
G cis-moll *n*
I do diesis minore *m*

cabaletta *n.* —*cf.* also Musical Forms
List
F cabalette *f*
G Cabaletta *f*
I cabaletta *f*

cable *n.* (chord for microphone, *etc.*) —
cf. also Recording List
F câble *m*
G Kabel *n*
I cavo *m*

cadence *n.* —*cf.* also Cadence List
F cadence *f*
G Kadenz *f*
I cadenza *f*

cadenza *n.* (in concerto, *etc.*)

F cadence *f*
G Kadenz *f*
I cadenza *f*

canary *n.* —*cf.* also Musical Forms List
F canarie *f*
G Canarie *f*
I canaria *f;* canario *m*

cane *n.* (used to make reeds) —*cf.* also Instrument Repair List
F roseau *m*
G Rohr *n*
I canna *f*

canon *n.* —*cf.* also Musical Forms List
F canon *m*
G Kanon *m*
I canone *m*

cantata *n.* —*cf.* also Musical Forms List
F cantate *f*
G Kantate *f*
I cantata *f*

canticle *n.* —*cf.* also Musical Forms List
F cantique *m*
G Gesang *m*
I cantico *m*

cantilena *n.* —*cf.* also Musical Forms List
F cantilène *f*
G Kantilene *f*
I cantilena *f*

canzone *n.* —*cf.* also Musical Forms List
F canzone *f*
G Kanzone *f*
I canzone *f*

canzonet *n.* —*cf.* also Musical Forms List
F canzonette *f*
G Kanzonette *f*
I canzonetta *f*

capriccio *n.* —*cf.* also Musical Forms List
F caprice *m*
G Capriccio *n*

I capriccio *m*

cardboard mute *n.* —*cf.* also Mutes List
F sourdine en carton *f*
G Kartondämpfer *m*
I sourdina di cartone *f*

carol *n.* —*cf.* also Musical Forms List
F carole *f*
G Carole *f*
I carola *f*

carry *v.* (to carry the voice) —*cf.* also Voice List
F porter la voix
G tragend
I (In Italian this concept doesn't make sense. You simply say "to sing" — "cantare.")

cartalige *n.* —*cf.* also Anatomy List
F cartilage *m*
G Knorpel *m*
I cartilagine *f*

carve *v.* —*cf.* also Instrument Repair List (Common Verbs)
F sculpter
G schneiden; schnitten
I intagliare

case *n.* (for an instrument)
F boîte *f*
G Koffer *m*
I astuccio *m*

cassation *n.* —*cf.* also Musical Forms List
F cassation *f*
G Kassation *f*
I cassazione *f*

cassette *n.* (for sound recording) —*cf.* also Recording List
F cassette *f*
G Kassette *f*
I cassetta *f*

castanets *n. / pl* —*cf.* also Instruments List (Percussion Instruments)
F castagnettes *f / pl*
G Kastagnetten *f / pl*

I castagnette *f / pl*; nacchere *f / pl*

castrato *n.* (singer) —*cf.* also Voice List
(Specialty Types)
F castrat *m*
G Kastrat *m*
I castrato *m*

cat gut *n.* —*cf. gut string*

cautionary accidental *n.* (an
accidental printed in the music as a
reminder to the player) —*cf.* also *sharp;
flat* and *natural.*
F altération de précaution *f*
G Errinungsvorzeichen *n*
I alterazione di precauzione *f*

cavatina *n.* —*cf.* also Musical Forms
List
F cavatine *f*
G Kavatine *f*
I cavatina *f*

CD *n.* —*cf.* also Recording List
F disque compact *f*; CD *m*
G CD *f*
I CD *m*; compact disc *f*

cedar *n.* —*cf.* also Instrument Repair
List (Various Woods)
F cèdre *m*
G Zeder *n*; Zedernholz *n*
I cedro *m*

celesta *n.* —*cf.* also Instruments List
(Percussion Instruments)
F célesta *m*
G Celesta *f*
I celesta *f*

'cellist *n.* —*cf.* also Professions List
F violoncelliste *m / f*
G Cellist *m*; Cellistin *f*
I violoncellista *m / f*; violoncello *m / f*

Century *n.* (15th-Century; 16th-
Century, *etc.*) —*cf.* also Historical
Periods & Styles List
F siècle *m* (*ex.* quinzième siècle *m*;
seizième siècle *m*; *etc.*)
G Jahrhunderts *n* (*ex.* fünfzehnte
Jahrhunderts *n*; sechzehnte

Jahrhunderts *n; etc.*)
I secolo *m* (*ex.* quindicesimo secolo *m*;
sedicesimo secolo *m*; *etc.*)

ceramic *n.* —*cf.* also Instrument
Repair List (Various Materials)
F céramique *f*
G Keramik *f*
I ceramica *f*

chaconne *n.* —*cf.* also Musical Forms
List
F chaconne *f*
G Chaconne *f*
I ciaccona *f*

chains *n. / pl* —*cf.* also Instruments
List (Percussion Instruments)
F chaînes *f / pl*
G Ketten *f / pl*
I catene *f / pl*

chamber music *n.*
F musique de chambre *f*
G Kammermusik *f*
I musica da camera *f*

channel *n.* (in stereo recording, *etc.*) —
cf. also Recording List
F chaîne *f*
G Kanal *m*
I canale *m*

check *n.* —*cf.* also Finances List
F chèque *m*
G Scheck *m*
I assegno *m*

chest voice *n.* (of a singer) —*cf.* also
Voice List
F voix de poitrine *f*
G Bruststimme *f*
I voce di petto *f*

chimes *n. / pl* —*cf. bells;* also Instruments List (Percussion Instruments)

child prodigy *n.*
F enfant prodige *m*
G Wunderkind *n*
I bambino prodigio *m*

chin *n.* (of the face) —*cf.* also Anatomy

List
F menton *m*
G Kinn *n*
I mento *m*

choir *n*. (church choir, *etc*.)—*cf. also*
church choir; Voice List (Choral Types)
F chœur *m*
G Chor *m*
I coro *m*

[1] choral music *n*. —*cf. also* Historical
Periods & Styles List
F musique chorale *f*
G Chormusik *f*
I musica corale *f*

[2] choral score *n*. —*cf. also* Score List
F partition chorale *f*
G Chorpartitur *f*
I partitura *f*; partitura per coro *f*

[3] choral types *n*. —*cf.* individual
entries; also Voice List (Choral/Vocal
Types)

chorale *n*. —*cf. also* Musical Forms
List
F choral *m*
G Choral *m*
I chorale *m*

[1] chord *n*. (specifically on a lute;
mandolin; guitar, *etc*.)
F accord *m*
G Griff *m*
I accordo *m*

[2] chord *n*. (triad, *etc*.)
F accord *m*
G Akkord *m*
I accordo *m*

[3] chord progression *n*. —*cf. also*
progression
F enchaînement *f / pl*; enchaînement
d'accords *f / pl*
G Akkordfolgen *m*
I progressione *f*

choreographer *n*. —*cf. also*
Professions List
F chorégraphe *m / f*

G Choreograph *m*; Choreographin *f*
I coreografo *m*; coreografa *f*

choreography *n*. (in dance)
F chorégraphie *f*
G Choreographie *f*
I coreografia *f*

[1] chorus *n*. (in in a song)
F refrain *m*
G Refrain *m* (*N.B.* German uses this
term but the pronounciation is like
French.)
I ritornello *m*

[2] chorus *n*. (a singing group) —*cf.*
choir; also Vocal List (Choral Types)

Christmas carol *n*. —*cf. also* Musical
Forms List
F chant de Noël *m*
G Weihnachtslied *n*
I canto di Natale *m*

[1] chromatic *n*. (accidental) —*cf. also*
accidental
F altération accidentelle *f*
G Versetzungszeichen *n*
I alterazione *f*

[2] chromatic *adj*. (scale, *etc*.)
F chromatique (In French,
"chromatique" is used most often as an
adjective that modifies a specific noun.
Ex. "demi-ton chromatique;" "gamme
chromatique," *etc*.)
G chromatisch
I cromatico

chromatic timpani *n. / pl* —*cf. also*
Instruments List (Percussion Instru-
ments)
F timbales chromatiques *f / pl*
G chromatische Pauken *f / pl*
I timpani cromatici *m / pl*

church choir *n*. —*cf. also* Voice List
(Choral Types)
F chœur d'église *m*
G Kirchenchor *m*
I coro di chiesa *m*

circle of fifths *n*. (cycle of fifths)

F cycle des quintes *m*
G Quintenzirkel *m*
I circolo delle quinte *m*

cittern *n.* —*cf.* also Instruments List
(Historic & Ethnic Instruments)
F cistre *m*
G Cister *f*
I cetra *f*

¹clamp *n.* —*cf.* also Instrument Repair
List
F serre-joint *m*
G Klammer *f*
I morsa *f*

²clamp *v.* —*cf.* also Instrument Repair
List (Common Verbs)
F agrafer
G klammern; festklammern
I stringere

clarinet *n.* —*cf.* also Instruments List
(Woodwinds)
F clarinette *f*
G Klarinette *f*
I clarinetto *m*

clarinetist *n.* —*cf.* also Professions
List
F clarinettiste *m* / *f*
G Klarinettist *m*; Klarinettistin *f*
I clarinettista *m*/*f*; clarinetto *m* /*f*;
suonatore di clarinetto *m*; suonatrice di
clarinetto *f*

Classic *n.* (period) —*cf.* also Historical
Periods & Styles List
F classique *m*
G Klassik *f*
I Classico *m*

classical music *n.* —*cf.* also
Historical Periods & Styles List
F musique classique *f*
G Klassiche Musik *f*
I musica classica *f*

claves *n.*/ *pl* —*cf.* also Instruments List
(Percussion Instruments)
F claves *f* /*pl*
G Holzstäbe *m* /*pl*
I claves *f* /*pl*

clavichord *n.* —*cf.* also Instruments
List (Keyboards)
F clavicorde *m*
G Klavichord *n*
I clavicordo *m*

clean *v.* —*cf.* also Instrument Repair
List (Common Verbs)
F nettoyer
G reinigen
I pulire

clef *n.*
F clef *f* (sometimes spelled *"clé" f*)
G Schlüssel *m*
I chiave *f*

climax *n.* (of a phrase)
F apogée *m*
G Höhepunkt *m*
I apice *m* (Not really used in Italian.
One usually says "the high point of the
phrase"—"punto più alto della frase.")

¹closed position *n.* (voicing of a
chord) —*cf.* also *open position*
F position serrée *f*
G enge Lage *f*
I posizione stretta *f*

²closed-stacks *n.* (in a library) —*cf.*
also *open-stacks*; Research List
F archives *m*/ *pl*
G Archiv *n*
I archives *m* /*pl*

coach *n.* (generally for vocalists) —*cf.*
also Professions List; Vocal List
F répétiteur *m*; répétrice *f*
G Korrepetitor *m*; Korrepetitorin *f*
I ripetitore *m*; ripetitrice *f* (In Italian this
term is uncommon. Usually one would
simply say "maestro" *m*; "maestra" *f*.)

coaching session *n.* (interpretive
lesson, *etc.*) —*cf.* also Teaching List
F master-classe *f*; répétition *f*
G Korrepetition *f*
I lezione di interpretazione *f*

coda *n.* —*cf.* also Musical Forms List
F coda *f*
G Koda *f* (in-general); Reprise *f* (in

Sonata-allegro form)
I coda *f*

color *n.* (tone color; timbre of a pitch;
or instrument, *etc.*) —*cf.* also *tone color*
F couleur *f*
G Farbe *f*
I colore *m*

coloratura soprano *n.* (singer) —*cf.*
also Voice List (Specialty Types)
F soprano colorature *f*
G Koloratursopran *f*
I soprano leggero *m*

comic opera *n.* —*cf.* also Musical
Forms List
F opera buffa *m* (Spelling borrowed
fromItalian, but with French gender.
N.B. there is no accent for "opera" in
this case.)
G komische Oper *f*
I opera buffa *f*

commission *n.* (contract to write a
composition; choreography, *etc.*)
F commande *f*
G Auftrag *m*
I commissione *f*

comp ticket *n.* (complimentary ticket)
—*cf.* also *ticket;* Concert List
F billet de faveur *m*
G Freikarte *f*
I biglietto omaggio *m*

compact disk *n.* —*cf. CD;* also
Recording List

¹competition *n.* —*cf.* also Competi-
tion List
F concours *m*
G Wettbewerb *m*
I concorso *m*

²competition winner *n.* —*cf.* also
Competition List
F gagnant *m;* gagnante *f*
F Preisträger *m;* Preisträgerin *f*
I vincitore *m;* vincitricite *f*

competitor *n.* —*cf.* also Competition
List

F concurrent *m;* concurrente *f*
G Teilnehmer *m;* Teilnehmerin *f*
I concorrente *m* / *f*

composer *n.* —*cf.* also Professions
List
F compositeur *m;* compositrice *f*
G Komponist *m;* Komponistin *f*
I compositore *m* / *f*

compound *n.* (meter; time signature)
—*cf.* also Time Signatures List
F mesure composée *f* (*N.B.* In French,
"composée" is not followed by the word
"temps," as are most meters)
G zusammengesetzter Takt *m*
I tempo composta *f*

compressor *n.* —*cf.* also Recording
List
F compresseur *m*
G Kompressor *m*
I compressore *m*

¹computer *n.* —*cf.* also Recording List
F ordinateur *m*
G Computer *m*
I computer *m;* elaboratore *m*

²computer music *n.*
F musique par ordinateur *f*
G Computermusik *f*
I computer music *f*

¹concert *n.*
F concert *m*
G Konzert *n*
I concerto *m*

²concert dress *n.* (tuxedo; gown, *etc.*)
—*cf.* also Concert List
F tenue de concert *f*
G Abendgarderobe *f*
I vestito da concerto *m*

³concert fee *n.* (money paid to
performer) —*cf.* also Concert List
F tarif *m;* cachet *m*
G Gage *f*
I cachet *m;* onorario *m*

⁴concert pitch *n.* (A-440, *etc.*)
F diapason de chambre *m*

G Kammerton *m*
I diapason *m;* diapason da camera *m*
(*N.B.* In Italian you say "give the A"—
"da il la.")

concertmaster *n.* —*cf.* also Professions List
F premier violon *m /f*
G Konzertmeister *m;* Konzertmeisterin *f*
I primo violino *m /f*

¹concerto *n.* —*cf.* also Musical Forms List
F concerto *m*
G Konzert *n*
I concerto *m*

²concerto for orchestra *n.* —*cf.* also Musical Forms List
F concerto pour orchestre *m*
G Konzert für Orchester *n*
I concerto per orchestra *m*

³concerto grosso *n.* —*cf.* also Musical Forms List
F concerto grosso *m*
G Konzerto Grosso *n*
I concerto grosso *m*

condensor mic *n.* —*cf.* also individual entries: *contact mic.; electro dynamic mic;* also Recording List
F micro à condensateur *m*
G Kondensatormikrophon *n*
I microfono a condensatore *m*

conduct *v.*
F diriger
G dirigieren
I dirigere

conductor *n.* —*cf.* also Professions List
F chef d'orchestre *m /f*
G Dirigent *m;* Dirigentin *f*
I direttore (Usually followed by specific type; *i.e.* "direttore d'orchestra" *m/f;* "direttore d'coro" *m/f, etc.*)

consequent (of a phrase) *n.* —*cf.* also Musical Forms List
F conséquent *f*
G Comes *m*

I conseguente *m*

consonant *adj.*
F consonant
G konsonant
I consonante

consul *n.* (an official from an embassy or consulate) —*cf.* also Legal Subjects List
F consul *m*
G Konsul *m*
I console *m /f*

consulate *n.* (a diplomatic office) —*cf.* also Legal Subjects List
F consulat *m*
G Konsulat *n*
I funzionario del consolato *m;* console *m*

contact mic *n.* —*cf.* also individual entries: *condensor mic.; electro dynamic mic.;* also Recording List
F micro à contact *m*
G Kontaktmikrophon *n*
I microfono a contatto *m*

¹Contemporary *n.* (Period) —*cf.* also Historical Periods & Styles List
F contemporain *m*
G zeitgenössisch *adj.*
I contemporaneo *m*

²contemporary music *n.* —*cf.* also Historical Periods & Styles List
F Musique contemporaine *f*
G zeitgenössische Musik *f*
I musica contemporanea *f*

¹contra bassoon *n.* —*cf.* also Instruments List (Woodwinds)
F contrebasson *m*
G Kontrafagott *n*
I controfagotto *m*

²contra bassoonist *n.* —*cf.* also Professions List
F contrebassoniste *m /f*
G Kontrafagottist *m;* Kontrafagottistin *f*
I controfagotto *m;* controfagottista *m /f*

contract *n.* (legal contract, *etc.*)
F contrat *m*

G Vertrag *m*
I contratto *m*

contralto *n.* —*cf.* also Voice List
(Specialty Types)
F contralto *m*
G Kontralt *m*
I contralto *m*

contrary motion *n.*
F mouvement contraire *m*
G Gegenbewegung *f*
I moto contrario *m*

copper *n.* —*cf.* also Instrument Repair
List (Various Materials)
F cuivre *m*; cuivre rouge *m*
G Kupfer *n*
I bronzo *f*

copy *v.* (to duplicate a recording;
mastertape, *etc.*) —*cf.* also Recording
List
F faire une copie
G überspielen
I duplicare

copyist *n.* —*cf.* also Professions List
F copiste *m* / *f*
G Kopist *m*; Kopistin *f*
I copista *m*/*f*

¹copyright *n.* —*cf.* also *performance
rights; royalties;* Research List
F copyright *m*; droits d'auteur *m* / *pl*
(*N.B.* French often uses "droits
d'auteur" which is actually the same
word as royalties.)
G Copyright *n*; Uhreberrecht *n*
I copyright *m*; diritti d'autore *m* / *pl*
(*N.B.* Italian often uses "diritti
d'autore" which is actually the same
word as royalties.)

²copyright infringement *n.* —*cf.*
also Research List
F contrafaçon *f*
G Uhrheberrechtsverletzung *f*
I violazione del diritto d'autore *m*
(usually in *sing.*)

¹cork *n.* —*cf.* also Instrument Repair
List (Various Materials)

F liège *m*
G Kork *m*
I sughero *m*

²cork grease *n.* —*cf.* also Instrument
Repair List (Various Materials)
F graisse *f*
G Korkfett *n*
I grasso di sughero *m*

cornet *n.* —*cf.* also Instruments List
(Brass Instruments)
F cornet *m*
G Kornett *n*
I cornetta *f* (Don't confuse with the
Renaissance instrument, "cornetto," *m*
or "zink" in English.)

cornettist *n.* —*cf.* alsoProfessions List
F cornettiste *m* / *f*
G Kornettist *m*; Kornettistin *f*
I cornettista *m* / *f*; suonatore di cornetta
m; suonatrice di cornetta *f*

corps de ballet *n.* (ballet company)
F corps de ballet *m*
G Balletkorps *n*
I corpo di ballo *m*

costume *n.* (in an opera, *etc.*)
F costume *m*
G Kostüm n
I costume *m*

count *v.* (to count measures; beats, *etc.*)
F compter
G zählen
I contare

¹counter subject *n.* (in fugue, *etc.*)
F contresujet *m*
G Kontrasubjekt *n*
I controsoggetto *m*

²counter tenor *n.* (singer) —*cf.* also
Voice List (Specialty Types)
F haute-contre *f*
G Kontratenor *m*
I contraltista *m*

counterpoint *n.* —*cf.* also Musical
Forms List
F contrepoint *m*

G Kontrapunkt *m*
I contrappunto *m*

country dance *n.* —*cf.* also Musical
Forms List
F contredanse *f*
G Kontretanz *m*
I contradanza *f*

courante *n.* —*cf.* also Musical Forms
List
F courante *f*
G Courante *f*
I corrente *f*

court music *n.* —*cf.* also Historical
Periods & Styles List
F musique de cour *f*
G Hofmusik *f*
I musica di corte *f*

cowbell *n.* —*cf.* also Instruments List
(Percussion Instruments)
F cloche de vache *f*
G Herdenglocke *f*
I campanaccio *m*

crack *n.* (in an instrument, *etc.*) —*cf.*
also Instrument Repair List
F fissure *f* (small); font *f* (large)
G Riß *m*
I fessura *f*

credit card *n.* —*cf.* also Finances List
F carte de crédit *f*
G Kreditkarte *f*
I carta di credito *f*

crescendo *n.*
F crescendo *m*
G Crescendo *n*
I crescendo *m*

critic *n.* (a person who writes for a
newspaper; magazine *etc.*) —*cf.* also
Concerts List; Professions List
F critique *m*
G Kritiker *m*; Kritikerin *f*
I critica *f*

crook *n.* (used for natural horns)
F corps de rechange *m*
G Stimmbogen *m*

I ritorto *m*

crochet *n.* (British name for quarter
note) —*cf. quarter note*; also Notes List

crumhorn *n.* —*cf.* also Instruments
List (Historic & Ethnic Instruments)
F cromorne *m*
G Krummhorn *n*
I cromorno *m*

cue *n.* (indication from a conductor for
entrance, *etc.*) —*cf.* also *downbeat;
entrance*
F indication *f*; indication de rentrée *f*
G Einsatz *m*
I attacco *m*

curtain *n.* —*cf.* also Stage List
F rideau *m*
G Vorhang *m*
I sipario *m*

curve *n.* (of finger, *etc.*)
F courbe *f*
G Bogen *m*
I curvatura *f*

¹cut *n.* (one song on a CD, *etc.*) —*cf.*
also *track*
F plage *f*
G Spur *f*
I traccia *f*

²cut-and-paste *v.* (gluing together a
score or part)
F couper-coller
G schneiden und einfügen
I taglia e incolla

³cut-off *n.* (from a conductor)
F césure *f*
G Zäsur *f*
I chiusura *f*; chiusa *f*

¹cycle *n.* (song cycle, *etc.*) —*cf.* also
Musical Forms List
F cycle *m*
G Zyklus *m*
I ciclo *m*

²cycle of fifths —*cf. circle of fifths*

— 99 —

cyclic form *n. —cf.* also Musical
Forms List
F forme cyclique *f*
G zyklische Form *f*
I forma ciclica *f*

cymbal *n. —cf.* also Instruments List
(Percussion Instruments)
F cymbale *f*
G Becken *n*
I piatto *m*

— D —

d *n.* (name of note) —*cf.* also Note
Names List
F ré *m*
G d *n*
I re *m*

d-double flat *n.* (name of note) —*cf.*
also Note Names List
F ré double bémol *m*
G deses *n*
I re doppio bemolle *m*

d-double sharp *n.* (name of note) —
cf. also Note Names List
F ré double dièse *m*
G disis *n*
I re doppio diesis *m*

d-flat *n.* (name of note) —*cf.* also Note
Names List
F ré bémol *m*
G des *n*
I re bemolle *m*

d-flat major *n.* (key center) —*cf.* also
Keys List
F ré bémol majeur *f*
G Des-dur *n*
I re bemolle maggiore *m*

d-flat minor *n.* (key center) —*cf.* also
Keys List
F ré bémol mineur *f*
G des-moll *n*
I re bemolle minore *m*

d major *n.* (key center) —*cf.* also Keys
List
F ré majeur *f*
G D-dur *n*
I re maggiore *m*

d minor *n.* (key center) —*cf.* also Keys
List
F ré mineur *f*
G d-moll *n*
I re minore *m*

d-sharp *n.* (name of note) —*cf.* also
Note Names List
F ré dièse *m*
G dis *n*
I re diesis *m*

d-sharp major *n.* (key center) —*cf.*
also Keys List
F ré dièse majeur *f*
G Dis-dur *n*
I re diesis maggiore *m*

d-sharp minor *n.* (key center) —*cf.*
also Keys List
F ré dièse mineur *f*
G dis-moll *n*
I re diesis minore *m*

dampen *v.* (stop or deaden a note,
etc.)
F étouffer
G dämpfen
I stoppare; fermare

damper *n.* (on a piano, *etc.*)
F étouffoir *m*
G Dämpfer *m*
I smorzatore *m*

damping pedal *n.* (on a piano) —*cf.*
also *sustaining pedal*
F pédale sourdine *f*
G Dämpferpedal *n* Dämpfer *m*
I pedale del piano *m*

[1]**dance** *n.*

F danse *f*
G Tanz *m*
I ballo *m* (for classical); danza *f* (for popular)

²**dance music** *n.* —*cf.* also Historical Periods & Styles
F musique de danse *f*
G Tanzmusik *f*
I musica da ballo *f*

dancer *n.* —*cf.* also *balerina; prima balerina; principal dancer;* Professions List
F danseur *m;* danseur de ballet *m;* danseuse *f;* danseuse de ballet *f*
G Tänzer *m;* Tänzerin *f*
I ballerino *m;* ballerina *f*

dat (DAT) *adj.* —*cf.* also Recording List
F DAT (spoken using the names of each letter or as a single word)
G DAT (spoken as a single word)
I DAT (spoken as a single word)

de *n.* (c-flat solfege syllable in the key of c-major in American, movable-do system) —*cf.* also Solfege List
F do *m*
G ces *n*
I do *m*
N.B. Cf. important note given under the entry "solfege" regarding differences between European and American solfege systems. *Cf.* also Solfege List.

debut *n.* —*cf.* also *premier;* Concerts List
F début *m*
G Debüt *n*
I debutto *m*

deceptive cadence *n.* —*cf.* also Cadence List
F cadence rompue *f*
G Trugschluß Kadenz *f* (*N.B.* German uses the same term for deceptive and imperfect cadence.)
I cadenza d'inganno *f*

decibel *n.* —*cf.* also Recording List
F décibel *m*
G Dezibel *n*

I decibel *m*

decrescendo *n.*
F decrescendo *m*
G Decrescendo *n*
I decrescendo *m*

demisemiquaver *n.* (British name for thirty-second note) —*cf. thirty-second note;* Notes List

demo *n.* (demo recording) —*cf.* also Recording List
F démo *f*
G Demo *m*
I demo *m*

deposit *n.* —*cf.* also Finances List
F dépot *m*
G Anzahlung *f*
I deposito *m*

desk *n.* (stand) —*cf.* also Orchestral Terms List
F pupitre *m*
G Pult *n*
I leggio *m*

development *n.* —*cf.* also Musical Forms List
F développement *m*
G Durchführung *f*
I sviluppo *m*

dexterity *n.* (finger dexterity, *etc.*)
F dextérité *f*
G Fertigkeit *f*
I abilità *f;* destrezza *f*

di *n.* (c-sharp solfege syllable in the key of c-major in American, movable-do system) —*cf.* also Solfege List
F do *m*
G cis *n*
I do *m*
N.B. Cf. important note given under the entry "solfege" regarding differences between European and American solfege systems. *Cf.* also Solfege List.

diaphragm *n.* —*cf.* also Voice List
F diaphragme *m*
G Zwerchfell *n*

I diaframma *m*

diatonic *adj.*
F diatonique
G diatonisch
I diatonico

diction *n.* —*cf.* also Voice List
F diction *f*
G Diktion *f*
I dizione *f*

digital *adj.* —*cf.* also Recording List
F digital; numérique; enregistrement
numérique *m*
G digital
I digitale

diminished *adj.* (interval) —*cf.* also
Intervals List
F diminué
G vermindert
I diminuito

diminution *n.*
F diminution *f*
G Verkleinerung *f*
I diminuzione *f* (for rhythmic diminu-
tion); diminuito *m* (for intervals)

dinner jacket *n.* (tuxedo) —*cf. tuxedo*

director *n.* (of an opera; theater, *etc.*)—
cf. also Professions List
F régisseur *m*
G Regisseur *m*; Regisseurin *f*
I regista *m*/*f*

dirge *n.* —*cf.* also Musical Forms List
F chant funèbre *m*
G Grabgesang *m*
I canto funebre *m*

dissonant *adj.*
F dissonant
G dissonant; mißtönend
I dissonante

distortion *n.* —*cf.* also Recording List
F distorsion *f*
G Verzerrung *f*
I distorsione *f*

dorian

divertimento *n.* —*cf.* also Musical
Forms List
F divertissement *m*
G Divertimento *n*
I divertimento *m*

¹divided *adv.* —*cf.* also Orchestral
Terms List
F divisé (*abv.* div.)
G geteilt (*abv.* get.)
I divisi (*abv.* div.)

²divided in 2 —*cf.* also Orchestral
Terms List
F divisé à 2 (*abv.* div. à 2)
G zweifach
I divisi a 2 (*abv.* div. a 2)

³divided in 3 —*cf.* also Orchestral
Terms List
F divisé à 3 (*abv.* div. à 3)
G dreifach
I divisi a 3 (*abv.* div. a 3)

²divided in 4 —*cf.* also Orchestral
Terms List
F divisé à 4 (*abv.* div. à 4)
G vierfach
I divisi a 4 (*abv.* div. a 4)

do *n.* (c-natural solfege syllable in the
key of c-major in American, movable-do
system) —*cf.* also Solfege List
F do *m*
G c *n*
I do *m*
N.B. Cf. important note given under the
entry "solfege" regarding differences
between European and American
solfege systems. Cf. also Solfege List.

dominant *n.* (scale degree; chord) —
cf. also Chords List
F dominante *f*
G Dominante *f*
I dominante *f*

dorian *n.* (church mode) —*cf.* also
Modes List
F dorien *m*
G Dorisch *n*
I dorico *m*

— 103 —

dot *n.* (for a quarter note; eighth note, *etc.*) —*cf.* also Notes List (Parts of a Written Note)
F point *m*
G Punkt *m*
I punto *m*

dotted *adj.* (quarter note; eighth note, *etc.*) —*cf.* also Notes List
F pointée
G punktiert
I con il punto (*N.B.* In Italian, you usually say the note with a dot, *i.e.* "nota con il punto.")

¹**double** *v.* (two or more instruments playing in unison, *etc.*)
F doubler
G verdoppeln
I raddoppiare

²**double appoggiatura** *n.* —*cf.* also *appoggiatura*
F appoggiature double *f*
G Anschlag *m*
I appoggiatura doppia *f*

³**double bar** *n.* (printed at the end of a piece, *etc.*)
F double barre *f*
G Doppelstrich *m*
I doppia stanghetta *f*

⁴**double bass** *n.* —*cf.* also Instruments List (Strings)
F contre basse *f*
G Kontrabaß *f*
I contrabasso *m*

⁵**double bass player / double bassist** *n.* —*cf. bass player;* also Professions List

⁶**double bass clarinet** *n.* —*cf.* also Instruments List (Woodwinds)
F clarinette contrebasse *f*
G Kontrabaßklarinette *f*
I clarinetto contrabasso *m*

⁷**double bass clarinetist** *n.* —*cf.* also Professions List
F joueur de clarinette contrebasse *m;* joueuse de clarinette contrebasse *f*

G Kontrabaßklarinetteist *m;* Kontrabaßklarinetteistin *f*
I clarinettista *m / f;* suonatore di clarinetto contrabasso *m;* suonatrice di clarinetto contra basso *f*

⁸**double concerto** *n.* —*cf.* also Musical Forms List
F double concerto *m*
G Doppelkonzert *n*
I concerto doppio *m*

⁹**double dot** *n.* (for a quarter note; eighth note, *etc.*) —*cf.* also Notes List (Parts of a Written Note)
F double point *m*
G Dopplepunkt *m*
I doppio punto *m*

¹⁰**double dotted** *adj.* (quarter note; eighth note, *etc.*) —*cf.* also Notes List
F double pointée
G dopplte punktiert
I doppio punto *m* (*N.B.* In Italian, you usually say the note with a double dot, *i.e.* "nota con il doppio punto.")

¹¹**double flat** *n.*
F double bémol *m*
G Doppel-Be *n*
I doppio bemolle *m*

¹²**double mute** *n.* —*cf.* also MutesList
F sourdine à double cône *f*
G Doppelkegeldämpfer *m*
I sordina a doppio cono *f*

¹³**double reed** *n.* (for oboe; bassoon, *etc.*) —*cf.* also *reed*
F anche double *f*
G Doppelrohrblatt *n*
I ancia doppia *f*

¹⁴**double sharp** *n.*
F double dièse *m*
G Doppel-kreuz *m*
I doppio diesis *m*

¹⁵**double stop; triple stop; quadruple stop** *n.* (violin, *etc.*)
F double-corde *f* / triple-corde *f* / quadruple-corde *f*
G Doppelgriff *m* / Trippelgriff *m* /

Quadruplegriff *m*
I doppia corda *f* / tripla corda *f* /
quadrupla corda *f*

[16] **double whole note** *n. —cf.* also
Notes List (Rhythmic Values)
F note carrée *f*
D Doppelganznote *f*
I breve *f* (note name) (*N.B.* In Italian,
they often distinguish between the *note*
itself, and the *duration* of that note. The
name of the *duration* of this note is:
breve *f.*) *Cf. double whole rest.*)
• *N.B.* The British name of this note is:
breve.

[17] **double whole rest** *n. —cf.* also
Rest List
F bâton de 2 pauses *f* (*N.B.* In French,
the names of the rests are not the same
as the corresponding notes. *Cf.* Notes
[individual entries and Notes List] for
comparison.)
G Doppelganze-Pause *f*
I pausa di breve *f* (*N.B.* In Italian the
rest is followed by the name of the note.
Ex. "pausa di ..." [followed by value.])
• *N.B.* The British name of this rest is:
breve.

down bow *n.* (violin, *etc.*) *—cf.* also
bowing; up bow
F tirer *v.* (*N.B.* In French, one usually
uses this verb for down bowing rather
than a noun.)
G Abstrich *m*
I arcata in giù *f*

downbeat *n.* (from conductor, *etc.*) —
cf. also *cue; entrance*
F battue *f*
G Abtakt *m*; (*N.B.* The phrase "auf die
eins" (on [the] one) is often used in
German.)
I battere *m*

downstage *n. —cf.* also Stage List
F sur le devant *m*
G im Vorgrund *m*
I ribalta *f*; proscenio *m*

draw *v.* (a bow, *etc.*)
F tirer (*N.B.* In French, one usually

indicates the bowing direction rather
than simply the concept of "drawing"
the bow. *Cf. down bow; up bow.*)
G ziehen
I tirare (*N.B.* In Italian you usually
simply say "to bow"—"dare l'arcata.")

dress rehearsal *n. —cf.* also Concert
List
F générale *f*; répétition générale *f*
G Generalprobe *f*
I prova generale *f*

dressing room *n. —cf.* also Concert
List
F loge *f*
G Garderobe *f*; Künstlergarderobe *f*
I camerino *m* (normally used in plural:
"camerini" *m / pl*)

drone *n.* (a long pedal tone, *etc.*)
F bourdon *m*
G Bordun *m*
I bordone *m*

drum stick *n. —cf.* also Drum Sticks
List and individual entries
F baguette *f*
G Schlegel *m*
I bacchetta *f*

drummer *n. —cf.* also *percussionist;*
Professions List
F bateur *m / f*
G Schlagzeuger *m*; Schlagzeugerin *f*
I batista *m / f*

dub *v. —cf.* also Recording List
F doubler
G verdoppeln
I riregistrare

duet *n. —cf.* also Musical Forms List
F duetto *m*
G Duett *n*
I duetto *m*

dulcian *n. —cf.* also Instruments List
(Historic & Ethnic Instruments)
F douçaine *f*
G Dulzian *m*
I dulciana *f*

dulcimer *n.* —*cf.* also Instruments List
(Historic & Ethnic Instruments)
F tympanon *m*
G Hackbrett *n*
I salterio tedesco *m*

duo *n.* —*cf.* also Musical Forms List
F duo *m*
G Duo *n*
I duo *m*

duple *n.* (meter; time signature) —*cf.*
also Time Signatures List
F mesure binaire *f*; mesure à deux
temps *f*
G Doppeltakt *m*
I tempo binario *m*

¹ **duration** *n.* (length of a composition)
F durée *f*
G Dauer *f*; Zeitdauer *f*
I durata *f*

² **duration** *n.* (of a note, *etc.*) —*cf. note
value; rest value*

¹ **dynamic marking** *n.*
F signe de nuance *m*
G dynamisches Zeichen *n*
I segno di dinamica *m*

² **dynamic microphone** *n.* —*cf.
electrodynamic mic*; also Recording List

dynamics *n.* / *pl* (*N.B.* In English we
tend to use this term in the plural, while
French, German and Italian all tend to
use it in the singular as given below.)
F nuance *f*; dynamique *f*
G Dynamik *f*
I dinamica *f*

— E —

e *n.* (name of note) —*cf.* also Note Names List
F mi *m*
G e *n*
I mi *m*

e-double flat *n.* (name of note) —*cf.* also Note Names List
F mi double bémol *m*
G eses *n*
I mi doppio bemolle *m*

e-double sharp *n.* (name of note) — *cf.* also Note Names List
F mi double dièse *m*
G eisis *n*
I mi doppio diesis *m*

e-flat *n.* (name of note) —*cf.* also Note Names List
F mi bémol *m*
G es *n*
I mi bemolle *m*

e-flat major *n.* (key center) —*cf.* also Keys List
F mi bémol majeur *f*
G Es-dur *n*
I mi bemolle maggiore *m*

e-flat minor *n.* (key center) —*cf.* also Keys List
F mi bémol mineur *f*
G es-moll *n*
I mi bemolle minore *m*

e major *n.* (key center) —*cf.* also Keys List
F mi majeur *f*
G E-dur *n*
I mi maggiore *m*

e minor *n.* (key center) —*cf.* also Keys List
F mi mineur *f*
G e-moll *n*
I mi minore *m*

e-sharp *n.* (name of note) —*cf.* also Note Names List
F mi dièse *m*
G eis *n*
I mi diesis *m*

e-sharp major *n.* (key center) —*cf.* also Keys List
F mi dièse majeur *f*
G Eis-dur *n*
I mi diesis maggiore *m*

e-sharp minor *n.* (key center) —*cf.* also Keys List
F mi dièse mineur *f*
G eis-moll *n*
I mi diesis minore *m*

[1] **ear** *n.* —*cf.* also Anatomy List
F oreille *f*
G Ohr *n*
I orecchio *m* (orecchie *pl* / *f*)

[2] **ear-training** *n.*
F solfège *m* (In French, the phrase "ear training" doesn't exist. They use the term *solfège* which implies the training itself.)
G Gehörbildung *f*
I solfeggio *m* (In Italian, the phrase "ear training" doesn't exist. They use the term "solfeggio" which implies the training itself.)

[1] **early** *adj.* (as in "early 19th-Century") —*cf.* also Historical Periods & Styles

F au début du... (Followed by the
century. *Ex.* "...au début du dix-
neuvième siècle.")
G früh... (Followed by the century, but
remember to keep in the proper case.
Ex. "...frühes neunzehnte Jahrhundert.")
I inizio del... (Followed by the century.
Ex. "...inizio del Diciannovesimo
secolo"); il primo... (Followed by the
century. *Ex.* "...il primo Ottocento.")

[2] **early music** *n.* (general term for
Medieval; Renaissance, *etc.*) —*cf.* also
Historical Periods & Styles List
F musique ancienne *f*
G Altmusik *f*
I musica antica *f*

ebony *n.* —*cf.* also Instrument Repair
List (Various Woods)
F ébène *f*
G Ebenholz *n*
I ebano *m*

edit *v.* —*cf.* also Recording List
F couper
G schneiden
I montare

edition *n.* (of music, *etc.*)
F édition *f*
G Ausgabe *f*
I edizione *f*

[1] **editor** *n.* (of a printed musical
edition, *etc.*) —*cf.* also Professions List
F éditeur *m*; éditrice *f*
G Bearbeiter *m*; Bearbeiterin *f*
I editore *m*; editrice *f*

[2] **editor** *n.* (of music; in a recording
studio, *etc.*) —*cf.* also Professions List;
Recording List
F monteur *m*; monteuse *f*
G Cutter *m*; Cutterin *f*
I produttore *m* / *f*; tecnico del suono *m*

effect *n.* —*cf.* also *special effects*
F effet *m*
G Effekt *m*
I effetto *m*

[1] **eighth note** *n.* —*cf.* also Notes List

(Rhythmic Values)
F croche *f*
D Achtelnote *f*
I ottavo *m* (note name)
(*N.B.* In Italian, they often distinguish
between the *note* itself, and the *duration*
of that note. The name of the *duration* of
this note is: croma *f.*) *Cf. eighth rest.*
• *N.B.* The British name of this note is:
quaver.

[2] **eighth rest** *n.* —*cf.* also Rest List
F demi-soupir *m* (*N.B.* In French, the
names of the *rests* are not the same as
the corresponding *notes. Cf.* Notes
[individual entries and Notes List] for
comparison.)
(*N.B.* In French, a quarter rest [*le soupir*]
is printed as normal but often in a
composer's manuscript they use the
19th-Century practice of hand-writing a
quarter rest like a "backwards" eighth
rest.)
G Achtel-Pause *f*
I pausa di croma *f* (*N.B.* In Italian the
rest is followed by the name of the note.
Ex. "pausa di ..." [followed by value.])
• *N.B.* The British name of this rest is:
quaver.

elbow *n.* —*cf.* also Anatomy List
F coude *m*
G Ellbogen *m*
I gomito *m*

electric *adj.* (non-acoustic instrument)
F electrique
G E- (Followed by the instrument
name; *Ex.* E-Gitarre; E-Piano, *etc.*);
elektro (followed by the instrument
name)
I elettrico *m*; elettrica *f* (Usually
preceded by the instrument name. *Ex.*
pianoforte elettrico; chitarra elettrica,
etc.)

(electro)dynamic mic *n.* —*cf.* also
individual entries: *condensor mic.; contact
mic.*; also Recording List
F micro électrodynamique *m*
G elektrodynamisches Mikrophon *n*
I microfono elettrodinamico *m*

elegy *n.* —*cf.* also Musical Forms List
F élégie *f*
G Elegie *f*
I elegia *f*

eleventh *n.* —*cf.* also Intervals List
F onzième *f*
G Undezime *f*
I undicesima *f*

embassy *n.* (diplomatic office of a country, *etc.*) —*cf.* also Legal Subjects List
F ambassade *f*
G Botschaft *f*
I ambasciata *f*

embellish *v.* (to ornament a note; phrase, *etc.*)
F embellir
G verzieren; verschönern (*N.B.* German usually uses the verb "verzieren," "to ornament." "Verschönnern" is lingustically correct, but sounds strange.)
I abbellire

embellished *adj.*
F ornementé
G verziert
I abbellimento *m* (In Italian the adjective isn't really used—they usually use the phrase "with embellishments"— "con abbellimenti." *m / pl*)

embellishment *n.* —*cf.* also *ornament (n.)*
F ornement *m*
G Verzierung *f*
I abbellimento *m*

embouchure *n.* (of a trumpet player, *etc.*)
F embouchure *f*
G Ansatz *m*; Embouchure *f*
I imboccatura *f*

encore *n.* —*cf.* also Concert List
F bis *m*
G Zugabe *f*
I bis *m*

ending *n.* (first; second, *etc.* in printed music)
F fois *f* (Ex. "première fois" *f*; "deuxième fois" *f, etc.*) (In French, one usually indicates which ending. Often you will also hear musicians refer to "encadrement première fois;" (*m*) "encadrement deuxième fois," (*m*) *etc.*, refering to the "bracket.")
G Endung *f* (Ex. "Erste Endung" *f*; "Zweite Endung," *f etc.*)
I finale *m* (Ex. "finale primo" *m*; "finale secundo" *m, etc.*)

engineer *n.* —*cf.* also Professions List; Recording List
F ingénieur *m*; ingénieur du son *m*
G Tonmeister *m*; Tonmeisterin *f*
I tecnico del suono *m*

¹ english horn *n.* —*cf.* also Instruments List (Woodwinds)
F cor anglais *m*
G Englisch Horn *n*
I corno inglese *m*

² english horn player *n.* —*cf.* also Professions List
F joueur de cor anglais *m*; joueuse de cor anglais *f*
G Englisch-horn Spieler *m*; Englisch-horn Spielerin *f*
I suonatore di corno inglese *m*; suonatrice di corno inglese *f*

engrave *v.* —*cf.* also Instrument Repair List (Common Verbs)
F graver
G gravieren
I cesellare

enharmonic *adj.* —*cf.* also Notes List
F enharmonique
G enharmonische
I enarmonico

ensemble *n.*
F ensemble *m*
G Ensemble *n*
I ensemble *f* (more for classical music); complesso *m* (more for pop music)

¹ entrance *n.* (in a piece; of a part in orchestra music, *etc.*) —*cf.* also *cue;*

— 109 —

downbeat
F entrée *m*
G Eintritt *n*
I entrata *f*

² **entrance** *n.* (the act of coming on to the stage) —*cf.* also Concert List
F entrée *f*; entrée sur scène *f*
G Eintritt *m*
I entrata *f*

epilogue *n.* —*cf.* also Musical Forms List
F épilogue *m*
G Epilog *m*
I epilogo *m*

episode *n.* —*cf.* Musical Forms List
F épisode *m*
G Episode *f*
I episodio *m*

equal temperament *n.* —*cf.* also Tuning List
F tempérament égal *m*
G gleichschwebende Temperatur *f*; gleichschwebende-temperierung *f*; wohltemperiert *adj.* (*N.B.* Although we are used to thinking "wohltemperiert" in English because of J.S. Bach's *Wohltemperiert Klavier*, the term sounds extremely antiquated and is virtually never used in modern speech.)
I temperamento equabile *m*

equalizer *n.* —*cf.* also Recording List
F égalisateur *m*
G Entzerrer *m*
I equalizzatore *m*

erase *v.* (erase a tape; track, *etc.*) —*cf.* also Recording List
F effacer
G löschen
I cancellare

estampie *n.* —*cf.* also Musical Forms List
F estampie *f*
G Estampie *f*
I estampida *f*

ethnic music *n.* —*cf.* also Historical Periods & Styles List
F musique ethnique *f*
G ethnische Musik *f*
I musica etnica *f*

etude *n.* (a musical study) —*cf.* also Musical Forms List
F étude *f*
G Etüde *f*
I studio *m*

euphonium *n.* —*cf.* also Instruments List (Woodwinds)
F euphonium *m*
G Baritonhorn *n*
I bombardino *m*

excerpt *n.* (part of an orchestral composition)
F extrait *m*
G Excerpt *n*; Auszug *m*; Stimmenauszug *m*
I estratto *m*

exhale *v.* —*cf.* inhale / exhale

¹ **exit** *n.* (from the stage) —*cf.* also Concert List
F sortie *f*
G Bühnenausgang *m*
I uscita *f*

² **exit** *v.* (from the stage) —*cf.* also Concert List
F quitter
G abgehen
I uscire, ("Egli esce di scena")

exposition *n.* —*cf.* also Musical Forms List
F exposition *f*
G Exposition *f*
I esposizione *f*

expression marking *n.* (allegro; pesante, *etc.*)
F signe d'expression *m*
G Vortragsbezeichnung *f*
I segno d'expressione *m*

Expressionism *n.* (compositional style) —*cf.* also Historical Periods & Styles List

F expressionnisme *m*
G Expressionismus *m*
I Espressionismo *m*

expressionistic *adj.*
F expressionistique
G expressionistisch
I esspressionistico *m* (Usually used in Italian as a noun.)

eye *n.* —*cf.* also Anatomy List
F œil *m* (yeux *m / pl*)
G Auge *n* (Augen *n / pl*)
I occhio *m* (occhi *m / pl*)

— F —

f *n.* (name of note) —*cf.* also Note Names List
F fa *m*
G f *n*
I fa *f*

f-double flat *n.* (name of note) —*cf.* also Note Names List
F fa double bémol *m*
G feses *n*
I fa doppio bemolle *f*

f-double sharp *n.* (name of note) — *cf.* also Note Names List
F fa double dièse *m*
G fisis *n*
I fa doppio diesis *f*

f-flat *n.* (name of note) —*cf.* also Note Names List
F fa bémol *m*
G fes *n*
I fa bemolle *f*

f-flat major *n.* (key center) —*cf.* also Keys List
F fa bémol majeur *f*
G Fes-dur *n*
I fa bemolle maggiore *m*

f-flat minor *n.* (key center) —*cf.* also Keys List
F fa bémol mineur *f*
G fes-moll *n*
I fa bemolle minore *m*

f-hole *n.* (of violin, *etc.*)
F ouïe *f*
G F-Loch *n*
I effe *f*

f major *n.* (key center) —*cf.* also Keys List
F fa majeur *f*
G F-dur *n*
I fa maggiore *m*

f minor *n.* (key center) —*cf.* also Keys List
F fa mineur *f*
G f-moll *n*
I fa minore *m*

f-sharp *n.* (name of note) —*cf.* also Note Names List
F fa dièse *m*
G fis *n*
I fa diesis *f*

f-sharp major *n.* (key center) —*cf.* also Keys List
F fa dièse majeur *f*
G Fis-dur *n*
I fa diesis maggiore *m*

f-sharp minor *n.* (key center) —*cf.* also Keys List
F fa dièse mineur *f*
G fis-moll *n*
I fa diesis minore *m*

fa *n.* (f-natural solfege syllable in the key of c-major in American, movable-do system) —*cf.* also Solfege List
F fa *m*
G f *n*
I fa *m*
N.B. Cf. important note given under the entry "solfege" regarding differences between European and American solfege systems. *Cf.* also Solfege List.

face *n.* —*cf.* also Anatomy List
F visage *m*

G Gesicht *n*
I faccia *f*

facsimile *n.* —*cf.* also Research List
F fac-similé *m*
G Faksimile *n*
I fac-simile *m*; facsimile *m*

¹ **false** *adv./adj.* (a wrong entrance; note, *etc.*)
F faute d'èntrée *f* (for an entrance);
canard *m /sl.* (for a note — *i.e.* "a duck" implying "a quack")
G falsch
I falsa entrata *f*; (for an entrance); stecca *f* (for a note); sbagliare *sl*

² **false relation** *n.* (harmonic relationship)
F fausse relation *f*
G Querstand *m*
I falsa relazione *f*

falsetto *n.* (of a singer) —*cf.* also Voice List
F fausset *m*
G Falsett *n*
I falsetto *m*

fantasy *n.* —*cf.* also Musical Forms List
F fantaisie *f*
G Fantasie *f*
I fantasia *f*

fe *n.* (f-flat solfege syllable in the key of c-major in American, movable-do system) —*cf.* also Solfege List
F fa *m*
G fes *n*
I fa *m*
N.B. Cf. important note given under the entry "solfege" regarding differences between European and American solfege systems. *Cf.* also Solfege List.

fee *n.* (paid to a performer) —*cf. concert fee;* also Concert List

feedback *n.* —*cf.* also Recording List
F réaction *f*
G Rückkoppelung *f*
I feedback *m*

¹ **felt** *n.* —*cf.* also Instrument Repair List (Various Materials)
F feutre *m*
G Filz *m*
I feltro *m*

² **felt stick** *n.* —*cf.* also Drum Sticks List
F baguette de feutre *f*
G Filzschlegel *m*
I bacchetta di feltro *f*

fermata *n.*
F point d'orgue *m*
G Fermate *f*
I corona *f*

festival *n.* (music festival, *etc.*)
F festival *m*; festival de musique *m*
G Fest *m*; Musikfest *n*; Musikfestspiel *n*; Musikfestival *n*
I festival *f*; festival musicale *f*

fi *n.* (f-sharp solfege syllable in the key of c-major in American, movable-do system) —*cf.* also Solfege List
F fa *m*
G fis *n*
I fa *m*
N.B. Cf. important note given under the entry "solfege" regarding differences between European and American solfege systems. *Cf.* also Solfege List.

fiberglass *n.* —*cf.* also Instrument Repair List (Various Materials)
F fibre de verre *f*
G Glasswolle *f*
I fibra di vetro *f*

field drum *n.* —*cf.* also Instruments List (Percussion Instruments)
F tambour *m*
G Rührtrommel *f*
I tamburo *m*

fifth *n.* —*cf.* also Intervals List
F quinte *f*
G Quinte *f*
I quinta *f*

figure *n.* (a melodic; harmonic; rhythmic grouping)

F figure *f*
G Figur *f*
I figura *f*

figured bass *n.* (baroque harpsi-chord notation, *etc.*)
F basse chiffrée *f*
G Bezifferter Baß *n*
I basso cifrato *m*; basso numerato *m*; basso figurato *m*

film music *n.* —*cf.* also *sound track*; Historical Periods & Styles
F musique de film *f*
G Filmmusik *f*
I musica per film *f*

filter *n.* —*cf.* also Recording List
F filtre *m*
G Filter *n*
I filtro *m*

finale *n.* —*cf.* also Musical Forms List
F finale *m*
G Finale *n*
I finale *m*

finalist *n.* (in a competition) —*cf.* also Competition List
F finaliste *m* / *f*
G Finalist *m*; Finalistin *f*
I finalista *m* / *f*

¹ finger *n.* (of the hand) —*cf.* also Anatomy List
F doigt *m*
G Finger *m*
I dito *m*

² finger *v.* (to write fingering into the music)
F doigter
G bearbeiten (this is also used for "to edit")
I ditteggiare

³ finger hole *n.* (on an open-hole flute; recorder, *etc.*)
F trou *m*
G Fingerloch *n*
I foro *m*

fingerboard *n.*

F touche *f*
G Griffbrett *n*
I tastiera *f*

fingering *n.* (indications written into the music for the performer)
F doigté *m*
G Fingersatz *m*
I diteggiatura *f*

fingernail *n.* —*cf.* also Anatomy list
F ongle *m*
G Fingernagel *m*
I unghia *f*

fingers *n.* / *pl* (names) —*cf.* individual finger names; also Teaching List

fingertip *n.* —*cf.* also Anatomy List
F bout du doigt *m*
G Fingerspitze *f* (this is the actual tip of the finger); Fingerkuppe *f* (this is the fatty part of the fingertip)
I polpastrello *m*

¹ first finger *n.* —*cf. index finger;* also Anatomy List

² first inversion *n.* (of a chord) —*cf.* also Chord List (Chord Inversions)
F premier renversement *m*
G erste Umkehrung *f*
I primo rivolto *m*

fix *v.* —*cf.* also Instrument Repair List (Common Verbs)
F réparer
G befestigen
I riparare

flag *n.* —*cf.* also Notes List (Parts of a Written Note) (*N.B.* The British name for a flag is *hook.*)
F drapeau *m*
G Notenfahne *f*
I codetta *f*

¹ flat *n.* (accidental) —*cf.* also *sharp; natural; cautionary accidental*
F bémol *f*
G Be *n* (often written simply as the letter "B" [upper case] or "b" [lower case])

I bemolle *m*

²flat *adj.* (out of tune, *i.e.* singing or playing too low) —*cf.* also *sharp*
F bas (chanter trop bas / jouer trop bas)
G tief (zu tief singen / zu tief spielen)
I calante (for singing and playing)

flautist *n.* (flutist) —*cf.* also Professions List
F flûtiste *m*/*f*
G Flötist *m*; Flötistin *f*
I flautista *m*/*f*; flauto *m*/*f*; suonatore di flauto *m*; suonatrice di flauto *f*

flexatone *n.* —*cf.* also Instruments List (Percussion Instruments)
F flexaton *m*
G Flexaton *n*
I flexaton *m*

florid counterpoint *n.* —*cf.* also Musical Forms List
F contrepoint fleuri *m*
G blühender Kontrapunkt *m*
I contrappunto florido *m*; contrappunto fiorito *m*

flugelhorn *n.* —*cf.* also Instruments List (Woodwinds)
F flicorne *m*
G Flügelhorn *n*
I flicorno *m*

flute *n.* —*cf.* also Instruments List (Woodwinds)
F flûte *f*
G Flöte *f*
I flauto *m*

flutist *n.* —*cf. flautist; also* Professions List

flutter tongue *n.*
F flutterzunge *m*
G Flatterzunge *f*
I frullato *m*

fog horn *n.* —*cf.* also Instruments List (Percussion Instruments)
F sirène de brume *f*
G Nebelhorn *n*
I corno da nebbia *m*

folia *n.* —*cf.* also Musical Forms List
F folia *f*
G Folia *f*
I follia *f*

folk music *n.* (traditional style; modern style)
F musique folklorique *f* (traditional style); folk musique *f* (modern style)
G Volksmusik *f*
I musica folcloristica *f* (traditional style); musica popolare *f* (modern style)

foot *n.* —*cf.* also Anatomy List
F pied *m*
G Fuß *m*
I piede *m*

footlights *n.* —*cf.* also Stage List
F rampe *f*/ *pl*
G Rampenlicht *n*/ *pl*
I luci della ribalta *f*/ *pl*

footstool *n.* (for classical guitar, *etc.*)
F tabouret *f*
G Fußbank *f*
I poggiapiede *m*

forearm *n.* —*cf.* also Anatomy List
F avant-bras *m*
G Unterarm *m*
I avambraccio *m*

foreign police *n.* —*cf.* also Legal Subjects List
F agent d'immigration *m*
G Fremdenpolizei *f*
I polizia *f* (Usually you say "ufficio immigrazione," *i.e.* the office where they work.)

form *n.* (musical) —*cf.* also Musical Forms List
F forme *f*
G Form *f*
I forma *f*

forte piano *n.* —*cf.* also Instruments List (Historic & Ethnic Instruments)
F forte-piano *m*
G Fortepiano *m*
I forte-piano *m*

four-four (4/4) *n.* (time signature in words as it is spoken in conversation) — *cf.* also Time Signature List
F mesure à quatre-quatre *f*
G vierviertel Takt *m*
I quattro quanti *m / pl*

¹ fourth *n.* —*cf.* also Intervals List
F quarte *f*
G Quarte *f*
I quarta *f*

² fourth finger *n.* —*cf. little finger;* also Anatomy List (Fingers)

³ fourth inversion *n.* (of a chord) — *cf.* also Chord List (Chord Inversions)
F quatrième renversement *m*
G vierte Umkehrung *f*
I quarto rivolto *m*

foyer *n.* (lobby outside a concert hall) —*cf.* also Stage List
F foyer *m*
G Foyer *n*
I ridotto

¹ free stroke *n.* (guitar fingering) (*N.B.* The Spanish term *tirando* [for free stroke] is generally understood by all classical guitarists regardless of their language.)
F pincé *m*
G Wechselschlag *m*
I libero *m* (tocco libero *m*)

² free-form *n.* (jazz)
F free-jazz *m*; jazz libre *m*
G Free Jazz *m*
I freejazz *m*

³ free-lance (musician) *adj.* (a musician without an on-going contract)
F indépendent
G freischaffend
I libero professionista

⁴ free piece *n.* (piece chosen by competitor in a competition) —*cf.* also Competition List
F morceau de choix *m*
G Stück eigener Wahl *m*
I brano a scelta *m*

¹ French horn *n.* —*cf.* also Instruments List
F cor *m*
G Horn *n*
I corno *m*

² French horn player *n.* (hornist) — *cf. horn player* also Professions List

frequency *n.* (of a pitch; in sound reproduction, *etc.*) —*cf.* also Recording List
F fréquence *f*; modulation *f*
G Frequenz *f*
I frequenza *f*

fret *n.* (guitar, *etc.*)
F frette *f*; sillet *m*; barrette *f / sl.*
G Bund *m*
I tasto *m*

frog *n.* (of a bow)
F talon *m*
G Frosch *m*
I tallone *m*

fughetta *n.* —*cf.* also Musical Forms List
F fughette *f*
G Fughette *f*
I fughetta *f*

fugue *n.* —*cf.* also Musical Forms List
F fugue *f*
G Fuge *f*
I fuga *f*

fundamental *n.* (of a harmonic, *etc.*)
F son fondamental *m*
G Grundtone *m*
I suono fondamentale *m*

— G —

g *n.* (name of note) —*cf.* also Note Names List
F sol *m*
G g *n*
I sol *m*

g-double flat *n.* (name of note) —*cf.* also Note Names List
F sol double bémol *m*
G geses *n*
I sol doppio bemolle *m*

g-double sharp *n.* (name of note) — *cf.* also Note Names List
F sol double dièse *m*
G gisis *n*
I sol doppio diesis *m*

g-flat *n.* (name of note) —*cf.* also Note Names List
F sol bémol *m*
G ges *n*
I sol bemolle *m*

g-flat major *n.* (key center) —*cf.* also Keys List
F sol bémol majeur *f*
G Ges-dur *n*
I sol bemolle maggiore *m*

g-flat minor *n.* (key center) —*cf.* also Keys List
F sol bémol mineur *f*
G ges-moll *n*
I sol bemolle minore *m*

g major *n.* (key center) —*cf.* also Keys List
F sol majeur *f*
G G-dur *n*
I sol maggiore *m*

g minor *n.* (key center) —*cf.* also Keys List
F sol mineur *f*
G g-moll *n*
I sol minore *m*

g-sharp *n.* (name of note) —*cf.* also Note Names List
F sol dièse *m*
G gis *n*
I sol diesis *m*

g-sharp major *n.* (key center) —*cf.* also Keys List
F sol dièse majeur *f*
G Gis-dur *n*
I sol diesis maggiore *m*

g-sharp minor *n.* (key center) —*cf.* also Keys List
F sol dièse mineur *f*
G gis-moll *n*
I sol diesis minore *m*

galliard *n.* —*cf.* also Musical Forms List
F gaillarde *f*
G Gagliarde *f*
I gagliarda *f*

galop *n.* —*cf.* also Musical Forms List
F galop *m*
G Galopp *m*
I galoppo *m*

gambist *n.* —*cf. viol da gambist* also Professions List

gauge *n.* (density of a string) —*cf.* also Strings List
F calibre *m*
G Saitenstärke *f*

I calibro *m*

gavotte *n.* —*cf.* also Musical Forms List
F gavotte *f*
G Gavotte *f*
I gavotta *f*

gear *n.* (of tuning key, *etc.*)
F engrenage *m*
G Zahnrad *n*
I ruoto dentata *f*

generation *n.* (of a recording) —*cf.* also Recording List
F génération *f*
G Generation *f*
I generazione *f*

generator *n.* —*cf.* also Recording List
F générateur *m*
G Generator *m*
I generatore *m*

germ *n.* (small compositional motive, *etc.*) —*cf.* also Musical Forms List
F germe *m*
G Keim *m*
I cellula *f*

German silver *n.* —*cf.* also Instrument Repair List (Various Materials)
F argentan *m*
G Neusilber *n*
I alpacca *f*

gig *n.* / *sl.* (non-serious performing job)
F cacheton *m* / *sl.* (from the word "cachet *m*," or "artist's fee.")
G Gig *m* / *sl.*
I lavoretto *m*; (This term doesn't really exist in Italian.)

gigue (jig) *n.* —*cf.* also Musical Forms List
F gigue *f*
G Gigue *f*
I giga *f*

gipsy song *n.* —*cf.* also Musical Forms List
F chant gitan *m*
G Zigeunerlied *n*

I canto gitano *m*

glass harmonica *n.* —*cf.* also Instruments List (Percussion Instruments)
F harmonica de verres *f*
G Glasharmonika *f*
I armonica a vetro *f*

glockenspiel *n.* —*cf.* also Instruments List (Percussion Instruments)
F carillon *m*; glockenspiel *m*
G Glockenspiel *n*
I campanelli *m*/ *pl*; glockenspiel *m*/ *pl*

glottal attack *n.* —*cf.* also Voice List (Vocal Attacks)
F attaque dure *f*
G harter Einsatz *m*; Glottisschlag *m*
I attacco duro *m*

[1]**glue** *n.* —*cf.* also Instrument Repair List (Various Materials)
F colle *f*
G Leim *m*; Klebstoff *m*
I colla *f*

[2]**glue** *v.* —*cf.* also Instrument Repair List (Common Verbs)
F coller
G leimen; kleben
I incollare

[1]**gold** *n.* —*cf.* also Instrument Repair List (Various Materials)
F or *m*
G Gold *n*
I oro *m*

[2]**gold plated** *adj.* —*cf.* also *silver plated*; Instrument Repair List (Various Materials)
F plaqué d'or *adj.*
G vergoldet *adj.*
I placcato oro *adj.*

gong *n.* —*cf.* also Instruments List (Percussion Instruments)
F gong *m*
G Gong *m*
I gong *m*

gown *n.* (women's concert apparel for

performing) —*cf.* also Concert List
F robe de soirée *f* (Not really used—
very general.) *cf. concert dress.*
G Abendkleid *n* (Not really used—
very general.) *cf. concert dress*
I abito di gala *m* (Not really used—
very general.) *cf. concert dress*

grace note *n.* —*cf.* also Notes List
F appoggiature *f*
G Vorschlag *m*
I appoggiatura *f*

grain *n.* (of wood) —*cf.* also Instrument Repair List
F grain *m*
G Maserung *f*
I venatura *f*

grand piano *n.*
F piano à queue *m*
G Flügel *m*
I pianoforte a coda *m*

green room *n.* (waiting room for the performer before a concert) —*cf.* also Stage List
F loge *f;* foyer des artistes *m*
G Künstlerzimmer *n*
I camerino *m*

Gregorian Chant *n.* —*cf.* also *plain chant;* Musical Forms List
F chant grégorien *m*
G Gregorianischer Choral *m*
I canto gregoriano *m*

group lesson *n.* —*cf.* also Teaching List
F cours en groupe *m*
G Gruppenunterricht *m*
I lezione collettiva *f*

grouping *n.* —*cf.* individual entries (*quintuplet; spetuplet; sextuplet; triplet*) also Groupings List

guiro *n.* —*cf. scraper;* also Percussion List

guitar *n.* —*cf.* also Instruments List (Plucked Instruments)
F guitare *f*

G Gitarre *f*
I chitarra *f*

guitarist *n.* —*cf.* also Professions List
F guitariste *m/f*
G Gitarrist *m;* Gitarristin *f*
I chitarrista *m/f*

gut string *n.* (cat gut) —*cf.* also Strings List
F corde de boyau *f*
G Darmsaite *f*
I corda di budello *f*

H

[1]hair *n.* —*cf.* also Anatomy List
F cheveux *m / pl*
G Haare *n / pl*
I capelli *m / pl*

[2]hair *n.* (of a violin bow, *etc.*)
F mêche *f*
G Haare *n / pl*
I crini (dell'arco) *m / pl*

[1]half (of a section) —*cf.* also
Orchestral Terms List
F moitié *f*
G Hälfte *f*
I metà *f*

[2]half cadence *n.* —*cf.* also Cadence
List
F demi-cadence *f*
G Halbschluß Kadenze *f*
I cadenza sospesa *f*

[3]half note *n.* —*cf.* also Notes List
(Rhythmic Values)
F blanche *f*
D Halbnote *f*
I metà *f* (note name)
(*N.B.* In Italian, they often distinguish
between the *note* itself, and the *duration*
of that note. The name of the *duration* of
this note is: minima *f*. *Cf. half rest*.)
• *N.B.* The British name of this note is:
minum.

[4]half rest *n.* —*cf.* also Rest List
F demi-pause *f* (*N.B.* In French, the
names of the *rests* are not the same as
the corresponding *notes*. *Cf.* Notes
[individual entries and Notes List] for
comparison.)
G Halbe-Pause *f*
I pausa di minima *f* (*N.B.* In Italian the

rest is followed by the name of the note.
Ex. "pausa di ..." [followed by value.])
• *N.B.* The British name of this rest is:
minum.

[5]half step *n.* —*cf.* also Intervals List
F demi-ton *m*
G Halbton *m*
I semitono *m*

hall rental *n.* (fee for concert hall) —
cf. also Concert List
F frais de location *m*
G Sallmiete *f*
I affito *m*

[1]hammer *n.* (of piano, *etc.*)
F marteau *m*
G Hammer *m*
I martello *m*

[2]hammer *n.* (carpenter's hammer) —
cf. also *mallet;* Drum Sticks List
F marteau *m*
G Hammer m
I martello *m*

hand *n.* —*cf.* also Anatomy List
F main *f*
G Hand *f*
I mano *f*

handbell *n.* —*cf.* also Instruments List
(Percussion Instruments)
F clochette *f*
G Handglocke *f*
I campanello *m*

[1]harmonic *n.* (produced on an
instrument via the subdivision of the
overtone series) —*cf.* also *artificial
harmonic; natural harmonic*

F harmonique *m*
G Flageolett *f*
I armonico *m*

²harmonic minor (scale) *n.* —*cf.*
also Scales List
F gamme harmonique mineure *f*
G harmonische moll Tonleiter *f*
I scala minore armonica *f*

³harmonic progression —*cf.*
progression

harmonium *n.* —*cf.* also Instruments
List (Keyboards)
F harmonium *m*
G Harmonium *n*
I harmonium *m*

harmonize *v.*
F harmoniser
G harmonisieren
I armonizzare

harmony *n.*
F harmonie *f*
G Harmonie *f*
I armonia *f*

harp *n.* —*cf.* also Instruments List
(Percussion Instruments)
F harpe *f*
G Harfe *f*
I arpa *f*

harpist *n.* —*cf.* also Professions List
F harpiste *m/f*
G Harfenist *m;* Harfenistin *f*
I arpista *m/f;* suonatore di arpa *m;*
suonatrice di arpa *f*

harpsichord *n.* —*cf.* also Instruments
List (Keyboards)
F clavecin *m*
G Cembalo *n*
I cembalo *m*

harpsichordist *n.* —*cf.* also
Professions List
F claveciniste *m/f*
G Cembalist *m;* Cembalistin *f*
I clavicembalista *m/f*

hat mute *n.* —*cf.* also Mutes List
F sourdine à calotte *f*
G Hutdämpfer *m*
I sordina a cappello *f*

¹head *n.* (of a note) —*cf. notehead;* also
Notes List

²head *n.* (of of the human body) —*cf.*
also Anatomy List
F tête *f*
G Kopf *m*
I testa *f*

³head *n.* (of guitar; lute, *etc.*)
F tête *f*
G Kopf *m*
I palletta *f*

⁴head voice *n.* (of a singer) —*cf.* also
Voice List
F voix de tête *f*
G Kopfstimme *f*
I voce di testa *f*

headphone *n.* —*cf.* also Recording
List
F casque *m*
G Kopfhörer *m*
I cuffia *f*

heart *n.*—*cf.* also Anatomy List
F cœur *m*
G Herz *n*
I cuore *m*

heavy *adj.* (gauge of a musical string)
—*cf.* also Strings List
F fort; fort tirant
G hart
I forte; tensione forte

heckelphone *n.* —*cf.* also Instru-
ments List (Woodwinds)
F heckelphone *m*
G Heckelphon *n*
I heckelphon *m*

helicon *n.* —*cf.* also Instruments List
(Historic & Ethnic Instruments)
F hélicon *m*
G Helikon *n*
I helicon *m*

hemeola *n.*
F hemiole *f*
G Hemiole *f*
I hemiolia *f;* emiolia *f;* emiola *f*

hemidemisemiquaver *n.* (British name for sixty-fourth note) —*cf. sixty-fourth note;* also Notes List

hi-hat *n.* —*cf.* also Instruments List (Percussion Instruments)
F hi-hat *f;* pédale hi-hat *f*
G Hi-hat *f*
I charleston *m*

high *adj.* (general range of a pitch; instrument, *etc.*)
F aigu
G hoch
I acuto

hip *n.* —*cf.* also Anatomy List
F hanche *f*
G Hüfte *f*
I anca *f*

historical period *n.* —*cf.* also Historical Periods & Styles List
F époque *f*
G Epoche *f*
I epoca *f;* periodo *m*

hoarse *adj.* —*cf.* also Voice List
F rauque
G heiser
I rauco

hocket *n.* —*cf.* also Musical Forms List
F hoquet *m*
G Hoketus *m*
I ochetus *m;* hoquetus *m*

hook *n.* (British name for the flag of a note) —*cf. flag;* also Notes List (Parts of a Note)

¹ horn *n.* —*cf. French horn;* also Instruments List

² horn player *n.* (hornist; French horn player) —*cf.* also Professions List
F corniste *m/f*
G Hornist *m;* Hornistin *f*

I cornista *m/f;* corno *m/f;* suonatore di corno *m;* suonatrice di corno *f*

hornist *n.* (French horn player) —*cf. horn player* also Professions List

humidity *n.*
F humidité *f*
G Feuchtigkeit *f*
I umidità *f*

humoresque *n.* —*cf.* also Musical Forms List
F humoresque *f*
G Humoreske *f*
I umoresca *f*

¹ hundred twenty-eighth note *n.* —*cf.* also Notes List (Rhythmic Values)
F quintuple croche *f*
D Hunderdachtundzwanzigstenote *f*
I centoventtottesimo *m* (note name) (*N.B.* In Italian, they often distinguish between the *note* itself, and the *duration* of that note. The name of the *duration* of this note is: centoventtottesimo *m. Cf. hundred twenty-eighth rest.*)
• *N.B.* The British name of this note (although rarely used) is: *semihemidemisemiquaver.*

² hundred twenty-eighth rest *n.* —*cf.* also Rest List
F soupir d'une quintuple croche *m* (*N.B.* In French, the names of the *rests* are not the same as the corresponding *notes. Cf.* Notes [individual entries and Notes List] for comparison.)
G Hunderdachtundzwanzigste Pause *f*
I pausa di centoventtottesimo *f* (*N.B.* In Italian the rest is followed by the name of the note. *Ex.* "pausa di ..." [followed by value.])
• *N.B.* The British name of this rest (although rarely used) is: *semihemidemisemiquaver.*

hurdygurdy *n.* —*cf.* also Instruments List (Historic & Ethnic Instruments)
F vielle à roue *f*
G Dreleier *f*
I organino *m*

hybrid *n.* (artificially constructed chord; scale, *etc.*)
F hybride *m*
G Misch— (followed by the subject. *Ex.*
Mischakkord *m*; Mischtonleiter *f, etc.*)
I accordo ibrido *m*

hymn *n.* —*cf.* also Musical Forms List
F hymne *m*
G Hymne *f*
I inno *m*

hypoaeolien *n.* (church mode) —*cf.*
also Modes List
F hypoéolien *m*
G Hypoäolisch *n*
I ipoeolio *m*

hypodorian *n.* (church mode) —*cf.*
also Modes List
F hypodorien *m*
G Hypodorisch *n*
I ipodorico *m*

hypoionian *n.* (church mode) —*cf.*
also Modes List
F hypoionien *m*
G Hypoionisch *n*
I ipoionico m

hypolocrian *n.* (church mode) —*cf.*
also Modes List
F hypolocrien *m*
G Hypolokrisch *n*
I ipolocrio *m*

hypolydian *n.* (church mode) —*cf.*
also Modes List
F hypolydien *m*
G Hypolydisch *n*
I ipolidio *m*

hypomixolydian *n.* (church mode)
—*cf.* also Modes List
F hypomixolydien *m*
G Hypomixolydisch *n*
I ipomisolidio *m*

hypophrygian *n.* (church mode) —
cf. also Modes List
F hypophrygien *m*
G Hypophrygisch *n*
I ipofrigio *m*

— I —

iconography *n.* —*cf.* also Research List
F iconographie *f*
G Ikonographie *f;* Bildneskunde *f*
Iiconografia *f*

imitation *n.* (of a fugal subject, *etc.*)
F imitation *f*
G Imitation *f*
I imitazione *f*

imperfect cadence *n.* —*cf.* also Cadence List
F cadence imparfaite *f*
G Trugschluß Kadenz *f* (*N.B.* German uses the same term for deceptive and imperfect cadence.)
I cadenza imperfetta *f*

Impressionism *n.* (compositional style) —*cf.* also Historical Periods & Styles List
F impressionnisme *m*
G Impressionismus *m*
I Impressionismo *m*

impressionistic *adj.* —*cf.* also Historical Periods & Styles List
F impressionnistique
G Impressionistisch
I impressionistico *m* (Usually used in Italian as a noun.)

impromptu *n.* —*cf.* also Musical Forms List
F impromptu *m*
G Impromptu *n*
I improvviso *m*

improvise *v.* (as in jazz)
F improviser (*N.B.* In French, one improvises *at* an instrument. *Ex.* "au

piano;" "à la guitare," *etc.*)
G improvisieren
I improvvisare

¹in tune *adj.* (to sing / play with precise pitch) —*cf.* also *out of tune*
F chanter juste / jouer juste
G rein singen / rein spielen
I cantare (for singing) / giusto (for playing)

²in unison —*cf.* also Orchestral Terms List
F unis
G zusammen; einfach
I unisono

incidental music *n.* —*cf.* also Historical Periods & Styles List
F musique de scène *f*
G Bühnenmusik *f*
I musica di scena *f*

index *n.* (finger) —*cf.* also Anatomy List (Fingers)
F index *m*
G Zeigefinger *m*
I Indice *m*

inflection *n.* (in a tone or pitch)
F inflection *f* (of a voice); altération *f* (of a note)
G Stimmfall *m* (in general); Tonfall *m* (for a voice); Modulation *f* (for an instrument)
I inflessione *f* (for a voice or an instrument)

infringement *n.* —*cf. copyright infringement;* also Research List

inhale *v.* / **exhale** *v.* —*cf.* also Voice

List
F inspirer / expirer
G einatmen / ausatmen
I inspirare / espirare

¹inlay *n.* (ornamentation on the wood of an instrument, *etc.*) —*cf.* also Instrument Repair List
F marqueterie *f*
G Einlegearbeit *f;* Intarsie *f*
I intariso *m*

²inlay *v.* —*cf.* also Instrument Repair List (Common Verbs)
F marqueter
G einlegen
I inserire

input *n.* (of an amplifier, *etc.*) —*cf.* also Recording List
F entrée *f*
G Eingang *m*
I entrata *f*

insurance *n.* (health; life, *etc.*) —*cf.* also Legal Subjects List
F assurance *f*
G Versicherung *f*
I assicurazione *f*

instrument *n.*
F instrument *m*
G Instrument *n*
I strumento *m*

instrumentalist *n.* —*cf.* also Professions List
F instrumentiste *m* / *f*
G Instrumentalist *m;* Instrumentalistin *f*
I strumentista *m* / *f*

instrumental music *n.* —*cf.* also Historical Periods & Styles List
F musique instrumentale *f*
G Instrumentalmusik *f*
I musica strumentale *f*

instrumentation *n.* (of a composition, *etc.*)
F distribution *f*
G Besetzung *f*
I organico *m*

interest *n.* (accrued from a bank account, *etc.*) —*cf.* also Finances List
F intérêts *m* / *pl* (normally used in plural)
G Zinsen *m* / *pl* (normally used in plural)
I interesse *m* / *pl* (normally used in plural)

interlude *n.* —*cf.* also Musical Forms List
F entr'acte *m* (slightly older spelling, but still used in music); entracte *m* (more modern spelling)
G Zwischenspiel *n*
I interludio *m*

intermediate *n.* / *adj.* (level of a student) —*cf.* also Teaching List
F (de niveau) moyen *m*
G mittelreif *adj.* (*N.B.* German uses this term only as an *adj.*)
I livello medio (*N.B.* This term implies *ability* more than a specific *level* and is rarely used in Italian in this sense.)

intermission *n.* —*cf.* also Concert List
F pause *f*
G Pause *f*
I intervallo *m*

interpretation *n.* (musical)
F interprétation *f*
G Interpretation *f*
I interpretazione *f*

interval *n.* (between two notes)
F intervalle *m*
G Intervall *n*
I intervallo *m*

interview *n.* —*cf.* also Concert List
F interview *f*
G Interview *n*
I intervista *f*

intonation *n.* (maintaining correct pitch while playing or singing)
F justesse *f*
G Anstimmen *n*
I intonazione *f*

introduction *n.* (in a piece of music)
—*cf.* also Musical Forms List
F introduction *f*
G Einleitung *f*
I introduzione *f*

invention *n.* —*cf.* also Musical Forms
List
F invention *f*
G Invention *f*
I invenzione *f*

¹inversion *n.* (of a chord; interval) —
cf. also individual entries (*first inversion;
second inversion, etc.*); Chord List (Chord
Inversions)
F renversement *m*
G Umkehrung *f*
I rivolto *m*

²inversion *n.* (in 12-tone music) —*cf.*
also Twelve-tone Music (Matrix
Divisions List)
F renversement *m*
G Umkehrung *f*
I inversione *f*

inverted *adj.* —*cf.* also Chord List
(Chord Inversions)
F renversé
G umgekehrt
I rivolti

invitation *n.* (to a concert; restaurant;
party, *etc.*)
F invitation *f*
G Einladung *f*
I invito *m*
(N.B. In German, and sometimes French
[though never in Italian], to "invite"
someone can mean not only an
invitation to accompany you, but can
also means that you are going to pay for
them [at a restaurant, *etc.*]. *Ex.* German:
"Ich lade Sie ein..."; French: "Je vous
invite..." Be careful of this term, it can
get you into the uncomfortable situation
of paying when that was not what you
intended.)

ionian *n.* (church mode) —*cf.* also
Modes List
F ionien *m*

G Ionisch *n*
I ionico *m*

ivory *n.* —*cf.* also Instrument Repair
List (Various Materials)
F ivoire *m*
G Elfenbein *n*
I avorio *m*

— J —

¹jack *n.* (of a harpsichord) —*cf. quill*

²jack *n.* (end of a cable plugged into amplifier, *etc.*) —*cf.* also Recording List
F fiche *f;* prise "jack" *f / sl;* fiche "jack" *f / sl*
G Stecker *m*
I spinotto *m*

¹jam *v.* (to improvise a performance as in jazz)
F jam
G jam
I jam

² jam *n.* (an improvised performance among several musicians as in jazz)
F bœuf *m / sl;* jam *f;* jam-session *f*
G Jam *m;* Jam-Session *m*
I jam-session *f*

jaw *n.* —*cf.* also Anatomy List
F mâchoire *f*
G Kiefer *m*
I mascella *f*

jew's harp *n.* —*cf.* also Instruments List (Percussion Instruments)
F guimbarde *f*
G Maultrommel *f*
I scacciapensieri *m / pl*

jig *n.* —*cf. gigue;* also Musical Forms List

joint (finger; arm, *etc.*) —*cf.* also *articulation;* Anatomy List
F articulation *f*
G Gelenk *n*
I articolazione *f*

jury *n.* (of a competition or audition)

—*cf.* also Competition List
F jury *m*
G Jury *f*
I giuria *f*

— K —

kazoo *n.* —*cf.* also Instruments List
(Percussion Instruments)
F mirliton *m*
G Mirliton *m*
I kazoo *m*

¹ **key** *n.* (of an instrument)
F touche *f* (on a keyboard); clé *f* (on a
wind instrument) (*N.B.* In French, "key"
is usually written as *clef*, but sometimes
as *clé*.)
G Taste *f* (on a keyboard); Klappe *f* (on
a wind instrument)
I tasto *m* (on a keyboard); chiave *f* (on a
wind instrument)

² **key** *n.* (tuning key on a guitar, *etc.*)—
cf. also *peg*
F cheville *f*; clé *f* (*N.B.* In French, "key"
is usually written as *clef*, but sometimes
as *clé*.)
G Wirbel *m*
I chiavetta *f*

³ **key** *n.* (specific names of key centers)
—*cf.* specific entries; also Key Centers
List

⁴ **key** *n.* (tonal center)
F ton de... *m* (Followed by name of key.
Ex. "...le ton d'ut.")
G Tonart *f*
I tonalità *f*

⁵ **key change** *n.* —*cf.* also *modulation*
F changement de tonalité *m*;
changement de clef *m* (*N.B.* In French,
"key" is usually written as *clef*, but
sometimes as *clé*.)
G Tonartwechsel *m*
I cambio di tonalità *m*

⁶ **key signature** *n.*
F armature *f*
G Vorzeichen *n*
I armatura *f*; armatura di chiave *f*

¹ **keyboard** *n.* (on piano, *etc.*)
F clavier *m*
G Tastatur *f*
I tastiera *f*

² **keyboard instruments** *n.* / *pl* —*cf.*
also Instruments List (Keyboards)
F claviers *m* / *pl*
G Tasteninstrumente *n* / *pl*
I strumenti a tastiera *m* / *pl*

knee *n.* —*cf.* also Anatomy List
F genou *m*
G Knie *n*
I ginocchio *m*

knuckle *n.* (of the hand) —*cf.* also
Anatomy List
F articulation *f*; articulation du doigt *f*;
jointure *f*
G Fingergelenk *n*
I nocca *f*

— L —

la *n.* (a-natural solfege syllable in the key of c-major in American, movable-do system) —*cf.* also Solfege List
F la *m*
G a *n*
I la *m*
N.B. Cf. important note given under the entry "solfege" regarding differences between European and American solfege systems. *Cf.* also Solfege List.

label *n.* (record company) —*cf.* also Recording List
F maison de disque *f*
G Aufnahmegesellschaft *f*
I casa discografica *f*

¹lacquer *n.* —*cf.* also Instrument Repair List
F laque *m*
G Lack *m*
I lacca *f*

²lacquer *v.* —*cf.* also Instrument Repair List (Common Verbs)
F laquer
G lackieren
I laccare

lament *n.* —*cf.* also Musical Forms List
F lamentation *f*
G Klage *f*
I lamento *m*

laminate *v.* (to glue layers of wood together) —*cf.* also Instrument Repair List (Common Verbs)
F lamifier (Don't be confused that the more logical "laminer" is wrong, as this refers to pressing metal.)
G laminieren
I incollare; (incollare degli strati di legno); (Don't be confused that the more logical "laminare" is wrong, as this refers to pressing metal.)

lamination *n.* (layering of wood) —*cf.* also Instrument Repair List
F lamification *f*
G Schichtung *f*
I (Used more as a verb. *Ex.* "incollare degli strati di legno.") laminazione *f* (more for metal)

larynx *n.* —*cf.* also Anatomy List
F larynx *m*
G Kehlkopf *m*
I laringe *f*

late *adj.* (as in "late 19th-Century," *etc.*) —*cf.* also Historical Periods & Styles List
F à la fin du ... siècle (Followed by the century. *Ex.* "...à la fin du dix-neuvième siècle.")
G späte (Followed by the century, but remember to keep in the proper case. *Ex.* "...spätes neunzehnte Jahrhundert.")
I fine del... (Followed by the century. *Ex.* " ...fin del Ottocento."); tarto... (Followed by the century. *Ex.* "...tarto Ottocento.")

lay *n.* —*cf.* also Musical Forms List
F lai *m*
G Leich *m*
I lai *m*

le *n.* (a-flat solfege syllable in the key of c-major in American, movable-do system) —*cf.* also Solfege List
F la *m*
G as *n*
I la *m*
N.B. Cf. important note given under the

leading tone

entry "solfege" regarding differences between European and American solfege systems. *Cf.* also Solfege List.

leading tone *n.* —*cf.* also *subtonic;* Intervals List
F sensible *f;* ton sensible *f*
G Leitton *m*
I sensibile *f*

learn by heart —*cf. play from memory;* also Teaching List

¹**leather** *n.* —*cf.* also Instrument Repair List (Various Materials)
F cuir *m*
G Leder *n*
I cuoio *m*

²**leather stick** *n.* —*cf.* also Drum Sticks List
F baguette de cuir *f*
G Lederschlegel *m*
I bacchetta di cuoio *f*

lecture *n.* (in a class, *etc.*) —*cf.* also Teaching List
F conférence *f*
G Vortrag *m*
I conferenza *f*

ledger line *n.* —*cf.* also Staff List
F ligne supplémentaire *f*
G Hilfslinie *f*
I taglio addizionale *m*

leg *n.* —*cf.* also Anatomy List
F jambe *f*
G Bein *n*
I gamba *f*

leit-motif *n.*
F leitmotiv *m*
G Leitmotiv *n*
I leit-motif *m;* motivo conduttore *m*

letter of introduction *n.* (written documentation necessary to gain entry into some private libraries) —*cf.* also Research List
F lettre d'introduction *f*
G Empfehlungsbrief *n*
I lettera di presentazione *f*

¹**level** *n.* (*volume of a recording, etc.*) — *cf.* also Recording List
F niveau *m*
G Pegel *m*
I livello *m*

²**level** *n.* (of a student) —*cf.* also individual entries: *amature; beginner; intermediate; advanced; professional;* also Teaching List
F niveau *m*
G Niveau *n*
I livello *m*

li *n.* (a-sharp solfege syllable in the key of c-major in American, movable-do system) —*cf.* also Solfege List
F la *m*
G ais *n*
I la *m*
N.B. Cf. important note given under the entry "solfege" regarding differences between European and American solfege systems. *Cf.* also Solfege List.

librettist *n.* —*cf.* also Professions List
F librettiste *m / f*
G Librettist *m;* Librettistin *f*
I librettista *m / f*

libretto *n.* —*cf.* also Vocal List
F livret d'opéra *m*
G Operntextbuch *n*
I libretto *m*

lid *n.* (of a piano)
F couvercle *m*
G Deckel *m*
I coperchio *m*

lied *n.* —*cf.* also Musical Forms List
F lied *m*
G Lied *n*
I lied *m*

light *adj.* (gauge of a musical string) — *cf.* also Strings List
F faible; faible tirant
G leicht
I bassa; tensione bassa

lighting *n.* (stage lighting, *etc.*) —*cf.* also Stage List

F éclairages *m* / *pl*
G Beleuchtung *f*
I illuminazione *f*

limiter *n.* —*cf.* also Recording List
F limiteur *m*
G Begrenzer *m*
I limitatore *m*

line *n.* (on the staff) —*cf.* also Staff List
F ligne *f*
G Linie *f*
I linea *f*

linear *adv.* (movement of a melody, *etc.*)
F linéaire
G linear
I lineare

lip *n.* —*cf.* also Anatomy List
F lèvre *f*
G Lippe *f*
I labbro *m*

litany *n.* —*cf.* also Musical Forms List
F litanie *f*
G Litanei *f*
I litania *f*

little *n.* (finger) —*cf.* also Anatomy List (Fingers)
F petit doigt *m*; auriculaire *m*
G kleiner Finger *m*
I mignolo *m*

liturgical drama *n.* —*cf.* also Musical Forms List
F drame liturgique *m*
G liturgisches Drama *n*
I dramma liturgico *m*

live *adj.* (radio or television broadcast) —*cf.* also Recording List
F en direct; live
G live (Followed by name of source. *Ex.* Live-Sendung, *etc.*)
I dal vivo; live; in diretta

lobby *n.* (outside a concert hall) —*cf.* foyer; also Concert List

locrian *n.* (church mode) —*cf.* also

Modes List
F locrien *m*
G Lokrisch *n*
I locrio *m*

low *adj.* (general range of a pitch; instrument, *etc.*) —*cf.* also *high; medium*
F grave
G tief
I grave

¹lower *v.* (to alter a pitch)
F baisser
G erniedrigen
I abbassare

²lower bout *n.* (of a guitar; violin, *etc.*) —*cf. bout*

lullaby *n.* —*cf.* also Musical Forms List
F berecuse *f*
G Wiegenlied *n*
I ninna nanna *f*

lungs *n.* / *pl* —*cf.* also Anatomy List
F poumons *m* / *pl*
G Lungen *f* / *pl*
I polmoni *m* / *pl*

lute *n.* —*cf.* also Instruments List (Historic & Ethnic Instruments)
F luth *m*
G Laute *f*
I liuto *m*

lutenist *n.* —*cf.* also Professions List
F luthiste *m* / *f*
G Lautist *m*; Lautistin *f*
I liutista *m* / *f*

luthier *n.* —*cf.* also *builder;* Instrument Repair List (General Terms); Professions List
 (N.B. All three languages distinguish between a"luthier" [someone who makes smaller instruments; *i.e.* violin; guitar] and a "builder" [someone who makes larger instruments; *i.e.* piano; organ.])
F luthier *m*
G Baumeister *m;* Baumeisterin *f*
(usually preceded by the specific

instrument name. *Ex.*
"Geigerbaumeister," *etc.*)
I liutaio *m*

lydian *n.* (church mode) —*cf.* also
Modes List
F lydien *m*
G Lydisch *n*
I lidio *m*

lyre *n.* —*cf.* also Instruments List
(Historic & Ethnic Instruments)
F lyre *f*
G Leier *f*
I lira *f*

[1]**lyric soprano** *n.* (singer) —*cf.* also
Voice List (Specialty Types)
F soprano lyrique *f*
G Lyriksopran *m*
I soprano lirico *m*

[2]**lyric tenor** *n.* (singer) —*cf.* also
Voice List (Specialty Types)
F ténor lyrique *m*
G lyrischer Tenor *m*
I tenore lirico *m*

— M —

ma *n.* (e-sharp solfege syllable in the key of c-major in American, movable-do system) —*cf.* also Solfege List
F mi *m*
G eis *n*
I mi *m*
N.B. Cf. important note given under the entry "solfege" regarding differences between European and American solfege systems. *Cf.* also Solfege List.

madrigal *n.* —*cf.* also Musical Forms List
F madrigal *m*
G Madrigal *n*
I madrigale *m*

mahogany *n.* —*cf.* also Instrument Repair List (Various Woods)
F acajou *m*
G Mahagoni *n*; Mahagoniholz *n*
I mogano *m*

main theme *n.* —*cf.* also *sub theme*; Musical Forms List
F thème principal *m*
G Hauptthema *n*
I primo tema *m*; tema principale *m*

¹ major *adj.* (interval) —*cf.* also Intervals List; Keys List
F majeur
G groß (*N.B.* Difference between "major" used as an *adj.* for intervals as opposed to keys/chords in German. *Cf.* ² *major* below.)
I maggiore

² major *adj.* (keys; quality of a chord, etc.) —*cf.* also Intervals List; Keys List
F majeur
G dur (*N.B.* Difference between

"major" used as an *adj.* for intervals as opposed to keys/chords in German. *Cf.* ¹ *major* above.)
I maggiore

³ major scale *n.* —*cf.* also Keys List; Scales List
F gamme majeure *f*
G dur Tonleiter *f* (*N.B.* "Dur" by itself as a noun is neuter.)
I scala maggiore *f*

make-up lesson *n.* —*cf.* also Teaching List
F rattrapage *f* (In French, this word is usually used as a verb rather than as a noun. *Ex.* "Je vais rattraper le cours.")
G Nachholstunde *f*
I recupero *m*

mallet *n.* —*cf.* also Drum Sticks List
F mailloche *f*
G Schlegel *m*
I mazza *f*

manager *n.* (concert manager, *etc.*) — *cf.* also Concert List; Professions List
F agent *m*
G Manager *m*; Managerin *f*
I manager *m* (usually for general concert management); agente *m* (usually for theatre or opera)

mandolin *n.* —*cf.* also Instruments List (Plucked Instruments)
F mandoline *m*
G Mandoline *f*
I mandolino *m*

mandolinist *n.* —*cf.* also Professions List
F mandoliniste *m*/*f*

G Mandolinist *m*; Mandolinistin *f*
I mandolonista *m / f*; suonatore di mandolino *m*; suonatrice di mandolino *f*

manual *n.* (on organ; harpsichord, *etc.*)
F clavier *m*
G Manual *n*
I manuale *m*

manuscript *n.* —*cf.* also Research List
F manuscrit *m*
G Manuskript *n*
I manoscritto *m*

maple *n.* —*cf.* also Instrument Repair List (Various Woods)
F érable *m*
G Ahorn *n*; Ahornnholz *n*
I acero *m*

maracas *n. / pl* —*cf.* also Instruments List (Percussion Instruments)
F maracas *m / pl*
G Maracas *f / pl*
I maracas *f / pl*

march *n.* —*cf.* also Musical Forms List
F marche *f*
G Marsch *m*
I marcia *f*

¹marimba *n.* —*cf.* also Instruments List (Percussion Instruments)
F marimba *m*
G Marimba *n*
I marimba *f*

²marimba player *n.* —*cf.* also Professions List
F joueur de marimba *m*; joueuse de marimba *f*
G Marimba Spieler *m*; Marimba Spielerin *f*
I suonatore di marimba *m*; suonatrice di marimba *f*

masque *n.* —*cf.* also Musical Forms List
F mascarade *f*
G Maskenspiel *n*
I masque *f*

mass *n.* —*cf.* also Musical Forms List
F messe *m*
G Messe *f*
I messa *f*

master *n.* (tape) —*cf.* also Recording List
F bande mère *f*
G Originaltonband *n*
I master *m*

masterclass *n.* —*cf.* also Teaching List
F master-classe *f*
G Masterklasse *f*; Meisterklasse *f*
I master-class *f*

matrix *n.* (in 12-tone music) —*cf.* also 12-Tone Music List
F matrice *f*
G Matrix *f*
I matrice *f*

mazurka *n.* —*cf.* also Musical Forms List
F mazurka *f*
G Mazurka *f*
I mazurca *f*

me *n.* (e-flat solfege syllable in the key of c-major in American, movable-do system) —*cf.* also Solfege List
F mi *m*
G es *n*
I mi *m*
N.B. *Cf.* important note given under the entry "solfege" regarding differences between European and American solfege systems. *Cf.* also Solfege List.

¹measure *n.* (bar)
F mesure *f* (N.B. The same word is used in French for meter.)
G Takt *m*
I battuta *f*; misura *f* (N.B. In Italian, *misura* is used for both *measure* and *bar*.)

²measure line *n.* —*cf. bar line*

³measure number *n.* —*cf. bar number*

mediant *n.* (scale degree; chord) —*cf.*

also Chords List
F médiante *f*
G Mediante *f*
I mediante *f*; modale *m*; caratteristica *f*

Medieval *n.* (Period) —*cf.* also
Historical Periods & Styles List
F moyen-âge *m*
G Mittelalter *n*
I MedioEvo *m* (*N.B.* This is usually
spelled with the capital letters, but still
as one word.)

¹**medium** *adj.* (general range of a
pitch; instrument, *etc.*) —*cf.* also *high;
low*
F médium
G mittle
I medio

²**medium** *adj.* (gauge of a musical
string) —*cf.* also Strings List
F moyen; moyen tirant
G mittel; mittel hart; Medium hard
(borrowed from English)
I media ; tensione media

¹**melodic** *adj.*
F mélodique
G melodisch
I melodico

²**melodic minor scale** *n.* —*cf.* also
Keys List, Scales List
F gamme mélodique mineure *f*
G melodische moll Tonleiter *f*
I scala minore melodica *f*

melodrama *n.* —*cf.* also Musical
Forms List
F mélodrame *m*
G Melodrama *n*
I melodramma *m*

melody *n.*
F mélodie *f*
G Melodie *f*
I melodia *f*

men's choir *n.* —*cf.* also Voice List
(Choral Types)
F chœur d'hommes *m*
G Männerchor *m*

I coro maschile *m*

mensural notation *n.* —*cf.* also
Notation List
F notation mensurale *f*
G Mensuralnotation *f*
I notazione mensurale *f*

¹**metal** *n.* —*cf.* also Instrument Repair
List (Various Materials)
F métal *m*; métaux *m* / *pl*
G Metall *n*
I metallo *m*

²**metal mute** *n.* —*cf.* also Mutes List
F sourdine en métal *f*
G Metalldämpfer *m*
I sordina di metallo *f*

¹**meter** *n.* (binary; ternary, *etc.*) —*cf.*
also Time Signatures List
F mesure *f* (*N.B.* The same word is used
in French for measure and bar.)
G Mensur *f*
I ritmo *m* (ritmo binario; ritmo ternario,
etc.); tempo *m* (tempo binario; ritmo
ternario, *etc.*) *m*; misura *f* (misura
binario; misura ternario, *etc.*) (*N.B.* In
Italian, *misura* is used for both *measure*
and *bar.*)

²**meter change** *n.* —*cf. time change;*
also Time Signature List

method *n.* (instruction book) —*cf.* also
Teaching List
F méthode *f*
G Lehrwerk *n*; Lernmethode *f* (*N.B.*
"Lernmethode" tends to refer to a style
or method of teaching rather than a
specific book, *etc.*)
I metodo *m*

¹**metronome** *n.*
F métronome *m*
G Metronome *n*
I metronomo *m*

²**metronome marking** *n.*
("Mälzel's Metronome," *abv.* "M.M.")
F indication métronomique *f*
G Metronomangabe *f*
I indicazione metronomica *f*

mezzo soprano *n.* (singer) —*cf.* also
Voice List (Traditional Types)
F mezzo-soprano *m*
G Mezzosopran *m*
I mezzosoprano *m*

mi *n.* (e-natural solfege syllable in the
key of c-major in American, movable-do
system) —*cf.* also Solfege List
F mi *m*
G e *n*
I mi *m*
N.B. *Cf.* important note given under the
entry "solfege" regarding differences
between European and American
solfege systems. *Cf.* also Solfege List.

mic. *n.* (*abv.* for microphone) —*cf.*
microphone; also Recording List

micro-tone *n.* (in quarter tone music,
etc.) —*cf.* also *quarter tone*
F microton *m*
G Mikroton *m*
I microtono *m*

¹microphone *n.* —*cf.* also individual
entries: *condensor mic.; contact mic.;
electrodynamic mic;* also Recording List
F micro *m;* microphone *m*
G Mikrophon *n*
I microfono *m*

²microphone stand *n.* —*cf.* also
Recording List
F pied de micro *m*
G Mikrofonständer *n*
I asta de microfono *f*

¹middle *n.* (finger) —*cf.* also Anatomy
List (Fingers)
F majeur *m*
G Mittelfinger *m*
I medio *m*

²middle c *n.* (on the piano)
F do de la serrure *f*
G Schloß c *n;* eingestrichenes c *n*
I do centrale *m*

military music *n.* —*cf.* also
Historical Periods & Styles List
F musique militaire *f*

G Militärmusik *f*
I musica militare *f*

minimalism *n.* (compositional style)
—*cf.* also Historical Periods & Styles List
F minimalisme *m*
G Minimal Music *f* (*N.B.* This spelling is
borrowed from English); Minimalismus
m
I minimaliso *m;* musica minimalista *f*

¹minor *adj.* (interval) —*cf.* also
Intervals List
F mineur *m*
G klein (*N.B.* Difference between
"minor" used as an *adj.* for intervals as
opposed to keys/chords in German. *Cf.*
² *minor* below.)
I minore

²minor *adj.* (keys; quality of a chord;
etc.) —*cf.* also Intervals List; Keys List
F mineur
G moll (*N.B.* Difference between
"minor" used as an *adj.* for intervals as
opposed to keys/chords in German. *Cf.*
¹ *minor* below.)
I minore

minor scale *n.* —*cf.* also Keys List;
Scales List
F gamme mineur *f*
G moll Tonleiter *f* (*N.B.* "Moll" by itself
as a noun is neuter.)
I scala minore *f*

minuet *n.* —*cf.* also Musical Forms
List
F menuet *m*
G Menuett *n*
I minuetto *m*

minum *n.* (British name for half note)
—*cf. half note;* also Notes List

mix *n.* (recording post-production
ballancing of tracks, *etc.*) —*cf.* also
Recording List
F mixage *m*
G Abmischung *f*
I missaggio *m*

mixed choir *n.* —*cf.* also Voice List

(Choral Types)
F chœur mixte *m*
G gemischter Chor *m*
I coro misto *m*

mixer *n.* (mixing board in recording studio) —*cf.* also Recording List
F melangeur *m;* melangeur de son *m*
G Mischpult *n*
I mixer *m*

mixolydian *n.* (church mode) —*cf.* also Modes List
F mixolydien *m*
G Mixolydisch *n*
I misolidio *m*

mode *n.* (Medieval church mode) —*cf.* individal entries; also Modes List
F mode *m;* mode ancien *m;* mode grégorien *m*
G Kirchentonart *f*
I modo; *m;* modo gregoriano *m*

modern notation *n.* —*cf.* also Notation List
F notation moderne *f*
G moderne Notenschrift *f*
I notazione moderna *f*

modulate *v.* (to change key centers) —*cf.* also *modulation*
F moduler
G modulieren
I modulare

modulation *n.* (change of tonal center in a piece) —*cf.* also *key change; transitory modulation*
F modulation *f*
G Modulation *f*
I modulazione *f*

monophonic *adj.* —*cf.* also Historical Periods & Styles List
F monophonique
G onodie
I monodico

morris dance *n.* —*cf.* also Musical Forms List
F mauresque *f*
G Moreske *f*

I moresca *f*

motet *n.* —*cf.* also Musical Forms List
F motet *m*
G Motette *f*
I mottetto *m*

mother of pearl *n.* —*cf.* also Instrument Repair List (Various Materials)
F nacre *f*
G Perlmutt *n*
I madre perla *f*

motion *n.* (harmonic; melodic, *etc.*) —*cf.* also *contrary; oblique; parallel*
F mouvement *m*
G Bewegung *f*
I moto *m*

motive *n.*
F motif *m*
G Motiv *n*
I motivo *m*

mouthpiece *n.* (of clarinette; trumpet, *etc.*)
F bec *m* (for woodwinds); bocal *m* (for brass)
G Schnabel *m* (for woodwinds); Mundstück *n* (for brass)
I becco *m* (for woodwinds); bocchino *m* (for brass)

[1] **movement** *n.* (harmonic; melodic, *etc.*) —*cf. motion*

[2] **movement** *n.* (section of a large composition, *i.e.* "first movement;" "second movement," *etc.*)
F mouvement *m*
G Satz *m*
I movimento *m*

multi-media *n.* (compositional style)
F multimédia *m*
G Multimedia *f*
I multimediale *f*

muscle *n.* —*cf.* also Anatomy List
F muscle *m*
G Muskel *m*
I muscolo *m*

¹music *n.*
F musique *f*
G Musik *f*
I musica *f*

²music dictation *n.*
F dictée musicale *f*
G Musikdiktat *n*
I dettato musicale *m*

³music paper *n.* —*cf.* staff paper

⁴music publisher *n.* —*cf.* also
publishing company
F maison d'édition musicale *f*
G Musikverlag *m*
I casa editrice di musica *f*

⁵music stand *n.*
F pupitre *m*
G Notenständer *m*
I leggio *m*

⁶music theory *n.*
F théorie musicale *f*
G Musiktheorie *f*
I teoria musicale *f*

⁷music therapist *n.* — *cf.* also
Professions List
F musicothérapeute *m /f*
G Musiktherapeut *m*;
Musiktherapeutin *f*
I musicoterapeuta *m /f*

⁸music therapy *n.*
F musicothérapie *f*
G Musiktherapie *f*
I musicoterapia *f*

¹musical comedy *n.* —*cf.* also
Musical Forms List
F comédie musicale *f*
G Musical *n*
I commedia musicale *f*

²musical saw *n.* —*cf.* also Instruments List (Percussion Instruments)
F scie musicale *f*
G singende Säge *f*
I sega *f*

musicality *n.*

F musicalité *f*
G Musikalität *f*
I musicalità *f*

musician *n.* —*cf.* also Professions List
F musicien *m*; musicienne *f*
G Musiker *m*; Musikerin *f*
I musicista *m/f*

musicologist *n.* —*cf.* also Professions List; Research List
F musicologue *m/f*
G Musikwissenschaftler *m*;
Musikwissenschaftlerin *f*
I musicologo *m*; musicologa *f*

musicology *n.* —*cf.* also Research List
F musicologie *f*
G Musikwissenschaft *f*
I musicologia *f*

mute *n.* (for winds; strings, *etc.*)
F sourdine *f*
G Dämpfer *m*
I sordina *f*

muted *adv.* —*cf.* also Orchestral Terms List
F sourdine; sourdines *pl*; avec sourdine; avec sourdines *pl*
G mit Dämpfer; gedämpft
I con sordina; con sordini *pl*

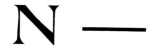

— N —

narrator *n.* —*cf.* also Professions List
F narateur *m;* naratrice *f;* récitant *m;* récitante *f*
G Sprecher *m;* Sprecherin *f;* Erzähler *m;* Erzählerin *f*
I voce recitante *f* (in music *Ex.* in *Peter and the Wolf*); narratore *m* (in film, theater, *etc.*)

nasal *adj.* —*cf.* also Voice List
F nasal
G nasal
I nasale

national anthem *n.* —*cf.* also Musical Forms List
F hymne national *m*
G Nationalhymne *f*
I inno nazionale *m*

nationalistic *adj.* (style) —*cf.* also Historical Periods & Styles
F nationaliste
G national
I nazionalistico (*N.B.* in music, you usually say "scuole nazionali.")

¹natural *n.* (chromatic alteration of a note)
F bécarre *m*
G Auflösungszeichen *n*
I bequadro *m*

²natural harmonic *n.* (*i.e.* a harmonic played on an open string, *etc.*)
—*cf.* also *artifical harmonic; harmonic*
F harmonique naturel *m*
G Flageolett *f*
I armonico *m*

³natural horn *n.* —*cf.* also Instruments List (Historic & Ethnic Instru-

ments)
F cor de chasse *m*
G Jagdhorn *n*
I corno di caccia *m*

¹neck *n.* (of the human body) —*cf.* also Anatomy List
F cou *m*
G Hals *m*
I collo *m*

²neck *n.* (of an instrument)
F manche *m*
G Hals *m*
I manico *m*

neighbor tone *n.*
F ton concomittant *m*
G Nebenton *m*
I tono secondario *m*

Neopolitan-sixth (chord) *n.*
F sixte Napolitaine *f*
G Neapolitanischer Sextakkord *m*
I sesta napoletana *f*

nerve *n.* —*cf.* also Anatomy List
F nerf *m*
G Nerv *m*
I nervo *m*

neume *n.* —*cf. nume*

nine-twelve (9/12) *n.* (time signature in words as it is spoken in conversation) —*cf.* also Time Signature List
F mesure à neuf-douze *f*
G neunzwölftel Takt *m*
I nove dodicesimi *m* / *pl*

ninth *n.* —*cf.* also Intervals List

F neuvième *f*
G None *f*
I nona *f*

nocturne *n.* —*cf.* also Musical Forms
List
F nocturne *f*
G Notturno *n*
I notturno *m*

node *n.* (on a singer's vocal chords; on
a tendon, *etc.*) —*cf.* also Anatomy List;
Vocal List
F nœd *m*
G Knoten *n*
I nodulo *m*

noise reduction *n.* —*cf.* also
Recording List
F suppression du bruit *f*
G Rauschunterdrückung *f*
I riduttore di rumore *m*

non-chord tone (passing tone;
neighbor tone, *etc.*)
F note de passage *f*; note étrangée *f*
G harmoniefremder Ton *m*
I nota accidentale *f*

normally *adv.* (after *ponticello, etc.*) —
cf. also Orchestral Terms List
F mode ordinaire
G gewöhnlich
I modo ordinario

nose *n.* —*cf.* also Anatomy List
F nez *m*
G Nase *f*
I naso *m*

notation *n.* —*cf.* also Notation List
F notation *f*
G Notenschrift *f*; Notation *f*
I notazione *f*

¹ note *n.* (c; d; e, *etc.*) —*cf.* also Notes
List
F note *f*
G Note *f*
I nota *f*

² note head *n.* —*cf.* also Notes List
(Parts of a Written Note)

F tête *f*
G Notenkopf *m*
I testa *f* (testa della nota *f*)

³ note value *n.* (sustained duration of
a note) —*cf.* also *rest value* (N.B. In
English we rarely use this term, but is
common in all three other languages.)
F valeur de la note *f*
G Notenwert *m*
I valore della nota *m*

nume (neume) *n.* (early Medieval
notation) —*cf.* also Notation List
F neume *m*
G Neume *f*
I neuma *m*

nut *n.* (of an instrument, *etc.*)
F sillet *m*
G Obersattel *m*
I capotastro *m*

nylon (string) *n.* —*cf.* also Strings
List
F corde en nylon *f*
G Nylonsaite *n*
I corda di nylon *f*

oak *n. —cf.* also Instrument Repair List
(Various Woods)
F chêne *m*
G Eiche *n;* Eichenholz *n*
I zuercia *f*

obligato *adj.*
F obligé
G obligat
I obbligato

oblique motion *n.*
F mouvement oblique *m*
G Seitenbewegung *f*
I moto obliquo *m*

¹oboe *n. —cf.* also Instruments List
(Woodwinds)
F hautbois *m*
G Oboe *f*
I oboe *m*

²oboe d'amore *n. —cf.* also
Instruments List (Woodwinds)
F hautbois d'amour *m*
G Oboe d'amoure *f*
I oboe d'amore *m*

oboist *n. —cf.* also Professions List
F hautboiste *m/f*
G Oboist *m;* Oboistin *f*
I oboista *m/f;* suonatore di oboe *m;*
suonatrice di oboe *f*

ocarina *n. —cf.* also Instruments List
(Historic & Ethnic Instruments)
F ocarina *m*
G Okarina *f*
I ocarina *f*

octave *n. —cf.* also Intervals List
F octave *f*

G Oktave *f*
I ottave *f*

ode *n. —cf.* also Musical Forms List
F ode *f*
G Ode *f*
I ode *f*

off-beat *n.* (a beat which falls between
the normal metric pulse—intrinsic in
jazz; ragtime, *etc.*)
F off-beat *f*
G Off-Beat *m*
I levare *f*

oil *n. —cf.* also Instrument Repair List
(Various Materials)
F huile *f*
G Öl *n*
I olio *m*

on stage *adj. —cf.* also Concert List;
Stage List
F en scène
G zur Bühne
I sul palco (general); in scena (more for
theater)

one-four (1/4) *n.* (time signature in
words as it is spoken in conversation) —
cf. also Time Signature List
F mesure à un-quatre *f*
G ein-viertel Takt *m*
I un quarto *m*

one-two (1/2) *n.* (time signature in
words as it is spoken in conversation) —
cf. also Time Signature List
F mesure à un-deux *f*
G ein-halb Takt *m*
I un mezzo *m*

¹**open** *adj.* —*cf.* also Orchestral Terms
List
F ouvert; ouverts *(pl.)*
G offen
I aperto

²**open position** *n.* (voicing of a
chord) —*cf.* also *closed position;* Chords
List
F position large *f*
G weite Lage *f*
I posizione lata *f*

³**open-stacks** *n.* (in a library) —*cf.*
also *closed-stacks;* Research List
F bibliothèque *f (N.B.* In French this is
simply refered to as a "library.")
G Bibliothek *f (N.B.* In German this is
simply refered to as a "library.")
I biblioteca *f (N.B.* In Italian this is
simply refered to as a "library.")

¹**opera** *n.* —*cf.* also Musical Forms List
F opéra *m*
G Oper *f*
I opera *f*

²**opera buffa** *n.* —*cf.* comic opera

³**opera chorus** *n.* —*cf.* also Voice List
(Choral Types)
F chœur d'opéra *m*
G Opernchor *m*
I coro d'opera *m*

operetta *n.* —*cf.* also Musical Forms
List
F opérette *f*
G Operette *f*
I operetta *f*

oratorio *n.* —*cf.* also Musical Forms
List
F oratorio *m*
G Oratorium *n*
I oratorio *m*

¹**orchestra** *n.*
F orchestre *m*
G Orchester *n*
I orchestra *f*

²**orchestra pit** *n.* —*cf. pit;* also Stage List

orchestral player *n.* —*cf.* also
Professions List
F musicien d'orchestre *m;* musicienne
d'orchestre *f*
G Orchestermusiker *m;*
Orchestermusikerin *f*
I orchestrale *m/f*

organ *n.* —*cf.* also Instruments List
(Keyboards)
F orge *m*
G Orgel *f*
I organo *m*

organist *n.* —*cf.* also Professions List
F organiste *m/f*
G Organist *m;* Organistin *f*
I organista *m/f*

¹**original** *n.* (in 12-tone music) —*cf.*
also Twelve-tone Music (Matrix
Divisions List)
F originale *m;* série originale *m*
G Grundgestalt *f*
I serie *f*

²**original manuscript** *n.* —*cf.* also
Research List
F manuscrit original *m*
G original Manuskript *n*
I manoscritto originale *m*

ornament *n.* (general term for all
ornaments) —*cf.* also *embellishment*
F ornement *m*
G Verzierung *f*
I ornamento *m*

ornamentation *n.* (general term for
all ornamentation)
F ornementation *f;* embellissement *m*
G Verzierung *f*
I ornamentazzione *m*

ornamented *adj.*
F ornementé
G verziert
I ornato; fiorito

oscillation *n.* (in phase of tone, *etc.*)
F oscillation *f*
G Schwingung *f*
I oscillazione *f*

ostinato *n.*
F basse obstinée *f*
G Ostinato *n*
I ostinato *m;* basso ostinato *m*

output *n.* —*cf.* also Recording List
F sortie *f*
G Ausgang *m*
I uscita *f*

out of tune (sing / play with inexact pitch) —*cf.* also *in tune*
F chanter faux / jouer faux
G falsch singen / falsch spielen
I stonare (for singing and playing)

ovation *n.* —*cf.* also Concert List
F ovation *f*
G Ovation *f*
I ovazione *f*

overdraw *v.* (a bank account) —*cf.* also Finances List
F mettre à découvert
G überziehen
I trarre allo scoperto

[1]**overtone** *n.*
F son harmonique *m;* son concomitant *m*
G Oberton *m*
I armonica *f*

[2]**overtone series** *n.*
F échelle harmonique *f*
G Obertonreihe *f*
I serie armonica *f*

overture *n.* —*cf.* also Musical Forms List
F ouverture *f*
G Ouvertüre *f*
I overture *f*

— P —

pad *n.* (of a clarinet, *etc.*)
F tampon *m*
G Filz *m*
I tampone *m*

padded stick *n.* —*cf.* also Drum
Sticks List
F baguette rembourrée *f*
G wattierter Schlegel *m*
I bacchetta imbottita *f*

palate *n.* (of the mouth) —*cf.* also
Anatomy List
F palais *m*
G Gaumen *m*
I palato *m*

palm *n.* (of the hand) —*cf.* also
Anatomy List
F paume *f*; paume de la main *f*
G Handfläche *f*
I palmo *m*; palmo della mano *m*

panpipes *n.* —*cf.* also Instruments
List (Historic & Ethnic Instruments)
F flûte de Pan *f*
G Panflöte *f*
I flauto di pan *m*

pantomime *n.*
F pantomime *f*
G Pantomime *f*
I pantomima *f*

[1]**parallel** *adj.* (octaves; parts, *etc.*) —*cf.*
also *motion*
F parallèle
G parallel
I parallelo

[2]**parallel (major)** *adj.* / *n.* (key
centers, *etc.*) —*cf.* also Keys List

F parallèle (majeur parallèle *f*)
G parallel (Paralleldurtonart *f*)
I parallela (parallela maggiore *f*)

[3]**parallel (minor)** *adj.* / *n.* (key
centers, *etc.*) —*cf.* also Keys List
F parallèle (mineur parallèle *f*)
G parallel (Parallelmolltonart *f*)
I parallela (parallela minore *f*)

parameter *n.* —*cf.* also Recording List
F paramètre *m*
G Parameter *m*
I parametro *m*

parody *n.* —*cf.* also Musical Forms List
F parodie *f*
G Parodie *f*
I parodia *f*

part *n.* (of a score) —*cf.* also Score List
F partie *f*
G Stimme *f*
I parte *f*

partita *n.* —*cf.* also Musical Forms List
F partita *f*
G Partita *f*
I partita *f*

passacaglia *n.* —*cf.* also Musical
Forms List
F passacaille *f*
G Passacaglia *f*
I passacaglia *f*

passage *n.* (a phrase or section of a
composition)
F passage *m*
G Passage *f*
I passaggio *m*

passepied *n.* —*cf.* also Musical Forms List
F passepied *m*
G Passepied *m*
I passepied *m*

¹passing chord *n.*
F accord de passage *m*
G Durchgangsakkord *m*
I accordo di passaggio *m*

²passing tone *n.*
F note de passage *f*
G Durchgangston *m*
I nota di passaggio *f*

passion *n.* —*cf.* also Musical Forms List
F passion *f*
G Passion *f*
I passione *f*

passport *n.* —*cf.* also Legal Subjects List
F passeport *m*
G Reisepaß *m*
I passaporto *m*

pastorale *n.* —*cf.* also Musical Forms List
F pastorale *f*
G Pastorale *f*
I pastorale *f*

pavan *n.* —*cf.* also Musical Forms List
F pavane *f*
G Pavane *f*
I pavana *f*

pedagogy *n.* —*cf.* also Teaching List
F pédagogie *f*
G Pedagogik *f*
I pedagogia *f*

¹pedal *n.* (of a piano) —*cf.* also *sustaining pedal; damping pedal*
F pédale *f*
G Pedal *n*
I pedale *m*

²pedal *v.* (pedaling on a piano; harp, *etc.*)
F pédaler

G treten (Pedal treten)
I pedale

³pedal tone *n.* (in composition)
F pédale *f*
G Pedalton *n*; Orgelpunkt *m*
I pedale (d'armonia) *m*

¹peg *n.* (at the end of a 'cello)
F pique *f*
G Stachel *m*
I puntale *m*

²peg *n.* (tuning peg of a violin; harp, *etc.*) —*cf.* also *key*
F cheville *f* (of wood, *i.e.* violin, *etc.*); bouton *m* (of metal, *i.e.* harp; piano, *etc.*)
G Wirbel *m* (of wood and metal, *i.e.* violin; harp, *etc.*)
I pirolo *m*; bischero *m* (of wood, *i.e.* violin, *etc.*); pirone *m* (of metal, *i.e.* harp; piano, *etc.*)

³peg box *n.* (of a violin; viola *etc.*)
F chevillier *m*
G Wirbelkasten *m*
I cavigliere *m*

pentachord *n.*
F pentacorde *m*
G Fünfklang *m*
I pentacordo *m*

pentatonic scale *n.* —*cf.* also Scales List
F gamme pentatonique *f*
G Pentatonik Tonleiter *f*
I scala pentatonica *f*

percussion (section) *n.* / *pl* —*cf.* also Instruments List (Percussion Instruments)
F batterie *f* / *pl*
G Schlagzug *n* / *pl*
I percussione *f* / *pl*

percussionist *n.* —*cf.* also *drummer*; Professions List
F percussionniste *m* / *f*
G Schlagzeuger *m*; Schlagzeugerin *f*
I percussionista *m* / *f*

¹perfect *adj.* (interval) —*cf.* also
Intervals List
F juste
G rein
I giusto

²perfect cadence *n.* (authentic
cadence) —*cf.* also Cadence List
F cadence paraite *f*
G authentischer ganz Schluß *f*
I cadenza perfetta f; cadenza autentica *f*

³perfect pitch *n.* —*cf.* also *relative
pitch*
F oreille absolue *f*
G absolutes Gehör *n*
I orecchio assoluto *m*

¹performance *n.*
F représentation *f*; performance *f*;
exécution *f*
G Aufführung *f*
I esecuzione *f*

²performance practice *n.*
(historical, *etc.*)
F pratique de l'exécution *f*
G Aufführungspraxis *f*
I prassi d'esecuzione *f*; pratica
d'esecuzione *f*

³performance rights *n.* / *pl*
(permission to perform a work) —*cf.*
also *copyright; royalties*
F droits d'execution *m* / *pl*
G Aufführungsrechte *n* / *pl*
I royalties *f*/ *pl*; diritti d'esecuzione *m*/
pl

performer *n.* —*cf.* also Concert List;
Professions List
F exécutant *m*; exécutante *f*; interprète
m/*f*
G Interpret *m*; Ausführender *m*;
Musiker *m*; Musikerin *f*; Künstler *m*;
Künstlerin *f* (*N.B.* "Musiker" and
"Künstler" are less literal, but more
commonly used in music.)
I interprete *m*/*f*

perigourdine *n.* —*cf.* also Musical
Forms List
F périgourdine *f*

G Perigourdine *f*
I perigordino *m*

period *n.* (a section in musical form)
—*cf.* also Musical Forms List
F période *f*
G Periode *f*
I periodo *m*

phlange *n.* —*cf.* also Anatomy List
F phalange *f*
G Fingerknochen *m*
I falange *f*

phrase *n.* (musical form) —*cf.* also
Musical Forms List
F phrase *f*
G Phrase *f*
I frase *f*

phrasing *n.* (execution of a phrase,
etc.)
F phrasé *m*
G Phrasierung *f*
I fraseggio *m*

phrygian *n.* (church mode) —*cf.* also
Modes List
F phrygien *m*
G Phrygisch *n*
I frigio *m*

pianist *n.* —*cf.* also Professions List
F pianiste *m*/*f*
G Pianist *m*; Pianistin *f*
I pianista *m*/*f*

¹piano *n.* —*cf.* also Instruments List
(Keyboards)
F piano *m*
G Klavier *n*
I pianoforte *m*

²piano reduction *n.* —*cf.* also Score
List
F réduction pour piano *f*; adaptation
pour piano *f*
G Klavierauszug *m*
I riduzione per pianoforte *f*;
adattamento per pianoforte *m*

³piano tuner *n.* —*cf. tuner;* also
Professions List

Picardy third cadence *n.* —*cf.* also
Cadence List
F cadence Picarde *f;* tierce picarde *f*
G Pikardische Terz Kadenz *f*
I cadenza frigia *f*

¹piccolo *n.* —*cf.* also Instruments List
(Woodwinds)
F piccolo *m;* petite flûte *f*
G pikkolo *f;* pikkolo flöte *f*
I flauto piccolo *m;* ottavino *m*

²piccolo trumpet *n.* —*cf.* also
Instruments List (Brass Instruments)
F clarino *m*
G Bach-Trompette *f*
I clarino *m*

¹pick *n.* (for a guitar, *etc.*)
F médiateur *m*
G Plättchen *n*
I plettro *m*

²pick-up *n.* —*cf. anacrusis*

³pick-up *n.* (for amplified instrument,
etc.)
F micro *m;* pick-up *m*
G Pickup *n;* Tonabnehmer *m*
I pick-up *m*

piece *n.* (of music, *etc.*)
F morceau *m;* pièce *f*
G Stück *n*
I pezzo *m*

pin *n.* (tuning peg of a harp; harpsichord, *etc.*) —*cf. peg; key*

pine *n.* —*cf.* also Instrument Repair
List (Various Woods)
F pin *m*
G Kiefer *n;* Kiefernholz *n*
I pino *m*

pipe *n.* (of an organ, *etc.*)
F tuyau *m*
G Pfeife *f*
I canna *f*

piston *n.* (of a trumpet, *etc.*)
F piston *m*
G Ventil *n*

I pistone *m*

pit *n.* (for an orchestra in a ballet, *etc.*)
—*cf.* also Stage List
F fosse d'orchestre *f;* parterre *m* (for
threater)
G Parterre *n*
I buca *f;* buca d'orchestra *f*

¹pitch *n.* (of a note)
F hauteur *f;* hauteur du son *f*
G Tonhöhe *f*
I altezza *f;* altezza del suono *f*

²pitch pipe *n.*
F diapason à bouche *m*
G Stimmpfeife *f*
I diapason *m;* corista *m*

placement (of the voice) *n.* —*cf.*
also Voice List
F pose de la voix *f*
G Führung der Stimme *f*
I messa di voce *f*

placing the voice *adv.* —*cf.* also
Voice List
F pose de la voix
G Ansatz der Stimme
I messa di voce

plagal cadence *n.* —*cf.* also Cadence
List
F cadence plagale *f*
G Plagelschluß Kadenz *f*
I cadenza plagale *f*

plagiarize *v.* —*cf.* also Research List
F plagier
G plagieren
I plagiare

plain chant *n.* (Gregorian Chant) —
cf. also *Gregorian Chant;* Musical Forms
List
F plain-chant *m*
G Choral *m*
I canto *m*

plastic *n.* —*cf.* also Instrument Repair
List (Various Materials)
F plastique *m*
G Plastik *m;* Kunststoff *m*

plated

I plastica *f*

plated *adj.* —*cf. gold plated; silver plated;* also Instrument Repair List (Various Materials)

¹play *v.* (instrument, *etc.*)
F jouer
G spielen
I suonare

²play-back *n.* —*cf.* also Recording List
F playback *m*; réécoute *f*
G Playback *n*; Rückspielen *n*
I playback *m*

³play from memory *v.* —*cf.* also Teaching List
F jouer par cœur
G auswendig spielen
I suonare a memoria

player piano *n.* —*cf.* also Instruments List (Keyboards)
F piano mécanique *m*
G Pianola *n*
I pianola *f*

plectrum *n.* (in harpsichord) —*cf. quill*; (for guitar; lute, *etc.*) —*cf. pick*

pluck *v.* (guitar, *etc.*) (*N.B.* The term "pluck," when used in all four languages in classical music, can have a negative connotation.)
F pincer
G zupfen
I pizzicare

pocket score *n.* (small study score; miniture score) —*cf.* also Score List
F partition de poche *f*
G Taschenpartitur *f*
I partitura tascabile *f*

point *n.* (tip of a bow, *etc.*)
F point *m*
G Spitze *f*
I punta *f*

pointer finger *n.* —*cf. index finger;* also Teaching List

pointillism *n.* (compositional style)
F pointillisme *m*
G Pointillismus *m*
I puntillismo *m*

¹polish *n.*
F crème à polir *f*; pâte à polir *f*
G Poliermittel *n*
I cera *f*

²polish *v.* —*cf.* also Instrument Repair List (Common Verbs)
F polir
G polieren
I lucidare

polka *n.* —*cf.* also Musical Forms List
F polka *f*
G Polka *f*
I polka *f*

polonaise *n.* —*cf.* also Musical Forms List
F polonaise *f*
G Polonaise *f*
I polacca *f*; polonaise *f*

poly-tonality *n.* —*cf.* also Historical Periods & Styles List
F polytonalité *f*
G Polytonalität *f*
I politonalità *f*

polyphonic *adj.* —*cf.* also Historical Periods & Styles List
F polyphonique
G polyphon
I polifonico

polyphony *n.* —*cf.* also Historical Periods & Styles List
F polyphonie *f*
G Polyphonie *f*
I polifonia *f*

polyrhythm *n.*
F polyrythmie *f*
G Polyrhythmus *m*
I poliritmia *f*

polyrhythmic *adj.*
F polyrythmique
G polyrhythmik

I poliritmico

popular music *n.* —*cf.* also
Historical Periods & Styles List
F pop musique *f*; musique pop *f*
G Popmusik *f*
I musica pop *f*; musica popolare *f*

portative organ *n.* —*cf.* also
Instruments List (Historic & Ethnic
Instruments)
F orgue portatif *m*
G Portativ *n*
I organo portativo *m*

position *n.* (sitting position; hand
position, *etc.*)
F position *f*
G Lage *f* (Sitzlage; Handlage, *etc.*)
I posizione *f*

poster *n.* (concert poster, *etc.*) —*cf.* also
Concert List
F affiche *f*
G Plakat *n*
I cartellone *m*

postlude *n.* —*cf.* also Musical Forms
List
F postlude *m*
G Nachspiel *n*
I postludio *m*

pot-pourri *n.* —*cf.* also Musical Forms
List
F pot-pourri *m*
G Potpourri *n*
I pot-pourri *m*

practice *v.* (N.B. The implication is to
practice alone, since if it is with 2 or
more people, the term is "to rehearse."
This is consistent in all 3 languages.) —
cf. also *rehearse*; Concert List; Teaching
List
F travailler (In French one "works at"
an instrument. *Ex.* "...au piano" "...à la
guitare," *etc.*)
G üben
I esercitarsi; studiare

pre-recorded *adj.* (radio or
television broadcast) —*cf.* also Recording List
F préenregistré
G Aufzeichnung *f* (N.B. This is used
only as a noun in German.)
I pre-registato

prelude *n.* —*cf.* also Musical Forms
List
F prélude *m*
G Präludium *n*
I preludio *m*

premier *n.* (première; first perfor-
mance of a piece) —*cf.* also *debut*;
Concerts List
F première *f*
G Erstaufführung *f*
I prima *f*

prepared *adv.* (prepared piano; guitar,
etc.)
F préparé
G präpariert
I preparato

¹press *n.* (newspaper; the "press" used
as a general term, *etc.*) —*cf.* also Concert
List
F presse *f*
G Presse *f*
I stampa *f*

²press agent *n.* —*cf.* also *publicist*;
Concert List; Professions List
F agent de presse *m* / *f*
G Werbeagent *m*; Werbeagentin *f*
I agente pubblicitario *m*

³press material *n.* —*cf.* also Concert
List
F dossier de presse *m*
G Reklame *f*
I materiale stampa *m*

⁴press release *n.* —*cf.* also Concert
List
F communiqué de presse *f*
G Pressemitteilung *f*; Verlautbarung *f*;
Presse-verlautbarung *f*
I comunicato stampa *m*

⁵press release photo *n.* —*cf.* also
Concert List

— 149 —

prima balerina

F photo de presse *f*
G Pressephoto *n*
I fotografia pubblcitaria *f*

prima balerina *n. / f* —*cf.* also
principle dancer (m); Professions List
F danseuse étoile *f*
G Primaballerina *f*
I prima ballerina *f*

prime *n.* (interval) —*cf. unison;* also
Intervals List

[1] **principal** *n.* (first violin; flute, *etc.* in
an orchestra or ensemble) —*cf.* also
concert master
F premier soliste *m / f* (winds); chef
d'attaque *m / f* (strings)
G erste Pult *m / f*; Stimmführer *m*;
Stimmführerin *f*
I primo *m* (primo violino *m*; primo
flauto *m, etc.*)

[2] **principal balerina** *n. / f* —*cf.*
prima balerina also Professions List

[3] **principal dancer** *n. / m* —*cf.* also
prima balerina (f); Professions List
F danseur étoile *m*
G Primoballerino *m*
I primo ballerino *m*

private lesson *n.* —*cf.* also Teaching
List
F cours particulier *m*
G Einzelunterricht *m*; Privatstunde *f*
(*N.B.* In German "Einzelunterricht" is a
private lesson given in a school [*i.e.* not
a group lesson], while "Privatstunde" is
also a one-on-one lesson [not a group
lesson] but it is *not* through a school
program.)
I lezione privata *f*

prize *n.* (award) —*cf.* also Competition
List
F prix *m*
G Preis *m*
I premio *m*

procenium *n.* (of a stage) —*cf. thrust;*
also Stage List

producer *n.* —*cf.* also Professions List;
Recording List
F réalisateur *m*; réalisatrice *f*
G Produzent *m*
I produttore *m*

professional *n. / adj.* (level of a
student) —*cf.* also Teaching List
F professionnel *m*; professionnelle *f*
(*N.B.* In French, "professional" doesn't
exist in this sense. The word
"professionnel" simply implies that you
are professionally working. It does not
refer to a "level.")
G Berufsmusiker *m*; Berufsmusikerin *f*;
Profi *sl. m / f*
I musicista di professione *m / f*

professor *n.* —*cf.* also *teacher;*
Professions List; Teaching List
F professeur *m / f*
G Professor *m*; Professorin *f*
I professore *m*, professoressa *f*; maestro
m; maestra *f* (*N.B.* The term maestro; —a
is used for a children's school teacher
but also for anyone having to do with
music or the arts.)

[1] **program** *n.* (radio; television, *etc.*) —
cf. also *station*
F émission *f*; programme *m*
G Sendung *f*
I programma *f*; trasmissione *f*

[2] **program** *n.* (printed for a concert) —
cf. also Concerts List
F programme *m*
G Program *f*
I programma *f*

[3] **program music** *n.* (≠ absolute
music) —*cf.* also *absolute music;*
Historical Periods & Styles List
F musique à programme *f*
G Programmusik *f*
I musica a programa *f*

[4] **program notes** *n.* —*cf.* also Concert
List
F commentaire *m*
G Programbeschreibung *f*
I note di sala *f / pl*

progression *n.* (chordal; harmonic, *etc.*) —*cf.* also *chord progression*
F progression *f*; marche *f* (marche des accords; marche d'harmonie, *etc.*)
G Folge *f* (Akkordfolge; Harmoniefolge, *etc.*)
I progressione *f*

prompter *n.* —*cf.* also Professions List; Voice List
F souffleur *m*/*f*
G Souffleur *m*; Souffleuse *f*
I suggeritore *m*; suggeritrice *f*

pronounce *v.* —*cf.* also Voice List
F prononcer
G aussprechen
I pronunciare

psalm *n.* —*cf.* also Musical Forms List
F psaume *m*
G Psalm *m*
I salmo *m*

publicist *n.* —*cf.* also *press agent;* Concert List; Professions List
F publicitaire *m* /*f*
G Publicist *m*; Publicistin *f*
I pubblicista *m* /*f*; agente pubblicitario *m* /*f*

publishing company *n.* —*cf.* also *music publisher*
F maison d'édition *f*
G Verleger *m*
I casa editrice *f*

pulse *n.* —*cf.* also Anatomy List
F pouls *m*
G Puls *m*
I polso *m*

pure tuning *n.*
F tempérament pur *m*
G reine Stimmung *f*
I temperamento naturale *m*

purfling *n.* (inlay around the edge of an instrument) —*cf.* also Instrument Repair List (General Terms)
F filet *m*
G Flödel *m*; Randeinlage *f*
I filetto *m*

¹ **Pythagorian comma** *n.*
F comma pythagorien *m*
G pythagoreische Komma *n*
I comma Pitagorico *m*

² **Pythagorian tuning** *n.*
F accord Pythagorien *m*
G Pythagoreische Stimmung *f*
I scala pitagorica *m* (*N.B.* In Italian you "tune with the Pythagorian Scale;" "accordato secondo la scala pitagorica" To say "accordatura pythagorica" sounds æsthetically ugly.)

— Q —

quadrille *n.* —*cf.* also Musical Forms List
F quadrille *f*
G Quadrille *f*
I quadriglia *f*

[1] **quadruple concerto** *n.* —*cf.* also Musical Forms List
F quadruple concerto *m*
G Quadrupelkonzert *n*
I concerto con quattro strumenti solisti *m*

[2] **quadruple stop** *n.* (violin, *etc.*) —*cf.* double stop

[1] **quarter note** *n.* —*cf.* also Notes List (Rhythmic Values)
F noire *f*
D Viertelnote *f*
I quarto *m* (note name)
(*N.B.* In Italian, they often distinguish between the *note* itself, and the *duration* of that note. The name of the *duration* of this note is: semiminima *f*.) *Cf.* quarter rest.
• *N.B.* The British name of this note is: *crochet.*

[2] **quarter rest** *n.* —*cf.* also Rest List
F soupir *m* (*N.B.* In French, the names of the *rests* are not the same as the corresponding *notes*. *Cf.* Notes [individual entries and Notes List] for comparison.)
G Viertel-Pause *f*
I pausa di semiminima *f* (*N.B.* In Italian the rest is followed by the name of the note. *Ex.* "pausa di ..." [followed by value.])
• *N.B.* The British name of this rest is: *crochet.*

[3] **quarter tone** *n.* —*cf.* also *micro-tone*
F quart de ton *m*
G Viertelton *f*
I quarto di tono *m*

quaver *n.* (British name for eighth note) —*cf.* *eighth note*; Notes List

quill *n.* (jack or plectrum in a harpsichord, *etc.*)
F tuyau *m*; tuyau de plume *m*; plectre *m*
G Federkiel *m*
I plettro *m*

quintuplet *n.* —*cf.* also Groupings List
F quintolet *m*
G Quintole *f*
I quintina *f*

— R —

ra *n.* (d-flat solfege syllable in the key of c-major in American, movable-do system) —*cf.* also Solfege List
F ré *m*
G des *n*
I re *m*
N.B. Cf. important note given under the entry "solfege" regarding differences between European and American solfege systems. *Cf.* also Solfege List.

racket *n.* —*cf.* also Instruments List (Historic & Ethnic Instruments)
F racket *m*
G Rankett *n*
I rankett *m*

ragtime *n.* —*cf.* also Musical Forms List
F ragtime *m*
G Ragtime *m*
I ragtime *m*

raise *v.* (a pitch, *etc.*)
F monter
G anheben
I alzare

range *n.* (of an instrument; voice, *etc.*)
F tessiture *f* (for instrument and voice); étendue *f* (for instrument and voice);
G Tonumfang *m* (for an instrument); Stimmumfang *m* (for a voice)
I estensione *f* (for instrument and voice)

rapsody *n.* —*cf.* also Musical Forms List
F rapsodie *f;* rhapsodie *f*
G Rhapsodie *f*
I rapsodia *f*

¹rattle (ratchet) *n.* —*cf.* also

Instruments List (Percussion Instruments)
F crécelle *f*
G Ratsche *f*
I raganella *f*

²rattle *v.* —*cf.* also Instrument Repair List (Common Verbs)
F tembler; vibrer
G scheppern
I vibrare

re *n.* (d-natural solfege syllable in the key of c-major in American, movable-do system) —*cf.* also Solfege List
F ré *m*
G d *n*
I re *m*
N.B. Cf. important note given under the entry "solfege" regarding differences between European and American solfege systems. *Cf.* also Solfege List.

realization *n.* (written or improvised version of a figured bass or other abreviated notation)
F réalisation *f*
G Aussetzung *f*
I realizzazione *f*

rebec *n.* —*cf.* also Instruments List (Historic & Ethnic Instruments)
F rebec *m*
G Rebec *m*
I ribecca *f*

recapitulation *n.* —*cf.* also Musical Forms List
F réexposition *f*
G Reprise *f*
I riesposizione *f*

reception *n.* (party after a concert)
F pot *m* / *sl.*; réception *f*
G Empfang *m*
I ricevimento *m*

recital *n.*
F récital *m*
G Vortrag *m*
I recital *m*; spettacolo musicale *m*

recitative *n.* —*cf.* also Musical Forms
List
F récitatif *m*
G Rezitativ *n*
I recitativo *m*

[1]record *v.* —*cf.* also Recording List
F enregistrer
G aufnehmen
I registrare

[2]record company *n.* —*cf. label;* also
Recording List

recorder *n.* —*cf.* also Instruments List
(Historic & Ethnic Instruments)
F flûte à bec *f*
G Blockflöte *f*
I flauto dolce *m*

[1]recording *n.* —*cf.* also Recording
List
F enregistrement *m*
G Aufnahme *f*
I registrazione *f*

[2]recording session *n.* —*cf.* also
Recording List
F séance d'enregistrement *f*
G Aufnahme *f*
I seduta di registrazione *f*

reed *n.* (for a clarinet *etc.*) —*cf.* also
double reed
F anche *f*
G Rohrblatt *n*
I ancia *f*

reel-to-reel *n.* (in sound recording,
etc.) —*cf.* also Recording List
F bande magnétique *f*; magnétophone
bobin à bobine *f*
G Tonbandmaschine *f*

I avvolgitore *f*

refrain *n.* (in a song, *etc.*) —*cf.* also
chorus; Musical Forms List
F refrain *m*
G Refrain *m* (N.B. The pronounciation
in German is identical to the French.)
I ritornello *m*

register *n.* (of an instrument; voice)
(N.B. This word in French, German, and
Italian is frequently interchangable with
"range" in English.)
F registre *m* (instrument); tessiture *f*
(for instrument and voice); étendue *f*
(for instrument and voice)
G Register *m* (instrument); Tonumfang
m (for an instrument); Stimmumfang *m*
(for a voice)
I registro *m* (both instrumental and
vocal); I estensione *f* (for instrument
and voice)

rehearsal *n.* (for concert, *etc.*) —*cf.*
also Concert List; Teaching List
F répétition *f*
G Probe *f*
I prova *f*

rehearse *v.* (for a concert, *etc.*) (N.B.
The implication is to rehearse with 2 or
more people, since if it is solo, the term
is "to practice." This is consistent in all
3 languages.) —*cf.* also *practice;* Concert
List; Teaching List
F répéter
G proben
I provare

reinforce *v.* —*cf.* also Instrument
Repair List (Common Verbs)
F renforcer
G verstärken
I rinforzare

[1]relative (major) *adj.* / *n.* (relation-
ship between tonal centers, *etc.*) —*cf.*
also Keys List
F relatif (relatif majeure *f*)
G gleichnamige (gleichnamige
Durtonart *f*)
I relativa (relativa maggiore *f*)

²relative (minor) *adj.* (relationship between tonal centers, *etc.*) —*cf.* also Keys List
F relatif (relatif mineure *f*)
G gleichnamige (gleichnamige Molltonart *f*)
I relativa (relativa minore *f*)

³relative pitch *n.* —*cf.* also *perfect pitch*
F oreille relatif *m*
G relatives Gehör *n*
I orecchio relativo *m*

Renaissance *n.* (Period) —*cf.* also Historical Periods & Styles List
F Renaissance *f*
G Renaissance *f*
I Rinascimento *m*

repeat sign *n.* (in printed music)
F reprise *f*
G Wiederholung *f*
I signo di ripetizione *m*; signo di ritornello *m*

requiem (mass) *n.* —*cf.* also Musical Forms List
F requiem *m*; messe des requiem *f*
G Requiem *n*
I messa di Requiem *f*

required piece *n.* (in a competition or audition) —*cf.* also Competition List
F morceau imposé *m*
G Pflichtstück *m*
I brano obbligatorio *m*

research *n.* —*cf.* also Research List
F recherche *f*; reserche musicale *f*
G Forschung *f*; Musikforschung *f*
I ricerca *f*; ricerca musicale *f*

resin *n.* —*cf.* also Instrument Repair List (Various Materials)
F résine *f*
G Harz *n*
I resina *f*

resolution *n.* (in an harmonic suspension, *etc.*)
F résolution *f*
G Auflösung *f*

I risoluzione *f*

resonance *n.* (of a hall; instrument, *etc.*)
F résonance *f* (of instrument; hall, *etc.*); vibration *f* (of a voice)
G Resonanz *f*
I risonanza *f*

¹rest *n.* (written quarter rest; eighth rest, *etc.*) —*cf.* individual entries; also Rest List
F silence *m*
G Pause *f*
I pausa *f*

²rest stroke *n.* (N.B. The Spanish term *appoyando* [for rest stroke] is generally understood by all classical guitarists regardless of their language.)
F buté *m*
G Anlegen *f*; Anlegenschlag *m*
I appagiato *m* (tocco appagiato)

³rest value *n.* (sustained duration of a rest) —*cf.* also *note value* (N.B. In English we rarely use this term, but is common in all three other languages.)
F valeur de la pause *f*
G Pausenwert *m*
I valore della pausa *m*

¹retrograde *n.* —*cf.* also Twelve-tone Music List (Matrix Divisions List)
F rétrograde *f*
G Krebsform *f*
I retrogrado *m*

²retrograde-inversion *n.* —*cf.* also Twelve-tone Music List (Matrix Divisions List)
F rétrograde du renversement *m*
G Krebsumkehrung *f*
I retrogrado dell'inversione *m*

reverb *n.* (of a hall or on a recording) —*cf.* also Recording List
F réverbe *f*
G Echo *n* (N.B. In German, something gives an echo. *Ex.* "...ein Echo geben.")
I riverbero *m*

review *n.* (in newspaper, *etc.*) —*cf.* also Concert List

F critique *f*
G Kritik *f*
I critica *f*

reviewer *n.* (a writer for a newspaper, *etc.*) —*cf. critic*

rhythm *n.* —*cf.* also Notes List
F rythme *m*
G Rhythmus *m*
I ritmo *m*

ri *n.* (d-sharp solfege syllable in the key of c-major in American, movable-do system) —*cf.* also Solfege List
F ré *m*
G dis *n*
I re *m*
N.B. Cf. important note given under the entry "solfege" regarding differences between European and American solfege systems. *Cf.* also Solfege List.

¹rib *n.* (bracing in an instrument) —*cf.* also Instrument Repair List
F contreéclisse *f*
G Stachel *m*
I fascia *f*

²rib *n.* (of the human body) —*cf.* also Anatomy List
F côte *f*
G Rippe *f*
I costola *f*

ricercar *n.* —*cf.* also Musical Forms List
F ricercare *m*
G Ricercar *n*
I ricercare *m*

riff *n.* —*cf. run*

rigadoon *n.* —*cf.* also Musical Forms List
F rigaudon *m*
G Rigaudon *m*
I rigaudon *m*

rim *n.* (of an instrument; snare drum, *etc.*)
F bord *m*
G Rand *m*

I orlo *f*

ring *n.* (finger) —*cf.* also Anatomy List (Fingers)
F annulaire *m*
G Ringfinger *m*
I annulare *m*

riser *n.* (terraced steps used by a chorus to stand during a concert) —*cf.* also Concerts List
F estrade *f*
G Treppenpodium *n*; Stufenpodium *n*
I pedana *f*

ritornello *n.* —*cf.* also Musical Forms List
F ritournelle *f*
G Ritornell *n*
I ritornello *m*

Rococo *n.* (Period) —*cf.* also Historical Periods & Styles List
F rococo *m*
G Rokoko *n*
I Rococò *m*

role *n.* (in an opera, *etc.*)
F rôle *m*
G Rolle *f*
I ruolo *m*; parte *f*

¹roll *n.* (of timpani, *etc.*)
F roulement *m*
G Wirbel *m*
I rullo *m*

²roll *v.* (to roll an "r," in singing; speaking, *etc.*) —*cf.* also Voice List
F rouler
G rollen
I arrotare la erre (This is only for "rolling an 'r'." For other consonants you use "arrotondare.")

romance *n.* —*cf.* also Musical Forms List
F romance *f*
G Romanze *f*
I romanza *f*

Romantic *n.* (Period) —*cf.* also Historical Periods & Styles List

F romantique *m*
G Romantik *f*
I Romantico *m*

rondo *n.* —*cf.* also Musical Forms List
F rondo *m;* rondeau *m*
G Rondo *n*
I rondò *m*

¹root *n.* (of a chord) —*cf.* also Chords List
F basse *f;* note de basse *f;* fondamentale *f;* son fondamentale *f*
G Grundton *m*
I suono fondamentale *m*

²root position *n.* (of a chord) —*cf.* also Chord List (Chord Inversions)
F état fondamental *m*
G Grundform *f*
I stato fondamentale *m*

rosette *n.* (of a guitar; lute, *etc.*)
F rosette *f*
G Rosette *f*
I rosa *f* (for guitar); rosette *f* (for lute)

rosewood *n.* —*cf.* also Instrument Repair List (Various Woods)
F bois de rose *m*
G Rosenholz *n*
I palissandro *m*

rosin *n.* (for a bow, *etc.*)
F colophane *f*
G Harz *n;* Geigenharz *n*
I pece *f*

rotary valve *n.* (for brass instruments, *etc.*)
F cylindre à rotation *m*
G Drehventil *n;* Zylinderventil *n*
I cilindro rotativo *m*

¹round *n.* —*cf.* also Musical Forms List
F ronde *f*
G Kanon *m*
I rondò *f*

²round *n.* (stage of a competition) —*cf.* also Competition List
F épreuve *f*
G Ausscheidung *f*

I selezione *f;* fase eliminatoria *f*
³round dance *n.* —*cf.* also Musical Forms List
F ronde *f*
G Reigen *m*
I girotondo *m*

¹row *n.* (in a hall) —*cf.* also Stage List
F rang *m*
G Reihe *f*
I fila *f*

²row *n.* (in 12-tone music) —*cf.* also Twelve-tone Music List
F série *f*
G Reihe *f*
I serie *f*

royalties *n.* / *pl* (fee paid to composer; recording artist, *etc.*)
F tantièmes *m/ pl;* droits d'auteur *m/ pl*
G Tantiemen *f/ pl*
I diritti d'autore *m/ pl*

run *n.* (scale; riff, *etc.*)
F trait *m;* riff *m/sl.* (*N.B.* The term "riff" is mostly used for rock; jazz, *etc.*)
G Lauf *m*
I veloce passaggio di note *m*

— S —

sackbut *n.* —*cf.* also Instruments List
(Historic & Ethnic Instruments)
F sackbut *m*
G Sackbut *f*
I sackbut *m*

sacred music *n.* —*cf.* also Musical
Forms List
F musique sacrée *f*
G Kirchenmusik *f*
I musica sacra *f*

saddle *n.* (on bridge of guitar;
mandolin, *etc.*)
F sillet *m*
G Sattel *m*
I osso del ponticello *m*; sella *f*

salon music *n.* —*cf.* also Historical
Periods & Styles List
F musique de salon *f*
G Salonmusik *f*
I musica da salotto *f*

sampler *n.* —*cf.* also Recording List
F sampler *m*; sound sampler *m*
G Sampler *m*; Sound Sampler *m*
I sampler *m*; sound sampler; *m*
campionatore *m*

sand *v.* —*cf.* also Instrument Repair
List (Common Verbs)
F poncer
G schmirgeln
I scantzvetrare

sarabande *n.* —*cf.* also Musical Forms
List
F sarabande *f*
G Sarabande *f*
I sarabanda *f*

saxophone *n.* —*cf.* also Instruments
List (Woodwinds)
F saxophone *m*
G Saxophon *n*
I sassofono *m*

saxophonist *n.* —*cf.* also Professions
List
F saxophoniste *m/f*
G Saxophonist *m*; Saxophonistin *f*
I sassofonista *m/f*

¹scale *n.* (c major scale, *etc.*) —*cf.* also
Keys List; Scales List
F gamme *f*
G Tonleiter *f*
I scala *f*

²scale length *n.* (the length of a
fingerboard, *etc.*)
F taille *f*
G Mensur *f*
I lunghezza *f*; estensione della tastiera *f*

¹scholarship *n.* (money granted for
studies)
F bourse *f*
G Stipendium *n*
I borsa *f*; borsa di studio *f*

²scholarship *n.* (serious research,
etc.) —*cf.* also Research List
F érudition *f*
G Gelehrsamkeit *f*
I erudizione *f*

¹score *n.* (printed orchestral or
chamber music) —*cf.* also Score List
F conducteur *m*
G Partitur *f*
I partitura *f*

²**score** *v.* (to arrange a piece)
F orchestrer
G bearbeiten
I orchestrare

³**score system** *n.* (of an orchestral score) —*cf. system;* also Score List

scraper *n.* (guiro) —*cf.* also Instruments List (Percussion Instruments)
F guiro *m*
G Guiro *m*
I guiro *m*

scroll *n.* (head of a violin, *etc.*)
F volute *f*
G Schnecke *f*
I riccio *m*

se *n.* (g-flat solfege syllable in the key of c-major in American, movable-do system) —*cf.* also Solfege List
F sol *m*
G ges *n*
I sol *m*
N.B. Cf. important note given under the entry "solfege" regarding differences between European and American solfege systems. *Cf.* also Solfege List.

seam *n.* (on an instrument between two pieces of wood; metal, *etc.*) —*cf.* also Instrument Repair List
F couture *f*
G Naht *f*
I giunzione *f*

¹**second** *n.* —*cf.* also Intervals List
F seconde *f*
G Sekunde *f*
I seconda *f*

²**second finger** *n.* —*cf. middle finger;* also Anatomy List (Fingers)

³**second inversion** *n.* (of a chord) — *cf.* also Chord List (Chord Inversions)
F deuxième renversement *m*
G zweite Umkehrung *f*
I secondo rivolto *m*

secondary dominant *n.* (tonal relationship in a composition) —*cf.* also

Chords List
F dominante de passage *f*
G Zwischendominante *f*
I dominante di passaggio *f;* dominante secondaria *f*

¹**section** *n.* (in an orchestra *i.e.* strings; winds, *etc.*)
F pupitre *m;* groupe *m*
G Gruppe *f*
I sezione *f*

²**section** *n.* (in a piece of music)
F partie *f*
G Absatz *m*
I sezione *f*

secular music *n.* —*cf.* also Musical Forms List
F musique profane *f*
G weltliche Musik *f*
I musica profana *f*

semibreve *n.* (British name for whole note) —*cf. whole note;* also Notes List

semi-finalist *n.* (in a competition) — *cf.* also Competition List
F demi-finaliste *f*
G Semifinalist *m;* Semifinalistin *f*
I semi-finalista *m /f*

semihemidemisemiquaver *n.* (British name for hundred twenty-eighth note) —*cf. hundred tewnty-eighth note;* also Notes List

semiquaver *n.* (British name for sixteenth note) —*cf. sixteenth note;* also Notes List

septuplet *n.* —*cf.* also Groupings List
F septolet *m*
G Septole *f*
I settimina *f*

sequence *n.* —*cf.* also Musical Forms List
F séquence *f*
G Sequenz *f;* Folge *f*
I sequenza *f*

sequencer *n.* (in MIDI) —*cf.* also

Recording List
F séquenceur *m*
G Sequenzer *m*
I sequencer *m*

serenade *n. —cf.* also Musical Forms
List
F sérénade *f*
G Serenade *f*
I serenata *f*

serial music *n.* (12-tone music) *—cf.*
also Historical Periods & Styles List;
Twelve-tone Music List
F musique sérielle *f*
G serielle Musik *f*
I musica seriale *f*

serious music *n.*
F musique sérieuse *f* (*N.B.* This term
doesn't really exist in French. One
usually says "musique pop," "musique
classique" or indicates some other
specific category.)
G ernst Musik *f*
I musica seria *f* (*N.B.* In Italian, one
usually says simply "musica classica" *f*
or indicates some other specific
catagory.)

serpent *n. —cf.* also Instruments List
(Historic & Ethnic Instruments)
F serpent *m*
G Serpent *m*
I serpentone *m*

seventh *n. —cf.* also Intervals List
F septième *f*
G Septime *f*
I settima *f*

sextuplet *n. —cf.* also Groupings List
F sextolet *m*
G Sextole *f*
I sestina *f*

shaker *n.* (guiro) *—cf.* also Instru-
ments List (Percussion Instruments)
F batteur *m*
G Schüttelrohr *n*
I shaker *m*

shape *n.* (of a phrase; melodic line,

etc.)
F forme *f*
G Form *f*
I forma *f* (for a phrase); linea *f* (for a
melody)

[1]**sharp** *n. —cf.* also *flat; natural;
cautionary accidental*
F dièse *m*
G Kreuz *n*
I diesis *m*

[2]**sharp** *adj.* (out of tune, *i.e.* singing or
playing too high) *—cf.* also *flat*
F trop haut (chanter trop haut / jouer
trop haut)
G zu hoch (zu hoch singen / zu hoch
spielen, *etc.*)
I crescere (for both singing and playing)

shawm *n. —cf.* also Instruments List
(Historic & Ethnic Instruments)
F chalumeau *m*
G Schalmei *f*
I cennamella *f*; ciaramella *f*

shim *n.* (under bridge, *etc.*) *—cf.* also
Instrument Repair List
F taquet *m*
G Ausgleichplättchen *n*;
Ausgleichsscheibe *f*
I spessore *m*

shorten *v.* (to shorten a breath; note,
etc.)
F abréger
G abkürzen
I abbreviare; accorciare

shoulder *n. —cf.* also Anatomy List
F épaule *f*
G Schulter *f*
I spalla *f*

si *n.* (g-sharp solfege syllable in the key
of c-major in American, movable-do
system) *—cf.* also Solfege List
F sol *m*
G gis *n*
I sol *m*
N.B. Cf. important note given under the
entry "solfege" regarding differences
between European and American

solfege systems. *Cf.* also Solfege List.

siciliana *n.* —*cf.* also Musical Forms
List
F sicilienne *f*
G Siziliano *m*
I siciliana *f*

side *n.* (the side of a violin; guitar, *etc.*)
—*cf.* also *bout;* Instrument Repair List
F côté *m*
G Zarge *f*
I fascia *f*

sight read *v.*
F à vue (jouer à vue / chanter à vue)
G vom Blatt (vom Blatt spielen / vom
Blatt singen)
I a prima vista (suonare a prima vista /
cantare a prima vista)

[1] **silver** *n.* —*cf.* also Instrument Repair
List (Various Materials)
F argent *m*
G Silber *n*
I argento *m*

[2] **silver plated** *adj.* —*cf.* also *gold
plated;* Instrument Repair List (Various
Materials)
F plaqué argenture
G versilbert
I placcato in argento

sing *v.*
F chanter
G singen
I cantare

singer *n.* —*cf.* also Professions List;
Voice List
F chanteur *m;* chanteuse *f*
G Sänger *m;* Sängerin *f*
I cantate *m/f*

singspiel *n.* —*cf.* also Musical Forms
List
F singspiel *m*
G Singspiel *n*
I singspiel *m*

siren *n.* —*cf.* also Instruments List
(Percussion Instruments)

F sirène *f*
G Sirene *f*
I sirena *f*

six-eight (6/8) *n.* (time signature in
words as it is spoken in conversation) —
cf. also Time Signature List
F mesure à six-huit *f*
G sechsachtel Takt *m*
I sei ottavi *m / pl*

[1] **sixteenth note** *n.* —*cf.* also Notes
List (Rhythmic Values)
F double croche *f*
D Sechzehntelnote *f*
I sedicesimo *m* (note name)
(*N.B.* In Italian, they often distinguish
between the *note* itself, and the *duration*
of that note. The name of the *duration*
of this note is: semicroma *f.) Cf.
sixteenth rest.*
• *N.B.* The British name of this note is:
semiquaver.

[2] **sixteenth rest** *n.* —*cf.* also Rest List
F quart de soupir *m* (*N.B.* In French,
the names of the *rests* are not the same
as the corresponding *notes. Cf.* Notes
[individual entries and Notes List] for
comparison.)
G Sechzehntel-Pause *f*
I pausa di semicroma *f* (*N.B.* In Italian
the rest is followed by the name of the
note. *Ex.* "pausa di ..." [followed by
value.])
• *N.B.* The British name of this rest is:
semiquaver.

sixth *n.* —*cf.* also Intervals List
F sixte *f*
G Seste *f*
I sesta *f*

[1] **sixty-fourth note** *n.* —*cf.* also
Notes List (Rhythmic Values)
F quadruple croche *f*
D Vierundsechzigstelnote *f*
I sesantaquattresimo *m* (note name)
(*N.B.* In Italian, they often distinguish
between the *note* itself, and the *duration*
of that note. The name of the *duration* of
this note is: sesantaquattresimo *m.) Cf.
sixty-fourth rest.*

• *N.B.* The British name of this note is: *hemidemisemiquaver.*

²sixty-fourth rest *n.* —*cf.* also Rest List

F seizième de soupir *m* (*N.B.* In French, the names of the *rests* are not the same as the corresponding *notes*. *Cf.* Notes [individual entries and Notes List] for comparison.)
G Vierundsechzigstel-Pause *f*
I pausa di semibiscroma *f* (*N.B.* In Italian the rest is followed by the name of the note. *Ex.* "pausa di ..." [followed by value.])
• *N.B.* The British name of this rest is: *hemidemisemiquaver.*

slapstick *n.* —*cf.* also Instruments List (Percussion Instruments)

F fouet *m* (*N.B.* This is literally "whip" in French, but is used in percussion termonology for slapstick.)
G Peitsche *f* (*N.B.* This is literally "whip" in German, but is used in percussion termonology for slapstick.)
I frusta *f* (*N.B.* This is literally "whip" in Italian, but is used in percussion termonology for slapstick.)

sleighbells *n.* / *pl* —*cf.* also Instruments List (Percussion Instruments)

F grelots *m* / *pl*
G Schellen *f* / *pl*
I sonagliere *f* / *pl*

slide *n.* (of a trombone, *etc.*)

F coulisse *f*
G Zug *m*
I coulisse *f*

¹slur *n.*

F liaison *f*
G Bindebogen *m*; Bindung *f*
I legatura *f*

²slur *v.* (to slur two notes, *etc.*)

F lier
G binden
I legare

snare drum *n.* —*cf.* also Instruments List (Percussion Instruments)

F caisse claire *f*
G Kleine Trommel *f*
I tamburo *m*; tamburo rullante *m*

¹soft attack *n.* —*cf.* also Voice List (Vocal Attacks)

F entrée douce *f*
G weicher Einsatz *m*
I attacco dolce *m*

²soft stick *n.* —*cf.* also Drum Sticks List

F baguette d'éponge *f*
G Schwammschlegel *m*
I bachetta di spugna *f*

sol *n.* (g-natural solfege syllable in the key of c-major in American, movable-do system) —*cf.* also Solfege List

F sol *m*
G g *n*
I sol *m*
N.B. Cf. important note given under the entry "solfege" regarding differences between European and American solfege systems. *Cf.* also Solfege List.

sold out *adj.* (concert, ballet, *etc.*) —*cf.* also Concert List

F épuisé
G ausverkauft
I esaurito

¹solder *n.* (soft metal alloy used to close seams on some brass instruments) Instrument Repair List (Various Materials)

F soudure *f*
G Lot *n*; Lötmetal *n*; Lötmittel *n*
I saldature

²solder *v.* —*cf.* also *weld*; Instrument Repair List (Common Verbs)

F souder
G löten
I saldare

¹solfege *n.*

F solfège *m*
G Solfeggio *f*
I solfeggio *m*
N.B. In French and Italian, they use the "fixed-do system" (*i.e.* the note c is

always named do). German also uses fixed-do, but they use the name for the note in German rather than the traditional solfege syllable.

"Fixed-do" is in drastic contrast to the practice in America, which uses a "moveable do system" *i.e.* the tonic of the key center is always called "do" (with the obvious exception of harmonic modulations, in which case the tonic of the new key center becomes do). *Ex.* in the U.S., in the key of D major, the note D is called do, in F minor, the note F is called do, *etc.*

In France and Italy you say the entire name of the note (with the words "sharp" or "flat") to say the name of a specific note. However, in *singing* solfege—you leave off the word "sharp" or "flat" but sing the note altered to the correct pitch. Thus, when singing a chromatic run with the notes "c, c#, d, d#" you would simply say "do, do, ré, ré," but sing the half step pitches. In German, you sing the entire name of the specific note.

Cf. Notes List (and individual entries) for chromatic listing of these notes with "sharp" and "flat" in French and Italian.

²solfege syllables *n.* —*cf.* individual entries; also Solfege List

solid *adj.* (*i.e.* not laminated wood) — *cf.* also Instrument Repair List
F massif
G massiv
I massiccio

solo *n.*
F solo *m*
G Solo *m*
I solo *m*

soloist *n.* —*cf.* also Professions List
F soliste *m/f*
G Solist *m*; Solistin *f*
I solista *m/f*

sonata *n.* —*cf.* also Musical Forms List
F sonate *f*
G Sonate *f*

I sonata *f*

sonatina *n.* —*cf.* also Musical Forms List
F sonatine *f*
G Sonatine *f*
I sonatina *f*

¹song *n.* —*cf.* also Musical Forms List
F chanson *f*
G Lied *n*
I canzone *f*

²song cycle *n.* —*cf.* cycle; also Musical Forms List

³song form *n.* —*cf.* binary form; ternary form; two-part song form; three-part song form; also Musical Forms List

sonority *n.* (of an instrument)
F sonorité *f*
G Klangfülle *f*
I sonorità *f*

¹soprano *n.* (singer) —*cf.* also Voice List (Traditional Types)
F soprano *m*
G Sopran *m*
I soprano *m*

²soprano clarinet *n.* —*cf.* also Instruments List (Woodwinds)
F petite clarinette *f*
G kleine Klarinette *f*
I clarinetto piccolo *m*

³soprano clef *n.* —*cf.* also Clef List
F clef d'ut 1 *f*
G Sopranschlüssel *m*
I chiave di soprano *f*

sordun *n.* —*cf.* also Instruments List (Historic & Ethnic Instruments)
F sordun *m*
G Sordun *m*
I sordone *m*

¹sound *n.*
F son *m*
G Klang *m*
I suono *m*

²**sound check** *n.* —*cf.* also Recording
List
F réglage *m*
G Sound check *m*
I prova del suono *f*

³**sound effect** *n.*
F effet bruitage *m*
G Klangeffekt *m*
I effetto sonoro *m*

⁴**sound hole** *n.* (of a guitar) —*cf.* also
f-hole
F ouïe *f*
G Schalloch *n*
I buca *f*

⁵**sound post** *n.* (of a violin, *etc.*)
F âme *f*
G Stimme *f*; Stimmstock *m*
I anima *f*

⁶**sound track** *n.* (for film, *etc.*) —*cf.*
also *film music*; Recording List
F colonne sonore *f*
G Tonstreifen *m*
I colonna sonora *f*

soundboard *n.* (of a piano; guitar,
etc.)
F table *f*; table d'harmonie *f*
G Boden *m*; Resonanzboden *m*
I tavola armonica *f*

soundbox *n.* (of a guitar, *etc.*)
F caisse *f*; caisse de résonance *f*
G Resonanzkasten *m*
I cassa *f*; cassa di rosonanza *f*

sousaphone *n.* —*cf.* also Instruments
List (Brass Instruments)
F sousaphone *m*
G Sousaphon *n*
I sousafono *m*

space *n.* (on the staff) —*cf.* also Staff
List
F interligne *f*
G Zwischenraum *m*
I spazio *m*

speaker *n.* —*cf.* also Recording List
F haut-parleur *m*

G Sprecher *m*
I altoparlante *m*

special effects *n./ pl* (in orchestra-
tion, *etc.*) —*cf.* also *effect*
F effets spéciaux *m/ pl*
G Spezialeffekte *m/ pl*
I effetti *m/ pl*

spinet *n.* —*cf.* also Instruments List
(Keyboards)
F épinette *f*
G Spinett *n*
I spinetta *f*

sponsor *n.* (organizer for concerts) —
cf. also Concert List
F sponsor *m*
G Sponsor *m*; Sponsorin *f*; Förderer *m*
(no *f* form)
I sponsor *m*

spotlight *n.* —*cf.* also Stage List
F projecteur *m*
G Scheinwerfer *m*
I riflettore *m*

spring *n.* —*cf.* also Instrument Repair
List
F ressort *m*
G Sprung *m*
I molla *f*

spruce *n.* —*cf.* also Instrument Repair
List (Various Woods)
F sapin *m*
G Fichte *f*; Fichtenholz *n*
I abete *m*

square notation *n.* —*cf.* also
Notation List
F notation carrée *f*
G Quadratnotenschrift *f*
I notazione quadrata *f*

¹**staff** *n.* (of music) —*cf.* also Staff List
F portée *f*
G Liniensystem *n*
I pentagramma *m*

²**staff paper** *n.* (blank music paper)
—*cf.* also Staff List
F papier à musique *m*

G Notenpapier *n*
I foglio pentagrammato *m*

¹stage *n.* —*cf.* also Stage List; Concerts List
F scène *f*
G Bühne *f*
I palcoscenico *m*

²stage *v.* (to organize an opera production) —*cf.* also Concert List
F mettre ("mettre en scène une pièce")
G setzen ("in Szene setzen");
veranstalten
I mettere ("mettere in scena")

³stage directions *n.* / *pl* —*cf.* also Stage List
F indications scéniques *f*/ *pl* (*N.B.* The accents are reversed between the words scène and scénique which naturally alters the pronounciation.)
G Regienweisung *f*
I didascalie ("didascalie in un testo drammatico")

⁴stage door *n.* —*cf.* also Stage List
F entrée *f*
G Bühneneingang *m*
I porta del palcoscenico *f*

⁵stage fright *n.* —*cf.* also Stage List; Concert List
F trac *m*
G Lampenfieber *n*
I paura dinanzi al pubblico *f*

⁶stage left *n.* —*cf.* also Stage List
F à gauche de la scène *f*; (côté) cours *f*
G Bühne links *n*
I a sinistra del palcoscenico *f*

⁷stage manager *n.* —*cf.* also Stage List
F régisseur *m*
G Inspizient *m*
I regista di scena *m*; direttore artistico *m*

⁸stage positions *n.* / *pl* —*cf.*
individual entries [*downstage; upstage; stage door; stage left; stage right; wings*]; also Stage List

⁹stage presence *n.* —*cf.* also Concert List
F présence sur scène *f*
G Bühneneindruck *m*; Bühne Ausstrahlung *f*
I presenza scenica *f*; portamento *m* (presence in-general)

¹⁰stage right *n.* —*cf.* also Stage List
F à droite de la scène *f*; (côté) jardin *f*
G Bühne rechts *n*
I a destra del palcoscenico *f*

staging *n.* (in an opera, *etc.*) —*cf.* also Stage List
F mis en scène *f*
G Inszenierung *f*
I messa in scena *f*

stain *v.* (to color wood, *etc.*) —*cf.* also Instrument Repair List (Common Verbs)
F teinter
G färben
I trattare (trattare il legno con un mordente)

standing room *n.* (an area for which inexpensive tickets for a concert are sold and the audience stands throughout the performance)
F places debout *f*/ *pl*
G Stehplatz *m*
I ingresso *m* (*N.B.* Traditional "standing room" is now officially illegal in Italy due to various fire codes.)

statement *n.* (bank statement) —*cf.* also Finances List
F relevé *m*; relevé de compte (— bancaire) *m*
G Kontoauszug *m*
I saldo *m*

station *n.* (radio; television, *etc.*) —*cf.* also *program*
F station *f*
G Sender *m*
I stazione *f*

¹steel drum *n.* —*cf.* also Instruments List (Percussion Instruments)
F steel-drum *m*
G Steel-Drum *f*

I tamburo di latta *m*

²steel plate *n.* —*cf.* also Instruments List (Percussion Instruments)
F feuille d'acier *f*
G Stahlplatte *f*
I lastra *f*

³steel string *n.* —*cf.* also Strings List; Instrument Repair List
F corde en acier *f*
G Stahlsaite *f*
I corda d'acciaio *f*

stem *n.* —*cf.* also Notes List (Parts of a Written Note)
F queue *f*
G Notenhals *m*
I gambo *m*

step *n.* (*i.e.* whole step; half step, *etc.*) —*cf.* also Intervals List
F ton *m* (In French, this is always qualified by the interval. *Ex.* "un ton;" "demi-ton," *etc.*)
G Ton *m* (In German, this is always qualified by the interval. *Ex.* "Ganzton;" "Halbton," *etc.*)
I tono *m* (In Italian "tono" automatically means a whole step. Anything else is qualified; *i.e.* a "half step" is a "semitono," *etc.*)

stool *n.* (sitting for a piano; harp, *etc.*) —*cf.* also *bench*
F tabouret *m*
G Stuhl *m*
I sgabello *m*; sedile *m*

¹stop *n.* (of an organ, *etc.*)
F registre *m*
G Register *n*
I registro *m*

²stop *v.* (to stop a note from sustaining or vibrating) —*cf. dampen*

stopped *adj.* (horns) —*cf.* also Orchestral Terms List
F bouché
G gestopft
I chiuso

¹straight *adj.* (*i.e.* non-arpeggiated chord; octave, *etc.*)
F ensemble (not common — usually one says "not arpeggiated": "non arpégé")
G simultan
I simultaneo (not common — usually one says "not arpeggiated": "non arpeggiato"); unito; simultaneo

²straight mute *n.* —*cf.* also Mutes List
F sourdine droite *f*
G Spitzdämpfer *m*
I sordina diritta *f*

strap *n.* (for a bassoon; guitar, *etc.*)
F sangle *f*
G Gurt *m*
I cinghia *f*; tracolla *f*

stress *v.* (to stress a note; syllable, *etc.*)
F accentuer
G betonen
I accentare; tracolla *f*

¹string *n.* (of a violin; guitar, *etc.*)
F corde *f*
G Saite *f*
I corda *f*

²string *v.* (to put strings on an instrument)
F changer les cordes (*N.B.* In French, you simply "change the strings.")
G besaiten; bespannen (*N.B.* In German you normally say "change the strings:" "...die Saiten wechseln," although one sometimes hears "besaiten" or "bespannen.")
I cambiare le corde (*N.B.* In Italian you simply "change the strings.")

strings *n.* / *pl* (section) —*cf.* also Instruments List (Strings)
F cordes *f* / *pl*
G Streicher *n* / *pl*
I archi *m* / *pl*

stomach *n.* (*N.B.* In French, German and Italian you distinguish between "stomach" [the organ] and "belly" [the outer portion of the body], while in

English we often use "stomach" for both.) —*cf. belly;* also Anatomy List
F estomac *m*
G Magen *m*
I stomaco *m*

strong *adj.* (a strong beat in a measure, *etc.*) —*cf.* also ≠ *weak*
F fort
G stark
I forte

strum *v.* (on a guitar, *etc.*) —*cf.* also *pluck*
F plaquer *sl.*
G schlagen *sl.*
I pennata *n.* (*N.B.* In Italian one usually says "dare la pennata," [play with a pick]. You can use the verb "strimpellare," but the conotation is someone who doesn't play very well *i.e.* "a plucker.")

student visa *n.* —*cf.* also Legal Subjects List
F visa d'étudiant *f*
G Studiumvisum *n*
I visto di soggiorno per studenti *m*

studio class *n.* —*cf.* also Teaching List
F studio-classe *f*
G Studioklasse *f*
I This word doesn't exist in Italian. You sometimes say "master-class" (borrowed from English). Studio class ("classe di studio") sounds æsthetically ugly in Italian.

¹study (étude) *n.* —*cf.* also Musical Forms List
F étude *f*
G Etüde *f*
I studio *m*

²study score *n.* —*cf.* also Score List
F partition d'analyse *f*
G Studienpartitur *f*
I partitura (*N.B.* In Italian, "partiture" is generally used for all types of scores.)

¹sub *n. / sl* (a stand-in for a performer) —*cf. substitute;* also Concerts List

²sub theme *n.* —*cf.* also *main theme;* Musical Forms List
F sous thème *f;* thème secondaire *m*
G Nebentheme *n;* Seitentheme *n*
I secondo tema *m;* tema secondario *f*

subdominant *n.* (scale degree; chord) —*cf.* also Chords List
F sous-dominante *f*
G Subdominante *f*
I sottodominante *f*

subject *n.* (musical theme, *etc.*) —*cf.* also Musical Forms List
F sujet *m*
G Subjekt *n;* Sujet *n* (from the French and pronounced as in French)
I soggetto *m*

submediant *n.* (scale degree; chord) —*cf.* also Chords List
(*N.B.* Only English uses the concept of "submediant," while French, German and Italian all use the concept of "superdominant.")
F sus-dominante *f*
G Oberdominante *f*
I sopra dominante *f*

substitute *n.* (sub. *sl.*) (stand-in for a performer) —*cf.* also Concerts List
F remplaçant *m;* remplaçante *f*
G Ersatzspieler *m;* Ersatzspielerin *f*
(*N.B.* In German the verb "einspringen" is usually used in this case.)
I sostituto *m;* sostututa *f*

subtonic *n.* (scale degree; chord) —*cf.* also *leading tone;* Chords List
F note sensible *f*
G Subtonica *f*
I sensibile *f*

suite *n.* —*cf.* also Musical Forms List
F suite *f*
G Suite *f*
I suite *f*

superimposition *n.* (simultaneously playing or writing two different chords; tonal centers, *etc.*)
F superposition *f*
G Schichtung *f*

supertonic

I sovrapposizione *f*

supertonic *n.* (scale degree; chord) —
cf. also Chords List
F sus-tonique *f*
G Obertonika *f*
I sopratonica *f*

support *v.* (to support the voice, *etc.*)
—*cf.* also *breath support*; Voice List
F appuyer
G stützen
I appoggiare

suspended cymbal *n.* —*cf.* also
Instruments List (Percussion Instruments)
F cymbale suspendu *f*
G hängendes Becken *n*
I piatto sospeso *m*

suspension *n.* (a suspended note in a
chord, *etc.*)
F suspension *f*
G Vorhalt *m*
I ritardo *m*

sustain *v.* (a pitch, *etc.*)
F soutenir
G aushalten
I sostenere

sustained *adj.* (a held note, *etc.*)
F tenue
G ausgehalten
I tenuta

sustaining pedal *n.* (on a piano;
celeste, *etc.*) —*cf.* also *damping pedal*
F pédale forte *f*
G Fortepedal *n*
I pedale del forte *m*; pedale di risonanza
m

sympathetic vibration *n.* —*cf.* also
vibration
F vibration par résonance *f*
G Sympathieschwingung *f*
I vibrazione simpatica *f*

symphonic poem *n.* (*N.B.* In
English we use the terms *symphonic
poem* and *program music* almost

interchangeably. This is not the case in
German, Italian and especially French.)
—*cf.* also Musical Forms List; *program
music*
F poème symphonique *f*
G sinfonische Dichtung *f*
I poema sinfonico *m*

symphony *n.* —*cf.* also Musical
Forms List
F symphonie *f*
G Sinfonie *f*
I sinfonia *f*

syncopate *v.*
F syncoper
G synkopieren
I sincopare

syncopation *n.*
F syncope *f*
G Synkope *f*
I sincope *f*

synthesizer *n.* —*cf.* also Recording
List
F synthétiseur *m*
G Synthesizer *m*
I sintetizzatore *m*

system *n.* (in full printed orchestral
score, *etc.*) —*cf.* also Score List
F système *m*
G System *n*
I sistema *f*

— 168 —

— T —

ta *n.* (b-sharp solfege syllable in the key of c-major in American, movable-do system) —*cf.* also Solfege List.
F si *m*
G his *n*
I si *m*
N.B. Cf. important note given under the entry "solfege" regarding differences between European and American solfege systems. *Cf.* also Solfege List.

tablature *n.* (lute; Baroque guitar; organ, *etc.*)
F tablature *f*
G Tabulatur *m*
I intavolatura *f*

table music *n.* —*cf.* also Historical Periods & Styles List
F musique de table *f*
G Tafelmusik *f*
I musica da tavola *f*

tabor *n.* —*cf.* also Instruments List (Percussion Instruments)
F tambour de provence *m*
G Tambourin *n*
I tamburino provenzale *m*

tails *n.* (tuxedo) —*cf. tuxedo;* also Concerts List

take off mutes —*cf.* also Orchestral Terms List
F enlevez les sourdines
G Dämpfern weg
I via sordini; tagliere la sordina

tambourine *n.* —*cf.* also Instruments List (Percussion Instruments)
F tambour de Basque *m*
G Tambourin *n*

I tamburino basco *m*

tape *n.* (*i.e.* cassette tape, *etc.*) —*cf.* also Recording List
F bande *f;* bande magnétique *f*
G Band *n;* Magnetband *n*
I nastro *m;* nastro magnetico *m*

tarantella *n.* —*cf.* also Musical Forms List
F tarentelle *f*
G Tarantella *f*
I tarantella *f*

te *n.* (b-flat solfege syllable in the key of c-major in American, movable-do system) —*cf.* also Solfege List
F si *m*
G b *n*
I si *m*
N.B. Cf. important note given under the entry "solfege" regarding differences between European and American solfege systems. *Cf.* also Solfege List.

teacher *n.* —*cf.* also *professor;* Professions List; Teaching List (*N.B.* The difference between a teacher and a professor in French, German and Italian is extreme. To be on the safe side, it is usually best to refer to any teacher as "professor" since calling a professor a teacher can be considered an insult. In Italy, the term "maestro" is always the best choice.)
F instituteur *m;* institutrice *f;* maître *m;* maîtresse *f;* (for grade school); professeur *m/f* (for upper level)
G Lehrer *m;* Lehrerin *f*
I insegnante *m /f* (in a grade school); maestro *m;* maestra *f* is used for a children's school teacher but also for

anyone having to do with music or the arts; professore *m*; professoressa *f* (for university or high school)

technique *n.* (on an instrument, *etc.*)
F technique *f*
G Technik *f*
I tecnica *f*

teeth *n.* / *pl* —*cf.* also Anatomy List
F dents *f* / *pl*
G Zähne *m* / *pl*
I denti *m* / *pl*

temperament *n.* (in tuning) —*cf.* also Tuning List
F tempérament *m*
G Temperatur *f*
I temperamento *m*

temperature *n.* (the relative warmth of a hall, *etc.*)
F température *f*
G Temperatur *f* (*N.B.* German uses the same word for temperament [re: the type of tuning] and temperature [re: the general warmth or coolness of a room.])
I temperature *f*

tempered tuning *n.* —*cf.* also Tuning List
F accord tempéré *m*
G temperierte Stimmung *f*
I accordatura temperata *f*; accordatura temperata *f*

temple block *n.* —*cf.* also Instruments List (Percussion Instruments)
F templebloc *m*
G Tempelblock *m*
I block cinese *m*

tempo *n.*
F tempo *m*
G Tempo *n*
I tempo *m*

¹tendon *n.* —*cf.* also Anatomy List
F tendon *m*
G Sehne *f*
I tendine *m*

²tendon sheath *n.* —*cf.* also

Anatomy List
F gaine *f*
G Sehnenscheide *f*
I guaina *f*

tendonitis *n.* —*cf.* also Anatomy List
F tendinite *f*
G Sehnescheidenetzündung *f*
I tendinite *f*

¹tenor *n.* (singer) —*cf.* also Voice List (Traditional Types)
F ténor *m*
G Tenor *f*
I tenore *m*

²tenor clef *n.* —*cf.* also Clef List
F clef d'ut quatrième ligne *f*
G Tenorschlüssel *m*
I chiave di tenore *f*

³tenor drum *n.* —*cf.* also Instruments List (Percussion Instruments)
F caisse roulante *f*
G Rührtrommel *f*
I tamburo rullante *m*

tenth *n.* —*cf.* also Intervals List
F dixième *f*
G Dexime *f*
I decima *f*

ternary form *n.* —*cf.* also *three-part song form*; Musical Forms List
F forme ternaire *f*
G dreitelige Form *f*
I forma ternaria *f*

tetrachord *n.*
F tétracorde *m*
G Tetrachord *m*
I tetracordo *m*

texture *n.* (of an orchestration, *etc.*)
F texture *f*
G Textur *f*
I tessitura *f*

theme *n.* (subject of a composition, *etc.*) —*cf.* also; *main theme*; Musical Forms List
F thème *m*
G Thema *n*

I tema *m*

theory *n.* —*cf. music theory*

¹third *n.* —*cf.* also Intervals List
F tierce *f*
G Terz *f*
I terza *f*

²third finger *n.* —*cf. ring finger;* also
Anatomy List (Fingers)

³third inversion *n.* (of a chord) —*cf.*
also Chord List (Chord Inversions)
F troisième renversement *m*
G dritte Umkehrung *f*
I terzo rivolto *m*

thirteenth *n.* —*cf.* also Intervals List
F treizième *m*
G Tredezime *f*
I tredicesima *f*

¹thirty-second note *n.* —*cf.* also
Notes List (Rhythmic Values)
F triple croche *f*
D Zweiunddreißigstelnote *f*
I trentaduesimo *m* (note name)
(*N.B.* In Italian, they often distinguish
between the *note* itself, and the *duration*
of that note. The name of the *duration* of
this note is: biscroma *f.*) *Cf. thirty-second
rest.*
• *N.B.* The British name of this note is:
demisemiquaver.

²thirty-second rest *n.* —*cf.* also Rest
List
F huitième de soupir *m* (*N.B.* In
French, the names of the *rests* are not the
same as the corresponding *notes. Cf.*
Notes [individual entries and Notes
List] for comparison.)
G Zweiunddreißigstel-Pause *f*
I pausa di biscroma *f* (*N.B.* In Italian
the rest is followed by the name of the
note. *Ex.* "pausa di ..." [followed by
value.])
• *N.B.* The British name of this rest is:
demisemiquaver.

thorax *n.* —*cf.* also Anatomy List
F thorax *m*

G Brustkorb *m*
I torace *m*

three-four (3/4) *n.* (time signature in
words as it is spoken in conversation) —
cf. also Time Signature List
F mesure à trois-quatre *f*
G drei-viertel Takt *m*
I tre quarti *m* / *pl*

three-part song form *n.* —*cf.* also
ternary form; Musical Forms List
F lied en trois parties *f*
G dreiteilige Liedform *f*
I canzone in forma tripartita *f*

¹throat *n.* —*cf.* also Anatomy List
F gorge *f*
G Kehle *f*
I gola *f*

²throat voice *n.* —*cf.* also Voice List
F voix de gorge *f*
G Kehlstimme *f*
I voce di gola *f*

through-composed *adj.* (form) —*cf.*
also Musical Forms List
F form ouverte
G durchkomponiert
I forma aperta

thrust *n.* (of a stage) —*cf.* also Stage
List
F avant-scène *f*
G Vorbühne *f*
I proscenio *m;* boccascena *m*

thumb *n.* —*cf.* also Anatomy List
(Fingers)
F pouce *m*
G Daumen *m*
I Pollice *m*

thunder machine *n.* —*cf.* also
Instruments List (Percussion Instru-
ments)
F machine pour le tonnerre *f*
G Donnermaschine *f*
I macchina per il tuono *f*

ti *n.* (b-natural solfege syllable in the
key of c-major in American, movable-do

system) —*cf.* also Solfege List.
F si *m*
G h *n*
I si *m*
N.B. Cf. important note given under the
entry "solfege" regarding differences
between European and American
solfege systems. *Cf.* also Solfege List.

ticket *n.* (for a concert, *etc.*) —*cf.* also
comp ticket (complimentary ticket);
Concert List
F billet *m*
G Karte *f*; Eintrittskarte *f*
I biglietto *m*

¹tie *n.* (bow tie for tuxedo) —*cf.* also
Concert List
F nœud papillon *m*
G Fliege *f*
I farfallino *m*; papillon *m*

²tie *v.* (to tie a note to another, *etc.*)
(*N.B.* In French, German and Italian, to
tie and to *slur* use the same verb but not
the same noun. The distinction rests on
whether the second note is the same [as
a "tie" in English] or different [as a
"slur" in English.])
F lier
G binden
I legare

timbre *n.* —*cf.* color; tone color

¹time change *n.* (meter change) —*cf.*
also Time Signature List
F changement de temps *m*; changement
de mesure *m*
G Taktwechsel *m*
I cambiamento di tempo *m*

²time signature *n.* —*cf.* also Time
Signature List
F mesure *f*; indication de la mesure *f*
G Takt *m*; Taktart *f*
I tempo *m* (*N.B.* Italian uses tempo to
mean both the speed of a piece and the
time signature of a piece.)

³time signatures *n.* (in words as
they are spoken in conversation) —*cf.*
individual entries; Time Signature List

⁴time value *n.* (duration of a note) —
cf. also Notes List
F valeur *f*; valeur de la note *f*
G Notenwert *m*
I valore *m*; valore della nota *m*

¹timpani *n.* —*cf.* also Instruments List
(Percussion Instruments)
F timbales *m / pl*
G Pauken *f / pl*
I timpani *m / pl*

²timpani stick *n.* —*cf.* also Drum
Sticks List
F baguette de timbales *f*
G Paukenschlegel *m*
I bacchetta per timpani *f*

timpanist *n.* —*cf.* also Professions List
F timbalier *m*
G Pauker *m*; Paukerin *f*
I timpanista *m/f*

tip (of a bow, *etc.*) —*cf. point*

tirando *n.* (guitar fingering) —*cf. free
stroke*

toccata *n.* —*cf.* also Musical Forms List
F toccata *f*
G Toccata *f*
I toccata *f*

tome *n.* —*cf. volume;* also Research List

tonality *n.*
F tonalité *f*
G Tonalität *f*
I tonalità *f*

¹tone cluster *n.*
F cluster *m*
G Tone cluster *m*
I cluster *m*

²tone color *n.* (timbre) —*cf.* also *color*
F timbre *m*
G Klangfarbe *f*
I timbro *m*

³tone deaf *adj.*
F on n'a pas d'oreille (In French "one
doesn't have an ear.")

G kein Gehör für Tonhöhen (In German "one has no hearing for pitches.")
I non ha orecchio (In Italian "one doesn't have an ear"); stonato *sl.* (This means literally "out of tune" but is often used in the sense of "tone deaf," and is very slang.)

⁴tone row *n.* (in 12-tone music) —*cf.* also Twelve-tone Music List
F série *f*
G Reihe *f*
I serie *f*

tonguing *n.* (articulation by flutists, *etc.*)
F coup de langue *m*
G Zungenstoß *m*
I colpo di lingua *m*

tonic *n.* (scale degree; chord) —*cf.* also Chords List
F tonique *f*
G Tonika *f*
I tonica *f*

touch *n.* (the feel of a piano's keys, *etc.*)
F toucher *m*
G Anschlag *m*
I tocco *m*

tour *n.* (concert tour, *etc.*) —*cf.* also Concert List
F tournée *f*
G Tournee *f*
I tournée *f*; tour *m*

tourdion *n.* —*cf.* also Musical Forms List
F tordion *m*
G Tourdion *m*
I tortiglione *m*

¹track *n.* (in multi-track recording) — *cf.* also Recording List
F piste *f*
G Spur *f*
I pista *f*

²track *n.* (one song or section of a CD or LP) —*cf. cut*

tranquilizer *n.* (medication) —*cf.* also Concert List
F tranquillisant *m*
G Beruhigungstablette *f*
I calmante *m*

transfer *n.* (moving money from one bank account to another) —*cf.* also Finances List
F transfert *m*
G Überweisung *f*
I bonifico *m*

transformer *n.* —*cf.* also Recording List
F transformateur *m*
G Wandler *m*
I trasformatore *m*

transition *n.* (in the compositional form of a piece)
F transition *f*
G Übergang *m*
I transizione *f*

transitory modulation *n.* —*cf.* also *modulation*
F modulation passagère *f*
G Ausweichung *f*
I modulazione di transizione *f*

translation *n.* (of a song text or other written words into another language) — *cf.* also Voice List
F traduction *f*
G Übersetzung *f*
I traduzione *f*

transpose *v.*
F transposer
G transponieren
I trasportare

transposition *n.*
F transposition *f*
G Transposition *f*
I trasporto *m*

treble clef *n.* —*cf.* also Clef List
F clef de sol *f*
G G-Schlüssel *m*; Violinschlüssel *m*
I chiave di violino *f*

triad *n.* —*cf.* also Chords List

F triade *f*; accord parfait *m*
G Dreiklang *m*
I triade *f*

triangle *n.* —*cf.* also Instruments List
(Percussion Instruments)
F triangle *m*
G Triangel *m*
I triangolo *m*

¹triple *n.* (meter; time signature) —*cf.*
also Time Signature List
F ternaire *f*; mesure à trois temps *f*
G Tripeltakt *m*
I tempo ternario *m*

²triple concerto *n.* —*cf.* also Musical
Forms List
F triple concerto *m*
G Tripelkonzert *n*
I concerto triplo *m*

³triple stop *n.* (violin, *etc.*) —*cf.* double
stop

triplet *n.* —*cf.* also Groupings List
F triolet *m*
G Triole *f*
I terzina *f*

tritone *n.* —*cf.* also Intervals List
F triton *m*
G Tritonus *m*
I tritono *m*

trombone *n.* —*cf.* also Instruments
List (Brass Instruments)
F trombone *m*
G Posaune *f*
I tromba *f*

trombonist *n.* —*cf.* also Professions
List
F trombiniste *m* /*f*; trombone *m*/*f*
G Posaunist *m*; Posaunistin *f*
I trombonista *m*/*f*; suonatore di
trombone *m*; suonatrice di trombone *f*

trumpet *n.* —*cf.* also Instruments List
(Brass Instruments)
F trompette *f*
G Trompete *f*
I tromba *f*

trumpeter *n.* —*cf.* also Professions
List
F trompettiste *m* /*f*; trompette *m*/*f*
G Trompeter *m*; Trompeterin *f*
I trombettist *m*; trombettista *f*;
suonatore di tromba *m*; suonatrice di
tromba *f*

¹tuba *n.* —*cf.* also Instruments List
(Brass Instruments)
F tuba *m*
G Tuba *f*
I tuba *f*

²tuba player *n.* —*cf.* also Professions
List
F tubiste *m*/*f*
G Tubist *m*; Tubistin *f*; Tuba Spieler *m*;
Tuba Spielerin *f*
I suonatore di tuba *m*; suonatrice di
tuba *f* (*N.B.* "tubista" doesn't work at all
in Italian, since this is someone who
makes pipes.)

tubular bells *n.* —*cf.* also Instru-
ments List (Percussion Instruments)
F cloches tubulaires *f* / *pl*
G Röhrenglocken *f* / *pl*
I campane tubolari *f* / *pl*

¹tune *n.* (a melody of a less classical/
serious nature)
F air *m*
.G Weise *f*
I aria *f*

²tune *v.* (to tune an instrument)
F accorder
G stimmen
I accordare

tuned *adj.* (an in-tune instrument) —*cf.*
also *untuned*
F accordé
G gestimmt
I accordato

tuner *n.* (piano tuner, *etc.*) —*cf.* also
Professions List
F accordeur *m*; accordeuse *f*
G Stimmer *m*; Stimmerin *f*
(Klavierstimmer *m*; Klavierstimmerin *f*,
etc.)

I accordatore *m*

¹**tuning fork** *n.*
F diapason *m*
G Stimmgabel *f*
I diapason *m*

²**tuning key** *n.* (on a guitar, *etc.*) —*cf.*
key

tuxedo *n.* (man's concert dress) —*cf.*
also Concert List
F smoking *m* (without tails); queue-
depie *f* (with tails)
G Smoking *m* (without tails); Frack *m*
(with tails)
I smoking *m* (without tails); frack *m*
(with tails)

twelfth *n.* —*cf.* also Intervals List
F douzième *m*
G Duodezime *f*
I dodicesima *f*

twelve-tone music *n.* —*cf.* also
serial music; Twelve-tone Music List;
Historical Periods & Styles List
F musique dodécaphonique *f*
G Zwölftonmusik *f*
I musica dodecafonica *f*

twist *n.* (of the neck on an instrument,
etc.) —*cf.* also Instrument Repair List
F gauchissement *m*
G Verwindung *f*; Krümmung *f*
I torsione *f* (*N.B.* "twisted" as an *adj.* is
"storto;" *i.e.* "a twisted neck" —
"manico storto.")

¹**two-four (2/4)** *n.* (time signature in
words as it is spoken in conversation) —
cf. also Time Signature List
F mesure à deux-quatre *f*
G zwei-viertel Takt *m*
I due quarti *m* / *pl*

²**two-part song form** *n.* —*cf.* also
binary form; Musical Forms List
F lied en deux parties *f*
G zweiteilige Liedform *f*
I canzone in forma bipartita *f*

³**two-two (2/2)** *n.* (time signature in

words as it is spoken in conversation) —
cf. also Time Signature List
F mesure à deux-deux *f*
G zwei-halb Takt *m*
I due mezzi *m* / *pl*

— U —

unison *n.* (prime interval, *etc.*) —*cf.*
also Intervals List
F unisson *m*
G Prim *f*
I unisono *m*

untuned *adj.* (an out-of-tune
instrument) —*cf.* also *tuned*
F désaccordé
G verstimmt
I scordato

up bow *n.* (violin, *etc.*) —*cf.* also
bowing; down bow
F pousser *v.* (*N.B.* In French, one
usually uses this verb for up bowing.)
G Aufstrich *m*
I arcato in sù *f*

upper bout *n.* (of a guitar; violin, *etc.*)
—*cf.* bout; side

upright piano *n.* —*cf.* also Instru-
ments List (Keyboards)
F piano droit *m*
G Wandklavier *n*
I pianoforte verticale *m*

upstage *n.* —*cf.* also Stage List
F arrière-scène *f*
G im Hintergrund *m*
I verso il fondo *m*; verso il fondo della
scena

— V —

value *n.* —*cf. note value; rest value*

valve *n.* (of a trumpet, *etc.*) —*cf.* also *rotary valve*
F piston *m*
G Ventil *n*
I pistone *m*

variation *n.* —*cf.* also Musical Forms List
F variation *f*
G Variation *f*
I variazion *m*

variations *n. / pl* —*cf.* also Musical Forms List
F variations *f/ pl*
G Variationen *f / pl*
I variazioni *m / pl*

vein *n.* —*cf.* also Anatomy List
F veine *f*
G Vene *f*
I vena *f*

velvet *n.* —*cf.* also Instrument Repair List (Various Materials)
F velours *m*
G Samt *m*
I velluro *m*

verse *n.* (in a song) —*cf.* also Musical Forms List
F couplet *m*
G Strophe *f*
I strofetta *f*

vibraphone *n.* —*cf.* also Instruments List (Percussion Instruments)
F vibraphone *m*
G Vibraphon *n*
I vibrafono *m*

vibraphonist *n.* —*cf.* also Professions List
F vibraphoniste *m /f*
G Vibrafonspieler *m;* Vibrafonspielerin *f*
I suonatore di vibrafono *m;* suonatrice di vibrafono *f*

vibration *n.* —*cf.* also *sympathetic vibration*
F vibration *f*
G Schwingung *f*
I vibrazione *f*

vibrato *n.*
F vibrato *m*
G Vibrato *n*
I vibrato *m*

video *n.* (a visual recording, *etc.*) —*cf.* also Recording List
F vidéo *f*
G Video *n*
I video *m*

vihuela *n.* —*cf.* also Instruments List (Historic & Ethnic Instruments)
F vihuela *f*
G Vihuela *f*
I vihuela *f*

vihuelist *n.* —*cf.* also Professions List
F vihueliste *m /f*
G Vihuelist *m;* Vihuelistin *f*
I suonatore di vihuela *m;* suonatrice di vihuela *f*

villanella *n.* —*cf.* also Musical Forms List
F villanesque *f*
G Villanella *f*
I villanella *f*

¹ **viol da gamba** *n. —cf.* also
Instruments List (Historic & Ethnic
Instruments)
F viol de gambe *f*
G Viole da Gamba *f*
I viola da gamba *f*

² **viol da gambist** *n. —cf.* also
Professions List
F joueur de viol de gamba *m;* joueuse
de viol de gamba *f*
G Viole da Gamba Spieler *m;* Viole da
Gamba Spielerin *f*
I suonatore di viola da gamba *m;*
suonatrice di viola da gamba *f*

¹ **viola** *n. —cf.* also Instruments List
(Strings)
F alto *m*
G Bratsche *f*
I viola *f*

² **viola d'amore** *n. —cf.* also
Instruments List (Strings)
F viole d'amour *f*
G Liebesgeige *f*
I viola d'Amore *f*

violin *n. —cf.* also Instruments List
(Strings)
F violon *m*
G Violine *f;* Geige *f*
I violino *m*

violinist *n. —cf.* also Professions List
F violiniste *m/f*
G Violinist *m;* Violinistin *f;* Geiger *m;*
Geigerin *f*
I violinista *m/f*

violist *n. —cf.* also Professions List
F altiste *m/f*
G Bratschist *m;* Bratschistin *f*
I violista *m/f;* suonatore di viola *m;*
suonatrice di viola *f*

violoncellist *n. —cf. 'cellist;*
Professions List

violoncello *n. —cf.* also Instruments
List (Strings)
F Violoncelle *m*
G Violoncello *n*

I violoncello *m*

virginal *n. —cf.* also Instruments List
(Keyboards)
F virginal *m*
G Virginal *n*
I virginale *m*

virginalist *n. —cf.* also Professions
List
F joueur de virginal *m;* joueuse de
virginal *f*
G Virginal-spieler *m;* Virginal-spielerin
f
I suonatore di virginale *m;* suonatrice di
virginale *f*

virtuoso *n.*
F virtuose *m/f*
G Virtuose *m;* Virtuosin *f*
I virtuoso *m*

visa *n. —cf.* also Legal Subjects List
F visa *m*
G Visum *n*
I visto *m*

¹ **vocal attacks** *n. —cf.* individual
entries *(aspirated attack; glottal attack; soft
attack);* also Voice List (Vocal Attacks)

² **vocal music** *n. —cf.* also Historical
Periods & Styles List
F musique vocale *f*
G Vokalmusik *f*
I musica vocale *f*

³ **vocal types** *n. —cf.* individual
entries; also Voice List (Choral/Vocal
Types)

vocalist *n. —cf.* also Professions List;
Voice List
F vocaliste *m /f*
G Sänger *m;* Sängerin *f*
I vocalist *m /f* (more for pop music);
corista *m /f* (more for choral music)

¹ **voice** *n. —cf.* also Voice List
F voix *f*
G Stimme *f*
I voce *f*

[2] **voice control** *n.*
F contrôl du souffle *m*
G Atemtechnik *f*
I tecnica vocale *f*

[3] **voice leading** *n.* (in part-writing, *etc.*)
F conduite des voix *f*
G Stimmführung *f*
I condotta delle voci *f*

[4] **voice types** *n.* —*cf.* individual entries; Voice List (Traditional and Specialty Types)

voicing *n.* (of parts in a composition)
F partie *f*
G Stimmführung *f*
I tessitura *f*

volta *n.* —*cf.* also Musical Forms List
F volte *f*
G Volte *f*
I volta *f*

[1] **volume** *n.* (relative loudness or softness of a sound, *etc.*)
F volume *m*
G Klangfülle *f*
I volume *m*

[2] **volume** *n.* (from a collection of books, *etc.*) —*cf.* also Research List
F volume *m;* tome *m*
G Band *m*
I volume *m*

waltz *n.* —*cf.* also Musical Forms List
F valse *f*
G Walzer *m*
I valzer *m*

¹warm-up *n.* (an exercise on an instrument; voice, *etc.*)
F échauffement *m;*
G Aufwärmübung *f*
I riscaldamento *m*

²warm-up *v.* (to physically prepare to play or sing)
F échauffer; *(N.B.* In French, to warm up an instrument is *chaufer.)*
G aufwärmen
I riscaldarsi

warp *v.* —*cf.* also Instrument Repair List (Common Verbs)
F (se) gauchir
G verziehen; krümmen
I curvare

washboard *n.* —*cf.* also Instruments List (Percussion Instruments)
F washboard *m*
G Waschbrett *n*
I asse per lavare *f*

weak *adj.* (a weak beat in a measure, *etc.*) —*cf.* also ≠ *strong*
F faible
G schwach
I debole

weld *v.* —*cf.* also *solder;* Instrument Repair List (Common Verbs)
F souder
G schweißen
I saldare

whisper mute *n.* —*cf.* also Mutes List
F sourdine à calotte *f*
G Huschdämpfer *m*
I sordina hush-hush *f;* sordina hush *f*

¹whole note *n.* —*cf.* also Notes List (Rhythmic Values)
F ronde *f*
D Ganznote *f*
I intero *f* (note name) *(N.B.* In Italian, they often distinguish between the *note* itself, and the *duration* of that note. The name of the *duration* of this note is: semibreve *f.)* *Cf. whole rest.*
• *N.B.* The British name of this note is: *breve.*

²whole rest *n.* —*cf.* also Rest List
F pause *f* *(N.B.* In French, the names of the *rests* are not the same as the corresponding *notes. Cf.* Notes [individual entries and Notes List] for comparison.)
G Ganze-Pause *f*
I pausa di semibreve *f* *(N.B.* In Italian the rest is followed by the name of the note. *Ex.* "pausa di ..." [followed by value.])
• *N.B.* The British name of this rest is: *breve.*

³whole step *n.* —*cf.* also Intervals List
F un ton *m*
G Ganzton *m*
I tono *m*

⁴whole tone scale *n.* —*cf.* also Scales List
F gamme de ton entière *f*
G Ganztonleiter *f*

I scala per toni interi *f*

¹wind machine *n.* —*cf.* also Instruments List (Percussion Instruments)
F machine à vent *f*
G Windmaschine *f*
I eolifono *m;* macchina del ventro *f*

²wind music *n.* —*cf.* also Historical Periods & Styles List
F musique pour instruments à vent *f*
G Blasmusik *f*
I musica per strumenti a fiato *f*

windpipe *n.* —*cf.* also Anatomy List
F trachée *f*
G Luftröhre *f*
I trachea *f*

winds *n. / pl* (section) —*cf. woodwinds;* also Instruments List

wings *n. pl* (side portion of a stage, backstge) —*cf.* also Stage List
F coulisses *f / pl* (N.B. French normally uses the same word for "backstage" as "wings.")
G Kulisse *f*
I dietro la quinta *f / pl* (N.B. Italian normally uses the same word for "backstage" as "wings.")

¹wire *n.* —*cf.* also Instrument Repair List (Various Materials)
F fil *m*
G Draht *m*
I filo *m*

²wire brushes *n. / pl* —*cf.* also Drum Sticks List
F balais *m / pl*
G Bessen *m / pl*
I spazzole *f / pl*

¹with hard stick (wooden stick) — *cf.* also Orchestral Terms List
F baguette en bois
G mit Holzschlägel
I bacchetta di legno

²with soft stick (sponge stick) —*cf.* also Orchestral Terms List

F baguette molle
G mit Schwammschlägel
I bacchetta di spugna

³with wood of the bow —*cf.* also Orchestral Terms List
F avec le bois
G mit Holtz
I col legno

withdraw *v.* —*cf.* also Finances List
F retirer
G abheben
I prelievo

without mute —*cf.* also Orchestral Terms List
F sans sourdine
G ohne Dämpfer
I senza sordina

women's choir *n.* —*cf.* also Voice List (Choral Types)
F chœur de femmes *m*
G Frauenchor *m*
I coro femminile *m*

¹wood *n.* —*cf.* also Instrument Repair List (Various Woods)
F bois *m*
G Holz *n*
I legno *m*

²wood block *n.* —*cf.* also Instruments List (Percussion Instruments)
F bloc *m;* wood bloc *m*
G Holzkasten *m*
I wood block *m*

wooden stick *n.* —*cf.* also Drum Sticks List
F baguette de bois *f*
G Holzschlägel *m*
I bacchetta di legno *f*

woodwinds *n.* (section) —*cf.* also Instruments List
F bois *m / pl;* vents *m / pl*
G Holzbläser *n / pl*
I legni *m / pl;* fiati *m / pl*

work visa *n.* —*cf.* also Legal Subjects List

— 181 —

world premiere

F permis de travail *m*
G Arbeitsbewilligung *f*
I permesso di lavoro *m*

world premiere *n.* —*cf.* also *premier;
debut;* Concerts List
F création mondiale *f*
G Uhraufführung *f*
I prima mondiale *f*

wound (string) *adj.* —*cf.* also Strings
List
F filé
G umsponnene; umsponnene Saite
I rivestita

wrist *n.* —*cf.* also Anatomy List
F poignet *m*
G Handgelenk *n*
I polso *m*

— X —

xylophone *n.* —*cf.* also Instruments
List (Percussion Instruments)
F xylophone *m*
G Xylophon *n*
I xilofono *m*

— Y —

youth orchestra *n.*
F orchestre jeunesse *m*
G Jugendorchester *n*
I orchestra giovanile *f*

— Z —

¹**zink** *n.* —*cf.* also Instruments List
(Historic & Ethnic Instruments)
F cornet à bouzuin *m*
G Zink *m*
I cornetto *m*

²**zink** *n.* —*cf.* also Instrument Repair
List (Various Materials)
F zinc *m*
G Zink *n*
I zinco *m*

zither *n.* —*cf.* also Instruments List
(Plucked Instruments)
F zither *f*
G Zither *f*
I cetra da tavolo *f*

List of Terms Catagorized from the
Dictionary of
Contemporary Music Terms in
English, French, German and Italian

by Anthony Glise

—Contents of Lists—

— Anatomy List —
(General Terms)

anatomy *n.*
F anatomie *f*
G Anatomie *f*
I anatomia *f*

arm *n.*
F bras *m*
G Arm *m*
I braccio *m*

artery *n.*
F artère *f*
G Ader *f*
I arteria *f*

back *n.*
F dos *m*
G Rücken *m*
I schiena *f*

back of the hand *n.*
F dos de la main *m*
G Handrücken *m*
I dorso della mano *m*

belly *n.* —*cf. also stomach*
N.B. F, G and I all distinguish between "stomach" (the organ) and "belly" (the outer portion of the body), while in English we often use "stomach" for both.
F ventre *m*
G Bauch *m*
I pancia *f*

blood *n.*
F sang *m*
G Blut *n*
I sangue *m*

bone *n.*
F os *m*
G Knochen *m*
I osso *m*

cartalige *n.*
F cartilage *m*
G Knorpel *m*
I cartilagine *f*

chin *n.*
F menton *m*
G Kinn *n*
I mento *m*

ear *n.*
F oreille *f*
G Ohr *n*
I orecchio *m*

elbow *n.*
F coude *m*
G Ellbogen *m*
I gomito *m*

eye *n.*
F œil *m* (yeux *pl*)
G Auge *n* (Augen *pl*)
I occhio *m* (occhi *pl*)

face *n.*
F visage *m*
G Gesicht *n*
I faccia *f*

fingernail *n.*
F ongle *m*
G Fingernagel *m*
I unghia *f*

fingertip *n.*
F bout du doigt *m*
G Fingerspitze *f* (this is the actual tip of the finger); Fingerkuppe *f* (this is the fatty part of the fingertip)
I polpastrello *m*

foot *n.*
F pied *m*
G Fuß *m*
I piede *m*

forearm *n.*
F avant-bras *m*
G Unterarm *m*
I avambraccio *m*

hair *n.*
F cheveux *m /pl*
G Haare *n /pl*
I capelli *m /pl*

hand *n.*
F main *f*
G Hand *f*
I mano *f*

head *n.* (of the human body)
F tête *f*
G Kopf *m*
I testa *f*

heart *n.*
F cœur *m*
G Herz *n*
I cuore *m*

hip *n.*
F hanche *f*
G Hüfte *f*
I anca *f*

jaw *n.*
F mâchoire *f*
G Kiefer *m*
I mascella *f*

joint *n.*
F articulation *f*
G Gelenk *n*
I articolazione *f*

knee *n.*
F genou *m*
G Knie *n*
I ginocchio *m*

knuckle *n.*
F articulatuion *f* (~ du doigt)
G Fingergelenk *n*
I nocca *f*

larynx *n.*
F larynx *n.*
G Kehlkopf *m*
I laringe *f*

leg *n.*
F jambe *f*
G Bein *n*
I gamba *f*

lip *n.*
F lèvre *f*
G Lippe *f*
I labbro *m*

lungs *n. / pl*
F poumons *m /pl*
G Lungen *f /pl*
I polmoni *m /pl*

muscle *n.*
F muscle *m*
G Muskel *m*
I muscolo *m*

nerve *n.*
F nerf *m*
G Nerv *m*
I nervo *m*

node *n.* (on a singer's vocal chords; on a tendon, *etc.*)
F nœd *m*
G Knoten *m*
I nodulo *m*

nose *n.*
F nez *m*
G Nase *f*
I naso *m*

palate *n.*
F palais *m*
G Gaumen *m*
I palato *m*

palm *n.* (of the hand)
F paume *f*; paume de la main *f*
G Handfläche *f*
I palmo *m*; palmo della mano *m*

phlange *n.* (*i.e.* joint)
F phalange *f*
G Fingerknochen *m*
I falange *f*

pulse *n.*
F pouls *m*
G Puls *m*
I polso *m*

rib *n.*
F côte *f*
G Rippe *f*

—Cadence List—

I costola f

shoulder n.
F épaule f
G Schulter f
I spalla f

stomach n. —cf. also *belly*
N.B. F, G and I all distinguish between "stomach" (the organ) and "belly" (the outer portion of the body), while in English we often use "stomach" for both.
F estomac m
G Magen m
I stomaco m

teeth n. / pl
F dents f / pl
G Zähne m / pl
I denti m / pl

tendon n.
F tendon m
G Sehne f
I tendine m

tendon sheath n.
F gaine f
G Sehnenscheide f
I guaina f

tendonitis n.
F tendinite f
G Sehnescheidenetzündung f
I tendinite f

thorax n.
F thorax m
G Brustkorb m
I torace m

throat n.
F gorge f
G Kehle f
I gola f

vein n.
F veine f
G Vene f
I vena f

windpipe n.

F trachée f
G Luftröhre f
I trachea f

wrist n.
F poignet m
G Handgelenk n
I polso m

thumb n.
F pouce m
G Daumen m
I pollice m

index n.
F index m
G Zeigefinger m
I indice m

middle n.
F majeur m
G Mittelfinger m
I medio m

ring n.
F annulaire m
G Ringfinger m
I anulare m

little n.
F petit doigt m; auriculaire m
G kleiner Finger m
I mignolo m

authentic cadence —cf. also *perfect cadence*
F cadence parfaite f
G authentischer Schluß m; Voll Kadenz f
I cadenza autentica f

cadence n.
F cadence f
G Kadenz f; Schluß m
I cadenza f

deceptive cadence n.
F cadence rompue f
G Trugschluß Kadenz f (N.B. German uses the same term for a deceptive and imperfect cadence.)
I cadenza d'inganno f

half cadence n.
F demi-cadence f
G Halbschluß Kadenze f
I cadenza sospesa f

imperfect cadence n.
F cadence impartaite f
G Trugschluß Kadenz f (N.B. German uses the same term for a deceptive and imperfect cadence.)
I cadenza imperfetta f

perfect cadence (authentic cadence) n.
F cadence parfaite f
G Voll Kadenz f; authentischer Schluß m
I cadenza perfetta f

Picardy third cadence n.
F cadence Picarde f; tierce picarde f
G Pikardische Terz Kadenz f
I cadenza frigia f

plagal cadence n.
F cadence plagale f
G Plagelschluß Kadenz f
I cadenza plagale f

—Chords List—
(General Terms)

closed position *n.*
F position serrée *f*
G enge Lage *f*
I posizione stretta *f*

inversion *n.*
F renversement *m*
G Umkehrung *f*
I rivolto *m*

inverted *adj.*
F renversé
G umgekehrt
I rivolti

open position *n.*
F position large *f*
G weite Lage *f*
I posizione lata *f*

—Chords List—
(Chord Inversions)
(Listed in Order of Inversion)

root position *n.*
F état fondamental *m*
G Grundform *f*
I stato fondamentale *m*

first inversion *n.*
F premier renversement *m*
G erste Umkehrung *f*
I primo rivolto *m*

second inversion *n.*
F deuxième renversement *m*
G zweite Umkehrung *f*
I secondo rivolto *m*

third inversion *n.*
F troisième renversement *m*
G dritte Umkehrung *f*
I terzo rivolto *m*

fourth inversion *n.*
F quatrième renversement *m*
G vierte Umkehrung *f*
I quarto rivolto *m*

—Chords List—
(Chord/Scale Degree Names)
(Listed Diatonically)

tonic *n.*
F tonique *f*
G Tonika *f*
I tonica *f*

supertonic *n.*
F sus-tonique *f*
G Obertonika *f*
I sopratonica *f*

mediant *n.*
F médiante *f*
G Mediante *f*
I mediante *f*; modale *m*; caratteristica *f*

subdominant *n.*
F sous-dominante *f*
G Subdominante *f*
I sottodominante *f*

dominant *n.*
F dominante *f*
G Dominante *f*
I dominante *f*

submediant *n.*
F sus-dominante *f*
G Oberdominante *f*
I sopra dominante *f*

subtonic *n.* —*cf.* also = *leading tone*
F note sensible *f*
G Subtonika *f*
I sensibile *f*

leading tone *n.* —*cf.* also = *subtonic*
F sensible *f*; ton sensible *f*
G Leittone *m*
I sensibile *f*

secondary dominant *n.*
F dominante de passage *f*
G Zwischendominante *f*
I dominante di passaggio *f*; dominante secondaria *f*

—Clef List—*

alto clef *n.*
F clef d'ut *f*; clef d'ut troisième ligne *f*
G Altschlüssel *m*
I chiave di contralto *f*

bass clef *n.*
F clef de fa *f*; clef de fa quatrième ligne *f*
G F-Schlüssel *m*; Baß-Schlüssel *m*
I chiave di basso *f*

clef *n.*
F clef *f*
G Schlüssel *m*
I chiave *f*

soprano clef *n.*
F clef d'ut 1 *f*
G Sopranschlüssel *m*
I chiave di soprano *f*

tenor clef *n.*
F clef d'ut quatrième ligne *f*
G Tenorschlüssel *m*
I chiave di tenore *f*

treble clef *n.*
F clef de sol *f*
G G-Schlüssel *m*; Violinschlüssel *m*
I chiave di violino *f*

---

*N.B. In French, clef is normally spelled *clef*, though sometimes spelled *clé*.

Cf. also *Staff List*

— Competitions List —

award ceremony n.
F remise des prix f
G Preisverleihung f
I premiazione f

competition n.
F concours m
G Wettbewerb m
I concorso m

competition winner n.
F gagnant m; -ante f
G Preisträger m; -in f
I vincitore m; vincitrice f

competitor n.
F concurrent m; -ente f
G Teilnehmer m; -in f
I concorrente m / f

finalist n.
F finaliste m / f
G Finalist m; -in f
I finalista m / f

free piece n. (piece chosen by competitor)
F morceau de choix m
G Stück eigener Wahl m
I brano a scelta m

jury n.
F jury m
G Jury f
I giuria f

prize n. (award)
F prix m
G Preis m
I premio m

required piece n.
F morceau imposé m
G Pflichtstück m
I brano obbligatorio m

round n. (stage of a competition)
F épreuve f
G Ausscheidung f
I selezione f; fase eliminatoria f

semi-finalist n.
F demi-finaliste f
G Semifinalist m; -in f
I semi-finalista m / f

— Concerts List —

(cf. also *Stage List* for related vocabulary)

agent n.
F agent m / f; impresario m
G Manager m; -in f; Agentur f (this implies more a company than an individual)
I agente m (usually more for theater); manager m (usually more for music)

audience n.
F public m
G Publikum n
I pubblico m

Beta-blocker n.
F bloqueur-beta m
G Beta-Blocker m
I Beta bloccante m (Usually used in plural: "Beta-bloccanti.")

bow n. (at the end of a performance)
F révérence f; salutation f
G Verbeugung f
I inchino m

bow v. (to bow at the end of a concert, etc.)
F révérence f (In French, one usually "gives" or "makes" a bow: "donner / faire une révérence." The verb is rarely used.)
G (sich) verbeugen
I inchinarsi

box office n.
F guichet m
G Kasse f
I biglietteria f

concert n.
F concert m
G Konzert n
I concerto m

concert dress n. (tuxedo; gown, etc.)
F tenue de concert f
G Abendgarderobe f
I vestito da concerto m

concert fee n. (paid to performer)

critic n. (from a newspaper, etc.)
F critique m
G Kritiker m; -in f
I critica f

debut n.
F début m
G Debüt n
I debutto m

dress rehearsal n.
F générale f; répétition générale f
G Generalprobe f
I prova generale f

dressing room n.
F loge f
G Garderobe f; Künstlergarderobe f
I camerino m (Normally used in plural: "camerini" m / pl)

encore n.
F bis m
G Zugabe f
I bis m

entrance n. (entering the stage)
F entrée sur scène f
G Eintritt m
I entrata f

exit n. (from the stage)
F sortie f
G Bühnenausgang m
I uscita f

exit v. (to leave the stage)
F quitter
G abgehen
I uscire ("Egli esce da scena")

gown n. (women's concert apparel)
F robe de soirée f (Not really used—very general.)
G Abendkleid n (Not really used—very general.)
I abito di gala m (Not really used—very general.)

concert fee n. (paid to performer)
F tarif m; cachet m
G Gage f
I cachet m; onorario m

198

intermission *n.*
F pause *f*
G Pause *f*
I intervallo *m*

interview *n.*
F interview *f*
G Interview *n*
I intervista *f*

manager *n.*
F agent *m*
G Manager *m; ~in f*
I manager *m* (usually for general concert management); agente *m* (usually for theater or opera)

on stage *adj.*
F en scène
G zur Bühne
I sul palco (very general); in scena (more for theater)

ovation *n.*
F ovation *f*
G Ovation *f*
I ovazione *f*

performance rights *n.*
F droits d'exécution *m / pl*
G Aufführungsrechte *n / pl*
I diritti di esecuzione *m / pl*

performer *n.*
F exécutant *m; ~e f;* interprète *m / f*
G Interpret *m;* Künstler *m; ~in f;* Musiker *m; ~in f* (*N.B.* "Künstler" and "Musiker" are less literal, but more commonly used in music.)
I interprete *m / f*

practice *v.* —*cf. also rehearse*
F travailler
G üben
I esercitarsi, studiare

premier *n.*
F première *f*
G Erstaufführung *f*
I prima *f*

press *n.* (newspaper; the "press" used as a general term, *etc.*)

F presse *f*
G Presse *f*
I stampa *f*

press agent *n.*
F agent de presse *m / f*
G Werbeagent *m; ~in f*
I agente pubblicitario *m*

press material *n.*
F dossier de presse *m*
G Reklame *f*
I materiale stampa *m*

press release *n.*
F communiqué de presse *f*
G Pressemitteilung *f;* Verlautbarung *f;* Presse-verlautbarung *f*
I comunicato stampa *m*

press release photo *n.*
F photo de presse *f*
G Pressephoto *n*
I fotografia pubblicitaria *f*

program notes *n.*
F commentaire *m*
G Programmbeschreibung *f*
I note di sala *f / pl*

publicist *n.*
F publicitaire *m / f*
G Publicist *m; ~in f*
I agente pubblicitario *m / f*

rehearsal *n.*
F répétition *f*
G Probe *f*
I prova *f*

rehearse *v.* —*cf. also practice*
F répéter
G proben
I provare

riser *n.*
F estrade *f*
G Treppenpodium *n;* Stufenpodium *n*
I pedana *f*

sold out *n.*
F épuisé

G ausverkauft
I esaurito

sponsor *n.*
F sponsor *m*
G Sponsor *m; ~in f;* Förder *m* (no *f* form)
I sponsor *m*

stage *n.*
F scène *f*
G Bühne *f*
I palcoscenico *m*

stage *v.*
F mettre (mettre une pièce sur la scène)
G setzen (in Szene setzen); veranstalten
I mettere (mettere in scena)

substitute *n.* (sub. *sl*)
F remplaçant *m; ~ante f*
G Ersatzspieler *m; ~in f; (N.B.* The verb "einspringen" is usually used in this case)
I sostituto *m; ~a f*

tie *n.* (bow tie for tuxedo)
F nœud papillon *m*
G Fliege *f*
I farfallino *m;* papillon *m*

tranquilizer *n.* (medication)
F tranquillisant *m*
G Beruhigungstablette *f*
I calmante *m*

tuxedo *n.* (man's concert dress)
F smoking *m* (without tails); queue-depie *f* (with tails)
G Smoking *m* (without tails); Frack *m* (with tails)
I smoking *m* (without tails); frack *m* (with tails)

world premier *n.*
F création mondiale *f*
G Uhrauffführung *f*
I prima mondiale *f*

— Drum Sticks List —

drum stick *n.*
F baguette *f*
G Schlegel *m*
I bacchetta *f*

felt stick *n.*
F baguette de feutre *f*
G Filzschlegel *m*
I bacchetta di feltro *f*

hammer *n.*
F marteau *m*
G Hammer *m*
I martello *m*

leather stick *n.*
F baguette de cuir *f*
G Lederschlegel *m*
I bacchetta di cuoio *f*

mallet *n.*
F mailloche *f*
G Schlegel *m*
I mazza *f*

padded stick *n.*
F baguette rembourrée *f*
G wattierter Schlegel *m*
I bacchetta imbottita *f*

soft stick *n.*
F baguette d'éponge *f*
G Schwammschlegel *m*
I bacchetta di spugna *f*

timpani stick *n.*
F baguette de timbales *f*
G Paukenschlegel *m*
I bacchetta per timpani *f*

wire brushes *n. / pl*
F balais *m / pl*
G Bessen *m / pl*
I spazzole *f / pl*

wooden stick *n.*
F baguette de bois *f*
G Holzschlegel *m*
I bacchetta di legno *f*

— Finances List —

bank account *n.*
F compte *m*; compte en banque *m*
G Konto *n*
I conto bancario *m*

bank card *n.* (This exists less in the U.S., but is very common in Europe. In the U.S. it is usually referred to as a "debit card." It is used exactly like a credit card, but the billing is automatically debited to your bank account.
F carte bancaire *f*; Carte Bleue *f* (trade name)
G EC-Karte *f* (trade name)
I carta bancomat *f*

bounce *v.* / *sl.* (a check)
F faire un chèque en bois *sl.* (to make a wooden check)
G platzen *sl.* (to explode a check)
I assegno scoperto *m* / *sl.*

budget *n.*
F budget *m*
G Haushaltsplan *n*; Budget *n*
I buget *f*

check *n.*
F chèque *m*
G Scheck *m*
I assegno *m*

credit card *n.*
F carte de crédit *f*
G Kreditkarte *f*
I carta di credito *f*

deposit *n.*
F dépôt *m*
G Anzahlung *f*
I deposito *m*

interest *n.* (accrued from a bank account, *etc.*)
F intérêts *m* / *pl*
G Zinsen *m* / *pl*
I interesse *m* / *pl*

overdraw *v.* (an account) —*cf.* also *bounce* (a check)

F mettre à découvert
G überziehen
I trarre allo scoperto

statement *n.* (bank statement)
F relevé (~ de compte bancaire) *m*
G Kontoauszug *m*
I saldo *m*

transfer *n.* (of money from one account to another)
F transfert *m*
G Überweisung *f*
I bonifico *m*

withdraw *v.*
F retirer
G abheben
I prelievo

— Form List —

antecedent (phrase) *n.* —*cf.* also *consequent*
F antécédent *m*
G Dux *m*
I antecedente *m*

binary form *n.*
F forme binaire *f*
G zweiteilige Form *f*
I forma binaria *f*

coda *n.*
F coda *f*
G Koda *f* (in-general); Reprise *f* (in Sonata-allegro form)
I coda *f*

consequent (phrase) *n.* —*cf.* also *antecedent*
F conséquent *f*
G Comes *m*
I conseguente *m*

cyclic form *n.*
F forme cyclique *f*
G zyklische Form *f*
I forma ciclica *f*

development *n.*
F développement *m*
G Durchführung *f*
I sviluppo *m*

episode *n.*
F épisode *m*
G Episode *f*
I episodio *m*

exposition *n.*
F exposition *f*
G Exposition *f*
I esposizione *f*

form *n.* (musical)
F forme *f*
G Form *f*
I forma *f*

germ *n.* (small motive, *etc.*)
G germe *m*

— Form List —

G Keim *m*
I cellula *f*

period *n.*
F période *f*
G Periode *f*
I periodo *m*

phrase *n.*
F phrase *f*
G Phrase *f*
I frase *f*

recapitulation *n.*
F réexposition *f*
G Reprise *f*
I riesposizione *f*

sequence *n.*
F séquence *f*
G Sequenz *f*; Folge *f*
I sequenza *f*

song form —*cf.* *three-part song form*; *two-part song form*

ternary form *n.*
F forme ternaire *f*
G dreiteilige Form *f*
I forma ternaria *f*

three-part song form *n.*
F lied in trois parties *f*
G dreiteilige Liedform *f*
I canzone in forma tripartita *f*

through-composed *adj.*
F form ouverte
G durchkomponiert
I forma aperta

two-part song form *n.*
F lied in deux parties *f*
G zweiteilige Liedform *f*
I canzone in forma bipartita *f*

— Groupings List —

quintuplet *n.*
F quintolet *m*
G Quintole *f*
I quintina *f*

septuplet *n.*
F septolet *m*
G Septole *f*
I sittimina *f*

sextuplet *n.*
F sextlet *m*
G Sextole *f*
I sestina *f*

triplet *n.*
F triolet *m*
G Triole *f*
I terzina *f*

—Historical Periods & Styles List—

aleatoric music *n.*
F musique aléatoire *f*
G aleatorische Musik *f*
I musica aleatoria *f*

avant garde music *n.*
F musique d'avant-garde *f*
G avantgardistische Musik *f*
I musica d'avanguardia *f*; musica d'AvanGuardia *f*

ballet music *n.*
F musique de ballet *f*
G Ballettmusik *f*
I musica per balletto *f*

Baroque *n.* (Period)
F baroque *m*
G Barock *m*
I Barocco *m*

Century *n.* (15th-Century; 16th-Century, *etc.*)
F quinzième siècle *m*; seizième siècle *m*; *etc.*
G fünfzehnte Jahrhunderts *n*; sechzehnte Jahrhunderts *n*; *etc.*
I quindicesimo secolo *m*; sedicesimo secolo *m*; *etc.*

choral music *n.*
F musique chorale *f*
G Chormusik *f*
I musica corale *f*

Classic *n.* (Period)
F classique *m*
G Klassik *f*
I Classico *m*

Contemporary (Period) *n.*
F contemporain *m*
G zeitgenössisch *adj.*
I contemporaneo *m*

contemporary music *n.*
F Musique contemporaine *f*
G zeitgenössische Musik *f*
I musica contemporanea *f*

court music *n.*
F musique de cour *f*
G Hofmusik *f*
I musica di corte *f*

dance music *n.*
F musique de danse *f*
G Tanzmusik *f*
I musica da ballo *f*

early *adj.* (as in early 19th-Century)
F au début du... (Followed by the century. *Ex.* "...au début du dix-neuvième siècle.")
G früh...(Followed by the century, but remember to keep in the proper case. *Ex.* "...frühes neunzehnte Jahrhundert.")
I inizio del... (Followed by the century. *Ex.* "...inizio del Diciannovesimo secolo"); il primo... (Followed by the century. *Ex.* "...il primo Ottocento.")

early music *n.* (general term for Medieval; Renaissance, *etc.*)
F musique ancienne *f*
G Altmusik *f*
I musica antica *f*

Expressionism *n.*
F expressionnisme *m*
G Expressionismus *m*
I Espressionismo *m*

expressionistic *adj.*
F expressionnistique
G Expressionistisch
I esspressionistico *m* (usualy used in Italian as a noun.)

film music *n.*
F musique de film *f*
G Filmmusik *f*
I musica per film *f*

historical period *n.*
F époque *f*
G Epoche *f*
I epoca *f*; periodo *m*

Impressionism *n.*
F impressionnisme *m*
G Impressionismus *m*
I Impressionismo *m*

impressionistic *adj.*
F impressionnistique
G Impressionistisch
I impressionistico *m* (usually used in Italian as a noun)

incidental music *n.*
F musique de scène *f*
G Bühnenmusik *f*
I musica di scena *f*

instrumental music *n.*
F musique instrumentale *f*
G Instrumentalmusik *f*
I musica strumentale *f*

late *adj.* (as in late 19th-Century, *etc.*)
F à la fin du... siècle (Followed by the century. *Ex.* "...à la fin du dix-neuvième siècle.")
G späte (Followed by the century, but remember to keep in the proper case. *Ex.* "...spätes neunzehnte Jahrhundert.")
I fine del... (followed by the century. *Ex.* "...fine del Ottocento."); tarto... (followed by the century. *Ex.* "...tarto Ottocento.")

Medieval *n.* (Period)
F moyen-âge *m*
G Mittelalter *n*
I MedioEvo *m* (*N.B.* Usually spelled with capital letters, but still as one word.)

military music *n.*
F musique militaire *f*
G Militärmusik *f*
I musica militare *f*

Minimalism *n.*
F minimalisme *m*
G Minimal Music *f* (*N.B.* spelling borrowed from English)
I minimaliso *m* (musica minimalista *f*)

nationalistic *adj.*
F nationaliste
G national
I nazionalistico (scuole nazionali *m*)

program music *n.*
F musique à programme *f*
G Programmusik *f*
I musica a programma *f*

Renaissance n. (Period)
F Renaissance f
G Renaissance f
I Rinascimento m

Rococo n. (Period)
F rococo m
G Rokoko n
I Rococò m

Romantic n. (Period)
F romantique m
G Romantik f
I Romantico m

salon music n.
F musique de salon f
G Salonmusik f
I musica da salotto f

serial music n. (12-tone music)
F musique sérielle f
G serielle Musik f
I musica seriale f

table music n.
F musique de table f
G Tafelmusik f
I musica da tavola f

vocal music n.
F musique vocale f
G Vokalmusik f
I musica vocale f

wind music n.
F musique pour instruments à vent f
G Blasmusik f
I musica per strumenti a fiato f

— **Instrument Repair List** —
(General Terms)

brace n. (a support in an instrument)
F contre-éclisse f
G Balken m; Sturz f
I catena f

builder n. N.B. All three languages distinguish between a "luthier" (someone who makes smaller instruments, i.e. violin; guitar) and a "builder" (someone who makes larger instruments i.e. piano; organ).
F facteur m / f (Usually followed with instrument, ex. facteur d'orgue.)
G Bauer m; ~in f (Usually preceeded with instrument, ex. Klavierbauer, etc.)
I costruttore m / f (Usually followed with instrument, ex. costruttore di pianoforti, etc.)

cane n. (used to make reeds)
F roseau m
G Rohr n
I canna f

clamp n.
F serre-joint m
G Klammer f
I morsa f

crack n.
F fissure f (small); font f (large)
G Riß m
I fessura f

glue n.
F colle f
G Leim m; Klebstoff m
I colla f

grain n. (of wood)
F grain m
G Maserung f
I venatura f

inlay n. (ornamentation on the wood of an instrument, etc.)
F marqueterie f
G Einlegearbeit f; Intarsie f
I intarsio m

lacquer n.
F laque m
G Lack m
I lacca f

lamination n. (layering of wood)
F lamination f
G Schichtung f
I (Used more as a verb. Ex. "Incollare degli strati di legno.") laminazione f (more for metal)

luthier n. N.B. All three languages distinguish between a "luthier" (someone who makes smaller instruments, i.e. violin; guitar) and a "builder" (someone who makes larger instruments i.e. piano; organ).
F luthier m
G Baumeister m; ~in f (Usually preceeded with instrument, ex. Gitarrenbaumeister, etc.)
I liutaio m

polish n.
F crème à polir f; pâte à polir" f
G Poliermittel n
I cera f

purfling n. (around the edge of an instrument)
F filet m
G Randeinlage f
I filetto m

seam n. (between two pieces of wood; metal, etc.)
F couture f
G Naht f
I giunzione f

shim n. (under bridge, etc.)
F taquet m
G Ausgleichplättchen n; Ausgleichsscheibe f
I spessore m

side n. (the side of a violin; guitar, etc.)
F côté m
G Zarge f
I fascia f

solid adj. (i.e. not laminated wood)
F massif
G massiv
I massiccio

spring n.
F ressort m
G Sprung m
I molla f

twist n. (of a neck, etc.)
F gauchissement m
G Verwindung f; Krümmung f
I torsione f (but "twisted" is "storto" adj. ("a twisted neck" — "manico storto")

bend *v.*
F dévier
G biegen
I piegare

brace *v.*
F consolider
G stützen
I irrobustire

break *v.*
F casser
G zerbrechen; zerreißen
I rompere

buzz *v.*
F sourdonner
G summen
I vibrare

carve *v.*
F sculpter
G schneiden; schnitten
I intagliare

clamp *v.*
F agrafer
G klammern; festklammern
I stringere

clean *v.*
F nettoyer
G reinigen
I pulire

engrave *v.*
F graver
G gravieren
I cesellare

fix *v.*
F réparer
G befestigen
I riparare

glue *v.*

F coller
G leimen; kleben
I incollare

inlay *v.*
F marqueter
G einlegen
I inserire

lacquer *v.*
F laquer
G lackieren
I laccare

laminate *v.*
F lamifier
G laminieren
I incollare ("Incollare degli strati di legno.")

polish *v.*
F polir
G polieren
I lucidare

rattle *v.*
F trembler; vibrer
G scheppern
I vibrare

reinforce *v.*
F rentorcer
G verstärken
I rinforzare

sand *v.*
F poncer
G schmirgeln
I scantzvetrare

solder *v.*
F souder
G löten
I saldare

stain *v.*
F teinter
G färben
I trattare (trattare il legno con un mordente)

warp *v.*

F (se) gauchir
G verziehen; krümmen
I curvare

weld *v.*
F souder
G schweißen
I saldare

brass *n.*
F cuivre *m*
G Messing *n*
I ottone *m*

ceramic *n.*
F céramique *f*
G Keramik *f*
I ceramica *f*

copper *n.*
F cuivre *m*; cuivre rouge *m*
G Kupfer *n*
I bronzo *f*

cork *n.*
F liège *m*
G Kork *m*
I sughero *m*

cork grease *n.*
F graisse *f*
G Korkfett *n*
I grasso di sughero *m*

felt *n.*
F feutre *m*
G Filz *m*
I feltro *m*

fiberglass *n.*
F fibre de verre *f*
G Glasswolle *f*
I fibra di vetro *f*

German silver *n.*
F argentan *m*
G Neusilber *n*
I alpacca *f*

gold *n.*
F or *m*
G Gold *n*
I oro *m*

gold plated *adj.* —*f. plated (gold)*

ivory n.
F ivoire m
G Elfenbein n
I avorio m

leather n.
F cuir m
G Leder n
I cuoio m

metal n.
F métal m
G Metall n
I metallo m

mother of pearl n.
F nacre f
G Perlmutt n
I madre perla f

oil n.
F huile f
G Öl n
I olio m

plastic n.
F plastique m
G Plastik n; Kunststoff m
I plastica f

[1] **plated (gold plated)** adj.
F plaqué d'or
G vergoldet
I placcato oro

[2] **plated (silver plated)** adj.
F plaqué argenture
G versilbert
I placcato in argento

resin n.
F résine f
G Harz n
I resina f

silver n.
F argent m
G Silber n
I argento m

silver plated adj. —cf. plated (silver)

velvet n.
F velours m
G Samt m
I velluro m

wire n.
F fil m
G Draht m
I filo m

wood n.
F bois m
G Holz n
I legno m

zink n.
F zinc m
G Zink n
I zinco m

ash n.
F frêne m
G Esche n; (~nholz n)
I frassino m

beech n.
F hêtre m
G Buche n; (~nholz n)
I faggio m

birch n.
F bouleau m
G Birke n; (~nholz n)
I betulla f

cedar n.
F cèdre m
G Zeder n; (~nholz n)
I cedro m

ebony n.
F ébène f
G Eben n; (~nholz n)
I ebano m

mahogany n.
F acajou m
G Mahagoni n; (~holz n)
I mogano m

maple n.
F érable m
G Ahorn n; (~holz n)
I acero m

oak n.
F chêne m
G Eiche n; (~nholz n)
I quercia f

pine n.
F pin m
G Kiefer n; (~nholz n)
I pino m

rosewood n.
F bois de rose m
G Rosenholz n
I palissandro m

spruce n.
F sapin m
G Fichte f; (~nholz n)
I abete m

—Instruments List—
(Woodwinds)

Often the names for instruments are kept in Italian (ex. piccolo is normally called "piccolo" in all three languages [with the same spelling], but for precision and gender qualification, the translated name is given. A safe option if you need to use a name, is to use the Italian name first and as a "back-up" know the native term.

alto clarinet *n.*
F clarinette alto *f*
G Altklarinette *f*
I clarinetto contralto *m*

bass clarinet *n.*
F clarinette basse *f*
G Baßklarinette *f*
I clarinetto basso *m*

basset-horn *n.*
F cor de basset *m*
G Bassetthorn *m*
I corno di bassetto *m*

bassoon *n.*
F basson *m*
G Fagott *m*
I fagotto *m*

clarinet *n.*
F clarinette *f*
G Klarinette *f*
I clarinetto *m*

contra bassoon *n.*
F contrebasson *m*
G Kontrafagott *n*
I controfagotto *m*

double bass clarinet *n.*
F clarinette contrebasse *f*
G Kontrabaßklarinette *f*
I clarinetto contrabbasso *m*

english horn *n.*
F cor anglais *m*
G Englisch Horn *n*
I corno inglese *m*

euphonium *n.*
F euphonium *m*
G Baritonhorn *m*
I bombardino *m*

flugelhorn *n.*
F flicorne *m*
G Flügelhorn *n*
I flicorno *m*

flute *n.*
F flûte *f*
G Flöte *f*
I flauto *m*

heckelphone *n.*
F heckelphone *m*
G Heckelphon *n*
I heckelphon *m*

oboe *n.*
F hautbois *m*
G Oboe *f*
I oboe *m*

oboe d'amore *n.*
F hautbois d'amour *m*
G Oboe d'amoure *f*
I oboe d'amore *m*

piccolo *n.*
F piccolo *m*; petite flûte *f*
G Pikkolo (–Flöte) *f*
I flauto piccolo *m*; ottavino *m*

saxophone *n.*
F saxophone *m*
G Saxophon *n*
I sassofono *m*

soprano clarinet *n.*
F petite clarinette *f*
G kleine Klarinette *f*
I clarinetto piccolo *m*

woodwinds *n.* / *pl*
F bois *m* / *pl*; vents *m* /*pl*
G Holzbläser *m* /*pl*
I legni *m* / *pl*; fiati *m* / *pl*

—Instruments List—
(Brass Instruments)

brass instruments *n.*/*pl*
F cuivres *m* /*pl*
G Blechinstrumente *m* / *pl*
I ottoni *m* / *pl*

cornet *n.*
F cornet *m*
G Kornett *n*
I cornetta *f* (Don't confuse with the Renaissance instrument, "cornetto," *m* or "zink" in English.)

(French) horn *n.*
F cor *m*
G Horn *n*
I corno *m*

piccolo trumpet *n.*
F clarino *m*
G Bach-Trompette *f*
I clarino *m*

sousaphone *n.*
F sousaphone *m*
G Sousaphon *m*
I sousafono *m*

trombone *n.*
F trombone *m*
G Posaune *f*
I trombone *m*

trumpet *n.*
F trompette *f*
G Trompete *f*
I tromba *f*

tuba *n.*
F tuba *m*
G Tuba *f*
I tuba *f*

—Instruments List—
(Percussion Instruments)

antique cymbal *n.*
F cymbale antique *f*
G Antike Zimbel *f*
I cimbal *m*

anvil *n.*
F enclume *f*
G Amboß *m*
I incudine *f*

bass drum *n.*
F grosse caisse *f*
G Große Trommel *f*
I gran cassa *f*

bells (chimes) *n.* / *pl*
F cloches *f* /*pl*
G Glocken *f* /*pl*
I campane *f* /*pl*

bones *n.*
F tablette *f*
G Brettchenklapper *f*
I tavoletta *f*

bongo *n.*
F bongo *m*; tambour bongo *m*
G Bongo *n*
I bongo *m*

bull roarer *n.*
F planchette ronflante *f*
G Schwirrholz *n*
I legno frullante *m*

castanets *n.* /*pl*
F castagnettes *f* /*pl*
G Kastagnetten *f* /*pl*
I castagnette *f* / *pl*; nacchere *f* /*pl*

celesta *n.*
F célesta *m*
G Celesta *f*
I celesta *f*

chains *n.* / *pl*
F chaines *f* / *pl*
G Ketten *f* /*pl*
I catene *f* /*pl*

chromatic timpani *n. / pl*
F timbales chromatiques *f / pl*
G chromatische Pauken *f /pl*
I timpani cromatici *m / pl*

claves *n. / pl*
F claves *f / pl*
G Holzstäbe *m / pl*
I claves *f / pl*

cowbell *n.*
F cloche de vache *f*
G Herdenglocken *f*
I campanaccio *m*

cymbal *n.*
F cymbale *f*
G Becken *n*
I piatto *m*

field drum *n.*
F tambour *m*
G Rührtrommel *f*
I tamburo *m*

flexatone *n.*
F flexaton *m*
G Flexaton *n*
I flexaton *m*

fog horn *n.*
F sirène de brume *f*
G Nebelhorn *n*
I corno da nebbia *m*

glass harmonica *n.*
F harmonica de verres *f*
G Glasharmonika *f*
I armonica a vetro *f*

glockenspiel *n.*
F carillon *m*; glockenspiel *m*
G Glockenspiel *n*
I campanelli *m / pl*; glockenspiel *m / pl*

gong *n.*
F gong *m*
G Gong *m*
I gong *m*

guiro *n. —cf. scraper*

handbell *n.*
F clochette *f*
G Handglocke *f*
I campanello *m*

harp *n.*
F harpe *f*
G Harfe *f*
I arpa *f*

hi-hat *n.*
F hi-hat *f*; pédale hi-hat *f*
G Hi-hat *f*
I charleston *m*

jew's harp *n.*
F guimbarde *f*
G Maultrommel *f*
I scacciapensieri *m*

kazoo *n.*
F mirliton *m*
G Mirliton *m*
I kazoo *m*

maracas *n. / pl*
F maracas *m / pl*
G Maracas *f / pl*
I maracas *f / pl*

marimba *n.*
F marimba *m*
G Marimba *n*
I marimba *f*

musical saw *n.*
F scie musicale *f*
G singende Säge *f*
I sega *f*

percussion instruments *n. / pl*
F batterie *f / pl*
G Schlagzeug *n. / pl*
I percussione *f / pl*

rattle (ratchet) *n.*
F crécelle *f*
G Ratsche *f*
I raganella *f*

scraper (guiro) *n.*
F guiro *m*

G Guiro *m*
I guiro *m*

shaker *n.*
F batteur *m*
G Schüttelrohr *n*
I shaker *m*

siren *n.*
F sirène *f*
G Sirene *f*
I sirena *f*

slapstick *n.*
F fouet *m*
G Peitsche *f*
I frusta *f*

sleighbells *n. / pl*
F grelots *m / pl*
G Schellen *f / pl*
I sonagliere *f / pl*

snare drum *n.*
F caisse claire *f*
G Kleine Trommel *f*
I tamburo *m*; tamburo rullante *m*

steel drum *n.*
F steel-drum *m*
G Steel-Drum *f*
I tamburo di latta *m*

steel plate *n.*
F feuille d'acier *f*
G Stahlplatte *f*
I lastra *f*

suspended cymbal *n.*
F cymbale suspendu *f*
G hängendes Becken *n*
I piatto sospeso *m*

tabor *n.*
F tambour de provence *m*
G Tambourin *n*
I tamburino provenzale *m*

tambourine *n.*
F tambour de Basque *m*
G Tambourin *n*
I tamburino basco *m*

temple block *n.*
F templebloc *m*
G Tempelblock *m*
I block cinese *m*

tenor drum *n.*
F caisse roulante *f*
G Rührtrommel *f*
I tamburo rullante *m*

thunder machine *n.*
F machine pour le tonnerre *f*
G Donnermaschine *f*
I macchina per il tuono *f*

timpani *n.*
F timbales *m / pl*
G Pauken *f / pl*
I timpani *m / pl*

triangle *n.*
F triangle *m*
G Triangel *m*
I triangolo *m*

tubular bells *n. / pl*
F cloches tubulaires *f / pl*
G Röhrenglocken *f / pl*
I campane tubolari *f / pl*

vibraphone *n.*
F vibraphone *f*
G Vibraphon *n*
I vibrafono *m*

washboard *n.*
F washboard *m*
G Waschbrett *n*
I asse per lavare *f*

wind machine *n.*
F machine à vent *f*
G Windmaschine *f*
I macchina del vento *f*; eolifono *m*

wood block *n.*
F wood bloc *m*; bloc *m*
G Holzkasten *m*
I wood block *m*

xylophone *n.*
F xylophone *m*

G Xylophon n
I xilófono m

—Instruments List— (String Instruments List)

double bass n.
F contre basse f
G Kontrabaß m
I contrabbasso m

strings n. / pl
F cordes f / pl
G Streicher n / pl
I archi m / pl

viola n.
F alto m
G Bratsche f
I viola f

viola d'amore n.
F viole d'amour f
G Liebesgeige f
I viola d'Amore f

violin n.
F violon m
G Violine f; Geige f
I violino m

violoncello n.
F violoncelle m
G Violoncell n
I violoncello m

—Instruments List— (Keyboard Instruments List)

baby grand (piano) n.
F crapaud m
G Stutzflügel m
I pianoforte a un quarto di coda m

clavichord n.
F clavicorde m
G Klavichord n
I clavicordo m

grand piano n.
F piano à queue m
G Flügel m
I pianoforte a coda m

harmonium n.
F harmonium m
G Harmonium n
I harmonium m

harpsichord n.
F clavecin m
G Cembalo n
I cembalo m

keyboards n. / pl
F claviers m / pl
G Tasteninstrumente n / pl
I strumenti a tastiera m / pl

organ n.
F orgue m
G Orgel f
I organo m

piano n.
F piano m
G Klavier n
I pianoforte m

player piano n.
F piano mécanique m
G Pianola n
I pianola f

spinet n.
F épinette f
G Spinett n
I spinetta f

upright piano n.
F piano droit m
G Wandklavier n
I pianoforte verticale m

virginal n.
F virginal m
G Virginal n
I virginale m

—Instruments List — (Historic & Ethnic Instruments List)

accordion n.
F accordéon m
G Ziehharmonika f
I fisarmonica f

alphorn n.
F cor des Alpes m
G Alphorn n
I Alphorn m

archlute n.
F archiluth m
G Erzlaute f
I arciliuto m

bagpipe n.
F cornemuse f
G Dudelsack m
I cornamusa f

baroque guitar n.
F guitare Baroque f
G Barok Gitarre f
I chitarra Barocca f

barrel organ n. (organ grinder's organ)
F orgue de Barbarie m
G Drehorgel f
I organetto di Barberia m; organetto m

cittern n.
F cistre m
G Cister f
I cetra f

crumhorn n.
F cromorne m
G Krummhorn n
I cromorno m

dulcian n.
F douçaine f
G Dulzian m
I dulciana f

dulcimer n.
F tympanon m
G Hackbrett n
I salterio tedesco m

forte piano n.
F piano-forte m
G Fortepiano m
I forte-piano m

helicon n.
F helicon m
G Helikon n
I helicon m

hurdygurdy n.
F vielle à roue f
G Dreleier f
I organino m

lute n.
F luth m
G Laute f
I liuto m

lyre n.
F lyre f
G Leier f
I lira f

natural horn n.
F cor de chasse m
G Jagdhorn n
I corno di caccia m

ocarina n.
F ocarina m
G Okarina f
I ocarina f

panpipes n.
F flûte de Pan f
G Panflöte f
I flauto di pan m

portative organ n.
F orgue portatif m
G Portativ n
I organo portativo m

racket n.
F racket m
G Rankett n
I rankett m

rebec n.
F rebec m
G Rebec m
I ribecca f

recorder n.
F flûte à bec f
G Blockflöte f
I flauto dolce m

sackbut n.
F sackbut m
G Sackbut f
I sackbut m

serpent n.
F serpent m
G Serpent m
I serpentone m

shawm n.
F chalumeau m
G Schalmei f
I cennamella f; ciaramella f

sordun n.
F sordun m
G Sordun m
I sordone m

vihuela n.
F vihuela f
G Vihuela f
I vihuela f

viol da gamba n.
F viol de gambe f
G Viole da Gamba f
I viola da gamba f

zink n.
F cornet à bouquin m
G Zink m
I cornetto m

—Instruments List — (Plucked Instruments)

guitar n.
F guitare f
G Gitarre f
I chitarra f

mandolin n.
F mandoline f
G Mandoline f
I mandolino m

zither n.
F zither f
G Zither f
I cetra da tavolo f

—Intervals List— (General List)

augmentation n.
F augmentation f
G Vergrößerung f
I eccedente adj. (For intervals, one usually says "eccedente," but modifying the noun "intervallo," i.e. "intervalo accendente."); aumento m (for rhythmic augmentation)

augmented adj. (intervals; chords, etc.)
F augmenté
G übermäßig
I eccedente

diminished adj. (intervals; chords, etc.)
F diminué
G vermindert
I diminuito

diminution n. (intervals; chords, etc.)
F diminution f
G Verkleinerung f
I diminuito adj. (For intervals, one usually says "diminuito," but modifying the noun "intervallo," i.e. "intervalo diminuito."); diminuzione f (for rhythmic diminution)

half step n.
F demi-ton m
G Halbton m
I semitono m

major adj. (intervals; chords, etc.)
F majeur
G groß
I maggiore

minor adj. (intervals; chords, etc.)
F mineur
G klein
I minore

perfect adj. (intervals; chords, etc.)
F juste
G rein
I giusto

step n. (i.e. whole step; half step, etc.)

F ton m (In French, this is always qualified by the interval. Ex. "un ton;" "demi-ton," etc.).
G Ton m (In German, this is always qualified by the interval. Ex. "Ganzton," "Halbton," etc.).
I tono m (In Italian "tono" automatically means a whole step. Anything else is qualified; i.e. a "half step" is a "semitono," etc.)

whole step n.
F un ton m
G Ganzton m
I tono m

—Intervals List— (Listed by Scale Degree — Listed Diatonically)

unison (prime) n.
F unisson m
G Prim f
I unisono m

second n.
F seconde f
G Sekunde f
I seconda f

third n.
F tierce f
G Terz f
I terza f

fourth n.
F quarte f
G Quarte f
I quarta f

fifth n.
F quinte f
G Quinte f
I quinta f

sixth n.
F sixte f
G Sexte f
I sesta f

seventh n.
F septième f
G Septime f
I settima f

octave n.
F octave f
G Oktave f
I ottave f

ninth n.
F neuvième f
G None f
I nona f

tenth n.
F dixième f

G Dezime f
I decima f

eleventh n.
F onzième f
G Undezime f
I undicesima f

twelfth n.
F douzième m
G Duodezime f
I dodicesima f

thirteenth n.
F treizième m
G Tredezime f
I tredicesima f

tritone n.
F triton m
G Tritonus m
I tritono m

— Keys List —
(General)

parallel (major) *adj.* / *n.*
F parallèle (majeure parallèle *f*)
G Parallel (Paralleldurtonart *f*)
I parallela (parallela maggiore *f*)

parallel (minor) *adj.* / *n.*
F parallèle (mineure parallèle *f*)
G Parallel (Parallelmolltonart *f*)
I parallela (parallela minore *f*)

relative (major) *adj. f*
F relatif (majeure rélatif *f*)
G gleichnamige (gleichnamige Durtonart *f*)
I relativa (relativa maggiore *f*)

relative (minor) *adj. f*
F relatif (mineure rélatif *f*)
G gleichnamige (gleichnamige Molltonart *f*)
I relativa (relativa minore *f*)

— Keys List —
(Names of Key Centers — Listed Chromatically from a-flat)

N.B. In French, they word "key" (in reference to a tonality) may be spelled as "clé" *f* or the more common "clef" *f*.

a-flat major *adj.* / *n.*
F la bémol majeur *f*
G As-dur *n*
I la bemolle maggiore *m*

a-flat minor *adj. n.*
F la bémol mineur *f*
G as-moll *n*
I la bemolle minore *m*

a major *n.*
F la majeur *f*
G A-dur *n*
I la maggiore *m*

a minor *n.*
F la mineur *f*
G a-moll *n*
I la minore *m*

a-sharp major *n.*
F la dièse majeur *f*
G Ais-dur *n*
I la diesis maggiore *m*

a-sharp minor *n.*
F la dièse mineur *f*
G ais-moll *n*
I la diesis minore *m*

b-flat major *n.*
F si bémol majeur *f*
G B-dur *n*
I si bemolle maggiore *m*

b-flat minor *n.*
F si bémol mineur *f*
G b-moll *n*
I si bemolle minore *m*

b major *n.*
F si majeur *f*
G H-dur *n*
I si maggiore *m*

b minor *n.*
F si mineur *f*
G h-moll *n*
I si minore *m*

b-sharp major *n.*
F si dièse majeur *f*
G His-dur *n*
I si diesis maggiore *m*

b-sharp minor *n.*
F si dièse mineur *f*
G his-moll *n*
I si diesis minore *m*

c-flat major *n.*
F do bémol majeur *f*
G Ces-dur *n*
I do bemolle maggiore *m*

c-flat minor *n.*
F do bémol mineur *f*
G ces-moll *n*
I do bemolle minore *m*

c major *n.*
F do majeur *f*
G C-dur *n*
I do maggiore *m*

c minor *n.*
F do mineur *f*
G c-moll *n*
I do minore *m*

c-sharp major *n.*
F do dièse majeur *f*
G Cis-dur *n*
I do diesis maggiore *m*

c-sharp minor *n.*
F do dièse mineur *f*
G cis-moll *n*
I do diesis minore *m*

d-flat major *n.*
F ré bémol majeur *f*
G Des-dur *n*
I re bemolle maggiore *m*

---

d-flat minor *n.*
F ré bémol mineur *f*
G des-moll *n*
I re bemolle minore *m*

d major *n.*
F ré majeur *f*
G D-dur *n*
I re maggiore *m*

d minor *n.*
F ré mineur *f*
G d-moll *n*
I re minore *m*

d-sharp major *n.*
F ré dièse majeur *f*
G Dis-dur *n*
I re diesis maggiore *m*

d-sharp minor *n.*
F ré dièse mineur *f*
G dis-moll *n*
I re diesis minore *m*

e-flat major *n.*
F mi bémol mineur *f*
G Es-dur *n*
I mi bemolle maggiore *m*

e-flat minor *n.*
F mi bémol mineur *f*
G es-moll *n*
I mi bemolle minore *m*

e major *n.*
F mi majeur *f*
G E-dur *n*
I mi maggiore *m*

e minor *n.*
F mi mineur *f*
G e-moll *n*
I mi minore *m*

e-sharp major *n.*
F mi dièse majeur *f*
G Eis-dur *n*
I mi diesis maggiore *m*

e-sharp minor *n.*
F mi dièse mineur *f*

G eis-moll *n.*
I mi diesis minore *m*

f-flat major *n.*
F fa bémol majeur *f*
G Fes-dur *n*
I fa bemolle maggiore *m*

f-flat minor *n.*
F fa bémol mineur *f*
G fes-moll *n*
I fa bemolle minore *m*

f major *n.*
F fa majeur *f*
G F-dur *n*
I fa maggiore *m*

f minor *n.*
F fa mineur *f*
G f-moll *n*
I fa minore *m*

f-sharp major *n.*
F fa dièse majeur *f*
G Fis-dur *n*
I fa diesis maggiore *m*

f-sharp minor *n.*
F fa fièse mineur *f*
G fis-moll *n*
I fa diesis minore *m*

g-flat major *n.*
F sol bémol majeur *f*
G Ges-dur *n*
I sol bemolle maggiore *m*

g-flat minor *n.*
F sol bémol mineur *f*
G ges-moll *n*
I sol bemolle minore *m*

g major *n.*
F sol majeur *f*
G G-dur *n*
I sol maggiore *m*

g minor *n.*
F sol mineur *f*
G g-moll *n*
I sol minore *m*

g-sharp major *n.*
F sol dièse majeur *f*
G Gis-dur *n*
I sol diesis maggiore *m*

g-sharp minor *n.*
F sol dièse mineur *f*
G gis-moll *n*
I sol diesis minore *m*

— Legal Subjects List —

ambassador *n.* (in an embassy, *etc.*)
F ambassadeur *m;* ~drice *f*
G Botschafter *m;* ~in *f*
I ambasciatore *m;* ~trice *f*

consul *n.* (an official from an embassy or consulate)
F consul *m*
G Konsul *m*
I console *m / f;* funzionario del consolato *m /f*

consulate *n.* (a diplomatic office)
F consulat *m*
G Konsulat *n*
I console *n*

embassy *n.* (diplomatic office of a country, *etc.*)
F ambassade *f*
G Botschaft *f*
I ambasciata *f*

foreign police *n.*
F agent d'immigration *m*
G Fremdenpolizei *f*
I polizia *f* (general for police) (Usually you say "ufficio immigrazione," *i.e.* the office where they work.)

insurance *n.* (health; life, *etc.*)
F assurance *f*
G Versicherung *f*
I assicurazione *f*

passport *n.*
F passeport *m*
G Reisepaß *m*
I passaporto *m*

student visa *n.*
F visa d'étudiant *f*
G Studiumvisum *n*
I visto di soggiorno per studenti *m*

visa *n.*
F visa *m*
G Visum *n*
I visto *m*

work "black" *v.* (to work illegally in a country without a work visa)
F travail au noir
G Schwarzarbeiten
I lavoro in nero

work visa *n.*
F permis de travail *m*
G Arbeitsbewilligung *f*
I permesso di lavoro *m*

— Modes List —

(Listed Diatonically from the note "a")

aeolian *n.*
F éolien *m*
G Äolisch *n*
I eolio *m*

locrian *n.*
F locrien *m*
G Lokrisch *n*
I locrio *m*

ionian *n.*
F ionien *m*
G Ionisch *n*
I ionico *m*

dorian *n.*
F dorien *m*
G Dorisch *n*
I dorico *m*

phrygian *n.*
F phrygien *m*
G Phrygisch *n*
I frigio *m*

lydian *n.*
F lydien *m*
G Lydisch *n*
I lidio *m*

mixolydian *n.*
F mixolydien *m*
G Mixolydisch *n*
I misolidio *m*

hypodorian *n.*
F hypodorien *m*
G Hypodorisch *n*
I ipodorico *m*

hypophrygian *n.*
F hypophrygien *m*
G Hypophrygisch *n*
I ipofrigio *m*

hypolydian *n.*
F hypolydien *m*

G Hypolydisch *n*
I ipolidio *m*

hypomixolydian *n.*
F hypomixolydien *m*
G Hypomixolydisch *n*
I ipomisolidio *m*

hypoaeolien *n.*
F hypoéolien *m*
G Hypoäolisch *n*
I ipoeolio *m*

hypolocrian *n.*
F hypolocrien *m*
G Hypolokrisch *n*
I ipolocrio *m*

hypoionian *n.*
F hypoionien *m*
G Hypoionisch *n*
I ipoionico *m*

— Musical Forms List —

allemande *n.*
F allemande *f*
G Allemande *f*
I allemanda *f*

antiphon *n.*
F antienne *f*
G Antiphon *f*
I antifona *f*

arabesque *n.*
F arabesque *f*
G Arabeske *f*
I arabesca *f*

aria *n.*
F aria *f*
G Arie *f*
I aria *f*

bagatelle *n.*
F Bagatelle *f*
G Bagatelle *f*
I bagatella *f*

ballad *n.*
F ballade *f*
G Ballade *f*
I ballata *f*

ballet *n.*
F ballet *m*
G Ballett *m*
I balletto *m*

barcarole *n.*
F barcarolle *f*
G Barkarole *f*
I barcarola *f*

binary form *n.*
F forme binaire *f*
G zweiteilige Form *f*
I forma binaria *f*

bolero *n.*
F boléro *m*
G Bolero *m*
I bolero *m*

bourée *n.*
F bourrée *f*
G Bourrée *f*
I bourrée *f*

branle *n.*
F branle *m*
G Branle *m*
I brando *m*; branle *m*

bridal song *n.*
F chant nuptial *m*
G Brautlied *n*
I canto nuziale *m*

burlesque *n.*
F burlesque *f*
G Burleske *f*
I burlesca *f*

cabaletta *n.*
F cabalette *f*
G Cabaletta *f*
I cabaletta *f*

canary *n.*
F canarie *f*
G Canarie *f*
I canaria *f*; canario *m*

canon *n.*
F canon *m*
G Kanon *m*
I canone *m*

cantata *n.*
F cantate *f*
G Kantate *f*
I cantata *f*

canticle *n.*
F cantique *m*
G Gesang *m*
I cantico *m*

cantilena *n.*
F cantilène *f*
G Kantilene *f*
I cantilena *f*

canzone *n.*
F canzone *f*

G Kanzone f
I canzone f

canzonet n.
F canzonette f
G Kanzonette f
I canzonetta f

capriccio n.
F caprice m
G Capriccio n
I capriccio m

carol n.
F carole f
G Carole f
I carola f

cassation n.
F cassation f
G Kassation f
I cassazione f

cavatina n.
F cavatine f
G Kavatine f
I cavatina f

chaconne n.
F chaconne f
G Chaconne f
I ciaccona f

chorale n.
F choral m
G Choral m
I chorale m

Christmas carol n.
F chant de Noël m
G Weihnachtslied n
I canto di Natale m

comic opera n.
F opera buffa m (Spelling borrowed from Italian but with French gender. N.B. There is no accent for "opera" in this case.)
G komische Oper f
I opera buffa f

concerto n.
F concerto m

G Konzert n
I concerto m

concerto for orchestra n.
F concerto pour orchestre m
G Konzert für Orchester n
I concerto per orchestra m

concerto grosso n.
F concerto grosso m
G Konzerto Grosso n
I concerto grosso m

country dance n.
F contredanse f
G Kontretanz m
I contraddanza f

courante n.
F courante f
G Courante f
I corrente f

cycle n.
F cycle m
G Zyklus m
I ciclo m

dirge n.
F chant funèbre m
G Grabgesang m
I canto funebre m

divertimento n.
F divertissement m
G Divertimento n
I divertimento m

double concerto n.
F double concerto m
G Doppelkonzert n
I concerto doppio m

duet n.
F duetto m
G Duett n
I duetto m

duo n.
F duo m
G Duo n
I duo m

elegy n.
F élégie f
G Elegie f
I elegia f

epilogue n.
F épilogue m
G Epilog m
I epilogo m

estampie n.
F estampie f
G Estampie f
I estampida f

etude (study) n.
F étude f
G Etüde f
I studio m

fantasy n.
F fantaisie f
G Fantasie f
I fantasia f

finale n.
F finale m
G Finale n
I finale m

folia n.
F folia f
G Folia f
I follia f

fugue n.
F fugue f
G Fuge f
I fuga f

fughetta n.
F fughette f
G Fughette f
I fughetta f

galliard n.
F gaillarde f
G Gagliarde f
I gagliarda f

galop n.
F galop m

G Galopp m
I galoppo m

gavotte n.
F gavotte f
G Gavotte f
I gavotta f

gigue (jig) n.
F gigue f
G Gigue f
I giga f

gipsy song n.
F chant gitan m
G Zigeunerlied n
I canto gitano m

hocket n.
F hoquet m
G Hoketus m
I ochetus m; hoquetus m

humoresque n.
F humoresque f
G Humoreske f
I umoresca f

hymn n.
F hymne m
G Hymne f
I inno m

impromptu n.
F impromptu m
G Impromptu n
I improvviso m

interlude n.
F entract m; ent'acte m
G Zwischenspiel n
I interludio m

introduction n.
F introduction f
G Einleitung f
I introduzione f

invention n.
F invention f
G Invention f
I invenzione f

jig n. —cf. gigue

lament n.
F lamentation f
G Klage f
I lamento m

lay n.
F lai m
G Leich m
I lai m

lied n.
F lied m
G Lied n
I lied m

litany n.
F litanie f
G Litanei f
I litania f

liturgical drama n.
F drame liturgique m
G liturgisches Drama n
I dramma liturgico m

lullaby n.
F berceuse f
G Wiegenlied n
I ninna nanna f

madrigal n.
F madrigal m
G Madrigal n
I madrigale m

march n.
F marche f
G Marsch m
I marcia f

masque n.
F mascarade f
G Maskenspiel n
I masque f

mass n.
F messe m
G Messe f
I messa f

mazurka n.
F mazurka f
G Mazurka f
I mazurca f

melodrama n.
F mélodrame m
G Melodrama n
I melodramma m

minuet n.
F menuet m
G Menuett n
I minuetto m

morris dance n.
F mauresque f
G Moreske f
I moresca f

motet n.
F motet m
G Motette f
I mottetto m

musical comedy n.
F com édie musicale f
G Musical n
I commedia musicale f

national anthem n.
F hymne national m
G Nationalhymne f
I inno nazionale m

nocturne n.
F nocturne f
G Notturno n
I notturno m

ode n.
F ode f
G Ode f
I ode f

¹ opera n.
F opéra m
G Oper f
I opera f

² opera buffa n. —cf. comic opera

operetta n.
F opérette f
G Operette f
I operetta f

oratorio n.
F oratorio m
G Oratorium n
I oratorio m

overture n.
F ouverture f
G Ouverture f
I overture f

parody n.
F parodie f
G Parodie f
I parodia f

partita n.
F partita f
G Partita f
I partita f

passacaglia n.
F passacaille f
G Passacaglia f
I passacaglia f

passepied n.
F passepied m
G Passepied m
I passepied m

passion n.
F passion f
G Passion f
I passione f

pastorale n.
F pastorale f
G Pastorale f
I pastorale f

pavan n.
F pavane f
G Pavane f
I pavana f

perigourdine n.
F périgourdine f
G Perigourdine f
I perigordino m

plain chant n.
F plain-chant m
G Gregorianischer Gesang m
I canto gregoriano m

polka n.
F polka f
G Polka f
I polka f

polonaise n.
F polonaise f
G Polonaise f
I polacca f

postlude n.
F postlude m
G Nachspiel n
I postludio m

pot-pourri n.
F pot-pourri f
G Potpourri n
I pot-pourri m

prelude n.
F prélude m
G Präludium n
I preludio m

psalm n.
F psaume m
G Psalm m
I salmo m

quadrille n.
F quadrille f
G Quadrille f
I quadriglia f

quadruple concerto n.
F quadruple concerto m
G Quadrupelkonzert n
I concerto con quattro strumenti solisti m

ragtime n.
F ragtime m
G Ragtime m
I ragtime m

rapsody n.
F rapsodie f; rhapsodie
G Rhapsodie f
I rapsodia f

recitative n.
F récitatif m
G Rezitativ m
I recitativo m

requiem mass n.
F requiem m; messe des requiem f
G Requiem n
I messa di Requiem f

ricercar n.
F ricercare m
G Ricercar n
I ricercare m

rigadoon n.
F rigaudon m
G Rigaudon m
I rigaudon m

ritornello n.
F ritournelle f
G Ritornell n
I ritornello m

romance n.
F romance f
G Romanze f
I romanza f

rondo n.
F rondo m (rondeau)
G Rondo m
I rondò m

round n.
F ronde f
G Kanon m
I rondò f

round dance n.
F ronde f
G Reigen m
I girotondo m

sacred music n.
F musique sacrée f
G Kirchenmusik f
I musica sacra f

sarabande n.
G Sarabande f
G Sarabande f
I sarabanda f

secular music n.
F musique profane f
G weltliche Musik f
I musica profana f

serenade n.
F sérénade f
G Serenade f
I serenata f

siciliana n.
F sicilienne f
G Siziliano m
I siciliana f

singspiel m
F singspiel m
G Singspiel n
I singspiel m

sonata n.
F sonate f
G Sonate f
I sonata f

sonatina n.
F sonatine f
G Sonatine f
I sonatina f

song n.
F chanson f
G Lied n
I canzone f

study (étude) n.
G Etüde f
I studio m

suite n.
F suite f
G Suite f
I suite f

symphonic poem n.
F poème symphonique m
G sinfonische Dichtung f
I poema sinfonico m

symphony n.
F symphonie f
G Sinfonie f
I sinfonia f

tarantella n.
F tarentelle f
G Tarantella f
I tarantella f

ternary n.
F forme ternaire f
G dreiteilige Form f
I form ternaria f

theme n.
F thème m
G Thema n
I tema m

three-part song form n.
F lied en trois parties f
G dreiteilige Liedform f
I canzone in forma tripartita f

toccata n.
F toccata f
G Toccata f
I toccata f

tourdion n.
F tordion m
G Tourdion m
I tortiglione m

triple concerto n.
F triple concerto m
G Tripelkonzert n
I concerto triplo m

two-part song form n.
F lied en deux parties f
G zweiteilige Liedform f
I canzone in forma bipartita f

variation n.
F variation f
G Variation f
I variazioni f

variations n. / pl
F variations f / pl
G Variationen m / pl
I variazioni m / pl

villanella n.
F villanesque f
G Villanella f
I villanella f

volta n.
F volte f
G Volte f
I volta f

waltz n.
F valse f
G Walzer m
I valzer m

— Mutes List —
(Various Types)

cardboard mute *n.*
F sourdine en carton *f*
G Kartondämpfer *m*
I sordina di cartone *f*

double mute *n.*
F sourdine à double cône *f*
G Doppelkegeldämpfer *m*
I sordina a doppio cono *f*

hat mute *n.*
F sourdine à calotte *f*
G Hutdämpfer *m*
I sordina a cappello *f*

metal mute *n.*
F sourdine en métal *f*
G Metalldämpfer *m*
I sordina di metallo *f*

straight mute *n.*
F sourdine droite *f*
G Spitzdämpfer *m*
I sordina diritta *f*

whisper mute *n.*
F sourdine à calotte *f*
G Huschdämpfer *m*
I sordina hush *f*; sordina hush-hush *f*

— Notation List —

mensural notation *n.*
F notation mensurale *f*
G Mensuralnotation *f*
I notazione mensurale *f*

modern notation *n.*
F notation moderne *f*
G moderne Notenschrift *f*
I notazione moderna *f*

notation *n.*
F notation *f*
G Notenschrift *f*; Notation *f*
I notazione *f*

nume (neume) *n.*
F neume *m*
G Neume *f*
I neuma *m*

square notation *n.*
F notation carrée *f*
G Quadratnotenschrift *f*
I notazione quadrata *f*

— Notes List —
(Rhythmic Names)

(Listed in Order of Duration)

N.B. In French, the names of the notes are not the same as the corresponding rests. *Cf.* Rests List for comparison.

double whole note *n.* (*N.B.* British: breve)
F note carrée *f*
G Doppelganznote *f*
I breve *f N.B.* In Italian, they often distinguish between the note itself, and the duration of that note. The duration of this note in Italian is: longa *f*

whole note *n.* (*N.B.* British: semibreve)
F ronde *f*
G Ganznote *f*
I semi breve *f N.B.* In Italian, they often distinguish between the note itself, and the duration of that note. The duration of this note in Italian is: intero *f*

half note *n.* (*N.B.* British: minum)
F blanche *f*
G Halbnote *f*
I minima *f N.B.* In Italian, they often distinguish between the note itself, and the duration of that note. The duration of this note in Italian is: metà *f*

quarter note *n.* (*N.B.* British: crochet)
F noire *f*
G Viertelnote *f*
I semiminima *f N.B.* In Italian, they often distinguish between the note itself, and the duration of that note. The duration of this note in Italian is: quarto *m*

eighth note *n.* (*N.B.* British: quaver)
F croche *f*
G Achtelnote *f*
I croma *f N.B.* In Italian, they often distinguish between the note itself, and the duration of that note. The duration of this note in Italian is: ottavo *m*

sixteenth note *n.* (*N.B.* British: semiquaver)
F double croche *f*
G Sechzehntelnote *f*
I semicroma *f N.B.* In Italian, they often distinguish between the note itself, and the duration of that note. The duration of this note in Italian is: sedicesimo *m*

thirty-second note *n.* (*N.B.* British: demisemiquaver)
F triple croche *f*
G Zweiunddreißigstelnote *f*
I biscroma *f N.B.* In Italian, they often distinguish between the note itself, and the duration of that note. The duration of this note in Italian is: trentaduesimo *m*

sixty-fourth note *n.* (*N.B.* British: hemidemisemiquaver)
F quadruple croche *f*
G Vierundsechzigstelnote *f*
I semibiscroma *f N.B.* In Italian, they often distinguish between the note itself, and the duration of that note. The duration of this note in Italian is: sesantaquattresimo *m*

hundred twenty-eighth note *n.* (*N.B.* British: semihemidemisemiquaver)
F quintuple croche *f*
G Hunderdachtundzwanzigstenote *f*
I centoventottesimo *m N.B.* In Italian, they often distinguish between the note itself, and the duration of that note. The duration of this note in Italian is: centoventottesimo.

—Notes List—
(Parts of a Written Note)

beam n.
F barre f
G Notenbalken m
I linea di raggruppamento f

dot n.
F point m
G Punkt m
I punto m

double dot n.
F double point m
G Dopplepunkt m
I doppio punto m

flag n. (N.B. The British name for a flag is hook)
F drapeau m
G Notenfahne f; Fähnchen f
I codetta f

note head n.
F tête f
G Notenkopf m
I testa f (testa della nota f)

stem n.
F queue f
G Notenhals m
I gambo m

—Note Names List—
(Pitches)

(listed chromatically from a-double flat)

a-double flat n.
F la double bémol m
G ases n
I la doppio bemolle f

a-flat n.
F la bémol m
G as n
I la bemolle f

a n.
F la m
G a n
I la f

a-sharp n.
F la dièse m
G ais n
I la diesis f

a-double sharp n.
F la double dièse m
G aisis n
I la doppio diesis f

b-double flat n.
F si double bémol m
G heses n
I si doppio bemolle m

b-flat n.
F si bémol m
G b n
I si bemolle m

b n.
F si m
G h n
I si m

b-sharp n.
F si dièse m
G his n
I si diesis m

b-double sharp n.

F si double dièse m
G hisis n
I si doppio diesis m

c-double flat n.
F do double bémol m
G ceses n
I do doppio bemolle m

c-flat n.
F do bémol m
G ces n
I do bemolle m

c n.
F do m
G c n
I do m

c-sharp n.
F do dièse m
G cis n
I do diesis m

c-double sharp n.
F do double dièse m
G cisis n
I do doppio diesis m

d-double flat n.
F ré double bémol m
G deses n
I re doppio bemolle m

d-flat n.
F ré bémol m
G des n
I re bemolle m

d n.
F ré m
G d n
I re m

d-sharp n.
F ré dièse m
G dis n
I re diesis m

d-double sharp n.
F ré double dièse m
G disis n

I re doppio diesis m

e-double flat n.
F mi double bémol m
G eses n
I mi doppio bemolle m

e-flat n.
F mi bémol m
G es n
I mi bemolle m

e n.
F mi m
G e n
I mi m

e-sharp n.
F mi dièse m
G eis n
I mi diesis m

e-double sharp n.
F mi double dièse m
G eisis n
I mi doppio diesis m

f-double flat n.
F fa double bémol m
G feses n
I fa doppio bemolle f

f-flat n.
F fa bémol m
G fes n
I fa bemolle f

f n.
F fa m
G f n
I fa f

f-sharp n.
F fa dièse m
G fis n
I fa diesis f

f-double sharp n.
F fa double dièse m
G fisis n
I fa doppio diesis f

— Orchestral Terms —

g-double flat *n.*
F sol double bémol *m*
G geses *n*
I sol doppio bemolle *m*

g-flat *n.*
F sol bémol *m*
G ges *n*
I sol bemolle *m*

g *n.*
F sol *m*
G g *n*
I sol *m*

g-sharp *n.*
F sol dièse *m*
G gis *n*
I sol diesis *m*

g-double sharp *n.*
F sol double dièse *m*
G gisis *n*
I sol doppio diesis *m*

a 2 (English bastardization from the Italian —*cf.* "*divided in*…" followed by number)
F à 2
G zu 2
I a 2

at the bridge
F sur le chevalet
G am Steg
I sul ponticello

at the fingerboard
F sur la touche
G am Grifbret
I sul tasto; sulla tastiera

at the frog
F du talon
G am Frosch
I al tallone

at the point (of the bow)
F de la pointe
G an die Spitze
I punta d'arco

bells in the air
F pavillon en l'air
G Schalltrichter auf
I campane in aria

brassy *adj.*
F cuivré
G schmetternd
I metallico

desk (stand) *n.*
F pupitre
G Pult
I leggio

divided *adv.*
F divisé (div.)
G geteilt (get.)
I divisi (div.)

divided in 3
F div. à 3
G dreifach
I div. a 3

divided in 4
F div. à 4
G vierfach
I div. a 4

half (of a section)
F la moitié
G die Hälfte
I la metà

in unison
F unis
G zusammen; einfach
I unisono (unis. *abbr.*)

muted *adv.*
F sourdine (~s *pl.*)
G mit Dämpfer; gedämpft
I con sordina (~ sordini *pl.*)

normally *adv.* (after ponticello, *etc.*)
F mode ordinaire
G gewöhnlich
I modo ordinario

open *adj.*
F ouvert(~s *pl.*)
G offen
I aperto

stopped *adj.* (horns)
F bouché (~s *pl.*)
G gestopft
I chiuso

take off mutes
F enlevez les sourdines
G Dämpfer weg
I via sordini; tagliere la sordina

with hard stick (wooden stick)
F baguette en bois
G mit Holzschlegel
I bacchetta di legno

with soft stick (sponge stick)
F baguette molle
G mit Schwammschlägel
I bacchetta di spugna

with wood of the bow
F avec le bois
G mit Holtz
I col legno

without mute
F sans sourdine
G ohne Dämpfer
I senza sordina

— Professions List —

N.B. As in English, all three languages normally use a specific name for an instrumentalist (*i.e.* a "piano player" is usually called a "pianist"). However, some of the more rare instrumentalists are usually referred to as a "[instrument name...]player" (*i.e.* a "marimba player" rather than the correct, but sometimes strange-sounding "marimbist").

accompanist *n.*
F accompagnateur *m;* -trice *f*
G Begleiter *m;* ~ in *f*
I accompagnatore *m* ~trice *f*

accordionist *n.*
F accordéoniste *m f*
G Akkordionspieler *m;* ~ in *f*
I fisarmonicista *m f*

agent *n.*
F agent *m f;* impresario *m*
G Manager *m;* ~in *f;* Agentur *f* (this implies more a company than an individual)
I agente *m* (usually more for theater);
manager *m* (usually more for music)

arranger *n.*
F arrangeur *m;* -euse *f*
G Bearbeiter *m;* -in *f*
I arrangiatore *m;* -trice *f*

artist *n.*
F artiste *m f*
G Künstler *m;* -in *f*
I artista *m f*

balerina *n.* (female dancer) —*cf.* also *dancer*
F danseuse *f* (~ de ballet *f*)
G Tänzerin *f*
I ballerina *f*

ballet master *n.* / *m* (male ballet instructor)
F maître de ballet *m*
G Ballettmeister *m*
I maestro di ballo *m*

ballet mistress *n.* / *f* (female ballet instructor)
F maîtresse de ballet *f*
G Ballettmeisterin *f*
I maestra di ballo *f*

bass clarinetist *n.*
F joueur *m;* -euse *f* (~ de clarinette basse)
G Baßklarinetist *m;* -in *f*
I clarinettista *m f;* suonatore di clarinetto basso *m;* -trice di clarinetto basso *f*

bass player *n.* (double bassist)
F contrebassiste *m f*
G Kontrabaßist *m;* -in *f*
I contrabassista *m f*

bassoonist *n.*
F bassoniste *m f*
G Faggottist *m;* -in *f*
I fagottista *m f;* fagotto *m f* suonatore di fagotto *m;* -trice di fagotto *f*

builder *n.* —*cf.* also *luthier*
N.B. All three languages distinguish between a "luthier" (someone who makes smaller instruments, *i.e.* violin; guitar) and a "builder" (someone who makes larger instruments *i.e.* piano; organ).
F facteur *m f* (facteur d'orgue)
G Bauer *m;* -in *f* (Usually preceeded with instrument name, *ex.* Klavierbauer, *etc.*)
I costruttore *m f* (costruttore di pianoforti, *etc.*)

'cellist *n.*
F violoncelliste *m f*
G Cellist *m;* ~ in *f*
I violoncellista *m f;* violoncello *m f*

choreographer *n.*
F chorégraphe *m f*
G Choreograph *m;* -in *f*
I coreografo *m;* -a *f*

clarinetist *n.*
F clarinettiste *m f*
G Klarinettist *m;* ~ in *f*
I clarinettista *m f;* clarinetto *m f;* suonatore di clarinetto *m;* -trice di clarinetto *f*

coach *n.* (generally for vocalists)

composer *n.*
F compositeur *m;* -trice *f*
G Komponist *m;* -in *f*
I compositore *m f*

concertmaster *n.*
F premier violon *m f*
G Konzertmeister *m;* ~ in *f*
I primo violino *m f*

conductor *n.*
F chef d'orchestre *m f*
G Dirigent *m;* -in *f*
I direttore (~ d'orchestra *m f;* ~ di coro *m / f, etc.)*

contra bassoonist *n.*
F contrebassoniste *m f*
G Kontragottist *m;* ~in *f*
I controfagottista *m f;* controfatoggo *m f*

copyist *n.*
F copiste *m f*
G Kopist *m;* -in *f*
I copista *m f*

cornettist *n.*
F cornettiste *m f*
G Kornettist *m;* -in *f*
I cornettista *m f;* suonatore di cornetta *m;* -trice di cornetta *f*

critic *n.* (from a newspaper, *etc.*)
F critique *m f*
G Kritiker *m;* -in *f*
I critica *f*

dancer *n.*
F danseur *m;* -seuse *f*
G Tänzer *m;* -in *f*
I ballerino *m;* -a *f*

director *n.*
F régisseur *m*
G Régisseur *m;* -in *f*
I regista *m f*

double bass clarinetist *n.*

double bassist *n.* —*cf. bass player*

drummer *n. cf.* also percussionist
F bateur *m f*
G Schlagzeuger *m;* -in *f*
I batterista *m / f*

¹editor *n.* (of a musical edition, *etc.*)
F éditeur *m;* -trice *f*
G Bearbeiter *m;* -in *f*
I editore *m*

²editor *n.* (of a recording, *etc.*)
F monteur*m;* -euse *f*
G Cutter *m;* -in *f*
I tecnico del suono *m;* produttore *m*

engineer *n.* (of a recording, *etc.*)
F ingénieur *m f* (~ du son *m / f*)
G Tonmeister *m;* -in *f*
I tecnico del suono *m f*

english horn player *n.*
F joueur *m;* -euse *f* (~ de cor anglais)
G Englisch-horn Spieler *m;* -in *f*
I suonatore di corno inglese *m;* -trice di corno inglese *f*

flautist *n.* (flutist)
F flûtiste *m f*
G Flötist *m;* -in *f*
I flautista *m f;* suonatore di flauto *m;* -trice di flauto *f*

guitarist *n.*
F guitariste *m f*
G Gitarrist *m;* -in *f*
I chitarrista *m f*

harpist *n.*
F harpiste *m f*
G Harfenist *m;* -in *f*
I arpista *m f;* suonatore di arpa *m;* -trice di arpa *f*

harpsichordist n.
F claveciniste m/f
G Cembalist m; ~in f
I clavicembalista m/f

horn player n. (hornist)
F corniste m/f
G Hornist m; ~in f
I cornista m/f; corno m/f; suonatore di corno m; ~trice di corno f

instrumentalist n.
F instrumentiste m/f
G Instrumentalist m; ~in f
I strumentista m/f

librettist n.
F librettiste m/f
G Librettist m; ~in f
I librettista m/f

lutenist n.
F luthiste m/f
G Lautist m; ~in f
I liutista m/f

luthier n. —cf. also builder
N.B. All three languages distinguish between a "luthier" (someone who makes smaller instruments, *i.e.* violin; guitar) and a "builder" (someone who makes larger instruments *i.e.* piano; organ).
F luthier m
G Baumeister m; ~in f (Usually preceeded with instrument name, *ex.* Gitarrenbaumeister, *etc.*)
I liutaio m/f

manager n.
F agent m
G Manager m; ~in f
I manager m (usually for general concert management); agente m (usually for theater or opera)

mandolinist n.
F mandoliniste m/f
G Mandolinist m; ~in f
I mandolinista m/f; suonatore di mandolino m; ~trice di mandolino f

marimba player n.

F joueur m; ~euse f (~ de marimba)
G Marimba Spieler m; ~in f
I suonatore di marimba m; ~trice di marimba f

music therapist n.
F musicothérapeute m/f
G Musiktherapeut m; ~in f
I musicoterapeuta m/f

musician n.
F musicien m; ~enne f
G Musiker m; ~in f
I musicista m/f

musicologist n.
F musicologue m/f
G Musikwissenschaftler m; ~in f
I musicologo m; ~a f

narrator n.
F narateur m; ~trice f; récitant m; ~e f
G Sprecher m; ~in f; Erzähler m; ~in f
I voce recitante f; narratore m

oboist n.
F hautboiste m/f
G Oboist m; ~in f
I oboista m/f; suonatore di oboe m/f

orchestral player n.
F musicien m; ~ienne f (~ d'orchestre)
G Orchestermusiker m; ~in f
I orchestrale m/f

organist n.
F organiste m/f
G Organist m; ~in f
I organista m/f

percussionist n. cf. also drummer
F percussionniste m/f
G Schlagzeuger m; ~in f
I percussionista m/f

performer n.
F exécutant m; ~e f; interprète m/f
G Interpret m; Künstler m; ~in f; Musiker m; ~in f (N.B. "Künstler" and "Musiker" are less literal, but more commonly used in music.)
I interprete m/f

pianist n.
F pianiste m/f
G Pianist m; ~in f
I pianista m/f

press agent n.
F agent de presse m/f
G Werbeagent m; ~in f
I agente pubblicitario m

prima balerina n. /f —cf. also principle dancer m
F danseuse étoile f
G Primaballerina f
I prima ballerina f

principal dancer n. /m —cf. also prima balrina f
F danseur étoile m
G Primoballerino m
I primo ballerino m

prompter n.
F souffleur m /f
G Souffleur m; ~in f
I suggeritore m/f

producer n.
F réalisateur m; ~trice f
G Produzent m
I produttore m

professor n. —cf. also teacher Cf. important note under the entry teacher in the main part of the dictionary for clarification of these different titles.
F professeur m /f
G Professor m; ~in f
I professore m; ~a f

publicist n.
F publicitaire m/f
G Publisist m; ~in f
I pubblicista m/f

saxophonist n.
F saxophoniste m/f
G Saxophonist m; ~in f
I sassofonista m/f

singer n.
F chanteur m; ~euse f
G Sänger m; ~in f
I cantante m/f

soloist n.
F soliste m/f
G Solist m; ~in f
I solista m/f

sponsor n.
F sponsor m
G Veranstalter m; ~in f
I sponsor m

teacher n. —cf. also professor; Cf. important note under the entry teacher in the main part of the dictionary for clarification of these different titles.
F instituteur m; ~trice f; maître m; ~tresse f; (for grade school); professeur m /f (for upper level)
G Lehrer m; ~in f
I insegnante m/f (in a grade school); maestro m; ~a is used for a children's school teacher but also for anyone having to do with music or the arts; professore m; ~oressa f (for university)

timpanist n.
F timbalier n
G Pauker m; ~in f
I timpanista m/f

trombonist n.
F tromboniste m/f; trombone m/f
G Posaunist m; ~in f
I trombonista m/f; suonatore di trombone m; ~trice di trombone f

trumpeter n.
F trompette m/f; trompette m/f
G Trompeter m; ~in f
I trombettista m; ~a f; suonatore di tromba m; ~trice di tromba f

tuba player n.
F tubiste m/f
G Tubist m; ~in f; Tuba Spieler m; ~in f
I suonatore di tuba m; ~trice di tuba f

tuner n. (piano tuner, etc.)
F accordeur m; ~euse f
G Stimmer m; ~in f

I accordatore m

vibraphonist n.
F vibraphoniste m/f
G Vibrafon Spieler m; ~in f
I suonatore di vibrafono m; ~trice di vibrafono f

vihuelist n.
F vihueliste m/f
G Vihuelist m; ~in f
I suonatore di vihuela m; ~trice di vihuela f

viol da gambist n.
F joueur m; ~euse f (~ de viol de gamba)
G Viole da Gamba Spieler m; ~in f
I suonatore di viola da gamba m; ~trice di viola da gamba f

violinist n.
F violiniste m/f
G Violinist m; ~in f; Geiger m; ~in f
I violinista m/f

violist n.
F altiste m/f
G Bratschist m; ~in f
I violista m/f; suonatore di viola m; ~trice di viola f

violoncellist n. —cf. 'cellist

virginalist n.
F joueur m; ~euse f (~ de virginal)
G Virginal-spieler m; ~in f
I suonatore di virginale m; ~trice di virginale f

vocalist n.
F vocaliste m/f
G Sänger m; ~in f
I vocalist m/f (more for pop music); corista m/f (more for choral music)

— Recording List —
(General Terms)

amplifier n. (for electric guitar; sound support, etc.)
F amplificateur m; ampli m/sl
G Verstärker m
I amplificatore m

analog adj. (non-digital recording)
F analogique
G analog
I analogico

bandwidth n.
F largeur de bande f
G Bandbreite f
I larghezza di banda f

boom n. (extension for a microphone stand; lighting, etc.)
F perche f
G Galgen m (Mikrophongalgen, etc.)
I asta f

cable n. (chord for microphone, etc.)
F câble m
G Kabel n
I cavo m

cassette n.
F cassette f
G Kassette f
I cassetta f

CD n. (compact disk)
F disque compact f; CD m
G CD f
I CD m; compact disc f

channel n. (in stereo recording, etc.)
F chaîne f
G Kanal m
I canale m

compressor n.
F compresseur m
G Kompressor m
I compressore m

computer n.
F ordinateur m
G Computer m
I computer m; elaboratore m

condensor mic n. —cf. microphone list (below)

contact mic n. —cf. microphone list (below)

copy v. (to duplicate a recording; mastertape, etc.)
F faire une copie
G überspielen
I duplicare

dat (DAT) adj.
F DAT (spoken using the names of each letter or as a single word)
G DAT (spoken as a single word)
I DAT (spoken as a single word)

decibel n.
F décibel m
G Dezibel n
I decibel m

demo n. (demo recording)
F démo f
G Demo m
I demo m

digital adj.
F (enregistrement) numérique; digital
G digital
I digitale

distortion n.
F distorsion f
G Verzerrung f
I distorsione f

dub v.
F doubler
G verdoppeln
I riregistrare

edit v.
F couper
G schneiden
I montare

editor n. (of a recording, etc.)
F monteur m; ~euse f
G Cutter m; ~in f
I tecnico del suono m; produttore m/f

(electro)dynamic mic n. —cf. microphone list (below)

engineer n.
F ingénieur m; ~ du son m
G Tonmeister m
I tecnico del suono m

equalizer n.
F égalisateur m
G Entzerrer m
I equalizzatore m

erase v. (erase a tape; track, etc.)
F effacer
G löschen
I cancellare

feedback n.
F réaction f
G Rückkoppelung f
I feedback m

filter n.
F filtre m
G Filter m
I filtro m

frequency n.
F fréquence f
G Frequenz f
I frequenza f

generation n. (of a recording)
F génération f
G Generation f
I generazione f

generator n.
F générateur m
G Generator m
I generatore m

headphone n.
F casque m
G Kopfhörer m
I cuffia f

input n.
F entrée f
G Eingang m
I entrata f

jack n. (end of a cable plugged into amplifier, etc.)
F fiche f; prise "jack" f / sl; fiche "jack" f / sl
G Stecker m
I spinotto m

label n. (record company)
F maison de disque f
G Aufnahmegesellschaft f
I casa discografica f

level n.
F niveau m
G Pegel m
I livello m

limiter n.
F limiteur m
G Begrenzer m
I limitatore m

live adj. (radio or television broadcast) — cf. also pre-recorded
F en direct; live
G live (followed by name of source in German, ex. Live-Sendung, etc.)
I dal vivo; live; in diretta

master n. (tape)
F bande mère f
G Originaltonband n
I master m

microphone stand n.
F pied de micro m
G Mikrofonständer n
I asta de microfono f

mix n. (i post-production, etc.)
F mixage m
G Aufnahme f
I missaggio m

mixer (mixing board) n.
F melangeur m; (~ de son m)
G Mischpult n
I mixer m

noise reduction n.
F suppression du bruit f
G Rauschunterdrückung f
I riduttore di rumore m

output n.
F sortie f
G Ausgang m
I uscita f

parameter n.
F paramètre m
G Parameter m
I parametro m

play-back n.
F playback m; réécoute f
G Playback n; Rückspielen n
I playback m

pre-recorded adj. (radio or television broadcast) —cf. also live
F préenregistré
G Aufzeichnung f (normally used in German only as a noun)
I pre-registato

producer n.
F réalisateur m; –trice f
G Produzent m
I produttore m

record v.
F enregistrer
G aufnehmen
I registrare

recording n.
F enregistrement m
G Aufnahme f
I registrazione f

recording session n.
F séance d'enregistrement f
G Aufnahme f
I seduta di registrazione f

reel-to-reel n.
F bande magnétique f; magnétophone bobine à bobine f
G Tonbandmaschine f
I avvolgitore f

reverb n. (of a hall or on a recording)
F réverbe f
G Echo n (In German, something gives an echo. Ex. "...ein Echo geben.")
I riverbero m

sampler n.
F (sound) sampler m
G (Sound) Sampler m
I (sound) sampler m; campionatore m

sequencer n. (in MIDI)
F séquenceur m
G Sequenzer m
I sequencer m

session n. —cf. recording session

sound check n.
F réglage m
G Sound check m
I prova del suono f

sound track n. (for film, etc.)
F colonne sonore f
G Tonstreifen m
I colonna sonora f

speaker n.
F haut-parleur m
G Sprecher m
I altoparlante m

synthesizer n.
F synthétiseur m
G Synthesizer m
I sintetizzatore m

tape n. (i.e. cassette tape, etc.)
F bande f; bande magnétique f
G Band f; Magnettband n
I nastro m; (nastro magnetico m)

track n. (in multi-track recording)
F piste f
G Spur f
I pista f

transformer n.
F transformateur m
G Wandler m
I trasformatore m

microphone n. (mic)
F micro m; microphone m
G Mikrophon n
I microfono m

condensor mic n.
F micro à condensateur m
G Kondensatormikrophon n
I microfono a condensatore m

contact mic n.
F micro à contact m
G Kontaktmikrophon n
I microfono a contatto m

(electrodynamic mic n.
F micro électrodynamique m
G elektrodynamisches Mikrophon n
I microfono elettrodinamico m

— Research List —

autograph manuscript *n.*
F manuscrit autographe *m*
G handschriftlich Manuskript *n*
I manoscritto autografo *m*

closed-stacks *n./pl* (in a library) —*cf.*
also *open-stacks*
F archives *f/pl*
G Archiv *n*
I archives *f/pl*

copyright *n.*
F copyright *m*; droits d'auteur *m/pl*
G Copyright *n*; Uhrheberrecht *n*
I diritti d'autore *f/pl*

copyright infringement *n.*
F contrafaçon *f*
G Uhrheberrechtsverletzung *f*
I violazione dei diritti d'autore *f*

facsimile *n.*
F fac-similé *m*
G Faksimile *n*
I fac-simile *m*; facsimile *m*

iconography *n.*
F iconographie *f*
G Ikonographie *f*; Bildneskunde *f*
iconografia *f*

letter of introduction *n.* (necessary
to gain entry into some private libraries)
F lettre d'introduction *f*
G Empfehlungsbrief *n*
I lettera di presentazione *f*

manuscript *n.*
F manuscrit *m*
G Manuskript *n*
I manoscritto *m*

musicologist *n.*
G Musikwissenschaftler *m*; -in *f*
I musicologo *m*

musicology *n.*
F musicologie *f*
G Musikwissenschaft *f*
I musicologia *f*

open-stacks *n.* (in a library) —*cf.* also
closed-stacks
F bibliotheque *f*
G Bibliothek *f*
I biblioteca *f*

original manuscript *n.*
F manuscrit original *m*
G original Manuskript *n*
I manoscritto originale *m*

plagiarize *v.*
F plagier
G plagieren
I plagiare

research *n.*
F recherche *f*; reserche musicale *f*
G Forschung *f*; Musikforschung *f*
I ricerca *f*

scholarship *n.* (serious research, *etc.*)
F érudition *f*
G Gelehrsamkeit *f*
I erudizione *f*

tome *n.* (a specific volume of a collection
of books) —*cf. volume*

volume *n.* (of a collection of books, *etc.*)
F volume *m*; tome *m*
G Band *m*
I volume *m*

— Rests List —
(Listed in Order of Duration)

N.B. In French, the names of the rests are
not the same as the corresponding notes. *Cf.*
Notes List for comparison in Italian.

double whole rest *n.*
F bâton de 2 pauses *f*
G Doppelganze Pause *f*
I pausa di breve *f*

whole rest *n.*
F pause *f*
G Ganze Pause *f*
I pausa di semibreve *f*

half rest *n.*
F demi-pause *f*
G Halbe Pause *f*
I pausa di minima *f*

quarter rest *n.*
F soupir *m*
N.B. In French, a quarter rest (le soupir) is
printed as normal but often in a composer's
manuscript they use the 19th-Century
practice of hand-writing a quarter rest like a
"backwards" eighth rest.
G Viertel Pause *f*
I pausa di semiminima *f*

eighth rest *n.*
F demi-soupir *m*
G Achtel Pause *f*
I pausa di croma *f*

sixteenth rest *n.*
F quart de soupir *m*
G Sechzehntel Pause *f*
I pausa di semicroma *f*

thirty-second rest *n.*
F huitième de soupir *m*
G Zweiunddreißigstel Pause *f*
I pausa di biscroma *f*

sixty-fourth rest *n.*
F seizième de soupir *m*
G Vierundsechzigstel Pause *f*
I pausa di semibiscroma *f*

hundred twenty-eighth rest *n.*
F soupir d'une quintuple croche *m*
G Hunderdachtundzwanzigste Pause *f*
I pausa di centoventottesimo *m*

—Scales List—
(cf. also Keys List)

harmonic minor scale n.
F gamme harmonique mineure f
G harmonische moll Tonleiter f
I scala minore armonica f

major scale n.
F gamme majeure f
G dur Tonleiter f (N.B. "Dur" by itself as a noun is neuter.)
I scala maggiore f

melodic minor scale n.
F gamme mélodique mineure f
G melodische moll Tonleiter f
I scala minore melodica f

minor scale n.
F gamme mineure f
G moll Tonleiter f (N.B. "Moll" by itself as a noun is neuter.)
I scala minore f

pentatonic scale n.
F gamme pentatonique f
G Pentatonik Tonleiter f
I scala pentatonica f

scale n. (c major scale, etc.)
F gamme f
G Tonleiter f
I scala f

whole tone scale n.
F gamme de ton entière f
G Ganztonleiter f
I scala per toni interi f

— Score List —

choral score n.
F partition chorale f
G Chorpartitue f
I partitura f; partitura per coro f

piano reduction n.
F réduction pour piano f; adaptation pour piano f
G Klavierauszug m
I riduzione per pianoforte f; adattamento per pianoforte m

pocket score n. (small study score; miniture score)
F partition de poche f
G Taschenpartitur f
I partitura tascabile f

score n. (printed orchestral music)
F conducteur f
G Partitur f; Dirigierpartitur f
I partitura f

study score n.
F partition d'analyse f
G Studienpartitur f
I partitura (N.B. In Italian, "partiture" is generally used for all types of scores.)

system n. (in full printed orchestral score, etc.)
F système m
G System n
I sistema m

— Solfège Syllables List —

(Listed chromatically as sung from c-flat to c, assuming American "fixed-do" system, in the key of c-major)

N.B. In French and Italian, they use the "fixed-do system" (i.e. the note c is always named do). German also uses fixed-do, but they use the name of the note in German rather than the traditional solfège syllable.

"Fixed-do" is in drastic contrast to the practice in America, which uses a "moveable do system" i.e. the tonic of the key center is always called "do" (with the obvious exception of harmonic modulations, in which case the tonic of the new key center becomes do). Ex. In the U.S., in the key of D major, the note D is called do, in F minor, the note F is called do, etc.

N.B. That in France and Italy you say the entire name of the note (with the words "sharp" or "flat") to say the name of a specific note. However, in singing solfège—you leave off the word "sharp" or "flat" but sing the note altered to the correct pitch. Thus, when singing a chromatic run with the notes "c, c#, d, d#" you would simply sing "do, do, ré, ré," but sing the half step pitches. In German, you sing the entire name of the specific note.

de n. (c-flat in fixed-do system in c-major)
F do m
G ces n
I do m

do n. (c in fixed-do system in c-major)
F do m
G c n
I do m

di n. (c-sharp in fixed-do system in c-major)
F do m
G cis n
I do m

ra n. (d-flat in fixed-do system in c-major)
F ré m
G des n
I re m

re n. (d in fixed-do system in c-major)
F ré m
G d n
I re m

ri n. (d-sharp in fixed-do system in c-major)
F ré m
G dis n
I re m

me n. (e-flat in fixed-do system in c-major)
F mi m
G es n
I mi m

mi n. (e in fixed-do system in c-major)
F mi m
G e n
I mi m

ma n. (e-sharp in fixed-do system in c-major)
F mi m
G eis n
I mi m

fa n. (f in fixed-do system in c-major)
F fa m
G f n
I fa m

fe n. (f-flat in fixed-do system in c-major)
F fa m
G fes n
I fa m

fi n. (f-sharp in fixed-do system in c-major)
F fa m
G fis n
I fa m

se n. (g-flat in fixed-do system in c-major)
F sol m
G ges n
I sol m

sol n. (g in fixed-do system in c-major)
F sol m
G g n
I sol m

si n. (g-sharp in fixed-do system in c-major)
F sol m
G gis n
I sol m

le n. (a-flat in fixed-do system in c-major)
F la m
G as n
I la m

la n. (a in fixed-do system in c-major)
F la m
G a n
I la m

li n. (a-sharp in fixed-do system in c-major)
F la m
G ais n
I la m

te n. (b-flat in fixed-do system in c-major)
F si m
G b n
I si m

ti n. (b in fixed-do system in c-major)
F si m
G h n
I si m

ta n. (b-sharp in fixed-do system in c-major)
F si m
G his n
I si m

— Staff List —

ledger line n.
F ligne supplémentaire f
G Hilfslinie f
I taglio addizionale m

line n. (on the staff)
F ligne f
G Linie f
I linea f

space n. (on the staff)
F interligne f
G Zwischenraum m
I spazio m

staff n. (of music)
F portée f
G Liniensystem n
I pentagramma m

Cf. also Clefs List

— Stage List —
(cf. also Concerts List for related vocabulary)

backdrop n.
F toile de fond f
G Hintergrund m
I fondale f

backstage n.
F coulisse f
G Hinterbühne f
I dietro le quinte f/pl

blocking n.
F mis en scène f
G Regieprobe f, Blocking n
I movimenti m/pl (~ di scena m/pl)

box office n.
F guichet m
G Kasse f
I biglietteria f

curtain n.
F rideau m
G Vorhang m
I sipario m

downstage n.
F sur le devant f
G im Vorgrund m
I ribalta f; proscenio m

footlights n.
F rampe f
G Rampenlicht n/pl
I luci della ribalta f/pl

foyer n. (lobby)
F foyer m
G Foyer n
I ridotto m

green room n. (waiting room for the performer before a concert)
F loge f; foyer des artistes m
G Künstlerzimmer n
I camerino m

pit n. (for an orchestra in a ballet, etc.)
F fosse d'orchestre f; parterre m (for the theater)
G Parterre n
I buca f; ~ d'orchestra f

spotlight n.
F projecteur m
G Scheinwerfer m
I riflettore m

stage n.
F scène f
G Bühne f
I palcoscenico m

stage directions n./pl (instructions given by director, etc.)
F indications scéniques f/pl (N.B. The accents are reversed between the words scène and scénique which naturally alters the pronunciation.)
G Regienweisung f
I didascalie f/pl

stage door n.
F entrée f
G Bühneneingang m
I porta del paccoscenico f

stage fright n.
F trac m
G Lampenfieber n
I paura dinanzi al pubblico f

stage left n.
F à gauche de la scène f
G Bühne links n
I a sinistra del palcoscenico f

stage lighting n. (stage lighting, etc.)
F éclairages m/pl
G Beleuchtung f
I illuminazione f

stage manager n.
F régisseur m
G Inspizient m
I regista di scena m; direttore artistico m

stage presence n.
F présence sur scène f
G Bühneneindruck m; Bühne

Ausstrahlung f
I presenza scenica f; portamento m (presence in-general)

stage right n.
F à droite de la scène f
G Bühne rechts n
I a destra del palcoscenico f

staging n. (in an opera, etc.)
F mis en scène f
G Inszenierung f
I messa in scena f

thrust n. (of a stage)
F avant-scène f
G Vorbühne f
I proscenio m

upstage n.
F arrière-scène f
G im Hintergrund m
I verso il fondo m

wings n. /pl
F coulisses f /pl
G Kulisse f
I dietro le quinte f /pl

— **Strings List** —

gauge (of a string) n.
F calibre m
G Saitenstärke f
I calibro m

gauges adj. (listed in order of density of strings)

light adj. (gauge/density of a string)
F faible; faible tirant
G weich
I tensione bassa

medium adj. (gauge/density of a string)
F moyen; moyen tirant
G mittel
I tensione media

heavy adj. (gauge/density of a string)
F fort; fort tirant
G hart
I tensione forte

gut string n. (cat gut)
F corde de boyau f
G Darmsaite f
I corda di budello f

nylon string n.
F corde en nylon f
G Nylonsaite f
I corda di nylon f

steel string n.
F corde en acier f
G Stahlsaite f
I corda d'acciaio f

wound string n.
F corde filé f
G umsponnen Saite f
I corda rivestita f

— **Teaching List** —
(General Terms)

advanced n. (level of a student) —cf. list "Levels of Students" below

amature n. —cf. list "Levels of Students" below

assignment n. (weekly assignment, etc.)
F devoir m
G Aufgabe f
I compito m

beginner n. —cf. list "Levels of Students" below

coaching session n. (interpretive lesson, etc.)
F master-classe f; répétition f
G Korrepetition f
I lezione di interpretazione f

group lesson n.
F cours en groupe m
G Gruppenunterricht m
I lezione collettiva f

hand n.
F main f
G Hand f
I mano f

intermediate n. —cf. list "Levels of Students" below

lecture n. (in a class, etc.)
F conférence f
G Vortrag m
I conferenza f

level (of a student) n.
F niveau m
G Niveau n
I livelo m

make-up lesson n.
F rattrapage f (In French, this word is usually used as a verb rather than as a noun. Ex. "je vais rattraper le cours.")
G Nachholstunde f
I recupero m

masterclass n.
F master-classe f
G Masterklasse f; Meisterklasse f
I master-class f

method n. (instruction book)
F méthode f
G Lehrwerk n; Lernmethode f (N.B. "Lernmethode" tends to refer to a method of teaching rather than a specific book, etc.)
I metodo m

pedagogy n.
F pédagogie f
G Pedagogik f
I pedagogia f

play from memory v
F jouer par cœur
G auswendig spielen
I suonare a memoria

practice v. —cf. also 'rehearse'
F travailler (In French one "works at" an instrument. Ex. "...au piano;" "...a la guitare," etc.
G üben
I esercitarsi; studiare

private lesson n.
F cours particulier m
G Einzelunterricht m; Privatstunde f (N.B. In German Einzelunterricht is a private lesson given in a school [i.e. not a group lesson], while Privatstunde is also a one-on-one lesson [not a group lesson] but it is not through a school program.)
I lezione privata f

professional n. —cf. list "Levels of Students" below

professor n. —cf. also teacher
F professeur m /f
G Professor m; ~in f
I professore m; ~a f

rehearsal n.
F répétition f
G Probe f
I prova f

rehearse v. —cf. also practice
F répéter
G proben
I provare

studio class n.
F studio-classe f
G Studioklasse f
I master-class (Cf. note in main dictionary concerning this word in Italian.)

teacher n. —cf. important note under the entry teacher in the main part of the dictionary for clarification of these different titles.
F instituteur m; ~trice f, maître m; ~tresse f, (for grade school); professeur m/f (for upper level)
G Lehrer m; ~in f
I insegnante m/f (in a grade school); maestro m; ~a f is used for a children's school teacher but also for anyone having to do with music or the arts; professore m; ~oressa f (for university and high school)

technique n. (on an instrument, etc.)
F technique f
G Technik f
I tecnica f

— Teaching List —
(Level of a Student)
(listed in order)

amature n.
F amateur m
G Amateur m; ~in f
I dillettante m /f

beginner n.
F débutant m; ~ante f
G Anfänger m; ~in f
I principiante m

intermediate adj. (level of a student)
F (de niveau) moyen m; ~enne f
G mittelreif adj.
I livello medio (N.B. This term implies ability more than a specific level and is rarely used in Italian in this sense and if so, only as an adj.)

advanced adj. (level of a student)
F avancé m; ~ée f, supérieur m; ~eure f
G vortschreitend (N.B. German uses this term as an adj.)
I livello avanzato m (N.B. This term implies ability more than a specific level and is rarely used in Italian in this sense.)

professional n. (level of a student)
F professionnel m /f (In French, "professional" doesn't exist in this sense, since the word "professionnel" simply implies that you are professionally working. It does not refer to a "level.")
G Berufsmusiker m; ~in f, Profi m /f /sl
I musicista di professione m /f

— Time Signatures List —
(General Terms)

compound meter n.
F mesure composée f (N.B. In French, "composée" is not followed by the word "temps.")
G zusannmengesetzter Takt m
I tempo composta f

duple meter n.
F mesure binaire f, mesure à deux temps f
G Doppeltakt m
I tempo binario m

time change (meter change) n.
F changement de temps m; changement de mesure m
G Taktwechsel m
I cambiamento di tempo m

time signature n.
F mesure f; indication de la mesure f
G Takt m; Taktart f
I tempo m (N.B. Italian uses tempo to mean both the speed of a piece and the time signature of a piece.)

triple meter n.
F mesure binaire f, mesure à deux temps f /
ternaire f, mesure à trois temps f
G Tripeltakt m
I tempo ternario m

— Time Signatures List —
(Listed in words as they are spoken in conversation. Listed in order of ascending meter.)

one-two (1/2) n.
F mesure à un-deux f
G ein-halbTalkt m
I un mezzo m

two-two (2/2) n.
F mesure à deux-deux f
G zwei-halbTalkt m
I due mezzi m /pl

one-four (one-quarter) (1/4) n.
F mesure à un-quatre f
G ein-viertel Talkt m
I un quarto m

two-four (two-quarter) (2/4) n.
F mesure à deux-quatre f
G zwei-viertel Talkt m
I due quarti m /pl

three-four (three-quarter) (3/4) n.
F mesure à trois-quatre f
G drei-viertel Talkt m
I tre quarti m /pl

four-four (4/4) n.
F mesure à quatre-quatre f
G vier-viertel Talkt m
I quattro quanti m /pl

six-eight (6/8) n.
F mesure à six-huit f
G sechs-achtel Talkt m
I sei ottavi m /pl

nine-twelve (9/12) n.
F mesure à neuf-douze f
G neun-zwölftel Talkt m
I nove dodicesimi m /pl

— Tuning List —

equal temperament *n.*
F tempérament égal *m*
G gleichschwebende Temperatur *f*; gleichschwebende-temperierung *f*; wohltemperiert *adj.* (*N.B.* Although we are used to thinking "wohltemperiert" in English because of J.S. Bach's *Wohltemperiert Klavier*, the term sounds extremely antiquated and is virtually never used in modern speech.)
I temperamento equabile *m*

pure tuning *n.*
F tempérament pur *m*
G reine Stimmung *f*
I temperamento naturale *m*

Pythagorian tuning *n.*
F accord Pythagorien *m*
G Pythagoreische Stimmung *f*
I accordato secondo la scala pitagorica *m* (In Italian you "tune with the Pythagorian Scale." To say "accordatura pythagorica" aesthetically ugly.)

tempered tuning *n.*
F accord tempéré *m*
G temperierte Stimmung *f*
I accordatura temperata *f*; accordatura temperata *f*

— Twelve-tone Music List —

matrix *n.*
F matrice *f*
G Matrix *f*
I matrice *f*

matrix divisions (in general order of common use):

original *n.*
F série original *m*: original
G Grundgestalt *f*
I serie *f*

inversion *n.*
F renversement *f*
G Umkehrung *f*
I inversione *f*

retrograde *n.*
F rétrograde *f*
G Krebsform *f*
I retrogrado *m*

retrograde-inversion *n.*
F rétrograde du renversement *m*
G Krebsumkehrung *f*
I retrogrado dell'inversione *m*

row *n.*
F série *f*
G Reihe *f*
I serie *f*

twelve-tone music *n.* (*cf.* also matrix divisions)
F musique dodécaphonique *f*
G Zwölftonmusik *f*
I musica dodecafonica *f*

— Voice List — (General Terms)

action *n.* (in an opera; play, *etc.*)
F action *f*
G Handlung *f*
I trama *f*

break *n.* (in a voice)
F mue *f*
G Stimmbruch *m*
I muta *f*

breath *n.*
F souffle *m*
G Luftstoß *m*
I fiato *m*; respiro *m*

breath support *n.*
F appui du souffle *m*
G Atemstütze *f*
I appoggio sulla maschera *m*

carry the voice *adv.*
F porter la voix
G tragend
I (In Italian this concept doesn't make sense. You simply say "cantare"—"to sing.")

chest voice *n.*
F voix de poitrine *f*
G Bruststimme *f*
I voce di petto *f*

coach *n.* (singing coach)
F répétiteur *m*; ~trice *f*
G Korrepetitor *m*; ~in *f*
I ripetitore *m*; ~trice *f*

diaphragm *n.*
F diaphragme *m*
G Zwerchfell *n*
I diaframma *m*

diction *n.*
F diction *f*
G Diktion *f*
I dizione *f*

exhale *v.* —*cf.* inhale /exhale

falsetto *n.* (of a singer)
F fausset *m*
G Falsett *n*
I falsetto *m*

head voice *n.*
F voix de tête *f*
G Kopfstimme *f*
I voce di testa *f*

hoarse *adj.*
F rauque
G heiser
I rauco

inhale *v.* / **exhale** *v.*
F inspirer / expirer
G einatmen / ausatmen
I inspirare / espirare

nasal *adj.*
F nasal
G nasal
I nasale

node *n.* (on a singer's vocal chord)
F nœd *m*
G Knoten *n*
I nodulo *m*

placement of the voice *n.*
F pose de la voix *f*
G Führung der Stimme *f*
I messa di voce *f*

placing the voice *adv.*
F pose de la voix
G Ansatz der Stimme
I messa di voce

prompter *n.*
F souffleur *m* / *f*
G Souffleur *m*; ~in *f*
I suggeritore *m* / *f*

pronounce *v.*
F prononcer
G aussprechen
I pronunciare

roll *v.* (to roll an "r," *etc.*)
F rouler

228

— Voice List —
(Choral Types)

— Voice List —
(Vocal Types—Traditional)
(Listed by Range)

— Voice List —
(Specialty Vocal Types)
(Listed by Range)

G rollen
I arrotare la erre (This is only for "rolling an 'r'." For other consonants you use "arrotondare.")

singer n.
F chanteur m; ~euse f
G Sänger m; ~in f
I cantate m / f

support v. (to support the voice, etc.) —f. also Voice; breath support
F appuyer
G stützen
I appoggiare

throat voice n.
F voix de gorge f
G Kehlstimme f
I voce di gola f

translation n. (of a song text or other written words into another language)
F traduction f
G Übersetzung f
I traduzione f

vocalist n.
F vocaliste m / f
G Sänger m; ~in f
I vocalist m / f (more for pop music) corista m / f (more for choral music)

voice n.
F voix f
G Stimme f
I voce f

voice control n.
F contrôl du souffle m
G Atemtechnik f
I tecnica vocale f

boy's choir n.
F chœur de garçons m
G Knabenchor m
I coro di fanciulli m

church choir n.
F chœur d'église m
G Kirchenchor m
I coro di chiesa m

men's choir n.
F chœur d'hommes m
G Männerchor m
I coro maschile m

mixed choir n.
F chœur mixte m
G gemischter Chor m
I coro misto m

opera chorus n.
F chœur d'opéra m
G Opernchor m
I coro d'opera m

women's choir n.
F chœur de femmes m
G Frauenchor m
I coro femminile m

soprano n.
F soprano m
G Sopran m
I soprano m

mezzo soprano n.
F mezzo-soprano m
G Mezzosopran m
I mezzosoprano m

alto n.
F alto m
G Alt m
I contralto m

tenor n.
F ténor m
G Tenor f
I tenore m

baritone n.
F baryton m
G Bariton m
I baritono m

bass n.
F basse f
G Baß m
I basso m

castrato n.
F castrat m
G Kastrat m
I castrato m

lyric soprano n.
F soprano lyrique f
G Lyriksopran m
I soprano lirico m

coloratura soprano n.
F soprano coloratura f
G Koloratursopran f
I soprano leggero m

contralto n.
F contralto m
G Kontralt m
I contralto m

counter tenor n.
F haute-contre f
G Kontratenor m
I contraltista m

lyric tenor n.
F ténor lyrique f
G lyrischer Tenor m
I tenore lirico m

basso buffo n.
F basse bouffe f
G Baß-Buffo m
I basso buffo m

— Voice List —
(Vocal Attacks)

aspirated attack *n.*
F attaque murmurée *f*
G gehauchter Einsatz *m*
I attacco sul fiato *m*

glottal attack *n.*
F attaque dure *f*
G harter Einsatz *m*
I attacco duro *m*

soft attack *n.*
F entrée douce *f*
G weicher Einsatz *m*
I attacco dolce *m*